To Tammi, for always being there for me, making me a better person, and giving my life such great joy. I love you.

EVERY

PICTURE

HAS A

STORY

TO TELL

J.W. Woodward

MASCOT BOOKS

www.mascotbooks.com

Every Picture Has a Story to Tell

For more information, please contact:
Mascot Books, an imprint of Amplify Publishing Group
620 Herndon Parkway, Suite 220
Herndon, VA 20170
info@mascotbooks.com

Library of Congress Control Number: 2023918237

CPSIA Code: PRV1223A

ISBN-13: 978-1-63755-867-6

Printed in the United States

1

JACK

EXPOSED THROUGH THE WAIST-HIGH SLIT of her burgundy dress, Tess's muscled thigh flexes as she shifts her weight from one foot to the other. The spotlight brightens her beautiful blue eyes, partially lighting the pool and landscape below, which remains eerily dark further beyond. Her robust calves tense as she braces in expectation of the upcoming booms of thunder. My heart races at the speed of the lightning from the surrounding storm as I watch Tess saunter across the room. More deep reverberations, followed by grand bursts of light that glimmer off Tess's long, wavy silver hair that flows with the gentle sway of her head and settles across her pale bare shoulder. Her body freezes in anticipation of the next flurry of photos and the boisterous roars of thunder that mimic the turmoil of our past year.

More rumbling and brilliant lights span across the eastern sky, briefly exposing the crashing waves beneath. Heavy rains sweep sideways across the blooming landscape, beating the colorful petals vigorously, making me think of the fragility of our lives. Tess flinches slightly as a lightning bolt strikes downward to touch the ocean, but she remains focused, flashing those sweet little dimples for the next shutter click. The trees battle to stay upright against the wind, much like we do against the struggles of life. Limbs pushed to the ground by the sheer force of the storm fight gallantly to rise again, like our attempts to rebound from unexpected setbacks. The radiant lights of the sky strive to remain alive before the next rumble reaches its arms around the house, rattling every window of the sunroom, making us both wince momentarily. The following dramatic light show paints a beautiful mosaic of the scenic coastline just yards away from the room. The beauty disappears quickly like beautiful moments of our lives that we try so hard to cling to.

I love the way the burgundy dress clashes so beautifully with Tess's ivory skin. The blackness gives way to another temporary explosion of illumination as Tess slowly slides the thin straps over her shoulders, lowering the fabric to the top of her chest, exposing the outer edges of her large blush-colored areolas. Her head eases backward, letting the thick silver spread across her back, displaying the front of her neck wrapped in a diamond choker. The windows rattle with another deep rumble. Tess's arms fall to her sides, allowing the dress to ease downward and expose her plentiful breasts. My eyes are entranced by my beautiful wife. My yearning is overwhelming. My excitement overflowing.

Her triceps become taut as she wiggles the dress over her hips and lets it fall to her burgundy-painted toes. Now fully exposed except for the small animal print material fitted tightly around her waist. Adorned with multiple diamond studs and a silver hoop dangling from each ear, three bracelets stacked on her left arm, and her ever-present two-strand silver chain with a 'T' dangling around her right ankle. And a sweet, dimpled smile. Not just a smile but the sweetest of all smiles. The smile that melted my heart the first time I saw it. The smile that has helped me through every challenge in my life, including the one enveloping us now. That beautiful smile that has always made my life brighter.

Outside the disturbance begins to ease but inside the sunroom the intensity of my desire is rising to even higher levels. How I wish Tess could see herself through my eyes, to see the perfection and beauty that she is to me. But Tess is much too hard on herself.

She playfully cups her full breasts with her pretty hands and shares a teasing smile. Her multiple rings sparkle with the flash of the camera. I love the burgundy nails against her fair skin as she lifts her mounds higher. When she drops her hands, I notice her quick glance downward and know she is wishing that her breasts stood firm instead of resting against her body. She jokes about resetting them back up to where they belong but my heart pounds with excitement at the sight of their natural shapeliness. The little freckle on the inside of her cleavage is just one of the countless little details about Tess that I treasure. Too often I catch her staring into the mirror and inhaling, trying to make her stomach pooch disappear as she runs her finger across the small life-giving scar below. I see the small curvature as a perfect complement to what I tell her is my little curvaceous five-foot-three-inch package of dynamite. I kiss her scar when we lay in bed and talk about life. I am thankful for its part along with her courage in bringing our two babies into this world.

Spinning around to look out the window, Tess leans forward slightly to accentuate what she calls her "big ole butt." It looks amazing to me wrapped in the tiny cloth of wild animal print, exposing much of her fleshy cheeks. I click the shutter faster as the love of my life parades around the room in her leopard heels that highlight her already alluring legs. Tess worries about every faint sign of varicose veins and attempts all home remedies to smooth any dimple that she sees as a massive onslaught of cellulite on what she says are her "thick thighs." The first time one of my photos showed a dimple on her backside cheek because of the way she was leaning, I thought she was going to throw my camera in the trash. I cherish the curvy body that Tess has worked diligently to keep in shape through years of dedicated exercise. I can never get enough of seeing her in shorts, skirts, dresses, or sexy nightgowns; anything that will allow me to enjoy those amazing gams.

I know I can be a little obsessive in my desire to capture her through my lens and impress her image forever in my mind. Tess says that sometimes she feels as if the paparazzi are chasing her, and I smile as I think of the accuracy of that assessment . . . as I snap a few more shots. Tess spins around again and runs her hands up through the beautiful waves of her silver hair, highlighting her pretty neck along with her shoulder and back muscles.

We both have become creative over the years by using anything available as a prop to enhance the fun of our sessions. Tess lifts a leg over the wicker chair and holds one of my old cameras as we continue with some playful shots. The storm begins to quickly move out. She takes one hand and effortlessly flips and spins her hair up into a messy bun on top of her head, wonderfully presenting her gorgeous eyes and prominent cheek bones. She drops her chin and offers me a most tantalizing look. Damn, I love that girl! She excites me more every year of our marriage. As usual, I begin to speed up at the end of our session as my desire to have Tess in my arms grows, but she is committed to ensuring I take enough time to get all the shots I want and discussed with her leading up to this session. And she likes to tease me by making me wait a little longer to have her in my arms.

Over the years Tess has sweetly learned not only the poses I enjoy but the positions that she feels enhance her look enough for her to better enjoy perusing the pictures with me later. I am always searching and thinking of new ways to seize her character and beauty in our photos. She stumbles a bit stepping down from the chair and I capture the laugh that follows, thinking that I haven't seen enough of Tess's smile over the last year. That this modest "good southern girl" has progressed to such adventurous play in front of the camera over the years still amazes me. Tess says it's because I give her assurance with my passion for her and the way that I see her. But I believe it's much more her love for me along with her desire to do almost anything to make me happy, which is also being tested right now. Tess has gifted me more joy than I ever could have imagined.

I am craving her badly as we near the end of this set of photos and Tess begins adding a few more playful poses bending both knees and stooping slightly, granting me the bonus of seeing the little dimples I love just below her knees. This is her way of tantalizing me a bit more by making me wait to feel her touch. This is the final straw; I need Tess in my arms.

Outside is now calm but I am churning with desire inside. I hand Tess her black silk gown as a cover-up before I fill our wine glasses. She eases back onto the wicker couch, and I remove the leopard heels as we lean back on the overly plush cushions. Her thighs peep at me through the opening in the gown as we listen to the now soft patter of rain mixed with the sound of smooth jazz coming from the wireless speaker. I am captivated by her eyes as I massage her pretty but tired feet. She makes me smile when reminding me how much harder it is to be the model rather than just standing behind the camera and clicking the shutter. I lean in to steal her bold dark lipstick with a long kiss to her delicate lips and thank her for being so wonderful to me. She gives me the usual sweet response, "I'm so glad you want me like you do." We finish our drinks and make our way through the French doors to the master. I taste more of her burgundy lips as I loosen the softly tied belt of silk at her waist. Our tongues waltz together beneath soft moans as I slowly move the silk across the slope of her shoulders, exposing the sexy little mole that I tell her adds to her look of a Hollywood star. That always causes an eye roll from her. My fingertips gently trace the curve of her lower back, keeping the cool material in contact with her skin. My hands guide the silk over the slope of her round bottom, pausing there for an extra moment. Lowering to my knees my lips follow the path of the robe along the front side of her body. Downward between her breasts which press gently against the sides of my cheeks. My lips lightly brush over her hardened tips and my kisses leave a trail of moisture down her stomach and across her adorable outie belly button. I feel a slight squirm as I nibble on her sides, finding one of her ticklish areas. Finally I let the negligee glide across the backs of her legs to a soft landing over her dark red painted toes, inhaling her scent through the entire journey and trying to hold onto it as if it gives me life.

I pause to wrap my hands firmly around her pretty ankles and feel the jewelry move beneath my grip. Slowly I begin retracing my path upwards, my hands moving over her hard calves, across her taught hamstrings, and back over her curved hips until my fingers find the top of the small leopard band. The only thing left between me and the promised joy that I deeply need. With a gentle pull I slide the silky animal cloth over the roundness of her backside and my lips follow the spotted material fervently down to her pretty little feet. She deliberately steps out of them one foot at a time with her hand holding steady to my shoulder for extra support as my hands cling to the sides of her legs.

I begin a wonderful return journey upward and I feel her fingers tighten on my shoulders. My hands find her voluptuous backside and hold firmly as my lips travel from the tops of her feet over her shin, across her soft knees, and melt against the velvet flesh of her inner thighs. I feel a small tremble through her body as her hands guide me to the destination of both our desires. Tess raises one heel off the ground, bringing her toes to a point as she slightly opens her knee and most generously offers me the wonderful gift of her. A move that always gets me. I am lost in the unique scent and feel of her most supple skin, her passion, her inner love. Like the floating mist left from the departed storm, her taste moves across my lips, over my tongue, and through my entire body as if her intimate soul has surrounded and engulfed me. Her knees begin to weaken, and her hands cup my cheeks persuading me back to her now-smeared burgundy lips. We share the mixed intimate flavors of our devotion as I gently lay her back to the cool sheets of the king bedding. I pause to admire her disheveled silver hair strewn across the pillow and resting over her fair skin. I strive to permanently etch into my mind the image of her naked body lying in the moonlight that has broken through the departing storm clouds. She is beautiful, and I whisper those words to her. I need her. I love her with all my heart. I wonder if I will ever again be able to give her all of myself like she deserves.

2

TESS

I AWAKEN TO THE WONDERFUL aroma of coffee with hints of caramel and chocolate floating over my pillow. A long easy stretch before pushing upward, placing the fluffy pillow against my back as Jack offers me the warm mug. One sip proves that my nose is not lying. Caramel mocha-flavored coffee with a dab of creamer, two squirts of double chocolate syrup, and whipped topping with a few sprinkles of cinnamon powder. Heavenly! Jack leans in to kiss the topping from my lip after the first sip and whispers, "Good morning, beautiful." My eyelids struggle to stay open against the post-storm sunshine gleaming through the double French doors on what is a gorgeous morning.

I stretch my legs, "I was sure I heard a noise last night and almost woke you."

Jack nuzzles my ear, "Probably just the unfamiliar sounds of the first night away from home."

Through the middle of another yawn, "I thought you wanted to get up early to watch the sun rise."

With a grin Jack proudly announces, "I did. You are my sunshine, and I am watching you rise."

He loves his corny jokes and his ability to make me laugh is one of my favorite things about him. "I love you corny."

"You were sleeping too peacefully to disturb earlier but I'm already on my second cup and couldn't keep my hands off you or you would still be resting."

"You won't ever hear me complaining about getting morning loving." Mm, I love the feel of his beautiful hands across my body. I remember thinking how sexy his hands and arms were as he drove me to the movies on our first date. For the first time, I notice that his cheeks look thinner after the surgery, but he has worked hard to get back into shape in a short amount of time. I take some credit for that by wearing skimpy outfits and joining him in our modest home gym. Yes, I was willing to dress like those twenty-year-old hussies with zero body fat strutting around the gym in their sports bras and what looks like underwear on their tight little butts. The little minxes that all of us mature women curse while trying to work out five days a week in our sweatpants to lose a pound. But for some crazy reason, my man was motivated by this old girl rolling around the yoga mat dressed like a floozie.

Jack unhooks the clip from my head, the one that I unconsciously put in at some point every night to keep him from pulling my hair out as he snuggles close to me. He lays on the pillow beside me and buries his face under the thick strands of silver. He calls it his silk blankie. I never dreamed he would love the color as much as he does when I decided to go natural a few years ago.

With a muffled voice from under his silk blankie, "Are we going to walk on the beach?"

With a slightly smaller yawn, "Once my eyes are open and the caffeine kicks in."

"No rush, but you know how fast the days go when we are on vacation." I know that he wants to take advantage of every minute we have together, as he always does—but even more so on this trip.

I enjoy the flavor of another sip from my warm mug and can feel Jack's energy as he flips to the other end of the bed and begins to kiss and rub my feet. "I love your toes painted dark colors."

I share a smile, "Why do you think I chose burgundy?"

"Because of that pretty new dress." He raises a brow proudly like he had gotten the correct answer to a pop quiz.

"And that too, a lady has to match."

He spins back up to the head of the bed and wraps both arms around me. "I loved last night." With a kiss to my cheek, "You are so good to me. I love you."

"I love you too, let's get ready for our walk," knowing that there will be no peace until we get going.

"Want another cup for the road, or rather the sand," with another little chuckle.

"Better not, I don't want to have to pee as soon as we get to the beach." Jack looks at me mischievously and I know he is thinking naughty thoughts of me on the beach.

I'm rustling through the drawer trying to decide on one of my too many bathing suit choices when I hear, "Are you going to wear the black one with the little skirt thing?"

A smile creeps across my face, "Yes of course I am." I will never understand the vision Jack has of me, but I am thankful for it.

Then with the sweetest voice like a child asking for a toy he adds, "Hair down to blow in the wind maybe."

A sigh, "Yes baby, for a little bit at least."

The damp sand is cool from last night's storm and squishes between our toes as the coastal breeze brushes gently against our faces. Our hands intertwine and there is not another person in sight, which is perfect in my world. I love my family and friends but alone with my hubby is my happy place. We shuffle through many life memories as we walk the deserted beach wondering how the last twenty-eight years have passed so quickly. Laughing at our crazy times together and thinking it seems like just yesterday that we were building sandcastles with our two toddlers.

I spin around, wrap my arms around Jack's neck and plant a big kiss on his lips. "I'm so glad that we came back here this year." Jack had suggested that we try visiting some place new, thinking that we needed a complete change of scenery with all the happenings from this past year. I didn't want that. I don't like change. I like steady and consistent and that is what Jack has always given me.

"Me too, baby."

I squeeze Jack's hand, "We better head back so we can go into town for our supplies. I'm ready to lock ourselves in and everyone else out for the next two weeks." We have always only stayed one week on our trips here, but Linda, the homeowner, had graciously offered the house two weeks this time, almost as if she had a sixth sense of our need. Linda always made a point to know everyone else's business so maybe she had heard something about our situation. Regardless, I was thankful to have the extra time.

Jack turns me around to hug me and kiss my neck from behind as we gaze out over the ocean. He gives me a big squeeze, "Maybe a couple of pictures on the way back?"

Laughing, "I thought you would never ask." He is rarely without his camera and never wants to miss an opportunity to photograph me. I will never understand it.

3

JACK

AS I PULL THE LEASED convertible into Sandy Toes, our favorite local restaurant, I proudly ask, "The car was a great idea, huh?" I had told Tess way more than she needed to know about the 1960 Impala during our travel down. How it became Chevrolet's best-selling model of the decade and how the tail fins on the elongated trunk were a special style for the model we rented, along with many other useless details. I knew she wasn't really listening to much of what I had to say about it and didn't really care about anything other than that it was bright red and pretty. And fun to ride in. I thought it would be a nice touch for our special vacation.

"It was a fun drive but look at me," laughing as she pulls the hair from her mouth, away from her cheeks, and off her clothes.

"You were gorgeous with your hair blowing in the wind, AND the car will make for a great photo session later," with a little wink.

She rolls her eyes toward me, "You do know I knew that was your plan as soon as you told me about the lease, right?"

"At least you had that new cute hair clip for when we got here."

"Never leave home without one," as she thoughtlessly spins the thick strands in her hand and clips the thick pile on top of her head.

I have always enjoyed the homey feeling of the Sandy Toes restaurant. The décor is beachy and fun with many trinkets and pictures signifying the town's history and that of the owner, Rohan. There is a large mural on the long street-side wall of all different sorts of shapes, sizes, and colors of legs from the knees down with feet buried in the sand to match the name on the front of the building. On either side of the mural are large corkboards with photos of locals and tourists capturing their special moments at the restaurant. Sort of a Sandy Toes Hall of Fame. There have not been many well-known celebrities visit the little strip of island. It is more of a quaint off-the-beaten-path town and has not been developed to allure tourists. But the few high-profile visitors had autographed their photos taken with Rohan and had a prominent position on the wall. There are only about fifteen hundred full-time residents and limited rental options on the island. Tess and I had stumbled across the hidden gem about fifteen years ago when driving around while staying in a larger, more touristy coastal town about thirty miles away. We fell in love with the people and the town almost instantly.

With the restaurant's long and thin structure most seats offer a gorgeous view through the large beachside windows and all seating on the covered porch facing the ocean fill up first. The few areas that can't provide a good sight line to the beach have been made into themed private rooms, small and cozy and a nice compromise to missing out on the preferred ocean view. There is also one large room across the entire back end of the building named Hurricane Hattie after Rohan's sweet but rambunctious wife of over forty years. The room and the restaurant are the main meeting place for most of the important happenings in town. And it's always spotless and ready to host whatever the need may be—Rohan sees to that.

The walls in the Hattie room are covered with photos from the town and its transformation over the years. I was proud to have one of my photos of a rather spectacular bad storm approaching the downtown area displayed on the wall. The storm had caused quite a bit of destruction, but people viewed it as a badge of courage that the town had not only survived but pulled together to help one another get back on their feet afterward. A feat that summarized what the people of the community are all about. There were only two photos of people on the wall, one of course was Hurricane Hattie herself. She is a small but spunky Indian lady that speaks her mind, one of the main reasons that Tess and she get along so well. The other was Sandy, the daughter of the founding father of the island and namesake of the town of Sandy Strips. She was in her now infamous pose. A troubling story too well known by the town's residents.

As we glance over the menu at our table on the deck, an accented voice carries across the way, "Miss Tess, Mr. Jack, so good to see you again." Rohan, the owner, shuffles quickly toward the table. He is such an affable person and he and I became friends on our very first visit many years ago. A few years back, I took marketing photos for Rohan's remodel and some food shots for his new menu as a favor. The no-charge part had made the penny-pinching Rohan very happy. Apparently, it had quite a positive impact on the business and Rohan has since embraced me even more.

I rise from my chair for the hug I know is coming, "Good to see you, my friend."

Rohan is from Mumbai and even though he had been on the southeast coast for two decades, he still carries much of his home accent. "I miss you both, good to have you back home." Tess loves the fanciness of his long, brightly-colored sherwani and matching turban and the way he interlocks his fingers in front of him when listening intently to someone talking. Tess smiles as our eyes meet while I am embraced in Rohan's hug.

Tess and I have taken at least one annual vacation to this secret little treasure spot for fifteen years and know most of the locals. Last year's personal challenges had kept us from making the trip for the first time since the discovery of our "home away from home."

"I have a new chef, he bakes great salmon, Miss Tess," Rohan offers proudly. Tess flashes another smile and I know that she is not only loving his accent, but the phrases that he uses from his homeland, even if we can't always determine what he means.

My sweet Tess has her own southern style of phrases, so she appreciates someone being creative with their speech. As a college basketball coach, I try to play a small part in helping my players with their classes and Tess thinks it's funny when my players tell her about me correcting their grammar in the middle of an intense practice. She laughs that her crazy sayings don't help me with the message I am trying to convey to help my players as they go out into the world. I admit that may be true, but the players have more fun with her stories when she visits practice than what they hear from me.

Our kids have had so much fun with some of Tess's sayings, many of which came from her dear grandmother. I remember during one of my son's competitions at school when he had a setback against the opposing team, Tess yelled out to him, "That's okay Sam, you hang in there like a hair in a biscuit!" As a player and a coach, I have heard many things from fans over the years and if there is nothing demeaning, I am typically just happy that parents care enough to be involved with their kids.

Apparently, other competitions like debates don't see parents' support in quite the same way, because the judge of this particular competition warned Tess that she would have to leave if she had another outburst like that. Never a dull moment with that girl.

"Thank you, Rohan, you made it easy for me to choose today," Tess offers sweetly.

"Mr. Jack, you want special? Want usual, right Mr. Jack?"

I don't even look at the menu, "The special sounds great my friend." The fresh fish sandwich with slaw and tater tots is always good with me, though it is definitely not on our regular eating program, but we ARE on vacation.

"Is my sweet Emma working today?" Tess asks, still pulling the hairs from around her face.

Rohan shakes his head while staring at the floor, "Oh, miss Tess, Emma didn't show up today and you know she never misses work. We very worried we can't get in touch with her." Rohan's brow wrinkles. "Emma has been here almost every day since she was eight, sweeping, taking out trash. I put her on payroll as soon as she was legal to work you know." Rohan tells us that story every year.

Little Emma stole our hearts the moment we first saw her. She almost always has a smile on her face and is full of energy. She grew up without her parents and was bounced around to different family members before moving out on her own. Rohan had told us that her mother was from Mexico and died during Emma's birth. Her father had left well before that. But Emma overcame her challenges with hard work and a great attitude. You would never know she had faced any of those hardships.

Emma has grown into a beautiful and determined young lady. She has the heart for being a caretaker to go along with her dreams of being a nurse. I don't think anyone that knows her doubts that she will accomplish her goal. Tess and Emma have grown very close over the years and stay in touch between our visits.

The best thing about Emma is her upbeat personality and the genuinely happy smile that she shares with everyone. She came to town all alone as an outsider but is now loved by everyone. Emma has the wonderful gift of making everyone that she meets feel better about their day.

I try to calm Rohan and Tess's worry, "She is almost twenty-three now and there are a lot of fun things for youngsters to do here at the beach. Tempting even for nice girls like Emma." I give Rohan a reassuring pat on the shoulder.

"I hope she calls soon, Mr. Jack. I tell her you and Miss Tess ask about her." Tess and I discuss how Emma has grown so much since we first saw her and couldn't believe that that much time had passed. We laugh as we remember the first time we spoke to her when she was about seven or eight years old. She was using the mini broom that Rohan had given her, pretending to sweep up around the tables. As soon as she saw Rohan walk back to the kitchen, Emma dropped the broom and came over to our table. She pulled a pencil from behind her ear and a piece of paper from her pocket and proudly said, "I will take your order now." We thought it was the cutest thing ever. After today's meal, and a couple of times during, Rohan checks on us, mostly to make sure Tess loves the salmon. Rohan tells us about his new chef, Marcus, who had been in a little trouble up north in the past but has been a model citizen since Rohan gave him a job almost two years ago. Rohan's former chef retired and after months of doing the cooking himself while searching, he decided to give Marcus the position because, nearing seventy, Rohan prefers visiting customers instead of spending the day in the kitchen. All the customers liked receiving the special attention from Rohan and most importantly, Hattie told him to find someone quickly so he wouldn't have to work such long hours. And Miss Hattie has the final say in those things.

I give Rohan a hug and tell him the food is fantastic as always and that we will see him again soon. And to please let us know once he finds Emma. I give a second reminder to the last part. As I hold the door open for Tess, I ask her the question that we have asked each other thousands of times, "Would you want that again?" We have used that question for meals, trips, haircuts, just about anything you can think of. Tess came up with it when we were first married and was still developing her cooking skills. She quickly discovered that I would never say anything to hurt her feelings when she asked if I liked something she had prepared, so Tess started asking if I would want it again. Tess confirms that not only would she want the salmon again, but that it was delicious, and assures me that she will be having it again before we leave.

4

TESS

JACK AND I DECIDE WE will ask the shop owners if they have seen Emma as we pick up our supplies. After giving it more thought, we decide that she must be helping someone in need or there is some other emergency that she is lending her assistance with, because that's the only thing she would put before work. But worriedly we agree that it is unlike her to miss work and not call.

Mateo and Celest are owners of The Founding Fathers, a farm that brings their fresh produce to town several days each week during the peak season. Their family also owns a farm-to-table restaurant about thirty miles away located in the middle of several acres of land where they grow their fruits and vegetables. The fresh peaches are our favorite. As we are making our selections at their produce stand in town, Celest, her head covered with one of her beautifully-colored signature scarves that I love, snatches a tomato from a customer and tells her if she doesn't think it is fresh, she shouldn't buy it. Mateo and Celest are nice, hard-working people, but Celest is not one to take any grief from anyone. Jack and I are careful to keep our chuckles under our breath and I mention to Jack that Celest may be a hot-tempered red head. But we both cannot remember a time when we saw her without a head wrap so we can't be sure. We load up on peaches, a bucket of strawberries, and a watermelon. I pick some colored peppers I can slice and cover with cream cheese to make one of our snack plate favorites. Jack sneaks off and adds a bouquet of flowers that I pretend not to see so he can surprise me later. I can be sweet too. Mateo and Celest say they have not seen Emma in a few days.

I easily coax Jack into stopping at Beachy Blessings, a newly opened shop. They have so many treasures that would look great in our sunroom back home. As I check out with a unique cross for my collection, I sweetly remind Jack that we have bought a memento each year we have visited. I also find a devotional that we can read together on the beach. I love it when Jack reads books aloud to me, something we have been doing for several years now. The owners whom we don't know well relay they have not seen Emma in a couple of days but comment on what a wonderful young lady she is.

There is hardly anyone stirring in town so when I catch movement from the corner of my eye on the sidewalk across the street, I automatically glance that way. Immediately, I shove Jack into the next store entrance, banging his shoulder on the door frame.

"Hurry, hurry," I whisper, pulling him behind a clothes rack and tugging on his shirt to duck down.

Jack looks confused while rubbing his shoulder, "What in the world is going on?"

"Shh. Keep your voice down," as I part the shirts on the rack to peek through the window.

Jack whispers this time, "What are we hiding from?"

"Not what, but who. It's BK!" BK and his long flowing blond hair is the owner of the beach rental store and self-proclaimed desire of all women breathing. "He is strutting down the sidewalk and I can't stand the thought of having to speak to him, or rather listen to him speak about himself. And I especially cannot stand to get a sweaty, suntan-lotion-smelling hug from him."

Jack chuckles, "He is a harmless surfer dude."

"Maybe, maybe not. But he doesn't really like you and he gives me the creeps."

Jack rubs his shoulder again but remains stooped and quiet. Suddenly, an irritated voice behind us blurts out, "Do you need help finding anything?"

We both jump and turn. Mrs. Blankenship, owner of the fanciest clothing store in town and not one to tolerate shenanigans, is obviously annoyed. I gather myself, "Um, no thank you. I dropped an earring, but I found it, so we are good."

Mrs. Blankenship stands with her hands on her hips, and I feel her eyes scan me up and down. I know she is thinking that my little sundress is too revealing for a woman of my age and my build. She is correct. Dressing a little more provocatively is one of the fun things I do for Jack when we travel. Her disgust is obvious. "You may be interested in one of our new dresses for this season."

Jack, always ready, has that look in his eyes. "Yes we are. Do you have anything shorter than this," as he slightly lifts the bottom of my dress.

I think Mrs. B's head is going to pop off her shoulders. "I certainly do not."

Jack adds, "Well thank you. Maybe we can try back later when you get more updated styles delivered."

Mrs. B spins around and walks back toward the register as Jack and I cautiously head out of the store, deciding not to push our luck by asking about Emma. I playfully punch Jack in the arm, "You didn't have to stir her up more than we already did by hiding behind her rack."

Jack winces, "You keep hitting that same arm and she doesn't need to be such a prude."

I look down at my dress, "Well, this is pretty revealing and not age appropriate."

Jack hugs me, "It's perfectly appropriate for a sexy lady like you and I am thankful for you wearing it to make me happy."

I pinch his butt, "You are a crazy man, but I am glad I make you happy."

Off to the small and only grocery store in town. A national chain is located on the mainland across a bridge which is the only access to the island. Only having one way on and off the island other than a boat gives me anxiety but I try not to let that enter my mind too often. Jack always likes to support the small independent businesses when possible, so he is fine with doing all our shopping at Food for Thought even if the selection is more limited. Ed, the owner, reminds Jack of the manager of the store where he worked during high school, which is a good memory for him. Jack has been looking through old pictures and reminiscing more than usual this past year. We try to buy everything on the list even though it is only a couple of miles back to our rental. We are both hoping to stay at the rental for a lot of private time together on this trip. Ed says that he saw Emma yesterday and she seemed like everything was fine.

One of our last stops is the local bookstore, Curl Up Books. We have a good selection of reading with us, but Jack and I are always up for a good bookstore visit, especially one locally owned and as unique as this one. And it is a great one, decorated eloquently with one section all local history, another all-beach reads—romance mostly with some mysteries—and one side holds a mixture of all genres including self-help and local authors. And of course, a children's section where we will pick up something for our grandbaby before leaving. There is nothing sweeter than reading a good book to our little cutie. All the bookshelves and counters are beautiful, restored antiques. There are many vintage accessories like old suitcases, a printing press, and even an old phone booth turned into a locked display for collectible books. We enjoy a short visit with Francis, the incredibly nice seventy-five-year-old owner. She can tell you about any book any time; a woman after my own heart. She goes on and on about how sweet Emma is when we ask about her. Francis's eyes tell me that she is not a fan of my mini sundress with the low-cut top, either, but she is too kind to say anything negative. I would never wear the things at home that I wear for Jack when we travel. I especially want to give Jack plenty of sexy looks with my outfits on this trip considering what we have been going through.

Jack mentions that he wants to stop at the drugstore to look for some beard oil for his goatee that has become fuller and grayer over the last year. I feel the heat rise in my cheeks when I remind him that I am his natural beard oil so not to worry as I will keep it in good shape. I surprise myself and Jack when I say naughty things like that. Jack decides to go next door for a bottle of wine while I browse one of my favorite clothing stores. A store more focused on comfortable and fun clothes instead of fancy ones. Aside from some of our fun date nights and our photo sessions, I prefer comfort over fancy every time.

As I bend over to put the last bags in the back of the car, I hear a whistle—my sweet and crazy husband, always treating me like I am something sexy, even though I'm not. This is a quiet time of day and we have seen very few people while shopping, so I decide to give my sweet guy a little surprise while he is gawking at me. Besides, extending our comfort zone with extra adventure is a big part of the reason we are on this trip. I know he will either have his camera ready, because he always does, or at least his phone to take a video so I want to give him something good.

I lean over slowly in my very short sundress, slowly rub my hands up my sides like a striptease, and slither my body back and forth, trying to emulate a sexy dancer. With my arms overhead, I roll my butt in circles and run my hands through my hair exposing the back of my neck. Jack loves that and gives me another construction worker's whistle showing his appreciation. Slowly I let my arms flow back down, gently brushing the sides of my body. Stopping with both hands on my butt, I give a couple of thrusting movements before bending over to place my hands on my knees. Another whistle. Then I really unleash the move that is going to rock his world. I hope he is capturing the moment with his phone, so he won't ask me to do it all again later. I start with a slow sway of my butt then move to some quicker shaking, and finally hard bouncing. I can feel the jiggle and I think of Jack kidding me that my butt walks me up the hills on our hikes. I feel more air on my panties and realize that my dress has bounced up over my big ole butt and stayed there. I keep going, knowing that my panties are showing. I am proud of myself giving him a fun start to this vacation.

Finally, while still bent over and my butt up in the air, I glance over my shoulder to blow him a kiss and see the shock on his face. I am the one SHOCKED and HORRIFIED when I turn and see Lucca, the neighbor to our rental whose wife had given me many massages over the years. He runs his hand through his wavy black hair pushing it back from his eyes before clapping and taking a few steps closer then wrapping both arms around me in a warm embrace. Lucca tries to hold back the huge smile fighting to come out, "It's so good to see you," with emphasis on the last four words. I feel the heat rise in my cheeks even though I should be well used to his limits-pushing jokes after all these years of our friendship.

I quickly try to deflect my overwhelming embarrassment by telling him how sorry I am that we couldn't come for Martina's service, and he acknowledges that he understands better than most with all we are going through. We have been in touch with several friends from the town since we had come to know them so well over the years and were devastated when Martina had passed so quickly from her battle with cancer. But we haven't shared much of our recent challenges with anyone here, or anyone back home, so I am curious as to how Lucca knows anything and how much. We talk of happy memories of our times spent together when Martina was here. I had expected Lucca to be more reserved than usual since my friend Victoria had told me during one of our recent phone conversations that he was battling depression. I was very wrong with that assumption.

Victoria had shared that Lucca had not reopened the massage business in the fitness building she owned, but she had been forcing him to come for workouts in hopes of getting him to talk about his loss. I'm not sure how the therapy had been going but Lucca must be pouring himself into the workouts because he looks fitter than I recall in his normal attire of a tight T-shirt and shorts. But I can't picture anything but Lucca's view of my big booty in the air during the whole conversation which lasts only about three to four minutes but seems much longer before Jack emerges from the wine shop .

I am even more happy than normal to see my husband, "Hi honey, look who I ran into."

Lucca reaches a hand to Jack, and they share one of those half-hugs that men do, "I was admiring the curves of that nice ride and walked up on Tess. I think I may have shaken her a bit." Good grief, I was shaking alright, shaking my big ass.

Jack proudly asks, "So how do you like her?"

With a quick side glance toward me Lucca responds, "She is a beauty for sure. I would love to take her for a ride sometime." Seriously, I am beyond embarrassed but not surprised as Lucca has always liked to joke. Jack and Martina were always the quieter, more reserved members while Lucca and I were more vocal when the four of us would get together.

Jack, while looking at the car, "Just say when and we can enjoy a ride together."

Together, oh my goodness. Where is my mind? Get control of yourself, Tess. I interject, "Lucca it was great to see you again, but we better get going since we have perishables."

"Oh, it was definitely my pleasure seeing you," Lucca gives another wide grin.

Jack pats the long trunk of the car as he walks around to the driver side, "Did you notice these big tailfins?"

Lucca winks, "Lots of junk in that trunk for sure."

I slip into the passenger seat and Lucca walks over to "check out the interior."

Jack hops in, "Can you believe what great shape she is in for her age?"

Another Lucca grin, "Mint condition, you can tell she has been well cared for."

Jack turns the key to show off the old radio and provide a little cool air on the warm day. I now realize that Lucca, standing next to the car, has a clear view down my low-cut dress that exposes way too much of my breasts and I can feel my nips trying to poke through the material. Jack always laughs that my pointers can fight through two layers of clothing and a breast pad. I give the front of my dress a couple of quick tugs and tell myself that it must be the direct blow of air conditioning making them stand at attention.

Lucca as usual tries to keep a fun time going, "I would love to hear her purr before you leave." I'm thinking this skit is never going to end. Please get me out of here Jack before I die from embarrassment or burst out with laughter, or both.

Jack revs the engine and begins backing out, "A good sound can make a special lady like this even more fun to ride."

Oh mercy, everything is relating to something completely different than this vehicle. My mind is producing images and thoughts that I shouldn't be having. That I never have. Finally, I am about to leave this exasperating situation when Lucca walks over to the driver side, giving him a clear view of my short dress riding up to my hips I try to wiggle the dress down to at least keep my panties from showing. Just as we are about to leave Lucca adds, "Why don't you guys come over for cocktails tonight?" Mercy sakes.

Jack touches my knee, "Whatever you say, baby."

My face feels like it's on fire, I'm embarrassed of my thoughts and I'm mad at myself for being aroused, but how can I say no with what Lucca has been through. "Sure, see you around seven."

Lucca smiles, knowing that had always been our meeting time for cocktails when Martina was alive. "Great, see you then."

As Jack steers to exit the parking lot, "Are you going to let those pretty locks down?"

I remove the clip, run my hands through my hair and let it flow freely in the wind.

The dress flapping against my hard nipples, the breeze flowing across my legs and up the dress over my warm panties, and the thought of going to Lucca's in a few hours. I wonder which one is stirring my hormones and making me on edge the most. I am ashamed of my thoughts. Thoughts that I never had before the challenges and conversations of this past year had let them sneak in.

5

JACK

I PAT TESS'S BACKSIDE AS we pass each other while putting groceries away in the kitchen. "He has always had it bad for you."

"Oh shush, you think everyone has it bad for me."

"Well, I'm right and . . . you didn't even ask who. I could have been talking about Rohan, BK, or many others."

Tess keeps putting up the groceries, "Lucca just likes to try to outwit me."

I know that's part of it, and I know that Tess is rarely flirty. Her sweet southern charm can be misinterpreted at times, but under her outgoing personality is really a shy girl. That's one of the many reasons I call her my "good girl." But if you didn't know her and Lucca well you could think they were being flirtatious, or at the very least, they were being inappropriate. "I know, you both do."

Tess keeps working, "Ha-ha. Hand me the paper towels and grab those empty bags."

"Oh, speaking of towels did you notice the water on the floor in the laundry room?"

Tess stops and looks at me puzzled, "Why in the world were you in the laundry room? I didn't know that you knew where it was."

"You are such a comedian. I was snooping around this morning like YOU trained me to do while waiting for the coffee to finish. That was a big storm last night, but if there was a leak from the ceiling over the washing machine, I can't figure out why it would have had dirt mixed in with it. Guess I better text Linda to be on the safe side."

Tess walks to the guest bathroom. "Speaking of towels again, I loved those turquoise and pink and teal flamingo towels that Linda had last time we were here. She must have changed them out because I haven't seen them in any of the rooms."

I steal a hug from Tess, "So, you have been snooping too?"

She laughs, "You know I have."

We met Rob and Linda on our first trip, and they have rented us their house every year since with the only exception being our missed trip last year. Linda makes sure that it is one of the more beautiful homes on the little island and we feel fortunate to have the standing rental. Rob travels quite often for work and Linda stays at Rob's sister's house on the mainland when we rent their place. Rob's sister had lost her husband in a military operation several years ago right before the birth of their son, John Robert, and was appreciative to have Linda and Rob help whenever possible.

Linda has exquisite taste, and the house is decorated beautifully with many amenities that you would only find at a high-end resort. Rob is a guy that works hard and plays hard so there are plenty of fun extras at the house that we have access to use. The three-story home is located at the end of the island with only a short walk down to the beach. The two neighbors on either side, including Lucca, are mostly blocked by the tall oaks and other mature landscaping. There is a pool and adjoining hot tub in the back and a game room upstairs. Rob has a boat, jet skis, surf boards, an outdoor kitchen, and just about anything else you can think of or need.

I hear a grumble under Tess's breath, "Oh, and I don't want anyone coming for repairs while we are here."

"Me neither, baby. It's probably nothing more than the hard rain with the wind, but you know how particular Linda is, so we better tell her." Linda has always been great about responding to any of the few issues or questions that we had during our stays. The house and the grounds were always immaculate, so I am sure that responding to fixing things is more about her personality than just being a good host.

Linda is a very accommodating person, and our standing routine has been for her to stop by for a quick visit over a glass of tea every year when we arrive. She apologetically canceled this year due to the bad storm.

Tess empties the last bag and kicks her shoes off. "You're right." Rob and Linda have always been good to us about working out our preferred time to stay and letting us use anything we want—they even practically insisted that we stay two weeks on this trip. And it looks like they added some extra toys this year, too. "Do you remember years ago when we tried the jet skis?"

I nod. "Do I remember? We were lucky to live through that adventure."

Tess laughs. "You're right and we just did it back then because we were afraid that we were getting old."

I put the last of the groceries into the cabinet, "Look at us now. Let's try not to go too wild on this trip."

I walk over and hug her from behind as she stares out the large window to the ocean. "What are you thinking, baby?"

"What to wear tonight." It makes me smile and reminds me of sitting in her apartment, helping her with her college homework only to find out later she wasn't listening to anything I was saying. Instead, she was thinking of what she was going to wear for our date later that night, which worked out just fine for me.

"Well, don't spend too much time on that. It's pool time, baby!"

We spend the remainder of the afternoon at the pool, which is one of our favorite benefits of the property and a big reason why we have rented from Rob and Linda for all these years. The mature trees and nice landscaping hide the neighbors from our view, granting a good deal of privacy. Upper decks on the neighboring houses can still be seen but there is enough distance that you don't have to worry about your neighbor trying to have a conversation while you are relaxing by the pool. We laugh that Linda is probably upset because the new neighbors are building onto their house, and she will not like anyone on the island upstaging her.

We enjoy a few snacks and a couple of frozen margaritas. Tess looks so good in her purple bikini. It is low cut at the waist, so low that I can see the edge of her life-giving scar. The top is also very revealing, exposing the outer edges of her areolas and revealing much more of her breasts than she would normally wear. She is much more comfortable wearing this suit at the private pool than on the beach in case we run into too many people, even if we don't know them. I bring over our second round of "margs." We were informed by our son, a recent college grad, that's what the cool kids call them. "You should book a massage while we are here. I'm sure Lucca will give you his best discount price."

Tess rolls her eyes. "Very funny, but it isn't as fun without you having one with me. Besides, I'm used to Martina's massages AND Victoria told me in our last conversation that he hasn't reopened the business."

I crack the shells on my fresh peanuts. "I know, I like getting them together, too, but I can edit our last set of photos, or I will be glad to go with you for support. I know that you could use one with all the stress you have been under."

Tess eases her sunglasses down slightly and gives me a stern stare. "I know what you are trying to do."

I lean back in my chair, toss a peanut in the air and catch it in my mouth. "Just trying to get you to relax and follow the doctor's advice."

Tess sits up from her lounger and places her drink on the table. "I know that she is supposed to be the greatest psychotherapist in America, maybe in the world, but her remedy sounds crazy . . . no, not crazy, but insane to me."

I turn to Tess. "I think so too but we have tried everything else baby, and I do mean everything." We had role played, used Tess's special oils, tried intimacy in every room at every time of day, even a little rendezvous out in the woods, and nothing helped.

Tess lowers the volume of the speakers from her phone. "I just don't think I could ever do it honey." Her eyes look down at the pool. "Don't be disappointed."

I love, appreciate, and respect Tess so much. She is the best thing that ever happened to me. I had been very open with Doctor Ladd out of desperation to get better and a desire to make Tess as happy as possible in every way. Tess is too sweet to admit she wouldn't be happy in that aspect of our lives if I never recovered, but I couldn't stand the thought of her having to live like that. Of us missing out on that special part of our life.

Our intimacy, while certainly not the only part of our closeness, has always been a big part of us. My desire for Tess has grown steadily over the years of our marriage, as much from the tightening of our bond as from her physical beauty. All of this made me more open with the doctor about my past, my fears, and my fantasies than I would have ever thought I could be with a stranger, or a friend for that matter.

I take Tess's hand in mine. "I'm not disappointed in you at all and I'm not sure that I could do it either. You know how I am so protective of you, but the 'expert' came to this as the best and only remaining option after months of meetings with us. And yes, she does have an incredible record of success for helping to correct this type of problem."

Tess looks at me sadly. "The thought has always repulsed me."

"Because you are a good girl who loves her husband. I know that you do and always will no matter what. I am certain nothing could ever change that for either of us." I want to believe that with all my heart.

She squeezes my hand. "Nothing could ever change that, but I am happy the way we are."

"I am happy with you too baby, but you aren't or at least can't continue to be as happy as you deserve to be with this part of your life missing. I'm afraid you will miss it and change over time."

Stiffening her back, "I believe that I can be fine for however long it is."

I try to hide my embarrassment from the issue after the surgery. "But it's not fair to you if we don't try everything we can, and I want you to be so much more than just fine."

She leans in for a long hug that makes everything good—for the moment, at least. "I will do my best to think about it but no promises."

I squeeze her a little more tightly. "It's ultimately your decision, baby . . . unless I can't do it if, or when, the opportunity presents itself." Which I think to myself could very well happen.

6

TESS

I CHOOSE A SHORT, WHITE skintight skirt and a just-as-tight purple and black button-up blouse. My silver necklace with a 'T' matching my anklet nestles deep down between my breasts and I worry I may be showing too much cleavage, but for some unknown reason, or one that I won't admit to myself, that is the choice I make. The 'T' rests on a black lace bra that props up my breasts a little more than usual. The final touches are black-heeled sandals that show off my burgundy toes and two toe rings, one on the second toe of each foot. The double-strand silver ankle bracelet hangs over the strap of my right shoe. I applied a more reserved dark blush on my cheeks and the faux diamond studded clip pulls my hair together at the top of my head while letting the lower part fan out below. Multiple diamonds and a couple of hoops in each ear. I refuse to allow myself to think of why I spent so much time and effort for a couple of drinks with an old friend.

Jack smiles at me. "Absolutely gorgeous. I couldn't have picked it out any better."

I force a smile past my underlying and unidentified concern. "That is saying a lot. Are you ready, baby?"

"I would follow you to the ends of the earth looking like that," as Jack rushes up to place both hands on my hips. I love the feeling of him holding me with such love and desire.

"You are a crazy man. Let's get going so we can get back for a night swim." I just want to get this over with and relax with my husband.

Jack flips the switch for the outside string lights around the pool on the way out. Nothing. The storm must have kicked a breaker. He runs back upstairs to check the box, but the outside lights are not listed, and he says all the breakers seem to be on. We don't want to be late, so he decides to text Linda on the walk over. She can have her repair person check that while looking at the leak, and then hopefully we won't have any further interruptions.

As Lucca opens the door to greet us, I hesitate at the entrance, thinking of Martina. Entering, I am reminded of her peaceful and calm personality. The room is a gentle mix of Bohemian colors with plenty of serenity. The atmosphere of dim lighting, scented candles, and the aroma of incense calms the nervousness that I shouldn't even be experiencing. Jack and I sink into the plush, light blue sofa piled with decorated pillows and two incredibly soft blankets hanging over the back of each end. Lucca sits across from us in a wicker hanging chair with dress shorts and a button-up shirt. That's about as dressed up as it gets for Lucca, and I envy the hanging chair. I have had Jack put similar chairs inside and out of each house that we lived in.

Lucca brings a round of fruity cocktails, the first being a Bohemian drink with gin, elderflower liqueur, and grapefruit juice. Over the next hour or so we talk through our fun times together, Martina's difficult struggle, then Lucca told us about a spat over boundary lines created by the new neighbor's addition to their house. It was Lucca's effort to reach a compromise in the boundary dispute that made Linda mad enough to not allow Rob to golf with Lucca any longer. There is plenty of laughter and a few tears as we share some of the memories. We try two other drinks during the conversations, one an easy Bellini which is my favorite of the night. Prosecco, fresh sliced peaches, and peach juice, a popular drink from Lucca's home country of Italy. I am feeling the effects of those drinks added to the margaritas we had much earlier, and I lean back onto Jack's shoulder. I am close to rolling to my side, which Jack knows will soon be followed by closing my eyes. Jack sits up and tells Lucca that Rohan said he is doing massages at home now. This rousts me from my near nap, and I excuse myself to the bathroom. Lucca follows behind, taking Jack to the room that he and Martina had remodeled into a massage room after she was diagnosed with lung cancer.

I hear Jack speaking to Lucca as we walk down the hall. "I've been trying to get Tess to have a massage while we are here. She needs it."

As I turn to enter the bathroom, I glance behind me. Seeing Lucca's stare, I tug my skirt downward as much as possible. Lucca refocuses on Jack. "It's truly amazing how much it can help the mind and body. We believed it enough to make it a life calling."

As Lucca reaches for the doorknob I hear Jack, "If it's too difficult for you, we can wait until another time."

"Not at all. You and Tess have been great clients and friends for a long time. We remodeled the room to let Martina work when she felt well enough. I just haven't had the heart to use it since she has . . . been gone."

Opening the door, Lucca takes a deep breath, "I think we did a pretty good job with it."

I return from the bathroom to find a room that is wrapped in serenity and love. Dim lighting, soft music, and a wonderful scent that is piped in at the flick of a switch. The two beds are covered with dark silk sheets with plush towels at the top and bottom as if ready to service a customer tonight. Oversized cushions cover one side of the large room and beautiful tapestries hide the work and supply station on the other side. I notice a towel warmer and a stone heater on the top of the counters. I am taken aback by the beauty and tranquility that envelopes the room. I turn to leave, stopping just short of the door. Tears well up in my eyes as I read the plaque on the wall written in script: "Keep spreading love and peace as we promised each other." Below it was signed: "I love you forever, Martina."

"She had that made from her handwriting just a couple of months before passing," Lucca struggles to get the words out.

My unfiltered mouth says the first thing to come in my mind, "I'm so sorry, Lucca . . . I hope that you WILL honor her by keeping that promise."

Jack and I take our place back on the couch. I had come out of the bathroom with the intent of calling it a night, but I just can't leave Lucca alone after the emotional tour of the room. Lucca offers another round of drinks, and I kid him that he should talk to Rohan about tending bar.

I prop my feet on the ottoman and lean back onto Jack's shoulder, wiggle my skirt down again, and take a sip. "Yum, this is my new favorite flavor of the night." Lucca looks like he is deep in thought then randomly darts out of the room leaving the chair swinging on the stand and yelling back, "What's wrong with me, I do need to honor her, and I have been a terrible host." Jack and I give each other a puzzled glance. Moments later Lucca returns with an arm full of supplies and throws a large pillow on the floor in front of the couch. "Off with those shoes," as he begins unbuckling my sandal. I sit up and attempt to withdraw my foot in protest, but Lucca is already unstrapping the second shoe and removing it before I can get the words out.

Now sitting up and more awake, I look down at Lucca. "You don't need to do this; we are here for a visit with you."

Lucca remains busy with organizing his supplies. "I don't have to, but I want to if I am not offending or forcing you."

A smile creeps onto my face. "You are not offending me at all, I just feel a little guilty."

"Please don't feel guilty, it's my pleasure and you're right, I need to honor her note on the plaque."

I lean back once more against Jack's shoulder, take his hand in mine, meeting his eyes with a little smile. I whisper, "You got want you wanted." Lucca sits cross-legged on the pillow in front of the sofa and gently picks up my left foot while sliding his other hand behind the bend of my knee to guide the foot to a little oval machine beside him. He explains that the machine with a soft glowing light provides a warming ultrasound that will relax the muscles and tendons. I am listening but more wondering about the view he is offered up my short skirt that rises even higher with the repositioning of my feet. The lights in the room are dim but the glow from the machine and the direction it is aimed is enough for Lucca to work and acts as a flashlight directly up my skirt to my white lace, partially-see-through panties. I try to inconspicuously wrangle the skirt down a little. He begins slathering scented lotion to the top and bottom of the right foot while my heel rests on his knee. Several moments in, Lucca uses his thumb and index finger to massage each of my painted toes. It is delightful.

"That feels fantastic." Soon, I feel more relaxed from the rubbing and the drinks, and I drift a little further down on Jack's shoulder without thinking of the skirt.

Lucca places a hand on my heel, moves his pillow forward slightly, and eases my foot into his lap as his hands move up to my calves. I squeeze Jack's hand a little tighter and he shifts over a bit to begin rubbing my shoulders. Lucca continues to caress my lower leg and around the front and back of my knee. The music is soothing, and the aroma of incense and oils is so relaxing. After several minutes, Lucca moves my foot to the pillow, repositions to his knees, and leans forward moving his hands up either side of my thigh with a little more pressure. From the angle of his reach and the shifting of my hips, his hands brush ever so slightly against the white lace with each stroke. More thoughts of what the doctor had suggested race through my mind. I try to fight back the images that I know I shouldn't be having. He continues the path from my knee up my thigh and under the skirt several more times before lowering back to his knees. My body relaxes into Jack.

Lucca removes my other foot from the machine and lifts it slightly to wipe with a towel, causing my knees to separate even more. I know that he has a clear view up my skirt but surprisingly it is not bothering me as much as before. I attribute that to being relaxed from the massage and the drinks. As Lucca goes through the process of placing the other foot in the warming container and begins to massage, Jack starts kissing my ears and neck, bringing chills to my body. Jack's hand runs across my chest and under the blouse which is unbuttoned far enough to give him plenty of access. Lucca continues with the other foot, placing it in his lap and moving up my lower leg again as Jack's hand moves under the black lace bra to massage my breast. I am so aroused. What am I doing? I shouldn't be letting this excitement happen, especially with all Jack and I are going through right now. As Lucca's hands move to my thigh, Jack pinches my swollen nipple. A chill rushes through my body as Lucca's hands move up my thigh, briefly disappearing under the skirt, and brushing against the lace as Jack twists and pulls a little harder. My back arches and I fight to not let the sounds come from my mouth. Lucca slows, letting his fingertips lightly take the last couple of trips up and down the inside of my thigh. I let out a breath of relief as Jack releases his grip on my strained nipple and slides his hand out of the bra. Lucca leans back. "I hope that was satisfactory."

A gravelly whisper eases past my lips, "Amazing." It is the only word I can get out.

As Lucca leaves the room Jack gives me a sweet kiss on the cheek. "Glad we came?"

No words come out, but my smile is all the answer he needs. Jack holds me tightly.

Lucca returns with water for everyone. "I never had the pleasure of working on you, but I remember Martina telling me that you had great leg muscles when she massaged you. She wasn't kidding."

"You are too kind, and the massage was fantastic, thank you."

"All thanks to you my dear, for getting me back in the groove. You should let me give you a full body experience while you are in town."

I offer a shy smile but no response.

7

JACK

MY EMOTIONS ARE MIXED AS we say our good-byes to Lucca and slowly start back home on the sandy path that connects the two houses. What am I doing? I have never been able to stand the thought of another man touching Tess, even for a massage. She has always chosen a female masseuse, just to make me more comfortable. Well, that and she is such a loving and loyal wife.

But here I was tonight, sitting with Tess while Lucca rubbed her legs, much too far up her skirt. And what did I do? I reached my hand down her bra and fondled her breasts during the massage. Even worse, I found myself getting excited inside. Unfortunately, not the full excitement of a recovery from surgery, but a sense of desire did race through my body.

I blame all the conversations with the doctor and the subsequent discussions, or attempted discussions, with Tess. I have never had any desire for another woman or anyone else involved in our special time, and just the thought of someone touching Tess just makes me ready to fight. Over this last year I have let too many thoughts creep into my head during therapy and during all the self-analyzing when alone in quiet times. I am convinced that it isn't by choice but out of desperation to get myself better, because the doctor told me that it would work. I just want to be everything Tess needs and deserves.

Along with the feelings of excitement tonight comes sentiments of failure. Failure that I am in this situation, that WE are in this situation. Thoughts of not being good enough for Tess. Thoughts that the doctor attributed to a hard-core military father that repeatedly delivered the message that I would never be good enough, in any area of life. The doctor said that message has seeped deep into my mind even though I thought I had beaten the words down by being committed to having successes in my family life and on the basketball court.

I certainly don't think of myself as anything great or as having accomplished amazing things, but I do have a wonderful wife and children along with a few athletic accomplishments. And I have a good job that I enjoy. I never really found myself feeling that I needed to prove my father wrong, but the doctor said that it was undoubtedly a motivation for me, even if it was deeply buried. So, I asked the doctor, knowingly or unknowingly what if it was motivational to me? What would be wrong with that? Doctor Ladd said that my insecurity was also an emotional force of me worrying about being a good enough father and husband. And good enough at my sport or my job. And most of all, my constant concern of making Tess happy.

I challenged the doctor's assessment. If I were insecure, I asked, why would trying something that involved other people in our sex life not make my insecurity worse? I was surprised by her quick and well-reasoned response.

Dr. Ladd said she had researched all she could about Tess and me before agreeing to help us. She went right into the story about a coaching decision I made during our last national championship basketball game. She was more knowledgeable about the details than I ever would have expected.

She went through the entire story of how our team was behind by twenty points in the first half of the title game. The other team had much taller players and was beating us badly by stopping our inside scoring with their height. They also were getting all the rebounds on missed shots.

Dr. Ladd perked up as she told the rest of the story that I remembered so well. I had decided to sit our two tallest players on the bench to start the second half of the game. I still recall the murmurs from the crowd when they noticed that our big guys were on the bench. I had decided that we could not beat the other team playing their style of game, so I went with smaller players who were fast and could shoot well from far away from the basket.

The taller players on the other team could not keep up with our speed. Even when our guys missed a long-range shot, the ball would bounce further away from the basket, allowing our quick players to track it down for another attempt.

The other coach never made the necessary adjustments in his game plan, and we roared back to win the game on a last-second basket. Dr. Ladd told me that everyone in the building thought I had lost my mind by taking out tall players when we were losing because of the other team's height.

Then she simply said, "Sometimes doing the thing that makes the least common sense is what works."

I saw her point and I did agree with her that I always, and I mean always, worry about Tess being happy in everyday life and in our intimate times. But why did that have to be a bad thing? What's wrong with wanting the love of your life to be happy? Doctor Ladd's diagnosis said that constant concern was part of what kicked in to give me a mental and emotional block of intimate performance after surgery. That my worries and fears about Tess's happiness along with the risks of the surgery combined to leave me unable to . . . well, to do what I need and want so badly: to make Tess happy.

I am not sure about all that, but I am admittedly desperate to do anything possible to overcome this issue and to make Tess satisfied in all ways. The doctor also said that Tess, due to her broken home and unreliable parents in her childhood, had buried her natural and normal fantasies because she wanted so badly to have a consistent traditional home life. That made me concerned that my issues of never being good enough were keeping Tess from being open about her needs and desires. I felt if I had done a better job of letting Tess know that everything with us would stay great no matter what, that she would have felt more comfortable sharing things that she may want to try. My selfish focus on my issues had spilled over to heighten Tess's fears.

It was all so much to process, not only for me but certainly for Tess, too. So, Tess and I have been trying to talk through it all. To be open about our fears, our dreams, and our fantasies whether acted upon or not. To make each other know that it is perfectly normal and okay to have certain thoughts if we share them and decide on any potential actions together. As the doctor advised.

But Tess is struggling even more than me to not only have discussions but to open her mind to any possibility that Doctor Ladd could be right. Tess likes things to be black and white with no gray area. She is not a risk-taker at all. Tess and I have built a great life, even if it is unknowingly influenced by our pasts, good and bad. So here we are, trying to figure it out . . . together. Trying to help me get better while holding onto the great life and marriage that we have.

And tonight creates even more questions. Why did I have the feelings that I did? Did Tess like it, too, or was she just trying to make me happy? Would she give me her honest feelings, or would she hide from her fears, and maybe even hide from her fantasies? The answers that I want so badly are not going to come easily.

One thing is for sure, Tess is so sexy and beautiful tonight, and it certainly seems that she enjoyed the massage. I finally admit to myself that I did, too.

8

TESS

MY KNEES ARE STILL WEAK as Jack and I arrive at the end of the sandy path, barefoot, and arms interlocked. On the other side of the gate, our feet feel the shift to concrete around the pool. Jack latches the gate behind us and asks, "Want to sit out by the pool before going in?"

Feeling aroused and on edge throughout every part of my body, I suggest, well, more like demand, that we go inside as I pull Jack's arm that direction. Once inside I can barely contain myself. I feel guilty at the reason why, but I am too worked up to think about that right now. I kiss Jack's lips while unbuttoning his shirt and throwing it to the floor. I run my hands over his body and kiss forcefully on his neck. Stepping over his shirt, I move my kisses to his sexy chest, which is an extra sensitive area for him, then kiss my way down Jack's stomach and sides, quickly pulling off his dress shorts, squeezing his little tight butt with force. Passion is running through my veins. I raise up and not so gently bite his bottom lip. Taking a step back I unbutton my blouse and fling it across the room. My insides are afire from being so aroused with no relief. I remove my bra and seductively massage my breasts in front of Jack. I know that drives him wild. I thrust my tongue deep into his mouth, taking his breath before pushing him down to the couch.

I wrangle out of my skirt and tight lace that is soaked from the tantalizing night, let them drop to my feet and, standing right in front of Jack's face, move my hand to smooth the wetness across my thighs ever so slowly. I keep my eyes locked on his sexy blues. I unclip my hair, fluff it and let it fall all around my face. Then I turn away from him and give him a much better movement of my butt than the one I gave Lucca earlier in the day.

I let Jack enjoy my backside for a moment before turning and guiding him by the shoulders to lie flat on the sofa. At least I did think of giving him a pillow. I lift one leg to place my knee on the couch beside his head and keep the other planted to the floor. I lower myself inches from his lips and whisper, "I need you to have me." These words and my actions are way out of the norm for me. Jack eagerly responds by raising his head to me and I smear the results of my earlier excitement across his soft lips.

My hands grasp my hubby's head, pulling him closer by the hair and telling him, demanding him, "More, baby." I am raging inside. I know he is happy to oblige, always, anytime, anywhere. I lower myself and aggressively push against his lips and begin to motion my hips back and forth with the inner part of my thighs pressing against his cheeks. Jack devotes himself to my core. He gasps for air, but I don't have the willpower to let him have it, I can't even slow down. I need it. I need him. My fingers grasp tighter to his hair, holding him close as I press harder to his face. I feel Jack's hands squeezing into the flesh of my backside as I watch the ocean under the moonlight out of the bay window.

The waves rise high and crash down with a violent force. They seem to become clearer and closer in my view and my body moves in connection with them. My hands unconsciously move to my breasts and begin pinching my aching, swollen nipples. I look down into Jack's loving eyes. Waves rising and falling faster and faster, becoming louder and louder. My passion rises higher and higher with the rolling waves until reaching high into the sky and breaking with one final mighty crash to the shore. The white suds flow beautifully and peacefully. I jolt back to the room with the sound of my own screams of ecstasy. Finally, a long exhale leaves my body limp against the sofa. It takes a moment for me to realize I am still suffocating my sweet husband. I slowly recover to ease my leg over Jack and onto the floor. Kneeling beside him, gently wiping my joy and my sweat off his glistening, rosy cheeks before sliding my tongue deeply into his mouth. We hold the kiss, letting our love tastes float between us until I begrudgingly lift away. "Get the bag, baby."

In the past we have dabbled with trying new toys, but not that often. The challenge of the past year had sent Jack on a mission to buy every crazy shape and size gadget that he thought I may like. I have never been a big fan of them and had repeatedly told Jack in the past that I only needed my man to make me happy. Words I regret now as it adds to his worry of not being able to give me that right now. Jack returns carrying the "special" bag and finds me sprawled naked on the couch with one foot on the floor and the other leg bent, my knee resting on the couch back, thighs gleaming in the moonlight from a mixture of my happiness, Jack's saliva, and both of our sweat. Enjoying the aftermath. I see the look in his eyes, and I know he wants this photo, but it will have to wait for my other needs at this moment.

Jack has the look of a cat with a feather hanging from its mouth and the canary nowhere to be seen. "You look amazing posed like that. Do you have a preference?"

"Everything is not a pose baby, and no, no preference. Surprise me . . . quickly."

And he does with one of the many instruments that we had not tried before. His salty lips meet mine again as he massages oil in the soft flesh below my scar. The touch of his hand is quickly igniting my inner waves again. He knows my body and my desires so well that his hand moves effortlessly and automatically to the right spots, with just the right amount of pressure. He smoothly exchanges his hand for the new plaything, and I hear a low hum. I am surprised by the natural fleshy feel as it slides up my inner thigh, brushing my inner folds, and finally pressing against my now extra sensitive tenderness. The device is pulsating between my legs, barely touching me, making my entire body rock with shivers before finally breaking through to flutter my insides. Jack masterfully guides the instrument in and out as the sound of the hum increases. My body flinches with each rhythmic change. Jack kisses my neck aggressively and then down my sides as he guides the device adeptly. My legs tense as my hips follow the thrusts. Jack moves downward, kissing and sucking my breasts as he thrusts the scepter deeper and harder. My legs open wide, my arms float over my head, my body on display for my husband, my eyes close and my mind begins playing a reel of thoughts and images.

Visions of Jack standing in front of me in his black underwear. His sexy chest and strong runner's legs, salt and pepper hair, strong thin jaw line, and his beautiful blues as he anxiously watches me undress. His gorgeous hands caressing my body with such familiarity. Strong arms wrapping around my body with such desire.

His chest brushes against my body as he leans over me, and I see his muscles flex as his kisses move to my other breast, finding their way to his favorite little freckle first. He continues to work magic, guiding the baton between my legs and his kisses become more aggressive. My back arches automatically, begging for more. My feet push into the couch, lifting my hips. I want it deeper. I feel my calves tighten. The thrusts are harder. Deeper. Jack's lips tighten and I feel his teeth against my swollen bud. Moans. Screams. Louder.

More images. Lucca's eyes looking up at me, his hands moving up my legs, repeated brushing against my wet lace, the growth and pulsing under my foot in his lap.

Once again, the waves rise to a crescendo and violently crash, my entire body convulses before the suds rush to the shore. My breath rushes out and all the tension leaves my body. I shiver with sensitivity as the shaft slowly exits and becomes silent. Everything is quiet. Jack tenderly wipes the sweat from my face and holds my hand as he sits beside me. Stillness. I'm so happy, unaware of how much time passes before I feel the soft blanket touching my skin. Jack offers me water. I love my husband. How could I not do everything possible to give him happiness?

9

JACK

I AWAKEN ON MY SIDE to the soft touch of Tess's hand across my chest and kisses to the back of my neck. She whispers in my ear, "I loved last night."

My eyes, not yet open, "Me too, baby." Big stretch. "It's still dark."

Her hand moves down my side and across my hip. "Thought we could have coffee and watch the sunrise we missed yesterday." I love her touch.

I stretch my arms and roll over for a hug. "Sounds good baby, I'll make the coffee."

"Unless you want some more of what you had last night." Tess gives an easy love tap to my backside as I roll out of bed.

I most definitely do want more of last night and I tell her that with my smile. I love her unusual aggression. Tess is a wonderful lover, but her tendency is to be submissive, letting me guide the time and direction of our lovemaking. Last night took me by surprise, and it was amazing!

Each with a mug in hand, our bodies entangle in the lounger on the upper deck facing the ocean. Beautiful hues of red, yellow, and orange peek above the calm waters. It is almost as gorgeous as the lady curled up beside me, messy hair dangling around her face, sipping her coffee, wearing one of my college T-shirts with a tiger logo . . . and nothing else.

She slides her hand in mine. "Want to spend the day at the beach, baby?"

"Sounds perfect." But, everything with her is perfect.

We settle into our loungers under the shade of the oversized umbrella with everything we need: music, cooler, snacks, books, magazines, and lotions. Over the years we have perfected taking everything necessary but nothing extra for our day on the beach. Some of our first vacations when the kids were small looked like we were moving onto the beach to live. Both of us with our arms full pulling a wagon, strapping all we could to our backs, and trying to not lose a child on the way down. We packed the kids with as much as we could too, and we filled the entire elevator with just our family. Within the first hour, someone either needed to pee or forgot something critical to their beach enjoyment. But somehow great fun was had, and everlasting memories were made.

I'm in my long, dark blue trunks with the same T-shirt Tess had worn earlier, I breathe in her lingering scent. Tess is wearing her one-piece black suit with a silver strap around the middle. It ties around the back of her neck and drops into a deep v-cut at the chest. It is cut high on the hips and backside exposing an ample portion of her voluptuous bottom. Topping it all off is the beautiful stark contrast of the black with her ivory skin. It's such an elegant suit and I love everything about it. Tess, maybe not so much as she keeps pulling the material out of her crack and pushing her boobs back inside the top. But she did prefer a one-piece that covered the small pooch of her tummy that she is so self-conscious of. It makes me sad that she worries so much about that. As I watch her pull up the top, I repeat what I had heard her say many times, "It's not always easy for a girl to look this good."

Laughter from Tess followed by, "Comfort over style would be my preference."

"Thanks for wearing it for me, you look so sexy."

"Only for you do I wear crazy things that I shouldn't."

I begin reading aloud to her from our newest mystery book. We read, snack, rest our eyes, and talk over the next few hours. I have never understood how time passes so quickly when I am with Tess. Walking back from cooling off in the ocean I am fixated on the water rolling off the back of Tess's suit and over her sexy butt, unaware of anything else's existence in the world. Tess's words break my focus, "Not alone anymore."

A couple we don't recognize approach from the beach house path. "Good afternoon, neighbors."

Tess squeezes my hand as we greet the strangers. I shake hands with Devin and introduce Tess and myself.

Devin motions, "This is my wife, Gabriella," and it doesn't take long at all for Tess and Gabriella to establish a connection with one another. Tess has always pointed out women to me that she thinks are pretty whether it's while watching online videos or when we are out. Tess says that she is crazy to make her husband look at beautiful women, but it doesn't matter because nobody compares to her in my eyes. The other thing that Tess has always said is that if people were able to come back as someone else after death, she would choose to be long and lean with tone muscles and beautiful dark skin and a full head of wild hair. She warned me if someone like that approaches me after she was gone that I better be nice to her because it may be Tess. She makes me laugh with her crazy thoughts. Well, Gabriella fits that description perfectly and I can't wait to laugh with Tess about it later.

As shy as Tess is about her own body, she is the opposite with her gregarious personality. Her smile and her laugh are contagious and whatever is floating around in her mind usually finds its way out quickly without a filter. Good or bad. Within the first few minutes she tells Gabriella that she is the most gorgeous woman she has ever seen. Turns out that Gabriella has the same outgoing personality, and they are off and running like longtime besties.

This leaves Devin and I time to get to know one another over a cold drink. He is from Texas, not as in cowboy hat and horse riding but the wealthy landowners of oil. Yet he is a down-to-earth guy, friendly, and easy to talk with. I'm guessing he is in his late forties, clean-shaven with a crisp business-type look even in his beach attire. A few inches shorter than me and obviously takes enough time off from work to lift weights. He and Gabriella met in her home country of Jamaica while he was there on a business marketing trip. Gabriella, not surprisingly from her good looks and the way she carries herself, is a former model and now vice president of the marketing firm that had presented a sales pitch to Devin at the time. They had hit it off quickly enough to marry six months later.

Devin, wanting to forge his own path, stepped away from the family land business and became involved in the tech industry. He worked at a startup firm in Silicon Valley, rising through the ranks quickly, eventually buying into the company. He expanded out on his own soon after and started a software company contracted by universities and some government agencies.

Tess and Gabriella return from their walk and Devin and I stand to what I think is a surrendering of our seats to the ladies, but Devin says he needs to get back for a business call. Tess politely offers Gabriella to stay with us until after the meeting.

Gabriella smiles and responds with her Jamaican accent, "I can't accept this time, but I promise I will see you very soon," and leans in for a quick cheek to cheek hug with Tess.

We settle back into our loungers, and I share my first impressions with Tess, "Devin is a nice guy."

Tess instinctively spins her hair and replaces the clip. "Yeah . . . that's good, but did you get a look at HER? I think that's the most beautiful woman I've ever laid eyes on."

I continue, "Devin invited us out on their boat, and I told him I would check with you."

Tess pops up in the chair. "Check with me? Why didn't you just say yes?"

"Maybe because you aren't crazy about boats."

"I can like boats for a chance to hang out with Gabriella. She's sweet and fun . . . and did you not get a look at her? Perfect cocoa skin, gorgeous dark hair, lean tone arms, legs for days, and a great personality. I want to go on that boat!"

"Whatever you say, baby."

A few more people wander into our area, some from the sparse rentals just down the beach and others from the nearby local houses. Although Tess prefers our earlier morning isolation, she is always up for a little people-watching. It is a great afternoon alternating between reading, music, short walks to cool off along the edge of the water, and even a quick nap to the sound of the waves. And of course, we enjoy a few snacks to carry us through lunch. We even have a few sing-a-longs to some of our favorite oldies, doing our best to make time stand still.

Back at the house we enjoy fresh seafood from the grill before heading to the pool. Without thinking I flip the pool lights again and I am surprised to see the pool area come to life. Linda must have sent someone while we were gone today, which works out perfectly for us not to have to deal with them. You can always count on Linda to take care of any need that arises when staying at her house.

The hundreds of tiny lights strung across the pool area and the surrounding wall provide a wonderful ambiance along with the solar tiki torches every six feet along the back wall. I try to replicate one of the peachy drinks that Tess liked from Lucca's and hand it to her as she walks by, linking her phone to the speaker. We are sipping our drinks with little umbrellas, listening to some of our beach favorites to get the full vacation vibe.

Since we are tucked in safely behind the pool wall and surrounding trees and bushes, Tess is brave enough to treat me with her tiniest swimsuit. A very skimpy white bikini, the bottoms, what little there is of them, tie with a string on the side of each of her curvy hips. Her bottom is basically bare as the string disappears in between those sweet buns and then there is just enough cloth to cover her hoochie—barely—and not one bit extra. The top is just as exciting: tying around her back and the back of her neck, leaving everything exposed except a small portion of her big round areolas and her hardened red tips. Pretty much the rest of her breasts are on display for me. As if it could get any better, the white basically turns see-through when wet. I feel like the luckiest man in the world. Tess says that she may as well be naked, and I agree with a smile that she should be.

She gifts me another great set of pictures while we play music and sip our drinks. Some photos are of her strutting in bright red open-toed heels, others posing as a glamorous movie star holding her umbrella drink on the lounger, and many others with various props in a variety of positions. I really like the ones lying on her stomach with her top untied, highlighting the downward curvature of her lower back before it rolls up over her nice round bottom. Her boobs squeeze out to her sides when lying flat and hang beautifully when rising to her elbows. I take shots from all angles. My favorites are when she pulls the straps back to playfully let the girls out in various poses around the pool while flipping, fluffing, and spinning that beautiful silver mane in a myriad of ways.

Lying topless on the lounger and straddling a chair are some of her bolder shots. She even pulls the bottoms to the side a few times saying with a laugh that it is pretty much all out there anyway. Tess does not like doing what she calls vulgar poses but does surprise me on occasion for a special treat. I'm sure she is trying to make this significant trip as special as she can for me, for us. The shots of her emerging from the ladder of the pool with water dripping from her skin and hair are epic. Tess is the best wife ever.

The music becomes louder as the night progresses and as we have a few more fancy drinks with tiny umbrellas. Tess and I have become the star singers of our own live concert under the lights at the pool. The drinks may contribute to the overconfidence of our singing voices as we belt out our favorite love ballads, but we are certain that we sound every bit as good as the star bands. Unsurprisingly, we sound even more amazing as the night draws on, at least in our own minds. Somewhere in the middle of one of our favorite duet songs, I barely hear a loud, rude sounding voice in the background. My first thought is: who is interrupting our best dance moves of the night?

"A-tin-shun, a-tin-shun, Sheriff Fry here," with a deep southern drawl.

I drop my imaginary microphone and as he approaches through the gate, I am furiously trying to find Tess's emergency cover-up. We have learned the hard way to keep a quick cover-up readily available when doing more risqué photos out and about. But between drinking, moving things around during photos, and the singing and dancing I don't see the wrap or any of our beach towels. As the short round man approaches, I nudge Tess to get in the pool. She gives me a puzzling look until she follows my eyes down to her skimpy see-through suit. Tess jumps in as the sheriff waddles up to within a few feet of me. Between not wanting him to see Tess in such a revealing outfit and our fun night interrupted, I am not very hospitable. Even less so given our history with this guy. The sheriff moves a little closer and I reluctantly lower the volume just as the duet is about to burst into chorus again. What a shame.

"Is the music too loud?" thinking I can't believe either of our neighbors would complain, and no one else lives close enough to hear.

With both hands resting on his service belt invisible under the overhang of his stomach, the sheriff gruffly replies, "Not about the music. Official town business of a more serious nature."

I admit, I am curious. "How can we help you, Sheriff?"

"You can start by get'n the little lady out of the water. All parties need to be interviewed." My mind flashes back to about twelve years ago before young Freddie became Sheriff Fry. He was about sixteen years old, and Tess and I were on one of our first vacations at Linda's house. Freddie was running around with his buddies, and they decided to "borrow" some of Rob's surfboards. Freddie, thinking he was the most qualified, told his friends that he would sneak into the pool area to get the boards. His friends quickly agreed since his dad was the sheriff, thinking they would not be at risk if he got caught.

Little Freddie had made it over the wall and was on his way to the storage area when he heard water running. We had just returned from the beach and Tess was in the outdoor shower. The shower area was boxed in with wooden planks on three sides while the wall with the shower head made the fourth side. Linda had it built to look vintage, so the planks had some gaps in them, which was fine since the pool area was gated. I came around the corner from starting the grill when I saw little Freddie with his pudgy, freckled face pressed against the planks. He never saw me coming, so when I spoke firmly and loudly from inches behind him, it startled Freddie bad enough that he collapsed to the ground. He rolled around attempting to get to his feet, crying and screaming how sorry he was. Once he finally made it to his feet, I saw just how badly I had scared him. Freddie's once dry shorts were soaked in the front and liquid was trickling down his leg. He ran away faster than some of the players on my basketball team trying to make their required time in full-court sprints. Little Freddie must have seen something he liked, because he has managed to show up at the oddest places on our vacations to get a glimpse of Tess every year since.

That history and the stress over the last few months mixed with the drinks and our private time being interrupted by this annoying kid who was now twenty-eight years old and had taken over as sheriff for his retired father, Frank, did not make me present my best self. "My wife has an uncanny ability to speak while in a pool."

I could only see that little kid with pee running down his leg and not a sheriff's uniform as he spoke nervously, "Mr. Walker, I'm a third generation lawman and have developed a keen sense of read'n people's faces and body language when conduct'n an interview." The sheriff tugs on his belt as he turns to look at Tess in the pool. "I'm gonna to need to have her come out of the water."

Not knowing how long he had been at the gate before we heard him, I am sure he probably saw how small that bikini was and wanted a better look for himself. He certainly wanted to use a keen sense of body language, but it had nothing to do with solving a crime.

"Why don't you let me know what this is about, and we will try to help," as I take a step closer to him.

"I don't want to have to haul you both back to the station for impede'n an assault investigation, but I will if I have to."

I snapped, "Who has been assaulted?"

Aiming his big belly toward Tess and leaning to get a better view he requests again for her to exit the pool. Then adds, "It's confidential, but I can tell you it's a bad one."

I'm no lawyer but even as a small college basketball coach I am pretty sure people don't get arrested for not getting out of a pool so a sheriff can use his instincts to solve a case. We are at a standoff. "Sheriff, I'm confident that your acute senses of interrogation will work through clear water. Ask your questions."

He straightens his sheriff's hat with a scowl. "I'm move'n you over to my suspicious list," as he makes a note on his pad.

My peacekeeper personality leads me to be comical in stressful situations sometimes. The drinks probably have a little influence also. Whatever the case, the words just come out, "I'm your huckleberry." A line from one of my favorite movies. I have quoted lines from that movie so many times that Tess knew them almost as well as I did. I know she is either ready to kill me or die laughing.

"You think it's a joke'n matter, huh? The night before last a person was whooped up on out behind your pool. And I think you may have some evidence."

I tried to be a little more courteous given the severity of the situation. "Obviously we would be glad to help, but we didn't hear or see anything especially during the big storm."

"I believe you are withhold'n evidence, Mr. Walker."

I am becoming more annoyed. "What evidence?"

Sucking in a breath and trying to puff out his chest, "Through some pretty intense interrogat'n and some high tech investigate'n I've discovered that you have pictures from that night."

The photos from the first night during the storm have not entered my mind. "Not sure what you are talking about, Sheriff."

"The witness said you had a big spotlight of some sort and take'n pictures out that way," pointing to the back of the pool toward the beach.

Oh crap. Remembering the burgundy dress, "Yes, um yes, we did take a few pictures of the storm that night, but I doubt we have anything helpful." I mumble through a longer than needed explanation about aperture, focus, and other photography jargon that I know he won't understand to buy some time for me to think.

Sheriff Fry wipes the sweat from his brow. "Just bring me them pictures and I will crack the case from there."

I'm thinking there is no way I am going to hand over pictures of Tess to the guy who has been stalking her for years. "They will need to be edited to give the best available view of the background area before they could be used to help you."

"Don't worry me and ole Ed can figure it out. Ed takes pictures at the fish'n competition every year. He has put the winner's photo on the wall at the club for the last twenty years. He's dang good with pictures."

I am ready to wrap up this conversation. "No offense to ole Ed, but I will do the edits and review to see if there is anything helpful and be more than happy to share if I find something you can use."

"Now Mr. Walker, you aren't a law man or experienced investigator like me. Better just let me handle it."

I can't help but wonder how much investigating has been needed in this small town, really. So, I try a different approach. "Someone not familiar with my new equipment could lose every photo if he wasn't careful. Then your evidence would be lost for good. Better let me handle this for you."

"Why don't me and you go have a look at'em right now? I'm used to work'n overtime to catch bad guys."

I'm convinced he knows exactly what's in my camera since he wants to see the pictures so badly. And I question that he has chased, much less caught, many bad guys on this little island.

I have had enough of this back and forth. "Not going to happen tonight. I need to take care of my little lady," with a wink. "It will take a good amount of time to go through the photos the right way."

"All right then but you better not be try'n to pull the wool over my eyes."

"I'm sure your keen senses would alert you if I was trying to do anything with wool or your eyes."

"All right then, I'll be back soon to check on your progress. You might get some kind of award if your pictures help capture the guy."

I start to ask if it was an 'award' or a 'reward' but stop myself. "That's quite the honor, Sheriff Fry. I will be in touch."

He gives one more strained look to see down into the pool and then tips his hat toward Tess. "Evening ma'am."

The sheriff waddles to the gate and I reach a hand to help Tess from the pool. "Well, that was a mood killer."

I grab a couple of towels from behind the hot tub that would have come in handy earlier. "Who do you think told him about the pictures?"

Tess wraps a towel around her shoulders. "You had to do it didn't you?"

"Do what?"

"Antagonize him with the 'I'm your huckleberry' comment."

Proud of my timing to insert that line, I can't hold back a chuckle. "Couldn't pass it up with the western sheriff vibe and all."

Tess continues to dry off. "What are we going to do?"

"I will go through the pictures in the morning to see what I can find. But he isn't getting photos of you, only something edited to show the background if there is anything."

"It's kind of scary to think of something like that happening right near us," as she places the cover-up around her drying body.

I suggest, "Why don't you go see Victoria tomorrow morning while I go through the photos. If anyone knows what's going on it will be her, and you want to take a class with her anyway."

"Sounds like a plan. Let's get some rest." Tess presses her cool wet lips to mine.

10

TESS

TIRED FROM THE ADVENTURES OF last night we finish a much-needed coffee from Linda's flamingo mugs and prep for our busy day ahead. I kiss Jack goodbye, tell him to let me know if he finds anything interesting in the pictures, and head out to old vintage red. The camera is always within reach, so Jack snaps a few quick photos of me getting in the car and then a few behind the wheel. I must give him credit. The man is able to remain focused on me regardless of what else is happening in the world. I give him one more smile, slightly pulling my "Jackie O" sunglasses below my eyes to let him know I need to get going. He takes it as a tease and the shutter clicks a few more times. He is relentless.

If I had a champion in my life other than Jack it would be Victoria, an elegant lady in her seventies, though she looks at least twenty years younger. A dear friend for over a decade. Lean and fit with a head full of long, thick black hair and beautiful unblemished skin from a great commitment to self-care. A body type and look that I long for. What I value more than any of that is her profound wisdom and quiet confidence in life. Her ever calm and soothing presence. She and her late husband were well-traveled before settling on this small island strip almost twenty years ago. Jack and I just happened to be in town when they first opened the Pilates studio a few years after the move, and I was her first membership signing even though we only visited for a week or so each year. Jack thought I was crazy for that, but she would send workout plans and beauty tips between our visits, and I ended up with a great friend, so it was well worth it. I just fell in love with her instantly and I think she always appreciated that, in some small way, I helped her get started by running my mouth around town about how great she was. We have grown even closer with our talks over the years.

We share a long embrace when I enter the studio that has since expanded to a connecting full-size gym with a spa that was once occupied by Lucca and Martina but now sits empty. Victoria looks into my eyes as we separate from the hug, smiles under her high cheek bones, and tells me I am more gorgeous than ever. I love her! I step back and lower my arms. "You are the gorgeous one!"

"Oh, stop that. I have told you forever that Steven would have killed for me to have all those curves," peeking around to my backside. "You are healthy and beautiful and just have a different bone structure than what you want."

Yeah, lucky for me the same bone structure that gives me my wide hips wouldn't allow me to birth my babies naturally and is keeping me from the long and lean look that I strive for. "I wish I could lose about ten to fifteen pounds." A wish I have held onto for the last twenty-three years.

"I did tell you lifting the heavier weights during your CrossFit time would bulk you up some honey," Victoria squeezes my bicep. "But I have to say, your muscles look fantastic." Victoria has such a gentle tone that she can speak the truth without offending you.

I laugh because Victoria certainly did warn me of that. "I am proud of the progress I made on building my muscles and Jack loves it too, but I feel much of my hard work is hidden by that same fifteen pounds I have been fighting to lose for so long."

"Well, let's burn some calories my sweet friend."

We jump right in with a warm-up and some stretching before cycling through the different machines she has accumulated over the years. We talk, laugh, and cry a little about all the happenings in town and our lives, including the challenge back home with Jack. Our conversation is only interrupted for me to catch my breath on occasion. Her workouts, even at her age, are still no joke. Finishing up, wiping sweat from our faces, I ask Victoria if she has heard anything about the incident near our rental.

"Oh honey, I got a text not long before you arrived that it was sweet little Emma. I meant to bring it up as soon as you walked through the door but got sidetracked by the excitement of seeing you. I'm afraid my mind is not quite as sharp these days."

My hands automatically cover my cheeks and my heart drops. "Oh my goodness, I didn't know. How is she? What happened?" Questions fire without cease from my lips.

She proceeds to explain the story of how Preacher Jones was looking for his grandson's kite that had blown away the afternoon just before the storm arrived. It was little Teddy's favorite, a specially ordered dragon kite with large wings and fire coming from its mouth. The preacher thought it had blown toward Rob and Linda's house but he couldn't find it before the lightning started, so he was searching in the area early the morning after and found Emma lying in the brush with bruises and cuts all over her. He called the paramedics and Sheriff Fry.

I try unsuccessfully to hold back the smirk from my face about the sheriff's inability to help.

"They say she was beaten badly with a stick or bat or something like that," Victoria says. "She is resting and recovering at the inland hospital."

We both wonder who would want to hurt Emma, such a sweet and kind soul.

Victoria continues, "I think the sheriff is working on the theory that it was a random act by a tourist or construction worker, but he is not anything like his dad, who most likely would have already solved the case by now."

I nod in agreement with that statement. "That's so awful. Jack and I will go visit her."

Victoria asks if I have time for the sauna and I am so happy that she does. My skin needs it, and I am not close to being done talking with her.

The heat feels wonderful on our muscles after the hard work out. Victoria shares a little smile. "I know you pretty well Tess."

I nod my head, "Yes, you definitely do."

Victoria reaches over to touch my hand. "How long are you going to wait before talking to me about what is churning around in your mind?"

"Wow, maybe you know me even better than I thought."

She squeezes my hand in hers. "Well?"

My eyes move to the floor. "When I played the conversation with you through my head on the way here, well . . . I think it is just too embarrassing to get it all out."

Victoria softens her touch and pats my hand. "Only share what you want, but you know you can talk to me about anything. And remember, holding in stress will cause wrinkles."

Laughing, "You certainly know how to make a girl talk."

I take a deep breath and let it all roll out: Jack's biopsy followed by his prostate cancer surgery last year and that he hasn't been "functioning" since then. That all the specialists say that everything is fine medically, and he must have a psychological block. That the first two psychologists lasted three months total because they were incorrectly treating us as if we had marital problems. The third: a psychotherapist deemed the best in America, maybe even the world, in her field.

I tell Victoria about the months of a combination of individual and couple's sessions. That I spat out our personal intimacy details to the doctor that I thought I would never share with anyone: fears, failures, and fantasies, all to do anything I could to help Jack. To help us. Even though I was worried that he didn't want me in that way anymore. But that didn't make sense in my own mind since he was still after me and telling me how beautiful I was every day.

Jack did the same. He even talked to the doctor about the bleeding he had after the biopsy which I know was traumatic for him. But we had even found a way to laugh about it at the time when he ran into the room saying he was bleeding "down there" and it was freaking him out. I told him that he was lucky he didn't have to bleed there every month for many years of his life, and now he better understood why I had been grouchy sometimes. With a little better spirit, he laughed and said he would never survive that monthly.

I was totally impressed with Doctor Ladd, the way she listened, and the things that she had us try, yet still nothing worked. I knew Jack had always overanalyzed every part of intimacy well before any of this. He was always concerned about making me as happy as possible, which is part of what makes him such a great husband and lover. And I have always been so happy with every aspect of that part of our life, since our first time. I don't understand how the man who isn't fazed by playing or coaching in championship basketball games can worry or be nervous about our intimacy after all these years.

I continue to share the story with Victoria. The doctor had called a final meeting. The final option that she had for us before closing the case. My hopes were high for some great resolution from the most renowned psychotherapist in the field, and this is the frustrating advice that she gives us. She says that if we open ourselves up to new ideas and play out some of the fantasies that she believes we have deeply buried, it will trigger a litany of mental, physical, and hormonal instincts that she is reasonably confident will cure Jack and make him whole again. And that it would help me to ignite more passion to explore some of my hidden fantasies that I refuse to acknowledge, which in turn would help both of us. The doctor went on to cite several psychological and scientific studies to support her theory, but it all sounded so completely ridiculous to me that I didn't even hear the information about the studies. I wanted to slap her, and I'm surprised I didn't.

Victoria smiled in agreement with that part.

I was mad that I couldn't fire her, or at least walk out and slam the door behind me. But these were her final words, the cure. The ridiculous cure from the so called world-renowned professional. I shared all the anger and sadness that followed those words. The endless attempted conversations with Jack that I didn't want to have about her advice. Uncontrollably I confess to Victoria all that I had been holding in for too long, the worry about Jack's health, the confusion of what was blocking him from getting better, the guilt of not being able to help him, and even the terrible thoughts and feelings from the massage last night, while I was WITH Jack. I blame those feelings on the conversations that the doctor made us have. I insist that I don't have buried fantasies. I cry profusely as I admit that all of Jack's passion and attention to detail is still giving me amazing experiences, but I DO miss that one part of my closeness with him. I stop talking due to exhaustion from the total release of emotions. And my tears.

"I know that you are sorry you asked." I try to force a smile as I wipe the tears and sweat from my face.

Victoria places a hand on my shoulder. "Let's get out of this heat before we melt."

I curl up in the plush chair in Victoria's office as I sip my lavender tea, a Victoria staple, as her soothing voice speaks as if I had not just poured out my soul to her. "Listen, my sweet girl."

She tells me she is glad I got all the toxic feelings out, that it wasn't good for me to hold them in. Without making me feel angry or demeaned she says she understands all of this is undoubtedly a lot to process for me, but that in the big picture of life it is not nearly as bad as how my emotions are receiving it. That I am a good person and that our marriage is beautiful, unlike any she has seen. That she knows I am a good southern girl raised to do things "right." Right based on the information I have learned from others, well-intended or not. She tells me that we make choices to do wrong every day, just like our town gossip session earlier or telling little white lies to make someone feel better. That we try to rank our rights and wrongs, but they really are unrankable and that none of us can live perfectly. That our hearts will guide us and that I have a good spirit and a true love of Jack and my marriage. She suggests that before I can assess what is acceptable with my learned values and influences, I should listen to my heart on what is most important to me. My rooted beliefs of what is acceptable or doing something "wrong," as she does the air quotes, for the man I love more than anything in the world. And for myself.

I protest, "But I don't want anyone else, ever!"

Victoria sips her tea. "Well, there you have your answer."

I quickly respond, "But, I want to help Jack and to have that part of our intimacy back."

Victoria tilts her head slightly. "Well, there you have your answer."

I stare into my cup. "I see what you are doing."

Victoria smiles. "I am not doing anything, sweetie. You are letting yourself walk through the choices that are important to you. And you need to get somewhere quiet and continue to search your soul for an answer that you can live with."

Victoria dabs her tea bag up and down in the cup. "Do you remember our conversations about Martina when she was first diagnosed with breast cancer?"

My eyes roam the room as my mind goes through our phone conversations last year. "Yes, I told you that I had always feared having a mastectomy because I was afraid that Jack wouldn't think I was as beautiful as he sees me now."

Victoria speaks in her familiar soothing voice, "And how do you think Jack is feeling about how you see him right now?"

"But I AM happy with him, with us, with our intimacy. I always have been."

Victoria smiles. "I know that you are. You two have always been so precious with your sweet love. But you must decide what you are willing to open your heart to, if anything, to get where you both want to be."

I let a puff of air exit my lips. "I don't like making difficult decisions. Jack has always partnered with me on the tough things."

Victoria assures me that he will with this one too if I share my deepest thoughts with him completely and give him the chance. Even if it's uncomfortable.

I am looking for excuses. "But I am afraid to even allow myself to consider those repulsive ideas. I'm sure that Jack already feels bad as it is without adding that to it."

Victoria responds to me with love but blunt honesty, as usual. "First of all, how repulsive is it to you really? You just told me that you had "thoughts" after the massage. And secondly, what if you were in a situation where you felt Jack wasn't happy? What would you be willing to try to make it better?" She pauses to let that thought move around my mind before continuing. "I think that is probably on his mind right now, but he can't get to you because you have been unwilling to be as open and honest about your deepest fantasies as you have with everything else over the years. Maybe, just maybe, the doctor hit a nerve."

I catch myself involuntarily wringing my hands together and ignore her question about the massage. "Victoria, you know that I do not like gray area. It's easier for me to see things in black and white. I like it that way and 'those things' have always been wrong in my eyes and not what I want."

Victoria lifts her eyes to me while sipping her tea. "Oh, my dear friend. It would be so nice if the world was that simple, wouldn't it? Not only are you beautiful and sweet, but you are a smart girl, and you know that it just doesn't work that way. Not much in life is just black and white."

I fight back more tears. "But what if even thinking or talking about these things ruins our marriage? My marriage is the greatest happiness in my life, and I love how committed and loyal we both have been to each other from the beginning."

Victoria embraces me with the tenderness of a mother. "Your marriage IS wonderful and will remain so whatever course you two decide together. But you must decide together."

I am still attempting to process all of that when Victoria continues, "My turn to share something very personal with you.

"As you know, Steven was diagnosed with cancer eight years ago and the doctors laid out in detail the ugly journey we were to face. After a few months of talking about the end and what we wanted for each other, Steven confided in me things that he had held in for a lifetime . . . a bucket list of suppressed secrets, if you will. We tried to do everything on the list that we could while he was still able. One of the wishes and the thing that was most shocking to me was for us to be with another couple. I was saddened, and even a bit angry at first, but after a deep soul search and many conversations together over the next several weeks I realized that I shouldn't be upset that he entrusted me with his deepest secrets and fantasies. We shared so many experiences together over our lives and this wasn't any different than the others. Just something to share with one another. We checked this off his list and it was not only something to share, but it brought us closer than ever. And the bonus of him being very happy in his final days. My only regret was that we waited so long to be open with each other. And I am thankful that I didn't miss out on the experience of sharing it with the man I love."

After a long pause, she takes my hand again. "Tess, people have different ideas and feelings about all things in life. You and Jack have a wonderful and strong marriage and just need to continue to support one another. No one else can decide for you. You may not know what to do right now but if you search together with an open mind, your heart will give you the answer at the right time."

I am lost in processing her story. A story that if it were anyone else sharing, I would just write them off as crazy. But Victoria's calm assurance will leave me with a lot to think about.

Victoria sighs. "Tess, there is one final twist to the story. The couple that we were with was Martina and Lucca."

My eyes widen but no words will come out. I inhale a deep breath as my mouth falls open. My heartbeat increases. My mind is racing.

"He is a good person, Tess. Respectful, kind, and yes, he's handsome too, as you know. And discreet." Victoria gives me a wink and a smile.

From this revelation to the feelings after last night's "foot massage," I wonder if I have misread Lucca's friendly banter over the years.

11

JACK

I AM STILL EDITING THE photos when Tess returns from the visit with Victoria, hugs me around the neck from behind, kisses my cheek, and tells me I am her favorite person. I treasure the way Tess loves me.

While I am still lost in the warmth of her love, Tess blurts out, "It was Emma that was beaten."

I wasn't sure that I heard her correctly. "What?! Oh no! Is she okay?"

"She is recovering at the hospital and we need to go see her."

"Whenever you are ready."

"But first, did you find anything?"

"As a matter of fact, I did discover a few interesting items in the background of some of the pictures. I've moved them over to a separate file. Let me show you. They are at two different timestamps, one earlier in the evening and one as we were wrapping up. See the first one?" I point to a figure in the dark. "That could be Emma."

"Then here is the second. It looks like a different person." I point out a taller figure captured in the brush area visible when the sky was bright with the lightning. "That may be the attacker and that looks like it could be dark hair sticking out the back of a hat. Hard to determine how tall, but wearing a dark blue or black jacket with what looks to be a picture on the sleeve."

It is too fuzzy to make out any details. We have a side shot of the person and a couple more from the back but no front views. "But Tess, all of them have you in the foreground and it will be difficult if not impossible to crop you out and still get a halfway decent image of the person. And there is NO way I'm giving that pervert sheriff photos of you nude or even almost nude."

"I know just what to do."

Tess's confidence shocks me. "You do, huh? Please share."

"You remember what I've always told you I wanted to be? This is my big chance to show you what a great private investigator I would make."

I laugh at what I think is a joke. Tess's look tells me that she is not kidding.

"Jack, you know I have told you for years that is my dream job."

Careful not to laugh this time, "Easy now, Tess, we are on vacation, and I am not going to spend it all running around trying to outdo Sheriff Fry, or let you do anything dangerous."

"It was Emma, baby. She was beaten, and we must help."

"I agree, but I don't know about you playing amateur detective." I try to stall. "We can figure out what to do after we go see her."

We walk into Emma's room and are heartbroken to see her lying in the bed disheveled with monitors and tubes hooked to her. Her body flinches even with our gentle hugs, but her smile tells us that she is genuinely happy to see us, and she clings to each of our hands as we sit and talk. Even in pain, she displays the sweet demeanor we are accustomed to seeing. We linger for a long visit and let her know we will be available for her in any way she needs. I feel she wants to ask us to stay longer but stops just short of letting the words out. We are not able to get much information from her about the attack or anyone she thinks it could have been and I don't want to push her. She either doesn't know much or just isn't saying. I can't help but wonder which it is. We tell her we will be back soon and to let us know if there is anything she needs. Emma pauses for a long moment but just smiles and thanks us for coming to visit.

Once back at the house I tell Tess that Linda has texted me to let me know the lights are fixed, not to worry about the leak from the night of the storm, and that the key to the storage with the floats is hanging beside the laundry room door. Linda is always responsive to all our needs. I want to relax with Tess in the pool, but she is a bit anxious to get started on crime fighting. I convince her that she can think of a plan while floating with a frozen daquiri. I don't really intend for her to have a plan; I just want to get her into the pool to relax. Finally, she relents and changes into her fun high-waisted fifties-style bathing suit with lots of flowery colors. I throw on my multicolored suit and, with a glance in the mirror, worry that I just don't look as sexy to Tess as she always does to me.

We toss our "Cadillac" of floats, a blow-up double lounger, into the water. In true Rob and Linda fashion the chair easily fits two adults and has all the extras, including drink holders, an attached pillow on the back, and a waterproof container to keep our phones dry. I rub plenty of lotion on Tess's body, maybe a little too much, just because I enjoy any chance to touch her curves and I don't want her beautiful skin to burn. I hold the float steady as she climbs on and places the drink with a tiny umbrella in the holder. I place my drink on the side of the pool, start our music, climb aboard with Tess, and steer to the side to pick up my plastic cup. I feel good about the effort since I don't dump Tess out while settling in beside her, though we did rock precariously at one moment. We float and talk for over an hour. Mostly about what happened with Emma and who may be the attacker. We solve nothing.

Just as we exit the pool and settle into the double lounger under an umbrella to dry off and read, I hear the front gate rattle. I pop up from our seat in time to see Javier, Linda's pool guy, come around the corner. "What are you doing here, Javier?"

I can see that he is startled. "Uh, um, I must have the wrong day. I'm sorry." He quickly exits, almost running.

Tess and I agree that is strange since we rarely see him during our stay, but assume his schedule is off from normal. And Tess says that I may have sounded a little irritated to him which may have made him leave so quickly. She is probably right after our earlier sheriff interruption. We settle back into our cozy mystery book.

Out of the blue it hits me, but I wish I would have thought before I let the words come out. "What about the big party at Sandy Toes tonight?"

Tess confesses that she knows I want to stay in for some fun alone time. But the look in her eye says that she wants to go to that party.

She is right, I do want to be alone with her, but I want to support her, and I know she is excited about trying to figure out who attacked Emma.

I could see the wheels of Tess's mind turning. "Yes, this is live music night and Rohan always has a good turnout. People come in from all over the area. We will be able to start our investigation there. "I'm telling you, baby, I know I will be good at this."

My thoughts bounce between supporting her and worrying about her. "But Tess, please remember that we are not real investigators."

I can see the determination and excitement in her face. "Well, we are going to be."

I shake my head knowing that there is no stopping her now, but I do have one request. "Only if you wear something fun for me. A level four.

Admittedly, it is a bit silly to name clothing in levels of sexiness, but it just innocently happened over the years. Level one was running errands or going on a walk and typically included yoga pants. Level two was comfy around the house clothes, like shorts and a tank. Level three was for going to the theater or a nice dinner out such as a nice dress or skirt and heels. Level four was reserved for out of town only, away from anyone we knew and was a shorter dress or a high slit and more cleavage than a level three, much more. Level five was the play around clothes for our photo shoots and some of the swimsuits she packed for this trip. I think Tess is beautiful in all levels but if we are going to spend our vacation as investigators, I think it only fair to go with a level four.

"You know I will, but that will change my strategy."

"Your strategy? Do you have a strategy?"

"Of course I do, but it was going to be low profile tonight. If I'm going to dress for you, I certainly won't blend in, at least not with the other mature ladies. I guess it will have to be more of a mingle strategy now. Try to get them talking to let something slip. And to see who doesn't show, that could mean they are hiding something because everyone in town loves the bands that Rohan books. And he offers very good drink specials to attract an extra-large crowd."

I run my hands through my hair that is past due for a cut. "Good grief, what are we getting into?"

She certainly is not going to blend in. Tess strolls out of our room with a white summer dress that is just above the knee on one side and lifts slightly higher up the other leg with a slit that rises almost to her hip. Two tiny straps hold up the scooped top that exposes a generous portion of her beautiful breasts. The back drops low to the gentle indention of the bottom of her spine. It hugs her curves in such an alluring fashion and with no bra, her nipples are captivatingly prominent in the night air. I notice when we are getting into the car that a light shining at just the right angle grants a pretty good outline to her little string panties. I can't find the words to describe how provocative the shape of her body is in the tightness of the dress, so I just take some photos.

Tess wearing this outfit changed the night from dread to desire. The fact that Tess would never wear anything like this out in public back home is not lost on me. The outfit is accentuated by multiple diamond studs and small hoops in each ear, shiny skin-toned lipstick, bright red painted toes and fingers, one arm covered in bracelets, multiple rings on her hands, and the always-present silver ankle bracelet dangling over open-toed high heels. Her thick silver hair is held behind her ears with a flowered headband. She is the beauty of summer.

As we are walking from the car to the front door of the restaurant, I scan Tess's body again and speak in a soft tone as if trying to keep anyone else from hearing, "Listen, if we are separated when the fire department arrives, meet me back at the car."

Tess looks so confused. "What? Why is the fire department coming?"

I know she thinks I have some elaborate plan since she is absorbed with thoughts of the investigation. I try to keep a serious look. "Because you are SMOKING HOT in that dress."

"Get inside and focus, you nut." She pulls my arm as she picks up the pace toward the door.

Sandy Toes is rocking with loud music when we arrive, and full of people dancing, singing, drinking, and everyone generally having a good time. Where does Rohan find all these people? Did my marketing work have a small part at least? I have my camera and pretend to be capturing pictures of the fun, hoping to begin a list of suspects that we may not have thought of or generally just trying to catch anything that may help. I guess Rohan would like to have some pictures for his wall or some other marketing idea. Tess is working the room, getting people to talk which is an effective strategy, especially when they are drinking and having a good time. I keep sneaking pictures of her throughout the evening for my own pleasure. Damn, I love seeing Tess from across a room like this and know that she is my lady. Her personality and smile instantly bring life into any room she enters. Watching her legs flex in the heels as she walks across the floor, her butt sway in the tight dress, and the silver hair sparkle in the lights is pure joy for me. We mix in some dancing for our own fun too. We have taken lessons in the past, mostly ballroom dancing, but that isn't really the right fit for tonight. I cannot sing at all, so I decline to join karaoke that takes place during the band's break.

The tight dress does not allow Tess any way to record or document anything she may hear, so she gathers tidbits of information and delivers them to me every so often with a sweet kiss and suggests that I focus on the information she is sharing instead of her scoop top. The dimples in her cheeks tell me that she is having fun.

I record Tess's information on a small notepad when I can sneak off to a corner. I am feeling pretty good about myself, like a detective in a 1980s TV show when I take the pad out of my pocket and flip it open. My outfit of a lightweight dress shirt untucked from my summer dress pants would have worked with *Hawaii Five-0*. And then I remember the sheriff taking his pad out at the pool and I decide that maybe I am not as cool as I feel. I don't have much time to process any of it, but we would decipher our notes later. I figure that's probably how all the good detectives do it anyway. Watching Tess working in that dress and seeing her smile is tearing me all to pieces.

I am ready to go well before Tess has completed her recon mission, so I spend some time with Rohan when he isn't greeting everyone and trying to sell more drinks. Turns out I can get a little information of my own. Tess will be so proud of me. The number of guys gawking, offering to buy drinks, asking Tess to dance, and brushing up against her is getting out of control as more alcohol is consumed, so I call an end to the investigation for the night. It does something to a man when he sees so many guys desiring his wife. It makes me want to protect her, maybe punch a few of these guys, and at the same time leaves me feeling lucky to have such a beautiful lady. I can't wait to be alone with my baby.

12

TESS

I CAN'T WAIT TO REVIEW our notes and pictures from our undercover mission, but watching me move around in this outfit all night has given Jack a one-track mind. I feel the same way seeing him in his button-down shirt showing a glimpse of his chest and his warm smile as he works as a faux private investigator just for me. I think back to our first date and how I couldn't help but smile seeing the happiness in his eyes every time he looked at me. He made me feel so beautiful and has been looking at me that way ever since. By the end of that first night, I was on my way to falling in love because he was such a kind person that made me laugh and feel so special. I still love that about him all these years later. He is a traditional gentleman with a kind heart, a sexy man, and has always worked hard for our family. I want him just as much as he wants me right now, but for some reason he just can't see it. And part of this struggle is the balance between letting him know I desire him and the fear of making him feel bad during his current challenge.

After parking old red back home, my gentleman husband steps over to open my door. I can sense that he wants to get inside quickly, and I decide a little more teasing may be fun as he starts toward the door. In his hurried state, Jack makes it a few steps before realizing I am not beside him. He turns to find me leaning against the car, with one knee bent showing my leg up to the waist. Head down at a slight angle, hair falling over one eye, and hands slightly behind resting on the hood of the car. Jack freezes in his tracks, and I feel him consume me with his eyes. Finally, slowly stepping toward me, he smiles. "Baby, you are the most gorgeous woman in the whole world."

I try to be mysterious and sexy as I slowly brush the hair back from over my eye and smile. "I bet you say that to all the girls." Being mysterious is not something that comes naturally to me. I am more of a "you get what you see" kind of girl. But I continue to attempt my sultry moves, opening my mouth slightly before biting my lower lip gently as I walk seductively around old red. I am sure that I am more funny than flirty, but it makes Jack happy, so I stay in my role play.

Jack takes another step and enters the game with me. "Would you like to come inside for a nightcap miss Tess?"

I lick my lips ever so slowly. "I'm not sure it's ladylike to come inside on the first date."

"I'm very trustworthy, but we can sit outside if you prefer." He continues to play.

"Well, maybe that would be more appropriate." I turn to the side and lean over the car revealing more cleavage.

Jack fights to keep his eyes on mine, which makes me clinch my jaw to hold back a laugh, and I tell him to aim a little higher to find my eyes. He pauses a moment then gently takes my hand. "I think you will be much more comfortable inside and I would like to show you my photo collection." Jack motions toward the door. "I'm sure you will like it."

I let a smile come through as I push my hair back over one ear, another move that I know tears him up. "I'm intrigued. Maybe just one quick drink while we look at your work. But you must promise to behave yourself." I lightly glide a finger down his nose and across his lips.

"Oh, I promise to be good." A little wink and mischievous smile with a motion toward the house.

I begin a slow saunter to the door, accentuating the sway of my butt with each step as my date, my sweet husband, follows closely behind.

Jack spins me and takes me in both arms, dipping me backward, and our lips came together for a long, wonderful, Hollywood movie kiss. He loves to have dramatic intimate moments.

"Ooh, Mr. Walker, I don't think this would count as behaving yourself."

Jack quickly leads me by the hand through the door. "I can't take it any longer, baby. You have had me in pieces all night."

I laugh. "Well, you flipped my skirt tonight too, baby." He likes it when I use that little saying.

He passionately attacks my neck as soon as we enter the front door. Having watched me in that dress all evening excited him even more than I thought. Jack frantically removes my dress in the hall, leaving on the heels which I am now wishing I had kicked off earlier. Normally the shoes would have been off in the car or even before, but my mind was processing all the information I had obtained on my first official day as a private eye. He leads me by the arm to the bedroom, removing my bra from behind before laying me on the bed. I reach up to unbutton his shirt and whisper in his ear. He smiles, steps out of the room, and returns with BOTH bags, finding me modestly and playfully covering my private parts with my hands. I want something different tonight. It isn't usually my first choice of our love play, but I enjoy the occasional times that we do break out the second bag. It is probably a good change for Jack and let's face it, nothing is required of me, and I receive all the pleasure. Though Jack always insists that he is the actual receiver of pleasure in this scenario.

He steers my body flat on my back, kissing each wrist before placing the restraints on firmly and attaching them to the bed. He deliberately slides his hands down my body as if to inspect every little thing about it, then forcefully removes my panties over my hips and down my legs. Again, kissing each ankle before applying the restraints and latching my ankles firmly to the bed. I love the look in his eyes as he adores my body.

I have complete trust in Jack, and it excites me knowing that I cannot possibly get free even if I want to. Bound and at the full mercy of my husband. Jack stands at the end of the bed as if to admire his handy work . . . and me. He climbs onto the bed and I feel his thigh muscles flex against my sides as he leans over and passionately kisses my lips. His blue eyes scream that they need me. I know what is coming next. I don't care for the blindfold as much as the rest of this play, but Jack says that it is supposed to heighten my other senses. I tell him my senses are heightened just fine when I can see him over me. I love looking at the muscles from his shoulders to his biceps to his chest when he hovers over me during our lovemaking. Even so, the lights go out for me.

For the next hour or so—I estimate as I have quickly lost track of time—Jack caresses, gropes, kisses, nibbles, and does about anything else you can think of to every inch of my body. The feel of his sexy hands and soft lips is heavenly. I feel something smooth and cool circle the outsides of my breasts and then down my sides. Something feathery brushes lightly across my tummy and over my mid-section before crossing my thighs slowly. A warmth pours over my chest; the warm lotion candle that is the patchouli scent that I have been smelling.

My anticipation is high not knowing what is next when he whispers how much he loves me into my ear. I love it when he takes his time to enjoy me like this and to tell me every little thing that he loves about me. I am so aroused that if I could break through the restraints, I would attack him instantly. He keeps me guessing which area will be the focus next. Lips to the tender lower portion of my hips, fingertips lightly brushing over my arms. Jack is attentive to every area. He leaves trails of desire and teasing from my ears all the way to my feet. Every muscle of my body is relaxed and on edge at the same time. Warm and cool. Enjoying and wanting. But that is what Jack loves about this, to tease me unmercifully and to take his time enjoying me. He says that I always want to get right to it during our lovemaking, and he likes to take it slow. To make a production of loving me.

I have always told him that our roles were reversed in the intimate part of our relationship, with him wanting all the foreplay and then to cuddle afterwards. I know what I want, and I want it right then, and then I'm ready to move onto the next thing. Like tonight, as soon as we have finished our love game I will want to get to work on my case and Jack will want to cuddle and talk about what I liked best. But right now, none of that is on my mind. My body is squirming as I pull uselessly to free my arms and legs as he teases and devours me. It is amazing. He is amazing.

Jack has already made me "happy" twice, once with his special kisses between my legs and once with those beautiful hands massaging oils into my most sensitive flesh. He loves the scented essential oil love potions that I make for us, except for one of my first attempts when I made the blend too spicy. My insides became a little warm, but Jack jumped up saying his penis was on fire. I promptly told him to get back on top of me, hot or not. He needed to finish what he started. He calls it my love voodoo. Tonight's mix is "Ooh La La." One of our favorite concoctions.

Jack tells me to relax and steps away for a moment before quickly returning. I feel something icy cold massaging my areolas and circling each nipple. My buds become so hard I think I could cut glass with them. It's chilling as it moves down my sides and up one thigh then the other before the tip rests against the flesh between my legs. I am not sure what this is, and I don't hear a hum. Jack's warm breath spreads across my neck knowing that's a connection straight to my innermost desires. Our bodies slide together with the slickness from the oils. The device has somewhat warmed with my body heat and is now just a slight chill, but feels wonderful as it presses the moist and tender skin between my thighs. Jack's lips move to my legs and his kisses remain commanding around the top of my inner thighs as the coolness ever so gently enters my body, and my muscles shiver with each small movement. His lips flow across my skin, first to my sides then back to my hips, and the cool cylinder begins to flow in and out of my body.

For an instant, I think of how I wish it was Jack that I feel entering me. My thought is interrupted, and I let out a moan as he moves up and nibbles my nipple with just the right force, then sucks it intensely as the thrusting becomes deeper and more forceful. The nibbling and flicking of the tip of my breast with his tongue is sending me over the edge, only slightly painful and wonderfully glorious as the long cool scepter moves deeper and more rapidly. Jack is masterful at touching me. My back arches, offering my breasts deeper into my husband's kisses. Smooth but forceful movements between my thighs at just the right pace, our oily skin glides across each other as Jack moves his kisses closer to the action. His fingers massage my tender lips that are wrapped around the shaft while his tongue roams my clitoris just above, finding another way to raise me to even higher sensations. Everything moves together in perfect unison to bring me unspeakable pleasure. My core is all consumed with Jack's focus, his passion, and his relentless eagerness to please me. The cool penetration, the massage from his fingers, the flicking of his tongue, and the scent of our love is joyously overwhelming.

All the yearning from seeing Jack playing detective for me, the laughter from our role play, and the relentless teasing and kissing while I am helplessly bound travels through every fiber of my body. My passion is raging, my blood boiling through my veins. All my happiness and pent-up passion comes rushing out like a volcanic eruption, with quick panting breaths and a long loud scream. My arms and legs finally stop pulling against the restraints. Jack leans in to place his lips to mine ever so gently, wraps an arm snuggly around me, and I feel safe and free, even though I am still bound. His head rests gently on my shoulder as my breath works to slowly return to normal.

I whisper faintly, "What was that baby?"

Quietly in my ear, "Hope you liked it."

"Thank you, it was wonderful." And I lie still for him to enjoy seeing the aftermath because I know that he likes that. I decide the investigation can wait a little longer.

13

JACK

KNOWING THAT TESS WILL BE chomping at the bit to get started on the investigation today after I sidetracked us last night, I am up early. I've set up a makeshift private eye office at Rob's desk in the corner of the great room. The flash drive with pictures, notes from last night, pen, notepad, a short encouraging poem, and freshly brewed coffee. I have written silly poems for Tess for many years. They aren't very good, but they make her smile and that is all that matters to me. Tess comes out of the bedroom with messy hair and a sleepy look and walks over to the window where I am enjoying the ocean view. She notices the desk, smiles, wraps her arms around my neck, and plants a sweet kiss on my cheek. "You are the best husband."

"I try hard."

"You don't have to try; you just are." With the sweetest smile, "Last night was so good."

"I certainly enjoyed it," as I wrap an arm around her shoulders.

Tess squeezes my hand as we stare out to the ocean. "Really, what was that?"

I offer a sly smile. "You never know what I may have in those bags."

Tess lets out one of her make-the-world-better laughs. "Truer words have never been spoken."

I turn toward the kitchen. "Would you like it black or one of your fancy drinks?"

Tess notices the poem, picks up the paper, and reads aloud.

"Good morning my beautiful wife
Thank you for giving me such a wonderful life.
Last night you were an amazing date.
And when we got home it was super great.
Without a doubt, you are the sexiest private eye.
You will solve the case and beat Sheriff Fry!"

Tess lets out another big laugh that I never tire of as she hugs me tightly and tells me she loves me more than ever.

She rubs her eyes. "I think I will grab a quick shower to wake myself up first. Then surprise me with the drink, like you did last night," with a playful grin.

"Oh, I will surprise you again for sure." I pat her on the backside as she turns back toward the room for a shower.

Tess had been gone a few minutes before there is a knock on the door.

"Good morning, Mr. Walker."

"Morning, sheriff," I sigh.

"I came by last night, but nobody was home," as he pushes his way in.

"Yea, we went out last night."

"I trust that you have some good news for me with the pictures."

"Not yet. As you so aptly noticed, we weren't home last night."

Tugging his pants up over his belly, "You do realize that I'm in the middle of a big investigation and I can't have you slow'n me up, don't you?"

The little bubble over my head read: "you aren't the only one in the middle of an investigation" and I couldn't hold back a grin.

"You think this is a game, Mr. Walker?"

"Not at all Sheriff, but we are on vacation and I'm sure you have plenty of angles you are working."

"You can just hand them pictures over and ole Ed will help me go through them. Don't know if I told you but he takes all the pictures at the annual fishin' tournament, so he is good at that stuff."

"I appreciate it Sheriff, but I will get through them today."

"I get the feeling that you are hide'n something Mr. Walker, and that is make'n me suspicious."

"Yea, you're right, I committed a crime on a young lady that we adore and took pictures of myself doing it from the second level deck while in the brush twenty yards away. Thought you said you were an ace investigator, Sheriff."

"Now look here Mister, don't get wise with me. Maybe you just don't want me to see sexed up pictures of the little lady but that ain't no reason to hold up official business. Besides, I've seen plenty of pretty women in my day," as he proudly puffs out his chest.

I wasn't sure if I was going to laugh or throw up. "I will let you know if I find anything."

"Alright then, but I'm not waitin' much longer. And, how did you know it . . ." His voice trails off.

It was at that moment Tess strolls into the room flipping her hair up into a knot with one hand and staring at her phone in the other wearing just her panties and a short robe . . . UNTIED! I was trying to get the words of warning out of my mouth when I hear, "Well, there's the little lady now. I didn't get to speak to you properly the other night because you were in the pool." He pauses with a wide smile crosses his face. "It's nice to see you now though." I really think his eyes are going to pop out of his head. I am sure he is having a flashback to peeking between the planks of the outdoor shower and I am just about to yell at him like I did that day.

Without a word, Tess turns, ties the robe, and disappears back into the bedroom in a flash. I make a mental note to remember to tell Tess the joke about disappearing in a "flash" later.

The sheriff tries to gather himself while still staring at the empty doorway Tess has passed through. "Yep, I'm gonna need those pictures soon Mr. Walker."

I walk over and open the front door. "Have a good day, Sheriff... and be sure to check your pants." I chuckle as he hesitates before exiting.

I give Tess the all-clear as the door closes behind the sheriff. "That Peeping Tom is beginning to get under my skin."

Tess heads toward the coffee. "Sorry, I was trying to give you a nice surprise in return for the wonderful night you gave me."

"Well, you surprised me AND that irritating sheriff. I thought he may have a heart attack right here and Linda wouldn't like that."

"Especially since the sheriff is her second cousin." Tess sniffs her coffee with a satisfying smile.

"What? I didn't know that. Guess we better be careful saying things about him around town. Everyone here is connected in some way." We both chuckle.

"It's part of the intelligence gained on last night's undercover." Tess now sounds like she is in a serious work mode.

"Intelligence? Undercover? You are really into this private eye business."

"Let's get to work." She grabs her mug and heads to the desk.

I still want to know who told the sheriff about us taking pictures and even what type of pictures they were. Who would know about that?

I put the flash drive I copied with only the relevant photos to the crime into our laptop. Tess suggests that we start with people that have dark shoulder-length hair. I agree but remind her that the photos aren't that clear since the focus is on Tess and the suspect is a far distance away. But it is a good place to start. We open the notebook and begin making our list of possibilities. It is a long list, and we admit that the attacker could be someone we do not know, but we plow ahead with our notes. We break that list down to people who are involved in Emma's life in some way, then further shave it down to people that she sees every day, giving us a shorter group to work with.

We then go through the pictures from last night's party to see who did not attend and cross reference that with our other lists. Seeing Tess in the photos makes it very difficult for me not to get sidetracked again. I tell her that I met the chef last night and he had a ponytail that would probably fall about shoulder length or a little longer when loosened, along with several tattoos that looked as if they could be gang related in nature. Tess raises a brow to that information. Furthermore, I was able to visit with Sara, one of the other waitresses that has been at Sandy Toes for several years. Tess and I know that she has been a mentor and friend to Emma since she was a little kid hanging around the restaurant. Sara did not have anything nice to say about the new chef, Marcus, so we moved him onto an even shorter list of suspects. He was an ex-con and from out of town, so it will be difficult to obtain much more information about him.

We talk through several other possibilities and decide we need to speak with some locals that we know and trust for more ideas and information, like Victoria, Rohan, and Lucca. I agree with Tess's idea for her to visit Emma alone. If Emma has something she wants to share, she may be more likely to do so with just Tess in the room. And Tess wants us to spend some time in town speaking to people on our own, but that is going to have to wait. I still want to enjoy our vacation time even if we aren't going to make any progress on my issue.

I lean over to smell Tess's hair "I'm ready for some fun, baby. Let's take a break from your private investigator work."

Tess moves over to sit on my lap. "I'm sorry, baby. We can do anything you want."

I tilt my head. "Anything?"

Another knock on the door and Tess's body tenses. "That better not be the sheriff again."

Devin and Gabriella are out for a walk and want to tell us what time they would like us all to go out on the boat.

Our plan will have to wait as Tess and I relax by the pool until it's time for our boat adventure.

14

TESS

GABRIELLA IS PREPARED AS HER beautifully braided hair holds tightly against the whipping wind that frees much of my hair from its clip, leaving wild strands blowing across my face. I don't care. The day is gorgeous, and we are on a small yacht skating across the water with our newest friends. The thoughts of how to keep the pictures from the sheriff and the investigation that I had on the walk over to the dock have faded into the clear blue sky above . . . for now.

We anchor well offshore, which gives us a panoramic view of the island strip that is our home away from home. Jack and I try to identify all the homes and businesses that we can along the shore. The view off the other side of the deck is a vast and endless sea that seemingly meets the clear blue sky off in the distance. The wind from our excursion is now a gentle salty breeze. It is quiet and peaceful and far away from the heaviness and concerns of life. A small staff consisting of the captain, a five-star chef, who is introduced to us as Chef B, and an assistant join the four of us on the journey.

Devin is showing Jack his deep-sea fishing skills which I know Jack has no interest in. Jack hasn't fished since our son was about six years old. Jack bought all the fishing supplies needed, a rod and reel, tackle box, floaters and sinkers—whatever those are—only to make one trip and our little guy didn't like it at all. But Jack, always being such a polite guy, shows interest in Devin's top-end fishing equipment, and they seem pretty content at the back of the boat.

I hear Jack ask Devin if he knows the story of how the island received its name, a story he loves to share. Gabriella and I eavesdrop as Jack talks about a wealthy man named Bartholomew Anderson that purchased the island along with three other adjacent strips back in the late 1800s. He had a vision to join all four islands with bridges from the mainland and build a community of high-end homes.

All four islands were only strips of high mounds of sand dunes at the time and Mr. Bartholomew drew up the plans so every house could have a beautiful view of the ocean and sunrise on one side and of the inlet waters and sunset on the other. He had a beautiful blonde-haired daughter named Sandy that he thought would be a great way of advertising the paradise he would be offering.

He placed her picture on billboards and in newspapers throughout the area. The advertisements, somewhat similar to the later Coppertone ads, showed Sandy and her flowing blond hair in a one-piece bathing suit with one of the top straps pulled down off the shoulder showing her tan lines. Mr. Anderson was ahead of his time when it came to advertising.

Unfortunately, he ran into financial difficulties trying to navigate the moving of the sand dunes and the building of bridges to allow the construction of large beach homes. The development had progressed to just one island, our little home away from home, while the other three strips remained undeveloped and unused.

Just as unfortunate as the financial trouble for Mr. Anderson and for Sandy was the simple name that he had given to the four islands, Sandy Strips. Between the photo on the billboards, which was racy for that era, and the fact that there was only one developed island, the name confused many into thinking that there was a burlesque club on the island and the pretty Sandy 'stripping' was the main attraction.

Understandably embarrassed and running low on funds, both Mr. Anderson and Sandy disappeared from the public eye and the island was not developed into the nice area it is now until a generation later. Interestingly, Frances from the bookstore is a distant relative of the family, but you won't find any books regarding that part of the town's history in her store.

Gabriella and I settle into the surprisingly plush seating and pick up right where we left off at the beach. We are two peas in a pod. Both of us are full of mischief and without a filter to even slow down what is on our minds before it exits our mouths. We speak briefly of the shock of Emma being attacked so close to our homes. She takes me through Devin's story of breaking away from his oil family to carve his own path in the technology field. He expanded to a new area, working directly with universities and some government agencies and was in Jamaica for help with marketing when he entered the meeting that would change his life—and Gabriella's. Devin had been committed to his work and never considered marriage until that fateful week in Jamaica. Gabriella laughs that for the first time in his career, he didn't know anything about the contract he signed that day, only that she had presented it and he was all in for anything to do with her.

Gabriella had been a model since her late teens, just like her mother who is a native of Jamaica. Gabriella saved her earnings to obtain her marketing degree and when she returned to Jamaica, she quickly worked herself into the vice president position in a large marketing firm where her father, an American, held an executive position. Her and Devin's paths had been set in motion to collide years ago.

However, they have vastly different personalities. Devin, quiet, reserved, and focused on business, and Gabriella a beaming source of beauty and energy. She is loose and free. The contrast worked perfectly together, and they were married six months after that first meeting.

Devin fights to pull the shark on his line up to the boat before disappointingly saying how small it is. To me it looks big enough to make me not want to fall overboard and I know Jack doesn't care anything about the size one way or the other. But Jack does take some photos of Devin with the fish that he promises to send to him later, along with plenty of Gabriella and I enjoying our drinks.

Chef B serves our dinner on the large pop-up table on the deck. The dinner consists of several choices of fresh seafood—thankfully none of which are shark—several sides, and fresh bread. It is one of the best meals I have had in a long time, and the best I've ever had on the ocean, though that experience is admittedly limited. Devin is excited to learn from me that Jack is in academics. How did that not come up in their conversation while fishing? What do guys talk about? I explain that he is one of the few basketball coaches in a Division 2 college that is also a part-time professor at the university. And in the same town, Jack had led his high school basketball team to their first state title along with two more championships playing at the college where he now coaches. If Devin thinks that is impressive the next part really blows his mind. I go on to share that Jack has won five additional championships as the coach at his alma mater and been named Division 2 Coach of the Year four times. Yes, he is somewhat of a local legend and hero at the small school in our little community.

Jack is a reserved and private person and will never brag about any of that, so I do it for him. Everyone is anxious to know if he will return to coaching from his medical leave, including me. Jack has used his time away from work to help his students remotely. But I know in his heart, he wants to return to the game and students that he loves so much.

Greater than his love for the game, which is saying a lot, is his love of molding and preparing the kids for their futures. His players and students are young men and women but since they often refer to us as their second set of parents, we fondly refer to them as our kids. He has impacted the lives of so many young men and women that still stay in touch with us years later. That was evident from the steady flow of messages and visits Jack had after his surgery.

I can see the surprise on the faces of Devin and Gabriella. Once people hear that Jack is a basketball coach, they automatically think that he is aggressive and abrasive, but as they have witnessed, he is the opposite. When not coaching, Jack is a soft-spoken and kind gentleman. He is smart and has so many other interests outside of sports.

I have always recognized this success to be from Jack's relentless commitment in life and genuine concern for people, but he is quick to push credit my way, as he usually does with everything. Jack jumps into the conversation to say that I am his motivation and the glue that holds it all together. He loves to brag about me, but I will miss his kind words this time because I am awestruck at the beautiful setting sun. A gorgeous painting of reds, oranges, and yellows spreads across the western sky. More beautiful than you can put into words. Jack captures the moment with a few clicks of the shutter. We finish our dessert and sit quietly before pulling anchor on a beautiful evening together.

15

JACK

WE HAVE DECIDED A LATE evening swim to some relaxing music will be a great way to cap off the night. It is such a pleasant evening. Tess and I play and chase each other in the pool like two teenagers. Out of breath from our shenanigans, we cuddle together on the built-in seats at one end of the pool. We share a kiss under the star-filled night sky. Tess's wet lips send warmth running through my entire body.

I debate whether to interrupt such a wonderful night together, but I know that not only do we need to discuss the challenge I am having, but that it is the main reason for choosing to come on vacation right now. So, I ask Tess if she has given any more thought to what Dr. Ladd advised and if she has any ideas on what we should do. Immediately I regret bringing it up as I can see the worry and sadness in her pretty blue eyes. We hold hands in silence for several minutes and I remain hopeful that she is gearing up for a discussion.

I almost let the opportunity pass because I don't want to ruin such a good evening, but the thought of not being able to please her in that one special way overwhelms my hesitation and my judgement, so I follow with, "What was your answer when the doctor pushed you to tell her a fantasy that you haven't shared?"

Tess shifts nervously beside me. "I have always told you that I don't have any fantasies."

I lean in closer to her. "I also know that Dr. Ladd didn't let you get by with that response."

After a pause, Tess reluctantly shares, "I told her that anything that makes you happy and excited is my fantasy."

I put my arm around Tess and hold her tightly. "You are the sweetest wife ever." Another moment passes before I press a little further. "Did she really let you get by with that vague answer?"

Tess hugs me sweetly before stepping out of the pool and glancing back over her shoulder. "Let's listen to something more fun." She changes the playlist from our soft jazz to seventies hits.

I can see the stress fade from her face as she starts to move teasingly at the edge of the pool and asks if I am going to make her dance alone. I scramble out of the pool to join her in some old school club dancing, and we crank the music a little louder. We momentarily catch a second wind after our relaxing afternoon of boating and dinner with our new friends. We sing and dance to our favorite oldies. At some point the songs change from upbeat and fun to more romantic love songs and we begin to undress each other during our slow dances. It seems like a great idea at the time. Finally, the tiredness catches back up to us, and we decide to settle into the hot tub not wanting the night to end.

Making out with my girl—Tess makes fun of me for using the phrase 'making out'—in the bubbly warm water under the stars is so romantic. I love these moments. It's so peaceful. Until Lucca comes stumbling through the gate calling frantically for me and Tess, interrupting the beautiful words of a love ballad.

"In the hot tub," I begrudgingly respond to his panicked pleas calling our names.

He redirects from the back steps and trots toward us in a rush. "Help me, he's coming to get me."

Tess and I speak in unison. "Who's coming to get you?"

Lucca bends over, hands to his knees to catch his breath. "Sheriff Fry, he is accusing me of the attack on Emma! I would never hurt Emma . . . or anyone else."

Tess responds before I can. "We know that Lucca."

Far removed from the relaxed and romantic mood just moments ago, I point toward the gate. "Here comes the ole Peeping Tom now."

Lucca looks back at us. "You know I didn't do this."

Tess and I nod in agreement as the sheriff approaches. "Lucca, I am officially placing you under arrest for the assault on Emma Lopez." The handcuffs clang together as the sheriff struggles to remove them from the belt hidden under the overhang of his stomach. I find myself thinking I hope he never needs to get to those cuffs in a hurry.

I object, "What evidence do you have, Sheriff?"

The sheriff looks at the bubbling water then around the pool to the clothes strewn across the area. With a satisfied look, "I already told you once Mr. Walker, I don't interview people that are in water."

Seriously? This guy never gives up. Tess knows that I am a private person, somewhat shy even, and certainly not one that would expose myself naked in front of strangers. I feel her hand reach for my arm as I push upward and she attempts to grab my hand, but it is too late. I pop up and out of the bubbles, showing everything, and I do mean everything. I stroll calmly past Lucca on my left and the sheriff directly ahead, grab two towels from the table and return to the hot tub without using either one. Everyone stares in shock and silence. I hold one towel up to block the sheriff's view of Tess, and without turning, resolutely state, "If you move from that spot sheriff, you will be conducting the rest of this interview from the bottom of the pool."

Tess, still in a bit of shock with me standing completely naked in front of her, hesitates as if to say something, then slowly steps from the water with a quick glance toward Lucca, who had an unblocked view of her from his angle. I wrap her in the towel that overlaps just above her breasts, leaving the bottom just far enough down on her legs to cover her intimate area, if she doesn't move much. I bend over, ass aimed right at the Sheriff, pick up the second towel and wrap it around my waste. I turn to face the sheriff. "Now that everyone is on dry land, what evidence do you have?"

Rattled and unsure where to let his eyes aim, the sheriff stutters, "I . . . I received a tip and discovered that Lucca and Emma have been stayin' together. I'm takin' him in."

I look at Lucca. "We will get to the bottom of this."

Sheriff Fry clamps the cuffs on Lucca's wrists and leads him through the gate.

"Let's get some rest baby, we're going to need it," as I put my arm around Tess, and we walk toward the house.

16

TESS

I SLEEP LATER THAN I planned considering all the happenings, probably because of emotional exhaustion or the effects of being on the boat all afternoon. Perhaps it was the sound of the pop-up overnight shower pelting the window or a combination of all of it. One thing for sure, I had a fun night with my husband even though I ran from a conversation that I should have had. One that we need to have. I feel so guilty about that. But dancing naked and singing had helped bury all that, at least until that stupid sheriff showed up.

I walk into the kitchen only to find Jack in the laundry room again. "You must be dying to use that washing machine."

"Morning baby, just got back from a run and thought I would check to see if there was a leak from last night's rain. Looks all clear."

I reach in the cabinet for a coffee mug. "Linda said not to worry about it, and we have a lot of work to do."

Jack closes in for a hug. "I know."

I put my hands to his chest. "Oh no you don't. I love you, but you are sweaty and I'm not." I lean in to give him a peck on the cheek.

Jack apparently had been thinking about the case on his run as he hesitantly mentions, "Lucca does have dark hair like in the pictures, baby."

My response may be a little too snippy. "You don't really believe he could have done that to Emma, do you? Besides I think he may be taller than the person in the pictures." I think of my conversation with Victoria, of how Lucca is a good person, but this isn't the time to share that story. Again, I see myself running from too many discussions, but I can't help it.

Jack takes a drink of water. "No, not really but we don't have much to go on, and just a friendly reminder, we really are not detectives."

A sarcastic tilt of my head, "Investigators investigate and that's what we are doing."

Knowing he is fighting a losing battle, "Are you going to see Emma?"

"First thing. What is my assistant going to do?"

"Assistant, huh?"

"Yeah, like that TV show you love and have watched a hundred times. The one where the detective and the assistant are in love, and he is a writer."

Jack smiles. "Not quite a hundred times. It is a great show but what does him being a writer have to do with anything?"

I place my hands on my hips ready to explain the obvious. "Well, you are an amateur photographer so both of you are a little artsy, both assist the real detective, and we are definitely in love."

Jack laughs. "Assist the real detective huh? Where do you want me to start boss?"

"I think you should start with Rohan. See what you can uncover about the convict chef and why Emma doesn't get along with him."

Jack leans over to stretch his legs and my heart flutters watching his muscles flex. "I don't like being away from you, can't we work as a team?"

"I won't be long at the hospital." I remind him that Emma didn't seem like she wanted to talk much last time.

Jack reluctantly agrees. "She may do better with just you there."

Sipping my coffee, "I hope so. I will try to set up a time to talk with

Victoria and then meet you in town for lunch."

Jack gives me sad puppy eyes. "Your assistant is not going to do as well when missing his sexy detective."

I can't resist his sweetness. "Okay, so let's meet at Victoria's for a workout together after we both finish the first part of our mission."

Jack's big smile makes me happy. "Now that is a good idea, boss."

I give him a love tap on the butt. "But you have to behave yourself."

"Who, me?" He turns and wraps both arms around me and gets his sweaty hug after all.

17

JACK

THE BREAKFAST RUSH HAD JUST finished when Rohan and I sit at a corner table, him with his usual diet soda and me with water. Rohan insists that we have a plate of his latest creation, fried fish toes. He is most excited that the toes theme matches the name of the restaurant. The new product is just fried fish, but they are cut to be shaped like toes and come in a spicy or mild selection. I am not so sure about the whole idea, but he says it isn't only the kids that would love them, but adults like crazy things too. We talk about the awful event with Emma and discuss his ex-con cook. Rohan sits with his fingers interlocked and seems surprised that Emma didn't like Marcus, and he assures me he will investigate it. Admittedly, he doesn't know much about Marcus's arrest other than it was a four-year sentence and he got out early. Marcus wanted to come to this area to take care of his elderly mother, or to just get her house eventually, depending on who was telling the story. Rohan did share some good information that he found out from Sara: Emma and her boyfriend Cody had broken up a few months ago. My boss will be proud of me for gathering that information. Rohan agrees to do a little digging for us, and for Emma. Great, we now have another assistant dragged into our nonexistent private eye office. I thank Rohan and let him get back to work, admitting that the fish toes are delicious, especially with his homemade tartar sauce. Everything is delicious with that tartar sauce.

I have time on my hands, so I walk through town taking photos. I'm not even sure why but it seems like something a good detective would do, or an assistant to the detective. As I stroll through the quaint seaside town that has been updated over the past few years, I think of how charming it all is. All the store fronts have been painted a bright happy color, sidewalks are clean, and creative hand-drawn names hang above the doors of the shops. Blooming pots of flowers sit every few feet on the sidewalk and wooden benches are placed under small shade trees in front of many of the shop entrances. All the storefront windows are decorated nicely, and you can barely pass anyone without receiving a smile and a greeting.

I walk by "What's the Scoop" and make a note on my little detective pad that Tess and I need to stop by one of our favorite spots later for some ice cream. The town is a step back into a simpler time. No wonder Tess and I have made this a home away from home over the years. I wonder if we are doing the right thing by getting involved in the Emma case. I can see that it is important to Tess, but I do not want her in any danger, or for us to make the whole town hate us.

Instinctively I wander into the small grocery store. It reminds me so much of the one where I worked through my high school days. A stress-free time. Before kids, career decisions, and before health issues. And before I became a detective— well, an assistant to the detective. The only thing on my mind back then was making a little cash to get new basketball shoes or rounding up friends for a pickup game.

Ed's voice startles me as I am inspecting the produce. I guess Ed to be in his mid to late fifties. He has owned the store for about twenty years, taking over after his father died from a heart attack at way too early of an age. I see Ed as a dedicated worker and a good person based on the way his store looks and how he treats his employees. I compliment him on the appearance of the produce department which he seems to appreciate more than I expected. A kind word is always good to offer.

Ed brings up Emma and I am surprised to hear that she has been working there a few nights a week when she is off from the restaurant. I doubt that Rohan knew about it, or he would have found a way to give her more hours. Ed is very concerned for her and is in the middle of sharing what a great person she is when Tess's call interrupts the conversation. Tess says that Emma was happy to see her but still in quite a bit of pain, and didn't offer much more information than she had during the first visit. Tess is on her way to the gym where she will fill me in more. I can't wait to see her in those tight yoga pants. I bid Ed a hurried farewell and rush off to see my wonderful wife at the gym. I miss her and am lost without her at my side.

18

TESS

I HAVE TRIED SO MANY different exercise routines at various gyms and at home over the years. CrossFit, yoga, Pilates, step classes, rebounding, and many more. I've visited gyms in our home area and out of town, but the one thing that has remained steady, at least since I turned thirty and after I had babies, is that I have worn yoga pants and not shorts for my workouts. No shorts, partly because I must tug them down over my thick thighs the whole time but also because I'm self-conscious of my big butt.

When working out at home with Jack I will dress like a floozie, sometimes to motivate him when he is too tired from long hours of work or recently to help him get back into the groove after his surgery. Jack has struggled with feeling older since the health issue arose, especially because he hit his fiftieth birthday in the middle of all of this. I see him checking his head in the mirror, noticing the newest grays and trying to determine how much his hairline has changed. He was so worried about his waistline that he started measuring his stomach and getting on the scales every few days. My goodness, when he found an age spot on his face you would think he was turning into a zombie. I think he is more handsome than ever and wish he wouldn't worry about any of that.

My efforts have proven to be quite an effective strategy as he is looking much stronger than in the few weeks after surgery and treatments. It makes me crazy that he can take the occasional break from exercise and barely gain a pound. He has been about the same weight since he was in high school with the lean and tone body that I love. Me, if I miss a week I see an instant gain directly to my butt, hips, or thighs, or all three.

I had called Victoria earlier and set up a private session with her for Jack and me in the original studio. I know that Jack will appreciate my surprise with short shorts and a tank top. Victoria looks so classy as always, dressed all in black with her hair tied up making her pretty cheek bones and eyes show up even more prominently than usual.

This part of the gym is small, maybe six to eight people could work out at a time, and she has kept it as it was on day one before her expansion. Many people ask why she doesn't convert it to an office or some other specialty area. She shared with me that she sometimes just uses it to meditate and be thankful for the leap of faith that her and Steven took together in opening the gym. Jack and I are honored that she shares it with us today.

Victoria helps me keep the surprise until the last minute by taking Jack up to the room early. I strut in and take off one of Jack's college T-shirts, revealing a loose tank top exposing too much of my boobs from the low-cut sides. My booty cheeks are pushing out of the shorts that are way too small and too tight. I can't hold back a grin at Jack's mouth hanging open as I stroll slowly across the room, bend over right in front of him and lay out my mat. The things I will do for that man. Victoria plays along, thinking that it is a sweet and fun surprise from me. From the look on his face, Jack thinks it is the greatest thing ever. I remind him that he needs to behave himself. That is a waste of breath.

Victoria leads us in yoga for stretching and warmup, then in some basic mat Pilates. Jack and I work up quite a sweat. I can feel Jack's eyes on me the entire time and I can't help but giggle inside when doing certain stretches that give him a view that I know is tearing him up. Besides the obvious downward dog, I strategically move my body around to give him the best view when spreading for a leg stretch or leaning over to show him some side boob. Our schedules rarely align for us to exercise together at a gym, but we have always laughed that he wouldn't be able to keep his eyes off me and that we would probably get kicked out of a class if we worked out together. I am certain we would be kicked out if I wore this outfit. Not just because of Jack but I would be removed for being too revealing, especially at my age.

As it is, Jack misses most of the cues to change exercises or switch sides of a stretch while watching me. Truthfully, I miss a few when checking Jack out too. I love watching my handsome guy. Thank goodness we are such good friends with Victoria and she lets us slide with our foolishness. I have seen her call out people in her classes several times, even asking them to leave for not paying attention. She sweetly tolerates our silly play.

Afterward in the sauna we discuss Emma and the events with Lucca last night. On my last trip to the sauna, I had unloaded so many emotions on poor Victoria, and she blew my mind with her story, which I haven't found the right time to share with Jack yet. I must quit dodging conversations. Even knowing Victoria as well as I have over the years it still amazes me to see that classy, toned, seventy-plus lady looking fabulous after a workout, even sweating in the heat of the sauna.

Victoria tries to recall things that have happened since our last visit. But she is adamant about one thing: Lucca did not do this and could not do it. A small part of me wonders if she could be blinded because of their relationship. Was I blind also? She confirms the Emma and Cody breakup and provides a time frame of about two to three months ago. She shares that Billy, Cody's cousin, had done something bad enough that Emma would not let him come to the loft any more, but Victoria doesn't know the details. She has seen Emma meeting Preacher Jones several times at his recently opened coffee shop, The Devotional Grind. She knew that Jack and I had helped Emma with applying for scholarship money and financial aid during one of our vacations, and Emma had been working so hard to become a certified nurse. Victoria continues to tell us that Emma was excited about her progress until a couple of months ago. No one knew what changed other than the trouble between her and Cody but none of us believed she would let that keep her from her goal.

Then there were Mateo and Celest from the farmer's market. Emma used to help them clean up their booths at the end of each week. Victoria says she heard that Celest told Emma that she didn't need her help any longer and has been even more ill-tempered than usual with everyone since. Victoria wonders if that could be a financial situation, but that didn't match with the reports that they were doing well at the farm and the restaurant.

Then we get off track to more gossip and less investigation when discussing Devin and Gabriella buying the house and land beside Rob and Linda. Victoria fills us in on the details. Devin built an addition to the house that created the need for a deed search and land survey to obtain town approval for the construction. The property survey had come back with mistakes from decades ago that the county said had to be corrected. Ultimately Rob and Linda lost several yards of beachfront, most of which was to the adjoining land owned by Lucca. Attorneys became involved with months of litigation, but the result was new property lines that put most of the pool house under Lucca's ownership. Linda and Rob had just remodeled the pool house into an apartment to become a beachfront rental, so the timing was terrible for them. Linda blamed Lucca and Devin, but they had nothing to do with the whole mess and both even tried to pitch in a fair price for the cost of the remodeled apartment. Linda refused the offer. She is a proud lady. She told Rob he could no longer be friends with Lucca or Devin but on one of their covert golf outings Lucca told Rob to use the pool house anytime he wanted. I know that Victoria has a solid source for much of her information.

It is time for Victoria to teach another Pilates machines class in the other part of the building, so we wrap up our conversation. I am getting hungry and from the look in his eyes, Jack is hungry too. But I know it isn't food that Jack is craving. I want Jack too; I liked watching his muscles flex during class. Even though he has trouble believing it, I love seeing my man do so many things, including working out. Jack wishes that he was some big bulky guy and blames his high school basketball coach for telling him that lifting heavy weights would mess up his jump shot. Jack stands right at six feet tall, and all the scouts said if he grew another two or three inches that he would be a highly recruited player by most Division 1 colleges. He didn't get any taller but did have a great career at our local Division 2 college in the town where we live. I told him that we may not have ended up together if he had gone far away to college, so it was all part of the plan for our happiness. And besides, I love his body build and lean muscles, even though he is always striving to get bigger and working hard in his attempt to have six-pack abs.

19

JACK

HAVING SPENT THE LAST SEVENTY-FIVE minutes watching Tess flex her muscles and bend over in that little outfit then wrapped only in a towel in the sauna, I am craving her badly. She has been so close to me but untouchable that whole time, which tested my resolve. We need to clean up before finding lunch, and lucky for me the old part of the building only has one shower, and Tess is in a hurry to eat and get on with the investigation.

The water running over her naked body is such a beautiful and provocative sight. Beads and small streams flow off her hair and over her shoulders across a line of four diagonal freckles between the shoulder blades, down to the curve of her lower back and over the voluptuous bubble mound below. My mouth fills with water as I follow the stream downward over her soft skin. I tell her how beautiful she is and how much I need her as I move to my knees for her, and steam begins gathering around us. I push my lips against her flesh and knead her beautiful round bottom intently with both hands. Sliding my hands to her curvy hips I turn her to face me and move my tongue across her navel and on to her pendent breasts. Cupping each, I suckle her pointed tips one at a time as the water pours over my lips. I ease to a sitting position on the shower floor and press my cheeks between Tess's strong thighs, drinking in the entire region as the streams pour over my face and into my mouth. Her body leans back against the shower wall and her fingers stretch wide, trying to brace herself to stay upright. Tess raises a leg, and it comes to rest on my shoulder, begging my kisses deeper into her. My hands dig into the round flesh of her backside, pulling her tighter to me, and I bury my face even further into her sweetness. I relentlessly show her my love and passion. Her hips move with me. Moans arise. A hand drops to grab my wet hair, pulling me tighter between her open legs. Her breath quickens. Her body is taut. Her fingers fight to dig into the wall tiles. A long moan. A glorious rush of water and her love drowns my face and fills me with her happiness.

20

TESS

I'M FEELING A LITTLE SINFUL with the smile on my face and the tingling between my legs as we take our seats at The Devotional Grind. Opened by Preacher Jones after his retirement from the church, the café walls are filled with beautiful crosses and framed Bible verses, and old-time gospel music comes through the speakers. My thoughts are in the shower with Jack when I notice Mr. Jones smiling at me from the register. Lord, please forgive me for having these thoughts in here. I'm trying hard to erase the image I have of Jack kneeling before me and giving me such pleasure. Get it together, Tess. I start thinking of why the preacher was in the brush behind our pool. Was he really searching for a lost kite? Why had he been meeting with Emma? Focus Tess, not on the tingle inside, but on the investigation. But the word "grind" in the name appeared to be flashing at me off the wall. An angel on one shoulder: you are a "good girl" Tess, listen to the music and be good. The little devil on the other is still in that shower with my leg hiked over Jack's shoulder, feeling his passion for me.

Preacher Jones greets us with his usual jovial smile in his bow tie and fedora with a feather in the side. We had visited his church a few times when he was still preaching and enjoyed his sermons. All indications pointed to him being a good person with many stories circulating of him helping others around town.

I accept the offer of the preacher's gentle handshake. "Hello Preacher, Jack and I are wondering if you have a minute."

With the calming persona of a preacher, he takes a seat at the table. "Of course, after the morning rush it slows down around here."

Jack and I don't believe that he is capable of too much harm, not only because he is a little frail, but because he is a good man, so I jump right into the questions. I can see the concern in his face as I rattle through what we want to know. Jack and I both assure him that we are trying to help Emma. We tell him that any information could be a tremendous help.

He sits his hat down on the table. "I will try to help where I can, but I can't betray Emma's trust." I am slightly surprised that he acted as if we knew about his meetings with Emma.

I try to sound reassuring. "And we wouldn't want you to."

I decide that the preacher's comment about not betraying Emma's trust moves him into the "not guilty" column. I hope that I am right in that thinking and decide to appeal to his sense of fairness. "Mr. Jones there is a man in jail that we believe to be innocent. Please share anything you can to help us get to the truth."

He looks surprised. "Who is in jail?"

"Lucca, the sheriff arrested him last night."

With conviction the preacher says, "Lucca didn't do this. He was helping her."

Jack and I share a puzzled look.

"He gave her a place to stay, why would the sheriff think he hurt her?"

"What do you mean he gave her a place to stay?"

Mr. Jones is still sorting his thoughts and not listening to the question. "Sheriff Fry sure isn't like his daddy."

We have heard that before.

He continues, "His father was a good sheriff and a good man. Helped the townspeople for years and kept everybody safe around here. Young Fry has a good heart, but he is just trying to make a name for himself by cutting corners."

I try to pull him back into the conversation, "Where did Lucca give her a place to stay?"

The preacher rubs his chin with his fingers, still processing the information we had shared. "In the old pool house of course, where else?"

Thinking that is impossible, "So, you are saying Emma has been living in the pool house behind Rob and Linda's place?"

"It's not old anymore. Rob and Linda remodeled it for a beachfront rental for some extra cash a couple of years ago." The preacher can't stop thinking of the sheriff. "Young Fry knows better; he knows Lucca didn't do this."

"Did Rob and Linda know she was there? They didn't mention it when we were setting up our rental dates."

"I don't think so because Emma asked me not to tell anyone. I figured it was okay to tell you since you are trying to help."

I wonder aloud, "How could they not know?"

The preacher went on to tell us that when they fixed it up, they left the side facing the house as storage out of need, but the one-bedroom unit faced the beach.

Curiously I ask, "But did they not go out there sometimes?"

"Not since the stir up over the survey. Rob told me Linda wouldn't step foot in it after it was determined to be mostly on Lucca's land, and they lost all that beachfront footage along with the rental income, as well as the cost of renovating.

Jack asks, "What about lights at night?"

"Lucca left a couple of lights on all the time so if you were walking by and someone was in there, you wouldn't know the difference."

Jack nods his head and confirms that the lights had been on during his early morning runs but he didn't think anything about it.

"Preacher, do you know why she needed a place to stay?"

"I assumed it was because of the breakup with Cody. She only told me because one time I had asked her to come by the shop as soon as she could for our meeting, but it took her a while to get here. She confessed that she wasn't living in the loft any longer."

My mind was racing, "Did she mention how she was getting to work?"

"She didn't say but I figured Lucca was giving her a ride and dropping her off down the road. With those tinted windows no one can see inside that Jeep. Lucca started coming in for a coffee more often. You know Emma would never buy a car because she was saving all she could for her nursing career."

"Thanks for your help, Mr. Jones. Please let us know if you think of anything else."

"Happy to do it." Preacher Jones pats me on the shoulder. "I hope you can get Lucca out, he's a good guy."

Everyone keeps telling me that. "We are going to do our best. By the way, the muffins are delicious."

As we reach the sidewalk in front of the shop, Jack leans in to give me a kiss, "Baby, you really are good at the detective stuff. You were firing away with great questions."

I can't hold back a smile. "Thank you honey. Let's pay Cody a visit."

21

JACK

TESS AND I DISCUSS POSTING bail for Lucca on the walk to Cody's. He is a longtime friend, but I am not sure yet that I want to make that commitment. There is still a lot that we don't know. Tess thinks we should since he doesn't have any other family in the area, or maybe no close family at all. We aren't sure. We agree to check about other family members with a text to Victoria and then make our decision.

Cody swings the door open; he seems agitated that his video game has been interrupted. The loft apartment is messy with clothes and pizza boxes strewn all around. Cody glances back at his game frozen with the barrel of a gun aimed at an unsuspecting target. "She's not here," running a hand through his unwashed hair. We had only met Cody a few times and were not sure if he would remember us. We admit that we know about the breakup and ask if we can talk for a minute. He reluctantly invites us in while throwing debris out of chairs so we can sit. He grabs a dirty T-shirt from the floor and pulls it over his head.

As Tess talks with Cody, my thoughts drift back to Tess excitedly telling me about the first time she had visited the loft. She and Victoria had made a surprise stop to invite Emma to lunch. I remember Tess laughing as she told me that for some reason, Emma seemed genuinely happy to go to lunch with two old ladies. Tess described how the apartment was immaculate, smelled of fresh flowers, and was decorated so cutely. Pictures of Cody and Emma sat along the entertainment stand with other pictures of the town and Sandy Toes. There was even one of Emma and Tess that I had taken on Emma's sixteenth birthday. Now it is a mess and the couple of pictures left behind were turned over where they once were lovingly displayed. A broken home rips my heart out.

My mind bounces back to the conversation just as the niceties come to an end and Tess jumps right in as is her preferred style. "Why haven't you been to see her?"

Cody raises an eyebrow. "She is the one who broke up with me."

Tess pounces, "So you can't go see her in the hospital?"

Cody's face says that he has no idea that Emma is in the hospital. He begins spitting all sorts of questions at us without waiting for a response. Is she okay, what happened, when? He is visibly shaken and the love he still has for her is apparent . . . or is he just a very good actor?

We question him about why they broke up and he admits it was all his fault. He was taking extra shifts to help them with their finances. He was exhausted and barely getting by with all the extra work. His cousin Billy who is a bouncer—or security manager, depending on who was telling the story—at Sand in your Boots, the honky-tonk bar on the outskirts of town, told him he could help. Billy got Cody started on some uppers which quickly progressed to more dangerous drugs. This worsened their financial struggles and eventually Cody lost his job at the plant and, in his own words, the best thing in his life, Emma. He said that he had been clean since the day Emma walked out the door sixty-four days ago but had only been able to find part-time work. "I threw it all away like an idiot. I would do anything to have her back." He seems genuinely sad, disheveled, and like he has given up on life. But he is sincere.

We praise him for the progress he has made and tell him not to ever give up. I told him, "You must fight for the one you love. We all make mistakes, but if you are willing to sacrifice anything for her you still have a chance."

Tess wraps her arm around mine and before closing the door behind us, I look at Cody. "Go see her."

Cody drops his head. "If she will let me."

22

TESS

THE PREACHER'S MUFFIN DID NOT fill me up, so we make a stop at What's the Scoop Ice Cream Shoppe. We both decided to try a different flavor than our usual. Trying new things seems to be the theme of this trip. Jack has strawberry cheesecake, and I try the pistachio. As we wait in line for the nice young lady to fill our cones, I enjoy the happy faces of the kids across the colorful room. They are full of smiles and excitement with no worries except wishing for a different flavor of ice cream from the one they chose. The business has squeezed as many chairs and tables into the area as possible, so everyone sits very close. Some of the little ones smile at each other while licking the sides of their cones. Others read the kids trivia on the walls, while some try to name the animals that have been painted between the trivia questions. Still others draw in the coloring books while cartoons play on the TVs mounted to the wall.

We walk on the beach, enjoying our cones until we get close to the backside of the fresh market. Jack and I look at each other and ask the question at the same time, "Would you want that again?" We are both surprised that we enjoyed the new flavors.

We turn up a side alley shortcut hoping to catch Mateo and Celest for some more peaches before they pack up for the day. Mateo is at the passenger door of the farm truck with the seat leaned forward when Jack calls out, "Hi Mateo, hope we aren't too late for some peaches." Mateo, startled, turns quickly toward us, dropping a small metal box spilling the contents into the alley.

I bend down to help him retrieve the paper which is mostly cash as he hurriedly scoops it up with both hands. Jack gathers up some bills that have blown a few feet away. "Too hard to come by to let it fly away."

Mateo nervously replies as he stuffs everything messily back in the box, "So true, thank you both."

"Can we still get some peaches, or have you packed up?"

Mateo hurriedly stuffs the box underneath a jacket on the floor behind the seat. "Happy to get some for you, follow me."

Celest is breaking down the displays when we approach with Mateo leading the way. "Did you get the boxes?"

He scrambles to pick out the peaches for us. "I will go back to get them in just a minute."

Celest has a beautiful multi-colored scarf on today and flashes a fake half-smile toward us. "We would never get home if I waited on him. I will go get them."

Mateo's nerves seem to be settling down a little and he asks Jack if he is ready for the big baseball game. Jack gives him the "I have no idea" look and asks why the game is a bigger deal than usual. Mateo explains that the Manatees team is coming from the inland to play at the local field and everyone will be there. Apparently the Manatees are a Double-A minor league team and the Disco Duckbills, the town team, are only a Single-A minor league team. All that means absolutely nothing to me, but Mateo seems very excited. He goes on to explain that baseball scouts and the press will be coming from all over to cover the game and look at prospects. And the most exciting news, according to Mateo, is that one of the players is family to someone in town and it is rumored the local player is about to be called up to the big leagues.

Mateo goes on to tell us the player is Rob's nephew, Robbie, that lives on the mainland. Everyone is coming to support them, and Rohan is throwing a post-game bash. Rohan never misses an opportunity to get more sales. Jack tells Mateo that the game is scheduled close to the time we are leaving, but we will try to make it. We wonder if Rob will make it back in time for the big event since Robbie is playing and he loves the Disco Duckbills so much.

Jack and I have been to a few of the local minor league games over the years and they did put on a good show. There was a wide variety of good food from food trucks all around and much more, but the real draw is the entertainment. I'm not a baseball fan but the music, yes, a lot of disco tunes due to the team's name, with the players dancing in the middle of the game makes it more fun to watch. They also have a drawing to let locals take a turn at cheerleading and dance with the players, which everyone loves. Mascots interact with the kids and the adults in the stands, and the announcer adds his humor to the mix. It is good entertainment that brings in crowds from surrounding areas, and it sounds like this will be a big event with extra hype. Jack looks it up on his phone and says that the original date had been the first night we were here, but the sudden shift of the path of the storm had caused a postponement.

Jack and I are thankful for a few clouds in the sky to block the sun as we eat our next snack under a shade tree at the park not far from the market. We always feel that we eat too much on vacation and try to cut back when we get home. I excitedly tell Jack what I saw in the metal box that Mateo dropped. An envelope filled with cash and the initials "EL" scribbled in the lower left corner.

Jack, as always, keeps a level head and does not jump to conclusions, much to my dismay many times. But I can tell he is intrigued. "Are you sure?"

I nod my head and mumble with a mouth full of peach, "Definitely."

Practical Jack adds, "Maybe the initials are for someone that works at the farm and not Emma."

"I guess it could be, but you have to admit that he seemed nervous," as peach juice spills down my chin.

Jack eases closer and tastes my peachy lips, lightly sucks my lower lip, then kisses down my chin, and onto my neck. "Too good to waste any."

"We at least need to find out more," as I take two of his fingers into my mouth, circle them with my tongue tasting peach juice. I tighten my lips around them as I ever so slowly pull them back out while staring into his beautiful blues. "You're right, too good to waste."

23

JACK

WE MAKE A QUICK STOP at the courthouse on the way out of town only to discover that Lucca's bail has not yet been set, so we head back home for a little time at the beach. As the wind blows across us in old red, Tess shares the surprising news about Lucca and Martina from her conversation with Victoria earlier. I am almost as shocked that it has taken her this long to share the news as I am at the fact that it happened. My mind churns through so many things on the drive back.

We settle back under the umbrella, still having a few hours before sunset to ourselves on the uncrowded portion of the beach. Tess is wearing the one-piece black suit again that is cut high up her sides and backside. I love how the low cut of the suit allows me to admire her beautiful breasts as she studies her notes on the case. At one point we both glance at the apartment-turned-Emma-hideout and I wonder why Lucca hasn't shared this information with us, or the sheriff for that matter. There are still things that are missing from this mystery we are trying to solve.

I gently pull Tess by the arm. "You need a break," as I lead her down to the water. We are waist deep in the water trying to keep our balance against the breaking waves. It is such a relief to just have fun together and not talk about my issue, the doctor's remedy, the sheriff, or anything else. Just me and Tess with no worries for a moment in time. Holding onto each other, laughing, playing like lovestruck teenagers. I am enjoying Tess's laugh as much as anything else we are doing. Until I see a shadow against the setting sun walking toward us. I nudge Tess and point to the shadow.

Tess scowls. "That better not be the stupid sheriff again."

I squint against the sun. "Can't be, not blocking enough light." We chuckle together.

As we stumble our way out of the undertow of the ocean, Lucca comes into view. He smiles, points at his chest then toward Tess, slightly turning his head for a moment, though just briefly. He chuckles and finally says, "You, um . . . you may want to put those up."

All sets of eyes instinctively follow Lucca's stare toward Tess and discover the waves had knocked the top of her suit down, exposing BOTH of her breasts. They are out, loud and proud. Lucca tries to hold in a laugh. "I don't know why both of you keep flashing me but I'm not complaining."

I feel my face warming as Tess is stuffing and tucking her boobs back into the suit and trying to pull it closed like a zip up hoodie. "What are you doing here?"

Lucca grins. "I came to thank my friend for bailing me out."

Tess leads the way back to the umbrella and I am pretty sure that both Lucca and I wish it was a longer walk. The waves had impacted the back of the suit almost as much as the front exposing her nice round bottom that is twisting with her every step on the walk back to our seats. Tess is still working on making sure the girls are tucked in safely and squeezing the salt water from her hair and doesn't think to worry about her backside.

I hand Lucca a cold drink. "We tried to post bail but were told that it wasn't set yet."

Lucca's brows rise slightly. "Who then?"

I lift my drink in a toasting gesture. "No idea but glad you are a free man."

Lucca bumps his cup against mine. "For now. I am as glad to be away from the sheriff's mouth as much as I am to be out of jail."

I laugh. "I bet he wasn't too happy to see you walk out of there."

Lucca smiles. "I thought his head was going to explode. Said he would have me back within seventy-two hours."

Tess and I enjoy the thought of Sheriff Fry so upset. "So, who do you think it was?"

Lucca lets out a sigh after a big gulp of his drink. "Bail or assault?"

"Either, both I guess."

"I wish I knew the answer to both, my friend."

Tess nods in agreement. "We do have some questions though."

I reach into the goodie bag. "Want some pretzels to go with that drink?"

Lucca chuckles. "I didn't go on a hunger strike in jail." But he takes the bag and begins eating like maybe he had.

Lucca goes on to explain how Emma came to stay in the pool house while marginally trying to fight his eyes from the plunging black suit and Tess's breasts. I even offer to change seats with him to hinder the view because he keeps losing his train of thought, all but acknowledging that we both can see his stares, but he quickly declines. Lucca continues that Emma had shown up at his door in the middle of the night a couple of months ago, too shaken to tell him what happened. Seeing she needed a friend more than an advisor he offered to let her stay in the extra room at his house. She had forced herself to go to work even though he could see she was having trouble hiding the hurt on her face. After a few nights, he told her that they needed to come up with a different arrangement because it wouldn't look good for either of them if people found out she was staying there.

When she finally told him of Cody's drug use, he came up with the idea of the pool house. Rob and Linda had not been in there since the survey dispute so he thought it would be safe until she could line up something better. Preacher Jones was right that Lucca had been her ride to work, which may explain why she was no longer at her other jobs, and Lucca even bought her a battery-powered bike that she hid in his storage area for times when he wasn't available.

When we ask why his storage area instead of the pool house, Lucca explains he was worried that Emma may be seen getting in the backside of the apartment storage through the brush from Rob's house and that Linda had changed the locks on the pool house storage area anyway and he didn't have a key. Lucca said that Linda told him she didn't want him to take any more of her stuff after stealing part of their land. Lucca laughed about that part and says that he certainly doesn't need extra storage to accumulate more things.

Lucca also shares that Rob had been partying more than usual and would show up at Lucca's at all hours of the night. Lucca would help him get back home and try to avoid being caught by Linda. He didn't think that was too different from the way Rob had always been other than the fact they couldn't get caught hanging out together by Linda.

We are happy to learn more, but this does nothing to explain why Emma was attacked. Lucca tells us that he was worried about her being depressed from the breakup and that he would go over many nights and peek into a window to make sure that she was okay. When we look at him with big eyes, he clarifies that there was a damaged blind from one of Rob's wild nights a while back and you could only see the main living area and the couch where Emma usually was. But he never thought of anything like this happening to her. I think of Cody and wonder if he had fooled us by acting like he was still in love with Emma. Or maybe Billy had gotten mad about Emma not letting him come to see Cody. Either way, Tess and I need to find answers because Sheriff Fry would be pushing to move forward with the case against Lucca.

Tess speaks up. "What about the evidence that Peeping Tom sheriff said he found?"

Lucca lifts his hands into the air. "An anonymous note of all things."

I sit up in the chair. "I am not surprised."

Lucca shakes his head. "Neither am I. He never has liked me though. He even questioned me about the disappearance of Rob's expensive golf clubs earlier, and I told him mine had been stolen with them. What a moron."

I agree. "That sounds exactly like his idea of great investigating."

Lucca continues, "Rob bought a new set of clubs for the few times we snuck off for a round, but I rented mine instead. I just don't see the point of buying another set right now since Rob and I can't sneak out to play often."

Half-jokingly I ask, "Did the super investigator sheriff ever find out who stole them?"

Lucca sits back in his chair. "Rob had some problems with the first construction workers stealing things from the apartment and from their pool area. He and Linda fired the whole crew and that pushed them back a few months on the remodel. Before all the survey drama, we both kept our clubs in the storage area behind the apartment because it was easier to just grab them both at the same time when we could play. I suspect both mine and Rob's clubs are being enjoyed by construction workers somewhere. At least they are getting used. To answer your question, no, the sheriff never did anything about the thefts."

Lucca pauses and struggles with the next part. He confesses that when the sheriff first threatened to prove it was him that assaulted Emma, he panicked and tried to use his true alibi. He had been in the house watching the storm come in and noticed our big studio light in the sunroom. He has been friends with us long enough to know what we were doing. He moved to the side window with his binoculars to watch Tess pose. He apologizes profusely, trying to justify it by saying Tess is so beautiful and that he has been lonely. At least that explains how the sheriff knew about the pictures.

Tess ignores Lucca's comments. "We need to figure this all out before the sheriff has everyone believing that you are guilty." She walks, as we stare, to a spot where she could see between the houses and through the trees to the setting sun. "We are going to solve the case," she pauses and adds, "It's gorgeous, isn't it?"

Without taking our eyes off Tess, Lucca and I speak in unison, "Beautiful."

24

TESS

THE ALMOST-FULL MOON HOVERS OVER the ocean as Jack and I hold hands while our toes sink into the cool sand at the edge of the water. We have the beach all to ourselves, at least in this little corner. The crashing of unseen waves in the darkness along with the gentle brushing of the suds over my feet stirs my insides, unknown, even dangerous, and yet I feel safe in the darkness as Jack's fingers tighten between mine. My mind drifts in the night air. The whole conversation with Victoria replays in my head. Lucca's hands on my leg flashes before my eyes along with the intoxication I felt. My overwhelming love for Jack embraces my body. The passion of our intimacy over the years rises from deep within me. The briefness of our lives flickers in the stars above. My desire to do anything to bring happiness to both Jack and I rushes through my body.

My own voice startles me by breaking through the soothing sounds of the ocean, "Schedule the massage." I feel as if the words dropped from the sky or washed in with the waves, or maybe they just appeared out of the darkness. But they came from my lips, unfiltered. A simple statement that I had uttered many times before about innocent massages over the years, but this time they meant something different. Entirely different. So much more. Life changing. Value challenging. Deep inside, I still question if I can go through with it. Do I truly want to? But the words had poured out of my mouth just as the emotions and feelings had as I stared at the waves through the bay window when Jack was giving his love to me. It all came out in three little words. Three defining words. Followed by four more: "Because I love you."

We walk silently back to the house as a light rain begins to fall. Jack and I entangle our bodies together on the same comfortable couch we shared in the sunroom after taking photos on our first night. The storm that engulfed us that night. The storm of health. The storm of Emma's beating. The storm of the doctor's remedy. The storm of Lucca's touch. The storm of our hearts. The storm of passion.

We lay quietly holding each other, clinging tightly, both not wanting to let go but knowing deep in our souls that nothing could separate us. Neither could survive without the other. Years of growing together and nurturing our love. Years of learning every detail of each other. Years of laughing and of crying. Years of pulling each other forward, lifting each other up. Years of commitment that wouldn't and couldn't be shattered. Years of true love.

25

JACK

TESS LAYS HER HEAD ON my shoulder, the silky silver feels cool across my chest. One leg is curled up and resting across my thighs as I caress her soft skin instinctively. She rubs her foot across my leg intuitively. The sky is like a canvas before us is being magnificently painted with beautiful colors, locking our gaze and leaving us speechless. Stunning yet serene. I cherish the feeling of Tess's breath tickling my neck. I love her so much. It feels as if I have loved her my whole life.

Tess whispers, "Emma gets out of the hospital today and asked if I could come to get her."

I pull Tess closer and pause before struggling to say, "I'll go see Lucca while you're gone."

Tess stares at the sky, long pause, "I'm going to make her talk to me today." Then she presses her lips to mine. We both cling tightly to hold onto the moment.

Tess shares a sweet wave as she pulls off in old red to pick up Emma. I walk over to Lucca's and find him on the deck staring at the ocean. He invites me to have a seat while he disappears in the house for a few minutes, before returning to the deck with two exotic coffee-flavored mixtures and sits beside me. "Hope you like the new drink I've been working on."

I tell him that if Rohan doesn't have an opening at the bar at Sandy Toes, then maybe Preacher Jones would like the help at The Devotional Grind. My insides churn as I sip the drink. I ask Lucca how he is holding up and if he has thought of an answer to the bail or the beating. He has no answers, but I am more stalling than looking for answers anyway. I need to let it come out before I have a change of heart. I know that could happen at any time. So, I begin.

I tell Lucca the whole story, surgery and complications, not physical but apparently psychological. If feels as if every word is a struggle to come out of my mouth. I share the stories of doctors, specialists, and therapists. The story of the "renowned expert" therapist and her diving deep into our fears and fantasies. The studies, the diagnosis, and then her advice as a last resort. I admit how insane it all sounds. I explain that we had been told that the doctor's methods were sometimes unconventional, but she had an incredible proven record of success. I tell him that I am not being completely selfish by only thinking of getting better, but that the doctor had mentioned Tess's deeply hidden fantasies and that she was missing out on things that she wanted to do but was afraid would put the life she loved in jeopardy. I had no idea if that is true or just the doctor's theory. I question whether I may have smothered Tess's desires over the years with my protectiveness. I admit that I am in a confused state of mind and that my thoughts of how—or even if—to move forward are in a constant battle.

I continue pouring it all out by acknowledging our long and close friendship over the years and that Tess always enjoyed his and Martina's company. That our hearts broke for him at Martina's passing. Finally, I force the words out, what we are asking of him, or in my view the amazing offer we are thinking of sharing with him. A "special" massage. It feels like someone else's words floating through the air. Lucca sits in silence, and I wonder if he may be in shock for a moment.

Finally, he scoots his chair forward and begins his own story.

Several years ago, he and Martina had hit a rough patch and were struggling. He couldn't pinpoint why. Lucca chuckles when he says that Martina and I were always the quiet ones, and it was hard to get information from us both. He discovered later that she had an affair or two; he wasn't sure how many. He was devastated but determined not to give up on their relationship. They had talked and searched their hearts, then talked some more. Finally they decided they were in a rut and had lost their passion, and that was the main reason for their unhappiness. Both were happy in their daily life and still in love with each other, but intimacy had become routine. He notes how hard this was to share with me or anyone. They both were willing to try to do anything to save the marriage.

They had gone to counseling like Tess and I had, and researched several ideas to help. After many months of attempting too many different things to remember, this ultimately led to inviting others into their private time, which Lucca says was a surprising decision to both he and Martina but they were desperate. He confesses to feeling like a failure as a man and being terrified. He wasn't sure if she would stay regardless of what they tried.

They concluded there was nothing to lose so they jumped in wholeheartedly. He speaks about the first attempt being uncomfortable and not enjoyable, but that there was enough of some spark to keep trying. Soon they were enjoying the experiences and were totally surprised by the positive impact it had on their own private intimacy. He warns me that every couple has different needs and experiences and reactions, but for them it allowed them to regain their passion for each other. A happy, fun, and passionate time, and made them closer than ever.

He goes on to share that he and Martina had come so close to inviting Tess and I several times, but ultimately didn't want to risk our friendship if we were offended or uncomfortable.

The same concern is going through my mind right now.

He laughs that Martina had desires for me AND Tess and wanted to tell us every time the four of us got together. He goes on to share many of the different scenarios that he and Martina enjoyed that surprised them. Knowing she was happy was all he needed but there were many other benefits that he never dreamed he would like.

He admits that he always loved Tess's fun and outgoing personality and knew it was obvious that he thought she is a sexy woman. Lucca says that he is genuinely honored, appreciative, and excited that he is even considered to have this conversation. He adds that he respects us both immensely and would never do anything to offend us or to damage our trust in him. Maybe Victoria was right about Lucca, about him being the right person to try this new adventure, this therapy with.

Feeling more comfortable after hearing his story I talk of things I would have never believed that I would talk about with anyone as we discuss possibilities of an intimate meeting. Safety is one of the topics, which apparently is simply understood by people that do this often as either using protection or providing recent test results. It feels so strange to talk so normally about these things. As I struggle to move the conversation forward, my protective side fights with the we-must-try-anything side. Back and forth. Plan it all versus spontaneous. Rules versus make it up as we go. Cancel this crazy idea versus we are so close to trying something that may help me get past this block and help Tess too. This is acceptable versus this is terrible. Keep talking versus shutting up and leaving before I change my mind. Different pieces of me won different parts of the battle. Finally, I am confident that Lucca and I are on the same page. Lucca is patient and understanding during the whole crazy conversation.

Lucca breaks the uncomfortable tension with a chuckle. "Just don't kick my ass."

I tilt my head, confused. "What?"

Lucca laughs. "I remember that drunk guy that was messing with Tess and Martina a few years back during the live music at Rohan's place."

I join him in laughter. "I did get a little mad."

"A little? You had that guy face down on the ground with his arm bent like a pretzel before the rest of us knew what was happening." Lucca mimicked moving his arm behind him with a scrunched face.

I smile. "That's not like me, and besides, I don't think we have to worry about you being a jerk like he was."

"That you don't. Nothing but respect from me." Another chuckle. "I don't want to see that side of you again."

26

TESS

I OPEN THE DOOR TO find Jack squeezed between the washing machine and the wall. "Really? You are obsessed with the washer."

"Something about that leak keeps bothering me."

I toss the keys on the kitchen island, wondering if it is the washer or his conversation with Lucca that is bothering him. "No kidding."

Jack steps back and looks at the washer as if it is an alien while he speaks, "Number one, Linda gets upset about any maintenance issues, but she didn't mention any more about the leak."

I agree, "That's true but we found out that her and Rob have been going through a lot. Maybe she had whoever fixed the breaker look at it while they were here."

Jack pushes the washer back into place. "True, but number two, I can't find any signs of water from the ceiling or wall, and it can't be the washer because we didn't use it that night."

I'm a little more curious now. "So, what are you thinking?"

"And I found this under the washer when I slid it out." He holds up an unmarked key and a small nail.

My detective mind is working hard, but I have nothing to offer so I shrug. I'm thinking Jack is about to say something wise or profound about the clue.

All he offers is, "I don't know but it's weird, huh?"

Okay, that's enough of the mystery washer business, so I begin to tell Jack about my conversation with Emma. When I got her in the car, I let it all out, everything we had discovered and told her that good people were in trouble. That Lucca was still facing charges, and everyone was trying to help find out who hurt her. I told Emma that momma Tess wanted some answers.

She told the story of her and Cody and the drugs. That she still loves him, but she couldn't be around that stuff, especially with a child.

Jack's eyes open almost as wide as mine when I heard it the first time. "Wait, what? Emma is pregnant?"

"She is. And that's why she was even more upset about Cody."

Jack eyes remain wide. "Does he know?"

I kick off my shoes. "She didn't tell him before they broke up for fear of losing the baby like her mom had before, so no, he does not know."

"Is the baby okay after the assault? She took quite a beating." Jack is searching for an explanation, and I understand why.

I walk over and plop down on the sofa. "Amazingly, they think the baby will be okay, but they had some scary moments when she was first admitted. Good thing Mr. Jones found her when he did."

Emma said that she had been meeting with the preacher since she found out she was pregnant. Seeking advice about life, tough decisions, and how to move forward. The preacher was the only one she had told before the doctor at the hospital.

Jack washes his hands and comes over to snuggle beside me. "So, the preacher did lie to us?"

I tilt my head. "Not really, he did say he wouldn't betray her trust from the beginning."

It looks as if Jack's eyes are watching a ping-pong ball bounce back and forth as he sits quietly for a moment. "So he was the only one that knew she was pregnant before the assault?" I can sense that he doesn't want to say the rest out loud.

I shrug.

"But why? That makes no sense."

I put my hands up in the air. "It sure doesn't. We are still missing something."

I continue to update Jack that she did confirm that she went to Lucca's for help, that he put her up at the pool house and gave her rides to work. And the bike with a basket to haul supplies. She is very upset that he is being blamed for the assault.

Jack leans over to pull my feet onto his lap for a rub. A move that is so automatic that he does it without a thought, and I love it. I can feel the pressure from his hands as he thinks about all this new information. "What did she say about Marcus?"

I let out a satisfying groan. His strong hands feel so good on my feet. "Only that he was too nosy, and that he was hateful."

Jack gives my foot a few kisses, "So where do we go from here?"

I think for a long moment. "Let's sit by the pool and go over it all again, I guess." Then hesitantly I follow that up with, "How did it go with Lucca?"

Jack looks through the bay window toward the ocean. "You get the snacks, and I will grab everything else."

I am not sure what to think about his avoidance of my question, but I am okay with the non-answer for now. I am still unsure what I think about the idea too. I put on the leopard bikini feeling that Jack needs a happy boost.

Jack stops on the way to try the mystery key on the two storage doors connected to the garage before we enter the pool area. No luck. "Are there any other doors you can think of?"

I start slowly walking toward the pool. "Not that I know of." Putting extra emphasis on the twisting of my butt, "Don't you see anything more interesting than doors?"

He rushes up and grabs my butt with both hands. "I sure do."

I am happy to see Jack's smile.

Pool time is a good reprieve from investigating and whatever the conversation with Lucca was. I decide I don't need to know right now, and I trust Jack, so we just focus on beach music and piña coladas for the next couple of hours. I love the feel of Jack's hands rubbing lotion on my body. He reapplies more times than needed because he enjoys it, and he can't stand the thought of my fair skin getting too much sun. The concern over my skin and the fact that we like cooler weather more than the heat is why almost all our other getaways are to the mountains instead of the beach. I remind him that most people think tan curvy looks better than white curvy, but he reassures me that he loves my ivory skin and curves just the way they are.

I let Jack take some pictures to further cheer his mood, even some with the girls out. And then I make him change places with me behind the camera as he strikes the poses for me. He likes behind the camera better, but I think he is the sexiest man alive, even if he has a hard time believing that. Probably because I don't carry on about it twenty-four seven like he does with me. It is fun making him do whatever poses I choose, and I understand why he likes to capture me for later viewing. He is impressed with my creativity for his photos including getting him to undress and hold his hat in front of his privates for a fun shot. I get some of his cute little butt too.

But Jack does go a little overboard with my photos, to put it mildly. My pictures are spread across the house in every room and even all over the inside of his pickup truck for goodness' sake. Most men want a man cave with car or sports stuff. My man has made a Tess cave, pictures of me everywhere including under the glass on the bar top, hanging from photo clips beside the exercise equipment, framed on the bookshelves, and his favorite, the row of huge 24x56 canvas wall prints.

A few years ago, I returned from a short trip to find that wall of pictures and I thought my head was going to explode. Mercy, it is way too much of me! But I reminded myself that I am thankful that he loves me like that. And that doesn't include all the photo albums and his latest project of scrapbooking to record all our trips with a story and yes, more photos of me. He always says, "Every picture has a story to tell."

Unknown to Jack, I am resting my eyes in the lounger, or sleeping as he calls it, when he calls out, “I wish I could find out what this key goes to.”

Jack can’t believe that I can fall asleep anywhere so easily since he must have perfect conditions to even think about going to sleep. I grunt, “I know baby,” before closing my eyes again.

27

JACK

WE ARE BACK AT OUR makeshift detective desk in the great room, reviewing our notes and taking another look at the picture file. I glance up from the laptop to see her reaction as I say, "Tess, maybe we should postpone the massage until we solve this."

"Oh, so now we ARE a real detective agency, and we ARE going to solve it." Tess is still in her leopard suit bottoms but the top has been replaced by a loose tank. She says the girls don't like to be bound any more than necessary. The looseness of the top gives me a great view of the sides of those beautiful breasts. The air conditioning is obviously making her a little cold. I am having difficulty focusing on the conversation as her backside jiggles on her way to the kitchen for a drink. "We have to solve it with so many things hanging in the balance."

The doorbell rings. "I'll get it," Tess says as she resets the clip in her hair. "Emma said she would stop by."

I feel my skin crawl as I hear the annoying voice that has become all too familiar on this trip. "I came to get my pi . . ." Sheriff Fry's voice trails off as he sees what Tess is wearing.

I rush to the door to support Tess and see her standing, back-stiffened with her nipples pointing through the material and directly at the sheriff. Tess's voice is harsh. "You should be out finding the real criminal."

After having looked at the photos again, I am not convinced that they will clear Lucca from being the person in the picture. And I'm still not willing to let the disgusting sheriff have the pleasure of seeing Tess so I speak up. "Still working on them."

Sheriff Fry takes a deep breath. "I'm the sheriff of this town and lead investigator and I'm not waitin' any longer."

Tess waves an arm. "Just let him have them Jack. Boobs are just globs of fat with a nipple on the end and the poor boy probably never gets to see any."

Shocked, I quickly disagree, "You aren't getting them without a warrant."

The sheriff hangs his thumbs on the belt below his belly, his face reddening, probably more upset at Tess's comment than mine. "I'll be back with a warrant, and I WILL get them." He storms out, unable to keep himself from taking one last peek at Tess before closing the door behind him.

I turn to Tess. "What are you thinking?"

She gives me a sweet tilted-head look that is her way of saying please. "If it will clear Lucca, we have to."

I protest, "It may not help because it is fuzzy enough to argue there is a possibility that it is him."

Her detective voice springs out, "Maybe the sheriff just wants to see if what we have can help or hurt his case."

"More likely, he just wants to gawk at you. You have been teasing him hard in those outfits for years." I laugh at my own joke.

She agrees, "Maybe that too. Does he really need a warrant to get them?"

Laughing, "I have no idea. I was just repeating what I heard on those old detective movies we have watched. It shook him up though." I mimic the sheriff trying to pull up his pants and puff out his chest and waddling toward the door.

Tess starts one of her out of control laughs and can't stop. "You are going to make me pee." Tess says when she laughs too hard that she is afraid she is going to pee like she did when she was a little girl. As always, her laugh brightens an otherwise disturbing moment.

Finally catching her breath, "Let's go see Preacher Jones again."

I wrap both arms around her and pull her as close as I possibly can. So tight that she can barely breathe. "That will have to wait, you have a massage scheduled."

28

TESS JACK

I SIT IN FRONT OF the mirror staring, but not really seeing myself. I am not sure if I can or if I even want to look into my own eyes. Who is this woman looking back at me? I have never come remotely close to considering anything like this in my whole life. What am I doing? Without even thinking, I apply a light blush across my cheeks and my fingers grip the small cylinder that runs across my lips giving them a glossy shine.

I sit in the chair beside the crisply made bed, staring intently at Tess. I love watching her get ready. She is so beautiful. She is always beautiful with or without makeup. Her thick silver hair is pinned behind her ears on each side. Cheekbones with only a slight blush and her puffy lips pucker as she glides the gold tube slowly over them producing a slight shine.

I wear a soft flowing black skirt that hangs loosely just above my knees and a thin white tank with no bra. Why bind up the girls when all my clothes will be coming off soon? I am embarrassed that there is a tingle deep inside my tummy as I run my hands through the thick mane one more time giving it a little fluff. Was it a tingle of nerves or something else that I didn't want to admit to myself? Why did I put on makeup and try on three outfits before selecting this one?

Tess gives me a sweet smile in the mirror. She slides back the chair and stands to face my direction as if seeking my approval. She always has my approval of how she looks and how she carries herself. Her skirt shifts back and forth above her knees as she steps toward me, sliding her bright red toes into the flat sandals with diamond studs across the top. I have a longing to be on the couch rubbing her feet. She leans over and gives me the sweetest kiss. "Ready?" I have no idea if I am ready.

The path to Lucca's seems much shorter than before. A breeze lifts my skirt and eases through the thin material of my top. I tell myself that's the reason the tips of my breasts are standing at attention. Jack's fingers intertwine with mine giving me a feeling of safety, even if only momentarily. Lucca opens the door with a kindness in his face. My steps inside are shaky.

We arrive at the door too quickly. Tess steps in first and Lucca greets us with a warm welcome and an invitation to sit. It feels as if I am watching other people as we sip our wine. I am not hearing any of the words passing through the air, until . . . "Would you like to get started?" reverberates around the room at a deafening level.

The massage room is even more sensual than the first time I was here and has been rearranged. One bed has been prepared for service and there are more cushions spread across the floor in place of the other bed. The sounds of a rain forest are soft, and wonderful scents float in the air, wrapping their arms all around me. It's warm, but not too warm, comfortable. Rows of candles flicker all over the dim room. My eyes find the bed covered in dark silky sheets and towels lying to the side, ready. The voice is soft but still startles me, "Take all the time you need. I'm ready when you are."

Tess and I gaze into each other's eyes for a long moment then share an even longer kiss. Then an even longer embrace. It was hard to break the contact of our bodies. I whisper, "Only what you want." She smiles sweetly as she looks again into my eyes. Her baby blues shouting that she loves me. She grasps the bottom of her shirt and ever so slowly raises her arms over her head. A move that I love during our photo sessions but felt altogether different in this moment. Another smile. "I love you, Jack," as she slides out of her skirt and panties in one smooth motion. She has exposed herself to me, and for me. For us.

I'm comfortable lying under the warm sheets draped over my bare skin. I take one more look around the room and then at the man I love. Jack stretches the scented mask over my eyes and the room goes dark, leaving me with only my thoughts and senses. I feel Jack's lips on my cheek. The tingle inside grows a little stronger as I hear the gentle opening and closing of the door once more. The scents of bergamot, lavender, sandalwood, and others that I can't determine drift over the room like a vapor of sensuality. I feel a gentle weight on the sheet at my lower back. A brush of slightly cooler air falls over my skin as the sheet separates from my body.

The shadowed outline of her body in the candlelight looks like a painting of beautiful rolling hilltops and valleys. The slope of her shoulders down to the curve of her lower back and over the roundness of her bottom. Descending downward across the back of her muscled legs. I rub the scented lotion into my hands while watching the other set of hands that will soon travel these slopes. I question whether I can go through with this. A brief glance between me and Lucca, a mixture of concern and excitement in his eyes. I wonder if I am about to put Lucca on the ground like the drunk guy at Rohan's. Then four hands begin spreading the warm oils over Tess's soft skin.

Fingers gently touch my heels and begin a path up the back of my legs. For an instant every muscle in my body tenses before letting go of the breath I was holding. Hands trace slowly up each leg and over my fleshy hump, easing down to my lower back, and up to my shoulders leaving a trail of creamy frankincense and lavender. Four strong yet soft hands begin kneading my neck and shoulders with just the right amount of pressure. My breath calms slightly. Firm grasps of hands move over my triceps, pausing to massage deeper before moving down my arms lying at my sides. A hand slides up and down the length of each arm while I feel the firm wrap of fingers around each wrist as if they were being momentarily restrained. For the first time I realize that I'm not sure which side of me Jack is on.

Lucca and I are synchronized as we reload with oils and massage Tess's back firmly and hear the first soft moans of approval. Moving from upper back to Tess's sides, brushing against her breasts that are pushed out against the table. Following the slope to the small of her back and over to her hips, squeezing the cheeks of her incredible butt together before letting them relax. First a soft feel over her exposed bottom followed by a more intense massage of her inviting flesh. Grasping and squeezing her firm roundness as if we had been waiting forever to touch it. I try not to think about her backside exposed completely to another man.

All tension has been released from my shoulders and back and the two men pour their attention to my butt, rubbing and squeezing it with four hands. Tracing from bottom to top, around the sides, and back again as if they needed to know everything about it. I lay silent, still enjoying every moment of the attention. Finally, they break away and fingers move lightly down the backs of my legs reaching my heels again. I hear more lotion from the bottle and the rubbing of hands together. A deep massage to my feet and toes. Another firm grip around my ankles and a slow pouring of oil over my legs raises the tingle inside to another level as the warm liquid glides down the insides of my legs.

Our fingers work deeply into her well-defined calves and hamstrings feeling the power from her commitment to exercise. Both sets of hands are now positioned to cover the entire back part of each leg. Very slow, long glides from calf to the lower slope of her voluptuous backside. Up and down, over and over, marveling at the strength and shapeliness of the skin under our hands. Our hands began to press between her thighs as they travel further upward with each pass. My heart skips when Tess parts her legs ever so slightly.

I feel hands push between my thighs and upward brushing against the moisture between my legs. Again and again, remaining slightly longer with each pass. The heat is increasing within me. My breath is shorter, quicker. I feel my flower opening. I want more. My desire lifts my butt up slightly. Then, as if it all was only to tease, another slow trail of fingers fades over my backside up to my shoulders. A whisper, "Let's turn you over." I anxiously but nervously roll my body over laying bare in front of two men. My emotions are conflicted, excitement against embarrassment, desire against shame, passion against feeling slutty, anticipation of another man wanting me against worry over Jack's heart being broken.

Tess lays completely bare below us, legs parted slightly. Beautiful, sexy, exposed. I long for her. Briefly, I have thoughts of throwing Lucca out of the room. Our hands roam over each of her shoulders, mine on the sexy mole, then move to brushing her cheekbones softly, over her sweet little ears, down the sides of her neck. Tess tilts her head back slightly as we take turns stroking down the front of her neck. Oil begins flowing more freely as my heart beats faster. Holding her hands in ours, we spread her arms from her sides. Her breasts shift with the movement. Rubbing her strong biceps and underarms, working down to the hands that lay against our chests. Each finger receiving its own special attention, then pressure to her palms, before gently lying her arms back to her sides. More oil pouring over her breasts and oozing over and down her sides. Sensual and arousing.

The feel of warm oil pouring onto my chest and flowing over my body. Two hands circle each breast searching my flesh, kneading, squeezing, and sliding around every inch. Palms move across my hard nipples before fingers pinch and pull the throbbing tips. My back arches with the tugs. My hips begin to shift. I am beginning to lose control. Just in time, a temporary respite as the two sets of hands move across my tummy and continue downward. I want to scream for more, but I hold the words inside. Their hands brush over the smoothly shaven mound below my stomach and light fingers glide across the tops of my legs.

Our fingertips trace a gentle line down to Tess's pretty little feet before beginning to work our way back up. Our hands move over each leg, across the indent of her shins, over her precious knees, and onto the muscles of her thighs. The force rocks her body slightly, causing her breasts to sway with the motion. Hands again pressing between her thighs, brushing between her legs at the peak of the up and down movement. Again, and again. Lingering longer each time. Until stopping and remaining there. I can hear Tess's breath deepen and feel her muscles tense. She is so beautiful in her intimate area. What am I doing letting someone else see . . . and touch this most private of areas? I begin to question if I can hold myself together!

The friction on my inner thighs and brushes against my flower have turned the small tingle into full raging fire. I feel my breaths increasing. My mind is racing with so many thoughts and desires I can't catch them all. Muscles tense with every stroke of their hands. Suddenly it all pauses, and my hips relax. A soft touch glides up each side and comes to rest on my breasts again. I try to calm my breathing. Warm kisses, hot even, press against both sides of my neck. A sensitive area for me and chills roll over my entire body. I try to lengthen my neck as my desire rises again.

Lucca and I are feeding upon the sides of Tess's neck in tandem as her moans grow louder and her body begins to squirm. Her neck lengthens for more. I see the chills across her skin and her nipples harden even more. Our hands squeeze her breasts. Finally, we move from her neck, allowing her to breathe. But it will be only a short respite. Lips maneuver down her chest until reaching her full fleshy mounds. My heat is rising, and the pace quickens. Every inch of her breasts is now under assault. Kissing, licking, sucking, and nibbling. Pulling her nipples forcefully with our lips. We can't consume her fast enough.

Wild beasts have descended upon my breasts. Any control that I had has now submitted to the wolves consuming my body. The pleasure is more than enough to overtake any pain. My back arches to offer more of me to their hunger. The focus of the licking and sucking of my flesh temporarily keeps me from noticing the hands moving across my stomach and landing between my legs. A hand on the inside of each upper thigh, massaging my most tender flesh. Palms fit neatly into the crevices of my inner thighs. Pressing my nether lips together. My hips begin to move involuntarily.

Our hands meet between Tess's legs at her most intimate area, but neither will relinquish the space they desire. Clashing together, fighting for the delicacy of the tender flesh we have encircled.

The wolves still feed intently on my breasts as a fury develops between my legs. My knees willingly bend outward opening my thighs wider, submitting to their desire, to their need. Offering what they crave so badly, and what I want to give them. I feel the penetration. One, then two, more. I'm not sure how many. I don't care. I am all theirs.

We are invading our prey relentlessly, wildly. As if we must have her for our survival. I can feel her warm, velvety soft skin inviting us in.

My head falls back from the edge of the bed, my back arches further, generously offering my breasts to their frenzy. My arms stretch above my head surrendering all to my hunters' desires. My body shivers violently. My passion flows uncontrollably, mixing with the beasts and the oils.

Our beautiful prey has one final shuttering throughout her body, then succumbs to us completely.

My body goes limp, lifeless, legs still sprawled wide, weak arms hang above my head. My aching chest heaves for breath.

Spread wide before her pursuers. Naked, exposed, beautiful, peaceful.

Satisfied, overtaken, I lay submissively for my huntsmen to view.

We gaze at the lovely creature conquered before us. Her panting finally beginning to slow. Neither of us can stop admiring what we just enjoyed. I shudder as I suddenly remember the agreement from the conversation with Lucca. There are only so many restrictions you can put on a friend, only so much you can ask of a man with a beautiful woman lying completely naked and at our mercy below us. I lean over, placing my chest on the table at Tess's feet, moving my hands up her legs and under her backside, enjoying her flesh resting on my palms. Her body jerks from the sensitivity of her previous satisfaction when my lips touch her open flower. I taste her intimacy through the mixture of oils. I swallow her passion. Her sweetness spreads across my lips and the sweat and lotion from her inner thighs moisten my cheeks. I smile as I think of Tess telling me that she is my natural beard oil.

I reluctantly glance up to see Lucca standing at Tess's side, his eyes lost in her beauty. His hand moves across her breasts once again, and she flinches from their tenderness. Lucca drops his shorts slightly as I continue to push my lips into her sweet nectar. Tess is shivering and moaning with every pass of my kisses between those beautiful legs. Lucca is lost completely in her lying before him, filled with more desire than a man can handle. He kisses her breasts gently so as not cause more pain as he moves his hand on himself. Flicking her nipple with his tongue, I feel a slight shake to the table as his hand moves faster. I am squeezing her backside with both hands to bring her closer to me. The sensitivity of Tess's body is telling me she needs a break.

I am ready to end this adventure when Lucca rises from her breast and his excitement sprays across Tess's chest. Lucca lays himself on her breast, smearing the cream around her nipple, almost triumphantly. I feel my fists clinch, but Tess's satisfied smile calms me. The white paste is puddled on her with smaller amounts making a trail up to her neck. Lucca inadvertently rubs the remainder of his passion to her shoulder as he places a kiss to her forehead and whispers, "Thank you so much, Tess" before excusing himself from the room. Tess offers a weak dimpled smile with no words.

She looks beautiful, happy, and so peaceful lying nude on the oil-covered sheets. I am slightly surprised that I can't help but think she is so sexy, covered in love and desire. Tess's arms finally move, her hand wipes the stickiness from her chin and neck. Then she uses both hands to smear the larger amount into her chest.

I help Tess to her feet; she is weak in her legs and her voice is gravelly. Her hair is matted in stickiness, and her chest is smeared with Lucca's love. I help her dress and Lucca brings her water and with a gentle touch to her shoulder, "Thank you again. I think Martina would be very pleased." Lucca stops at the door and adds, "I hope we can do it again . . . soon." The door clicks shut leaving Tess and I alone to take it all in.

29

JACK

I STAND IN THE DARK on the upper deck while Tess showers. Under the stars, listening to the ebb and flow of the water. Always the same, yet ever changing, much like life. Different seasons of our journey, some things remain the same, others constantly changing all around us. Some change within us. Have Tess and I just changed seasons, or have we changed our entire journey together? Has our whole world changed? The extreme range of emotions and flurry of thoughts are overwhelming me. I am not able to capture them all to even try to put any order to it. I slow my breaths and attempt to select one thought at a time, but it's like trying to catch the breeze blowing across the deck. Impossible.

First and foremost, I love my wife with all my heart. That's what matters the most. Am I sure that is all that matters though or am I trying to simplify it too much? Tess and I have always kept our marriage pure. We even joke that we are glad that we weren't high school sweethearts so we didn't have to go through the things that most teenagers do with breakups. Most of our family and friends thought our dating period of three months was too short and that our marriage wouldn't make it. We had proven them wrong.

We have never been a couple that fights or argues. Neither of us are made that way and we both experienced too much of that lifestyle in our childhoods. It could be part of what drove us for something better for ourselves and our family. Sure, we did some things wrong when finding our way through raising children, but the kids always saw loving parents and had a safe environment at home. We both enjoy ordinary peaceful days and I have always done my best to provide for and protect Tess. Have I let her down this time? I keep telling myself one thought at a time, but it is a useless endeavor. The thoughts are like snowflakes falling from the sky and I am trying so hard to catch them and hold onto them so I can study their shape and meaning. But they disappear as quickly as I catch them.

But Tess did seem happy and appeared to enjoy every minute of this night. Was she hiding her true feelings to sacrifice for what she thought I wanted all along? Or did she have those hidden fantasies, some that maybe she didn't even know until now? Had I helped open the door to them or created them from nothing? The doctor had told us that her recommendation for recovery was based on all the hours of sessions digging deep into our fears and fantasies. I know we didn't hide things from each other but maybe we had unknowingly hidden them from ourselves.

Someone else touching Tess was always a fear and a hot button for anger inside of me . . . a nightmare, in fact. But something about tonight had been exciting . . . in some ways. I felt a part of my passion return, a part that had been gone for almost a year. Only a part though, and I feel so guilty for that reaction.

I have always gotten so excited when I massage Tess, gifted with the chance to look at her beautiful body, to feel her, and to see and hear her pleasure. We had tried that method multiple times as part of our therapy and even though I loved it as much as ever, it had not been the cure. I search myself to know what was different about tonight.

Tonight, I saw so much passion in her. Raw and exposed. I saw her pleasure in a new way, her happiness. It was different, thrilling, even forbidden when

I saw my sexy little curvy girl offer herself in a way that completely excited someone else along with me. Someone else wanting and needing her so badly. Watching her body move, feeling her muscles tense, and listening to the sounds of her joy. Knowing that she only considered it all to make me whole again. To make us whole again. Because she loves me more than anything.

Her images and sounds dance through my mind, my heart, and my body. Seeing Tess, her beauty and her sweetness in normal daily life, captured in photos for a moment in time, and during our intimacy has always been so wonderful to me. Seeing her in the throes of passion tonight was amazing. The evidence of love was spread across her glimmering thighs and the excitement she created in another was painted across her chest.

She was so beautiful and vulnerable lying before us. Sexier than ever. I never believed I could want her even more than I always have, but I do. Is that wrong?

30

TESS

UNDER THE COVERS OF OUR bed my body is completely relaxed. Exhausted from the effects of the massage and the energy of the passion that roared through me just a few hours earlier. It was amazing and wonderful, but should I feel this way? Of course I shouldn't. I should be filled with guilt from another man's touch. From exposing myself to him. For letting him put his love all over my body. But it was only to help Jack, right? That's what I told myself at least. And part of me is ashamed. The problem is that it's only a "part" of me feeling shame.

Jack and I had walked back quietly on the sandy trail, holding hands but not speaking of the very reason that we went there or our experience. I worry about Jack not having a special friend to talk with besides me. He has always been such a private person. He has many "friends," but aside from me he doesn't let people get too close. Jack has been available to so many people over the years. He has been there to listen to their darkest secrets, fears, and failures without judgement. To help, advise, or just to sit with them. So many times, over the years I wished for him to have a confidante, but he always said I was all he needed when it came to personal things. I knew when he shared personal details with the doctor that he was desperate to get better.

Is Jack mad? Hurt? Excited? I need to know. I want so badly to ask our question before he does, before I have to give my answer. When will we talk about it? I still feel the ecstasy of four hands on my body when the heaviness of my eyes finally makes them drift shut. Dreaming deeply.

I feel the soft rub of a hand on the side of my butt, then down my leg. Massaging gently over my body. Don't wake up Tess, this dream feels too real, and too good. I roll to my back and the hand moves across my thigh. I want to feel those hands again. I need to. The hand moves up to my breasts and I flinch at their tenderness from the earlier devouring. The weight of a body moves over me, it's too dark for me to see a face. Please don't stop with just hands this time. I need more. I need it all this time. I need it deeply. Inside. My neck eagerly accepts kisses, it is a little tender too. Much of my body is sore but I want this. I tell myself again, don't wake up Tess. I fight to stay strong against the aching as the kisses move across my love-marked breasts. I'm so wet again, already. I open my legs wide, and a hand rubs the moisture of passion over my tender flesh. My body shakes with excessive sensitivity.

I am forced open from the push to enter my body. More than earlier, much more. My flower opens wide to accept the generous offering, eagerly accepting the insertion. I want it so badly. I need it. Forceful thrusting begins to shake my body. More pain as my breasts bounce with the movement. I gasp. The intensity increases substantially. My body rocks from the force. Screams of pain and passion bellow out from deep inside. Are they real or just in my dream? Did I awaken Jack with my noise?

I reach my hands up to the headboard to brace myself from the fury below. Finally, I dig my nails into his chest. I must brace for the pounding and the pain and the passion. Louder groans roar out of me. Everything is hard and furious as I push my heels onto the bed and raise my hips inviting him deeper. The sounds of our skin slapping together, over and over. It all seems so real, but I am too exhausted to be sure. Are the emotions and fantasies of the night deceiving me? My neck is sweating from the thickness of my hair. Droplets of sweat begin to form on my chest. My legs and butt are weary from the repetition of flexing and lifting. I want to feel his body against mine, so I pull him down to me, wrapping my arms and legs all around to hold him tightly.

One last powerful and magnificent push deep inside of me and our love gushes forth exploding into one another. Bringing us together. Meshing as one. My muscles collapse, overwhelmed. Weary beyond exhaustion. Our wet bodies slide from one another. A slight chill creeps across my sweat-covered skin and I curl up against Jack. As I drift off into the clouds of my dreams, I whisper in his ear with a tired but gratified smile, "The crazy doctor was right!"

31

JACK

I AWAKE TO THE SMELL of coffee and pancakes. As I walk toward the kitchen Tess bounces over to me, flings both arms around me and gives me the biggest, sweetest kiss. "I love, love, love having Johnny Bravo back!"

We, like many other couples, have had several silly nicknames for our private parts over the years. Tess used to curl up on the couch and watch the Johnny Bravo cartoon with Sam, our toddler, for hours on end. So much that I kidded her that Johnny Bravo was getting more attention from her than me. Eventually little Sam grew out of the Johnny Bravo phase and Tess has kidded me ever since that now my "Johnny Bravo" has her undivided attention. I laugh, "And he loves getting together with petunia again." That has been my name for her love area ever since I told her one day when I was intimately kissing her there that she was as pretty as a petunia.

Tess squeezes my butt. "And I love middle of the night sex."

She has always liked when we awoke from sleep and made love in a dreamy state then cuddled against one another. "Me too, baby." And I did like middle of the night intimacy, and afternoon, morning, night. I liked every time we could be close. I believe much of the reason Tess enjoyed the different times of our intimacy, including morning and afternoon being two of her favorite times, was due to our fatigue in the evening from raising children and our busy schedules early in our married life.

My heart is filled with joy from being one with her again last night after so long. From being able to give her all of myself. I am cautiously optimistic that we have made it past a breaking point. But I am almost afraid to talk about it for fear that it is a one-time reprieve and because of the reason it happened at all. That and Tess doesn't really enjoy talking about the details like I do. My biggest question is if it will take something like that all the time, or am I really cured? And at what cost to us?

Part of me wonders if the price was too high. Have we ruined the pureness that we have had for so many years? Even after recovering from the initial shock of the doctor's assessment, the attempted conversations about possibly following her advice had remained difficult to discuss. Though I knew we both were thinking about it. The actual act of following that advice has overwhelmed my emotions, thoughts, and my heart. In my quietest of times, I had thought there was no way I would do that. And yet, here we are.

Sure, I was excited about the massage, but that is because I was focused on the woman I love. Her beauty, her joy, her passion. But there were times during, and certainly after that my heart was crushed by what we were doing. Times I wanted to punch Lucca. Who was I? Who had we become? Would once be enough? Could we block it from our memories over time? Could we put the genie back in the bottle? Would Tess want to explore more? Would I? I just want answers, but I know they will not easily come. For now, I will just need to be happy that I was able to give Tess all she deserves once again. All of me, for the first time in what seems like forever.

I wrap both arms around Tess and she recoils slightly from the soreness of her breasts. "I'm sorry, baby."

She pulls me back when I try to ease the intensity of my hug. "That's okay honey. I'm so happy, I can take a little pain."

As we enjoy our delicious breakfast, I flip through the pictures I had taken earlier wandering around town as I waited on Tess to get back from seeing Emma. Tess sips a second cup of coffee as we shuffle through them, talking of all the things we had done while vacationing here over the years. But we had never done anything like last night here, or anywhere else for that matter.

There was Ed in his green apron sweeping off the front porch at the Food for Thought Grocery. The front of Curl Up Books was decorated to promote the newest releases, and the ladies at Beachy Blessings gift shop were touching up their window displays. The close-up shots of fruits and veggies at The Founding Fathers produce stand were beautiful with all the colors, if I did say so myself. Kids were all smiles walking out of What's the Scoop. And Sandy Toes, the main gathering spot, was between meal rushes and unusually quiet. I had taken several photos down the side alleys too. The alleys were always clean but showed the working aspect of the businesses that were hidden behind the well-presented shop fronts.

"Wait, go back." The urgency in Tess's voice startles me.

"Which picture, baby?" I zoom in on one of the alley shots of Sandy Toes and at the corner of the storage shed, which of course had a graffiti painting by a young local artist of dozens of kids sticking their toes in the sand, was Marcus. Marcus with his finger pointed in the face of someone with their back to the camera. But there is no doubt who the other person is with his hands held up in the air toward Marcus. The curly black hair and wiry build clearly identifies Cody.

I run my fingers across the hair on my chin. "I can't believe that I didn't notice that when I was taking it." I had been clicking away, thinking of memories of me and Tess over the years but not paying attention to what was in many of the shots.

"They don't look happy with each other," Tess says what I am thinking.

"Wonder what that was about?" Already knowing what Tess's response would be.

"I don't know but we need to find out." She grabs her detective notebook and begins to write.

The doorbell rings. I'm thinking "not the sheriff again" as Tess and I look at each other. Relieved, we find Devin at the door. "Come in, where's Gabriella?"

"I had to sneak off while she was on her conference call, and I don't have much time."

Tess and I speak at the same time, "Is everything okay?"

Devin hurriedly responds, "Oh . . . yes, nothing bad. I forgot to get your phone number when we were with you, so I had to come in person. Gabriella's birthday is today, and I would like to surprise her with a short cruise out to celebrate."

"That's a great surprise, how can we help?"

Devin laughs. "No, I meant all four of us. We had a great time on our last trip and Gabriella loves Tess. No offense meant Jack."

"None taken, I love her too."

"Gabriella has been wanting to get together with you guys, but I kept missing you. Sorry about the late notice."

Devin pauses. "There is one more favor I would like to ask though. Would you mind brining all your equipment for a full photo shoot?"

I look at him, puzzled. "I don't mind at all, but I do this for a hobby. I'm not a professional and Gabriella is used to having experienced photographers."

"You will be great, thanks. See you at the dock at about one, and sorry again about the short notice."

Tess smiles. "You know what that means don't you?"

After twenty-eight years together I sure do. "When do you want to go to shopping?"

Tess enjoys looking for treasures, especially in stores that she hasn't been in for a while. Our plan is to separate temporarily to let her find a gift and I will visit Rohan to see if I can find any information about Marcus and Cody. After a quick stop at Around the Brim to check out the latest hats, I go over to Sandy Toes.

Rohan is hustling about but glad to stop for a short visit. I show him the picture of Marcus and Cody behind the building. He isn't aware that Cody has been coming around and has no idea why they would be talking, much less arguing. We both fear that it could be something with drugs, so Rohan agrees to set a camera up outside to see if he can find out more.

Tess and I meet back up at The Devotional Grind for a latte and to check in with Mr. Jones again. Some of the garden club ladies are there having coffee and muffins and sharing the happenings around town. We sit a couple of tables over and wait for Mr. Jones to finish his work in the back of the store as we listen to the garden club conversation. With several members in the group, they certainly seem to be on top of everything going on with everyone in town and maybe beyond.

Mr. Jones joins us and lays his feathered fedora in the empty chair beside him. I shake his hand, compliment the fedora and tell him that I had tried to find a new hat down the street but couldn't decide on one without Tess there to help.

Tess laughingly adds that she is relieved I waited for her because I need help with things like that since the only hat I wear is my college hat with the 'T' on the front.

I pretend that the T is for Tess as much as our tiger mascot.

We ask again if he can think of anyone else that Emma may have told or if someone could have overheard them talking about her being pregnant or staying at the pool house. We try to speak quietly to keep anyone in the busy café from overhearing. The preacher says he and Emma met privately in his office in the back each time and that his workers would have been too busy to listen in even if they wanted to. I hate to ask the next question, but I must. "Mr. Jones, did you tell your wife about Emma's situation? We would completely understand because Tess and I share everything."

"Absolutely not. Part of being a preacher is having to keep things from her, sometimes to protect people that count on me for counsel."

I look apologetically at the preacher. "I'm sorry I had to ask but we think someone else had to know because of the timing of Emma's beating."

We all agree that maybe she had confided in someone else that she hadn't told the preacher about. On the way out we speak to Mrs. Jones who is behind the counter, "The preacher hasn't put you to work has he?"

"Not at all, I make my own latte so I can add extra milk and syrup," she says with a sly grin. "The preacher wants me to watch my sugar, so I slip back here when he is busy with other things."

Tess laughs. "A girl has to do what a girl has to do to get the right coffee drink. I like the extra cream too, Mrs. Jones."

We load up in old red and let the wind blow as we head back to get ready for our boat ride.

32

TESS

ME WITH GIFT IN HAND and Jack with two duffel bags, one of camera equipment and the other a mystery case, we board *The Gabriella*, Devin's beautiful yacht. I must admit I amaze myself with the ability to find a gift on such short notice, and Gabriella seems sincerely appreciative of my efforts.

Gabriella brings us drinks as Devin captains us out to sea. I notice there is no staff aboard for this trip. We anchor and enjoy another drink before Devin comes down the steps. "Let's get the party started."

Gabriella, who apparently has been let in on this part of the surprise by now, agrees, and promptly grabs my hand and shoots up from her seat to get changed. I soon find out that Devin had texted Jack with outfit suggestions to match Gabriella's as closely as he could. Jack picking out clothes for me to wear for a photo shoot in front of others is kind of scary. Really scary in fact. The first round is tame enough, but I am thankful that I had applied makeup to cover the lust marks on my breasts and neck from the wolves last night.

Gabriella left her hair down and loose for this trip, and I love her natural curls. We dress to fit the scene, light summery thigh-length dresses, white with a touch of bright yellows and pinks. I am happy that mine matches my hot pink toe polish applied freshly only a few hours earlier by Jack. Though he did almost make us late kissing all over my feet and toes while painting them. He can't help himself, but I love the attention from him. The tops are cut low, and both dresses are sleeveless. Our hair blows in the ocean breeze and the loose flaps on the bottom of the dresses lift occasionally. I know that Jack is capturing some good shots with this set. And I am having so much fun.

We hold our champagne glasses, pose standing and sitting, and Jack takes some individual photos along with plenty of us together. Then Gabriella says it is time to go below and change our wardrobe. As we slide into pin-up-looking throwback bathing suits that I think are a nice touch, I glance over and see Gabriella without her top. This is one of those times I wish my filter worked. "Wow, your boobs are so beautiful. I wish mine stood at attention like that." It just comes rushing from my mind and across my lips, unfiltered.

Gabriella, sharing many of my own personality traits doesn't flinch, only smiles, "Thank you, they should after years of having to watch everything that went in my mouth and all that exercise."

We laugh together. I pull my top from the small bag of clothes, and I am impressed at how well Jack and Devin coordinated the outfits. I put both hands under my heavy mounds and hoist them upward. "I tell Jack all the time that one day I am going to have mine reset to stand up where they are supposed to be. At least I have breasts now instead of a flat chest like when we were first married though. I looked like a cake topper with no titties in my wedding dress," I said, laughing with Gabriella.

"Don't you even think about having any work on those beauties." I'm not surprised that Gabriella says something polite, but she is more emphatic than I expected. "Yours are perfect. I would love mine to be big and natural like that."

Trying not to acknowledge the fact that I am standing topless discussing boobs with a woman I just met a few days ago, I offer my honest reply. "You are too sweet but yours are perfect, firm and taut, and the beautiful cocoa color is absolutely gorgeous." My little angel appears on my shoulder again like in the coffee shop: what are you thinking Tess, breaking down the details of her gorgeous breasts? She is going to think you are crazy.

Gabriella takes a few steps over to me without a smile, and I am thinking she is going to say get off the boat and swim home. But she reaches out and places both hands around my boobs with a gentle squeeze and a little jiggle. As her hands brush across the front, my nipples stiffen instantly. "These girls are sexy as hell."

I did not see that coming. I am stunned with too many thoughts bouncing around my mind to grab only one for a reply. Gabriella speaks again before I can, "It's only fair," she says as she straightens her back to offer hers for my touch. I try to move my arms up slower than I want so I don't look overly anxious. But that is a lie; I want to feel them. And they feel as wonderful in my hands as they look through my eyes, even more. So firm, a perfect handful, and encircling the hard tips are a gorgeous quarter-sized dark brown pigment. My hands stay a little longer than I intend, but not longer than I want. Gabriella meets my eyes with a smile. "I guess we better get upside for the next round before the guys coming looking for us." But it doesn't feel as if she really wants to leave. I know I don't.

The pin-up shots are fun as we use many boating props, vintage sunglasses, and old time poses to fit the mood and, as Jack would say, to tell a story.

One final wardrobe change. Somehow, I am not uncomfortable going back below because Gabriella is easy to be around and hasn't seemed altered at all by our earlier surprising exchange of feeling each other up. But I am uncomfortable with the next outfit. The white almost see-though string bikini. In front of Devin is bad enough but in front of this model with such a beautiful lean body is another. About four or five inches shorter, I feel stumpy and thick when standing next to her beauty, and my pale skin against her gorgeous cocoa color is not going to be good. All that apparently comes out of my mouth as we remove our pin-up suits.

"You must be joking." Gabriella is right next to me again. "I would die to have that pretty skin and your big naturals," as she gives them another squeeze. "And that nice round booty," as she gives it a love tap and holds on longer than I expect. Running her hand down the side of my leg, "And those strong sexy legs." She does a model spin in front of me. "Models are only required to be long. Look at my tiny butt and skinny legs. I have always wanted a figure like yours."

"I think you have had too much ocean air, but I love you for trying to make me feel better about this last set." I finish putting on my bikini even though it doesn't cover much more than me standing there naked and add, "Models are required to be beautiful too, not just long." Gabriella is most definitely long and beautiful.

Gabriella's bikini is even smaller than mine, which I didn't believe possible. It is leopard and blends with her skin making it appear that she has nothing on at first glance, which isn't far from the truth. Two tiny strips just barely cover her nipples leaving the rest of her perky breasts exposed. There is nothing covering her little butt besides the string that is hiding between her taut cheeks. And if the front part moves the tiniest in any direction, everyone will be seeing all her private parts.

My eyes scan up and down her body. I smile. "Now I am not worried, neither of those guys will notice that I am there much less my outfit."

Gabriella smiles. "You are the sweetest." She leans over and gives me a peck on the cheek. "I promise that Devin will notice you." She turns and her long brown legs start upstairs, leaving me at eye level to watch her butt twist up each step. She is a beautiful woman.

We make what are already racy photos even more so when Devin asks for some topless shots. I wonder what Jack is thinking. But we are on their boat, it is part of her birthday present, they are both so nice, and the request is just so casual that it sounds like someone asking you to smile. I am nervous and somewhat embarrassed, but surprisingly I also feel the tingle in my middle like last night. We are too far in to turn back at this point.

So many different poses, laying on loungers at every possible angle, standing with our hair blowing in the wind, and looking over the railing with our starkly contrasting butts sticking up in the air. Some with heels and some barefoot. Jack always has plenty of ideas for photos, but it has always just been of me.

He tells us that we are nearing the end and Gabriella whispers into my ear to just go with her lead on the last few. I think she means we will do something funny for the guys to wrap it up. I am so wrong about her humor.

Jack clicks the shutter rapidly as Gabriella leans over and kisses me on the cheek. She moves me in front of her facing the camera, reaches her arms around me, and places her hands on my bare breasts, smiling from over my shoulder. She then walks around, turning my backside toward Jack with Devin sitting behind him, and has me bend forward slightly before putting her hand on my butt while giving a surprised face toward the camera. I know Jack and Devin love this. If I don't let myself think of the camera, I am loving it too.

For the big finale, Gabriella places both hands on my face and turns us sideways to the camera. She places her lips on mine and holds the pose for Jack to have plenty of time to get the shot. She then shares a long, deep passionate kiss with me, taking me completely by surprise. And even more to my surprise, I like it. Maybe a little too much.

We all sit round the captain's chair as Devin guides us back toward land. Jack is telling Devin about Emma and our investigation and the sheriff wanting the pictures. My mind is replaying the conversation with Gabriella while picturing her naked body, the touches, and the kiss, not tuning into the details of Emma that I already know. Devin is extremely happy with the photos even though Jack tells him to wait until he receives the final product before judging.

As we disembark the boat, one of the many boating terms that Devin has taught us, he tells Jack he has some technology that may help with making the background shot of our potential suspect clearer. He invites us over later for dinner and to work on the pictures, which we are excited to accept. Maybe for more than one reason for me.

33

JACK

GETTING READY FOR DINNER, TESS and I talk about the steamy photo session on the boat. Neither of us really know how to process it but agree that we did enjoy our time with Devin and Gabriella. We laugh at what has taken place over the last couple of days as Tess slides into her skintight bright red dress. Damn, her curves and complexion look great in tight outfits and bold colors. She presses against her stomach, wishing it away as she looks into the mirror. I want her to see herself through my eyes so badly. The massage then the boat pictures back-to-back, add in Tess being a private detective and we wonder whose lives we are living. But we are just trying to enjoy our journey.

I watch her lips change to red with a few strokes of her hand and I go to get the polish remover, because I know the toes will have to match. I think of how happy I am that I can give all of myself to her again. Though I am still not sure if I am okay with the sacrifice we made to get there. The images from the massage keep flashing through my mind. Some make me sad, some mad, but others excite me. Is that normal? Am I a terrible person, an awful husband?

Tess places a foot in my lap, and I notice another one of the little details of her that I love so much. A lone freckle on the side of her calf, right in the groove of where the muscle flexes when she points her foot or wears heels. The freckle reminds me of how I treasure all the special little things of Tess. I am repainting her pretty toes to match the fire-red dress when I finally build up the courage to ask the question, "Would you want that again?"

"The boat pictures?" I know that she is stalling so I silently continue to move the brush over her tiny toenails. They are so small that it is a challenge to not smear polish on her toes.

I can see that Tess is trying to choose her words carefully. "Oh, you meant the massage. Well, it was . . . very provocative." A brief pause followed by, "And it did accomplish the goal for us."

"It seems to have done that." With a tilt of my head, I remind her that she hasn't answered the question.

She pauses again which tells me what the answer is, but I need to hear her say it. Tess is struggling to get the words out. "It was a lot of feelings I have never felt before." Quickly adding, "Not better than our intimacy."

I silently clean the excess polish off her toes with a Q-tip while waiting for her to continue.

Tess selects her words carefully when finally proceeding. "Part of me felt slutty, or dirty, but another part felt excited. I never thought of doing anything like that until we faced so much this past year."

I patiently let her work through the words. "It was an amazing feeling to think that I could have two people want me that badly. I mean, you know I don't see myself like you see me. I don't see a sexy woman, so it was different thinking another man wanted me like that." She seemingly unknowingly places her hands on the dress over her chest and I assume that she is thinking of the frenzy on her breasts from that night.

She continues, "And it did feel wonderful, being stimulated so many places at the same time. Her dimples appear briefly. "I guess that part was obvious." Another pause before finally delivering her answer. "So, yes, I would want it again." Then her words pour out speedily, "But only if you would, and not all the time, just as something special on occasion." Another pause before finishing with, "Would you? Did you enjoy it?"

I feel as if I had shown my answer the night before with our middle of the night intimacy, that I was able to give her what I hadn't been able to this past year. So, I answer plainly and honestly, "I have always told you that I love everything about our intimate time, scent, taste, feel, sound, and the closeness I have to you during and after. And I have also told you that I love seeing you so much that I wish I could float out of my body at times and see all of you when we are making love. That's what it was like. I loved seeing you. Your body in full view, the movements, the muscles tensing, the total enjoyment of the woman I love." Keeping my eyes with hers, "So, yes I would want that again."

We embrace for a long moment. I treasure every time I am gifted with holding Tess in my arms. I breathe in the wonderful scent of the lady I love.

Tess giggles. "What about today? Would you want that again?"

"You know I loved that, because I always want pictures of you. I'm not enamored with Gabriella quite the way you are." I chuckle at my upcoming observation. "And apparently she is just as enamored with you."

Tess blushes and slides on her open-toed leopard heels before leaning over to leave a red lip print on my cheek.

I clutch Tess's hand as we walk toward the door. "Let's go get those photos enhanced."

"And who knows what else we may get into," as Tess teasingly twists her butt through the door.

34

TESS

"YOU BOYS GOT QUITE A show this afternoon," Gabriella prods Jack as Devin moves shrimp and steaks around the grill top. The side deck of their house offers a view of the ocean on one side, and a beautiful sunset to the west.

Devin laughs, "You always put on a show, honey."

Gabriella keeps goading as Jack places the steaks on a plate and moves toward the screened porch to the back of the house. "What was your favorite set, Jack?"

Jack's face begins to color. "I loved all of them."

"But if you had to pick only one?" Gabriella enjoys the teasing and is not going to let him off the hook.

Jack struggles, trying to not say the obvious, but Gabriella is not backing down. I think the color on his cheeks is too cute for her to stop. "Come on, Jack, what were your top three pictures?"

Devin tries to save him. "Stop being so mean. You know we loved the topless shots and the kiss." He laughs and I can see that he is not the least bit surprised at Gabriella pulling that stunt during pictures.

"I just want to know what Jack's favorites were," Gabriella says with a sweet innocent look toward Jack.

Devin again comes to the rescue. "Did you bring the flash drive, Jack?"

After a great dinner, Devin starts enthusiastically explaining how the software is going to work to enhance the photos as his fingers click at a feverish pace across the laptop. Gabriella is not interested in the workings of the software and takes my hand. "Come on, baby, we can find something more exciting to get into."

As we walk behind Devin, the screen fills with my smile, silver hair flowing, and my BOOBS. Now I am the one blushing. "Oh goodness, we definitely can find something better to do."

Gabriella stops in front of the computer. "This looks like fun, maybe we should stay."

I place a hand on her shoulder and steer her toward the double doors to the living room. "You're funny. Let's go before I have to see another close-up."

Gabriella winks. "I like the real thing better anyway."

We blow kisses to the hubbies as we close the door behind us.

I wonder why I am not more embarrassed thinking of my pictures displayed in front of a man I have only known briefly. My thoughts go to lying naked on a table in front of Lucca only twenty-four hours ago. Not long ago I would have been appalled at myself and probably Jack at the thought of both of those things. Add in the mutual boob feeling-up with Gabriella and I had no idea who I was anymore. For some reason, even though I still did not feel sexy it doesn't bother me like it should have. Who am I becoming?

Gabriella and I have a great time learning more about each other as we pop open a second bottle of wine. In many ways it is as if we have been friends for years. We share stories of our pasts and dreams of things we want to do. Beauty tips, hairstyles, and eventually our talk moves to intimacy. I am even looser than my normal unfiltered self as we continue refilling our glasses. Devin passes through once and grabs a bottle of scotch and a box of cigars.

We whisper and laugh like young girls at a sleepover. Devin shakes his head as he passes, "Looks like Jack and I are behind on the party."

Our feet curl under us as we sit side by side on the couch, the conversation moves to something even more risqué as we go into more detail about sexual positions that we prefer and what Jack and Devin like. Gabriella catches me off guard with one of her patented out-of-nowhere comments. She leans in closer, looks over her shoulder toward the deck as if to make sure the coast is clear, and whispers, "Don't you sometimes just need the soft touch of another woman?"

She flashes her pretty smile and waits for my answer. I pause before smiling back and sheepishly confess that I have never known that touch. Gabriella sits up straight, a genuinely surprised look on her face. "Oh baby, you must experience the beauty of that." She gently takes my hand and places it between both of her hands. "I would love to show you how wonderful that feels."

My head is spinning, and it isn't the wine. At least it isn't all wine. Sure, we joked around, had some fun touching, and even shared a great kiss, but I thought all that was just her playful personality. I love that about her. And I enjoy looking at other women, even pointing them out to Jack many times. But I have never, ever fantasized or even thought of being with another woman. I have never entertained that thought or desire . . . until right this moment. I feel that tingle in my lady area again, and suddenly Gabriella looks even more gorgeous than before as the thought of how wonderful her kiss was races through my mind. Who am I? Where is all this coming from?

Sweetly and slowly, Gabriella leads me by the hand from the couch to the bedroom, looking back with such a wonderful smile as we walk. I follow willingly. Even anxiously. The room is romantic with low-lit lamps on either side of the bed. A bed that suddenly looks intimidating to me. She gently turns my shoulders to face her and her pretty brown eyes seem to absorb me. "You are so sexy in that dress, babe."

The smile comes across my lips easily, but I can't find any words to follow.

She takes one step closer, pressing our bodies together and placing her soft hands on my cheeks ever so gently. "Relax. I want you to enjoy your first time." Her soft lips mesh with mine and our tongues dance a beautiful waltz while her hands roam the curves of my body over the tight dress. I feel like I am floating across a beautiful ballroom without my feet touching the dance floor.

When our lips finally separate, a panic floods my thoughts. "This is wrong. I can't do this without Jack. It will hurt him. I need to get out of here. Just run, Tess!" But my legs won't move.

Gabriella slowly pulls my dress upward, wiggling it over my abundant hips and then over my head, leaving me with only two small pieces of leopard print and heels. More thoughts arise; maybe Jack will be okay with this. Afterall, we agreed to open up to our fantasies, to help Jack recover, and to live our lives to the fullest. To not be bound by narrow-minded influences.

I nervously follow her lead and kick off my heels. Gabriella begins to unbutton her silk top, but I surprise myself and take over for her as I lean in for another kiss. I love the softness of her lips. The resistance in my mind softens, "are you really doing this" and "Jack will love me no matter what." The sexy lady in front of me helps to justify the thoughts. The silk slides effortlessly from her lean shoulders. My hands move, seemingly on their own, to unbutton her skirt and it falls quickly to her feet. Her tan skin is magnificent against the zebra thong and bra. She takes my hand and leads me toward the bed that is inexplicably less intimidating than moments before.

Turning me gently, Gabriella unlatches the clasp from my top freeing my breasts to fall softly. She reaches around and cups them with her delicate hands and softly tugs my hardened tips while placing kisses on my neck. The feel of her soft lips and warm breath grows the tingle inside to a rumble. Another gentle turn, before gracefully easing me back until I feel the cool silk sheets meet my skin. We kiss as our hands search each other's bodies and her skin feels so soft against mine.

Gabriella pulls a decorative white box from the nightstand drawer before hovering over me with a long pause as if to enjoy the moment. She runs a hand lovingly through my hair and comments on its softness and thickness. We begin another slow dance with our tongues as I unhook her top wanting to feel her breasts against mine. Wanting to see them again. Her lips trace down the front of my neck before her body lifts to offer me her beautiful breasts with gorgeous dark circles around the perky tips. She graciously lowers them to my lips. I massage their firmness before smearing them with what is left of my red lipstick. A delectable Bolero dance with slow rises and falls moving from one side to the other. I need more and pull her closer, taking the whole of her beautifully formed firmness into my mouth. I can't get enough of them, of her. Where is this desire coming from? I think of how I kiss Jack's chest because I know that it is a sensitive area for him, but this is a selfish desire to have Gabriella. A pleasure that I want for me. One hand is on her breast with the other on her back keeping her close, though she doesn't seem to need the encouragement at all. I slide back slowly and only long enough to clutch her pointed tips between my lips, as if to not let her get away. Her thighs press harder against my sides while my tongue circles her brown nipples. Needing to breathe is the only thing that makes me release her.

Gabriella rises to her knees over me, and I see the marks I left on her perky beauties. She gazes into my eyes before sliding lower and removing the last small piece of material from my body. I feel the moisture of her kiss-covered chest slide over the wetness of my anticipation as she moves back up my body to return the favor of attention. She kisses and plays with the flesh of my chest for the longest time, yet not long enough. My hands on her back want to keep her there.

Gabriella raises up once again and I can see the moisture of her kisses glisten from my chest and the glimmer of my excitement smeared on her flat stomach that has been resting between my legs. She lifts my leg and rubs from foot to thigh and back as her lips follow her fingers. Then the other leg. I float above our dance floor once again, enjoying every moment. Her kisses move up my inner thigh and the first brush of her lips on my tenderness sends a shiver through my body. Softly and gently her lips press between my legs. Slow, long, and deliberate as her hands fondle my chest and pinch, twist, and pull my nipples. My back arches involuntarily, wanting more.

Our waltz becomes a rumba. Longer, deeper kisses. Her tongue discovering my deepest inner passion. Her hands move to cup the flesh of my backside, and I lift my hips for her. I want to grant her all access to me. Long strokes of her tongue followed by quick light suctions. Becoming faster and more intense. My thighs squeeze against her cheeks striving to keep her there. She brings me to a wonderous spin on the dance floor. My hips rise higher, pushing toward her lips. The grand finale of our dance and it feels as if Gabriella is spinning my body effortlessly through the air. I'm suspended in the spotlights high above the floor, I gasp for breath, I can't see where I am. Finally, I begin falling, completely trusting Gabriella and submitting to her will. With an exhilarating rush I release myself to her and she catches me and all my passion like a dancer smoothly catches their partner after a lift. Gabriella slowly dips my hips back down to the sheets with one more deep loving kiss. I shiver all over, multiple times. My chest rises and falls. That was amazing.

Gabriella's body rests against mine, our breasts pushing together. She shares the sweetest of smiles and then the taste of my happiness with her lips to mine. We slow dance again with our kiss. I surprise myself yet again as I gently guide her to roll over. My lips want to cover every inch of her wonderful body. My kisses move down her sides tasting her supple skin and tracing the bones across her thin hips. My fingers grasp the sides of her zebra thong, and her hands reach to my cheeks, gently lifting to pull my eyes to hers, whispering, "You don't have to do this my love." A big smile crosses my lips. "I want to, baby." I am surprised by my own words.

I slide her panties down, moving slowly to enjoy her long, tan legs. My lips trace over each of them as if trying to memorize their shape. I spread her legs slightly wider, press my cheeks to her inner thighs, and kiss her beautiful dark intimate lips that match the color of her areolas. I pause to enjoy her scent and the feel of her soft flesh, then began to taste her sweetness. I am not confident in what I am doing but I know what Jack does to make me feel good.

I am surprised by the velvety softness of her intimate skin as it melts into my lips. I have always wanted Jack to describe the feeling and the taste of when he makes love to me like this but now, I understand why he says he can't find the words. All I know is that she is glorious, and I want more. My hands roam all over her smooth skin as I search her inner love. Gabriella's hands cling to my hair and pull me tighter. I am so glad she does. Her hips move fluidly, and her moans become louder. Her excitement makes me happy—that is another thing that Jack tells me. Like a graceful dancer she lifts her leg and wraps it around my back to pull me even closer. Then her movements intensify as I consume her, an Argentine tango with hard crisp movements of her hips, legs, and hands. I love the pressure of her leg on my back, squeezing me tighter with each passing moment. I kiss her passionately, desperately . . . and she relinquishes her joy to me. I am so happy and excited. I never dreamed I could love intimacy with another woman like I am now. The softness of her skin. Her touch. Her scent. Her kisses searching my body. Her beauty and her passion.

Gabriella places her hands on my moist, flushed cheeks and pulls me closer, looking into my eyes. "That was amazing, babe. You are amazing." The sound of her sincerity makes my dimples appear. The following kiss is mixed with both of our intimate flavors and is wonderfully romantic. Gabriella reaches into the box that she pulled from the drawer earlier.

A wand with a wide soft tip and a curved shaft with nubs on the ends and sides appears. She guides me over with a giggle. "Not done yet, baby." She looks deeply into my eyes and the initial feeling from the humming device makes my entire body shudder. Gabriella's lips melt into mine as she sends waves of sensations and pleasure rushing through my veins. Intense vibrations and penetration as her lips explore the details of my body again. Her soft skin meshes against mine. I lose count of how many times she has brought me to ecstasy.

Our sweaty bodies lay against one another, her head rests on my shoulder as I allow my breath to subside. Why have I waited so long for this? My eyes scan her body wrapped around mine, trying to imprint the image in my mind. I notice the disheveled sheets of the bed wet from our passion. I look around the room at our clothes strewn across the floor and our shoes lying next to each other. And then to two small lights outside the sliding doors.

First dim, then glowing brighter, and dimming again as they move through the air. My eyes widen. Cigars!

35

JACK

OUR TOES WIGGLE IN THE cool night sand with the moon and stars hanging brightly overhead. Our vacation is going by quickly and I am full of so many mixed emotions from the recent events, especially what has happened the last two nights. I straighten out the blanket that I grabbed from the pool storage on the walk back from our night with Devin and Gabriella. I wrap my arm around Tess as I wonder how I am supposed to feel. I interrupt the soothing sound of the water easing onto shore, "The enhancement software was a big help."

Tess breaks her silence. "And you both watched me and Gabriella?" Tess ignores my lame attempt to talk about something other than the obvious.

I nod my head. "We did. And I am so sorry, baby. I knew it wasn't right. Maybe it was too much scotch. You know I don't usually drink a lot, especially liquor. I have always heard the expensive stuff goes down easy. And it sure did." I knew I was rambling and trying to justify my shame from watching her with Gabriella, but was hoping this would help Tess to forgive me. And to help me feel better about myself.

My sweet Tess lifts her head and looks into my eyes. "I am so sorry that I did that without you, or at least talking with you first. I knew that I shouldn't. I tried to think of the best way to end it without hurting Gabriella's feelings, but it all just happened so fast."

I pull Tess closer. "It's okay baby."

She snaps back. "No, it's not okay. We do everything together."

I place a hand on her knee. "I was shocked, and maybe a little hurt at first. But we have discussed trying new things so much over the last few months. And that is all you did. And all of this has been to help me get better . . . and to make sure you have all the happiness that you deserve."

Tess stares down at the blanket. "I'm so embarrassed."

I squeeze her leg gently. "It was beautiful. Why would you be embarrassed?"

Her face wrinkles with concern. "So many reasons. Not the least of which is that I'm supposed to be your good girl."

I lean against Tess. "You are my good girl. Why would you think you aren't?"

"Good girls don't do things like that. Especially in front of others." Her eyes stay downward.

I ask, "Things like having fun? Help your husband get better and make him happy?"

I can sense Tess wrestling with the words. "But we have never done these things before. And . . . this is different from last night."

I try to speak lightly and with a fun demeanor. "And we are still happy and closer than ever, so I don't see the problem." Even though I am struggling with both of the events right now. I wonder if I have messed everything up with us by trying these new things. I feel like maybe I should have just continued to fight through my performance block.

She turns to me and lets me look into those beautiful blue eyes. "Are you happy with me?"

"Happier than ever. I love you more every day."

"You don't think I'm a floozie?"

I can't hold in the chuckle. "You are not a floozie, baby. You did all this for me." I pause. "Well, maybe not all of it," with a smile. "You opened yourself up to try anything to help me, to get our full intimacy back, and along the way you discovered things you didn't know you liked. I love you more than ever, Tess."

She looks at her feet wiggling deeper into the sand. "But do you still desire me after all of this?"

I lean in to kiss her soft lips as I am feeling hopeful that she will rekindle the excitement from earlier tonight. Tess in that tight red dress and the images of her with Gabriella are driving me wild. I want another intimate moment with Tess right now. "More than ever."

The sand has been cooling to our toes, but the air is still warm, and it is so late at night—or early in the morning depending on your perspective—that I know we have the beach to ourselves. Tess rolls over and begins to kiss me passionately. It's sweet and romantic with a quiet peace surrounding us.

Tess never really likes talking about our sex in detail the way I do, so I have learned to not push her to do that over the years. She did share some of the struggle with her emotions and feelings of guilt after the last two experiences. But tonight is different in more ways than the obvious rendezvous with Gabriella. Tess talks in detail about some of the things that excited her the last couple of nights. She talks about the feeling of another woman and her first kiss with Gabriella. She talks of the thrill of having two men so aroused by her and how she felt sexy lying exposed on the table. And she talks some about the feelings she had with Gabriella. I am happy that she confides in me, and my desire for her is growing immensely from the conversation.

I try to reassure her that I don't believe we did anything wrong or bad and that I know she has stepped way out of her area of comfort to help us because she loves me. I tell her that I could see her joy and excitement each of those times and that she shouldn't feel bad for letting her passion out. "You deserve to be excited and happy in every way, baby."

From the images of her in my mind to the words coming from her mouth, I can't take anymore. I roll to my side and push against her soft plush lips with another long kiss. My hands roam the curves of her body over the tight red dress. Our lips stay locked as I slide one hand down to her leg. I let her catch a breath as I urgently move my kisses lower and push the red material over her waist, tasting the skin of her inner thighs. I feel the chills come to her body as my lips trace the soft crevices of her pantie lines and her hands grasp my hair.

Tess surprises me and rolls me over to my back. She swings her leg over my waist and straddles me while lifting the red dress over her head. Tess is a strong and independent woman but has always been submissive in our special time. Not just during our occasional bondage play, but she usually lets me lead the way during our special time. Everything from starting our play to choosing positions. Tess has been different on this trip, much more assertive. I love her passion, but I wish I could read her thoughts on all the reasons why. I don't think she is trying to keep anything from me, but maybe she just doesn't know why herself.

Tess leans in close, letting her breasts push against me and whispers in my ear, "Let's go inside."

Even with her new aggression, Tess is nervous about making love on the beach. I smile. "I can't wait that long. I need you right now."

She gently protests, "Someone may come."

I nuzzle into her neck and breathe in her wonderful scent as I kiss her soft skin. "It's late, we're okay."

Tess makes one last half-hearted plea. "But baby."

My hands free the girls from the leopard material and leave a wet trail of kisses across her chest.

Tess submits to my desires as she had submitted to hers the last two nights. She stands long enough to remove her panties, tossing them to the side. I am enthralled by the view of my gorgeous wife standing over me. Tess lowers herself again and quickly gains access to what she wants, tossing clothes every which way.

The salty breeze brushes over our bodies as we come together as one under the stars. The tastes and scents of my wife mixed with her earlier encounter, the feel of her nails digging into my skin, and the view of her hair blowing make me completely lost in the moment. The calm splashing of the water and our sounds of passion are the only noises interrupting the tranquility of the night.

Soft moans escape our lips and I feel Tess's thighs tighten around my body. The feel of her breasts brushing against my skin with her movement is so arousing that my joy flows into my beautiful wife. I hold Tess tightly and breathe her in as my mind tries to drift back from the euphoric place that she has taken me.

At some point I hear her whisper, "Baby . . . baby."

I'm so happy that Tess is wanting more. I like that she can't control her excitement.

She calls my name with a slightly louder whisper and digs her hands into my arms as she squirms against my body. It makes my heart flutter that she wants me, and I love it when she calls out during our intimacy, though I might need a minute to regroup for her.

Once again, "Jack." Her voice rises above the whisper from before. A loud whisper, if there is such a thing.

I hug her tightly, loving the passion that she is sharing. "I love you, Tess."

She forces her hands between our bodies and pushes on my chest. "Someone is here, Jack!"

My eyes quickly dart toward the direction she is looking . . . two flashlights!!

"Oh no . . . come on," as I pull her by the hand. "Stay low." The lights are close but not shining in our direction—yet.

The lights and the outlines of two people are closing in as I scoop up all our stuff. We scurry naked in the direction of the house and push our way into a small opening in the brush. The blanket snags on a twig and I lose my grip, but we must keep moving. My legs are being poked and scratched with each step, pushing through the bushes and deeper into hiding. I hold in a yell when my toe finds a stump, but we keep moving. We must get deep enough to not be seen, but the lights are now too close for us to keep making noise with our steps, so we stoop down and hold our positions quietly.

With much of the brush a little over waist high, we squat low to hide from the now searching lights. We both cover our mouths with a hand from the attack on our bare bums from the sticks and twigs below. They must have heard us and by now have probably discovered the blanket. Both lights scan over the vegetation, and we hold our breaths as we sink even lower. One part of us is concerned that this could be one of the crazies that attacked Emma. The other part is trying not to laugh as we wiggle to keep the uprising sticks out of our butts.

"Oh, my goodness! There are a pair of panties and a blanket." It's the voice of an elderly lady.

Tess glares at me for dropping her intimates and probably just the entire situation that we find ourselves in.

"Now honey, don't get upset. Kids are a little wilder today than we were young."

Tess and I look at each other with wide eyes. We know that voice. Tess looks at me and mouths, "Preacher Jones!" I know that I am in deep trouble now.

I try to mouth back that at least we know it isn't a crazy attacker. She either doesn't understand or doesn't care as she keeps giving me the evil eye.

Mrs. Jones snaps a stick from the plant in front of her and leans over to poke at something. She raises the stick with Tess's panties proudly flying on the end. "I'll teach this girl a lesson and throw these little things away."

It takes all my willpower to hold back the laugh bubbling up. I know if I start laughing that Tess will quickly follow and we will be caught in this very embarrassing situation. The Joneses mumble something inaudible to one another and shine the lights over our heads one last time before turning to leave. Tess and I remain perfectly still for several more minutes to make sure they get a safe distance away. And to make sure that Mrs. Jones isn't trying to trick these mischievous youngsters into showing themselves.

We carefully make our way back and at one point Tess steps on something that she describes as mushy gross, and I place my hand over her mouth just before the scream comes out. Pinching it with two fingers and holding it in the moonlight shows that it is one of the flamingo towels from Linda's. Once we finally make our way to the soft sand and see the lights far down the beach, we can't hold back the laughs any longer. Uncontrollable, it flows out of both of us. We just can't stop. Tess pauses just long enough to stammer out, "The preacher's wife has my panties on a stick." More laughter rolls out, then, "This is going to make me pee."

I fight through my tears of laughter and wipe my eyes. "At least you aren't going to pee in your sexy panties." More laughter.

Out of breath, we finally gain a little bit of control. Tess slips on her dress and I step into my shorts. Our fingers are intertwined, and I carry the blanket over one arm as we stroll up the sandy path back to the house.

Tess wiggles her butt. "I'm going to kill you. Twigs and leaves are still falling from my crack." The laughter returns.

36

TESS

HAVING SHOWERED OFF THE SAND, twigs, and leaves, we finally make it to the comfort of our bed. My body is exhausted, but I can't slow down the thoughts of all that had taken place tonight and this week. I have hidden from a preacher and his wife in the brush, NAKED. I have made love with another woman, something I had never, ever thought of doing. Add to that the thought of lying naked in front of another man just one night earlier and letting him, along with Jack, kiss all over my body. And even more, put their hands on me . . . and in . . . my special place, to make me . . . mm. Then I had jumped Jack and almost smothered him to death when we returned from the first massage.

Who am I? Have I turned into a terrible person in just the last few days? Am I a floozie? But the thing that scares me the most is . . . I liked it. All of it. Well, not so much hiding in the brush. But the feelings, the passion, and other people desiring me with vigor. It has all been so exciting. And the intimacy with Jack has been even more intense than before, which I didn't think was possible. And the greatest thing is that Jack is cured. It worked. The crazy doctor was right. That was the whole point of stepping out of our comfort zone and challenging our beliefs. So, all should be well, right? Jack is not upset with me at all, in fact he seems very happy, even excited.

So, what is my problem? Why am I disturbed? I know the answer, but I keep pushing it down deep inside because I shouldn't feel this way. I want more. More of all of it. More passion with Jack, more excitement to give him what he deserves from me. To give myself what feels so good. Am I awful feeling this way? Am I losing control of myself? Have I already? I need rest. I drift off to Lucca, Gabriella, and Jack, most of all Jack—all of them. And the case is still floating in my mind. Why were the Joneses out at that time of morning that far from their house? Why was Linda's towel in the brush? I think of how badly I want to solve the case to show others that I can do it. To prove it to myself. After staying home to raise our children and take care of Jack and the house, I need to prove that I can do something special that matters to me and helps someone else. Something to make a difference in the world.

37

JACK

ANXIOUS TO REVIEW THE EDITED pictures with Tess, I skip my morning run. The aroma of hot coffee floats over us as we snuggle together on the couch. I am still in some funny boxers that Tess bought me with a big tiger on the front—she has a lot of fun jokes about these—and one of my college T-shirts with the full face of a tiger logo imprinted on the front. Tess is also wearing one of my shirts unbuttoned, and a pair of her little black panties. She looks so adorable with her messy silver locks and the strands that have broken free from the clip to hang across her cheeks.

The pictures of our suspect are clearer now, but for many different reasons it had proven too difficult for the software to get a perfect view. It is a marked improvement, but it may have complicated things more than helped them. What we thought was hair is actually the dark collar of the jacket that is just a different pattern from the rest of it. The prior fuzziness had distorted the photo, and our imaginations must have led us to determine that it was hair. There are still what seem to be hair strands, but we can't be sure of the length or color. The suspect list has grown.

At least the jacket has come into better focus, but it is an angle that doesn't give us much to work with. The logo or ad on the sleeve seems to be some sort of animal instead of the completely unidentifiable picture before. Also coming into focus with the enhancements is a partial lettering or number on the sleeve. Maybe the letter 'E' or the number eight, it is difficult to say for sure, but it has a curved edge. We are also able to see a portion of a stick or club in the person's hand and are convinced this must be the attacker and the weapon used on Emma.

I brush a strand of hair from Tess's cheek, and we share a kiss. "And since Devin and I had some extra time, he enhanced some other photos for me."

Tess looks concerned thinking I am speaking of her photos.

"Relax, look at this one of Cody and Marcus."

But apparently her mind is still on Gabriella and last night and she asks, "So embarrassing, did you watch the whole time?"

I smile. "Every wonderful second." I try to sound light and happy, but I have been thinking about how much more comfortable Devin and Gabriella are with sexual adventures than Tess and I are. Maybe we are in over our heads.

"I'm so embarrassed." Her face grows flushed again.

"Would you want it again?" I think it may be too soon to ask but decide to go for it anyway.

Her cheeks shine a little brighter, but without hesitation, "Yes, yes, I think I would. Would you want me to?"

"Devin suggested that we join." I wait for her reaction.

"What . . . he did?"

"Twice actually, but I thought it was better to wait for another time since it was your first experience." That is true, but I was also feeling freaked out about the whole thing too.

Tess turns to make eye contact. "That was sweet of you. It probably would have overwhelmed me."

With a chuckle, "Well, it took a lot of willpower to tell him no." That statement is true, but if I am honest with myself, I wonder if I would have been able to overcome my inhibitions anyway.

She looks around as if working out a math problem in her head. "You said wait for another time. Does that mean you would be okay with me doing that again?"

"Of course, it was sexy seeing you so lost in that pleasure." It WAS so sexy seeing Tess with Gabriella.

She smiles. "And Gabriella."

"I believe you know that I was focused on you, baby, but yes, she is a former model and a very pretty lady."

"I believe you being more excited about me, but I will never understand how you see me like you do."

Laughing, "That's a good thing because you would probably be peacocking all around town if you did." Tess laughs with me, and I continue, "Because you are perfect." I pick the laptop back up. "See the paper Cody is holding?"

Tess tries to refocus on the case. "Yeah, so what is it?"

I zoom in. "The logo on the paper reminds me of the one from the clinic when we took Emma there for a cut on her finger a few years ago. It looks like he is holding it up for Marcus to see."

We have no idea what it could be, but agree that it is curious to say the least.

"I've got one more for you." I show her a picture of the garden club walking into the café. "Notice the time stamp at the bottom." Tess shrugs. I tell her to remember the conversation with Victoria and she looks so cute while replaying it in her mind. Her eyes brighten. "If that is the normal meeting time, they would have been at the café when Emma and the preacher were talking on some of the days Victoria mentioned seeing her there."

"You got it, Sherlock Holmes."

She shrugs. "So what does that mean?"

I hold my hands out. "No idea, but it seems like some good investigating to me. So, what do we do next?"

Tess says that she isn't sure.

I move my thumbs in the air mimicking a video game. "I need to dust off my old video game skills."

Tess laughs and I am sure that she is thinking of how poorly I played when trying to compete on the newest games when our son was in high school. "You will have to fake it then."

I know this isn't going to be good, but I am willing to make a fool of myself to help Tess since I can see how important all this is to her.

38

TESS

CODY DOESN'T SEEM ANY HAPPIER to see us than he was the last time. Jack does a good job of convincing him that he is interested in the newest video game, and I believe Cody is happy to have someone to play with. That is until he sees Jack play. I think of our son laughing when Jack couldn't get his character aimed in the right direction. Jack has played up his interest well enough that Cody looks very confused when Jack's character runs into walls and keeps getting killed in a matter of seconds.

I excuse myself to the bathroom while Cody works diligently to advise Jack on how to control his character. I try to keep an ear open as I peruse through Cody and Emma's bedroom. After a few minutes I hear Cody say that he better check on Miss Tess, and I scurry to the messy bathroom and instinctively pick up a load of towels, trying to not look guilty of snooping, which I most certainly am. I'm not sure why I think towels will help but it seems like a good idea. I wait. I hear Jack loudly proclaim that he has the bad guy on the run and needs Cody to come help. I peek around the corner of the bathroom door. No Cody. I look down at my arms full of laundry from the bathroom floor and I think I may throw up. Cody's dirty towels! I throw them down quickly and tiptoe back up the hall to the bedroom, trying to hold back gags while thinking of the towels.

Jack has bought me a little more time. I take out my phone and snap as many pictures as I can while trying to look through drawers and inside boxes on the dresser. Trying to find that paper Cody was holding, a clue, anything that may help point us to someone. I pick up a picture of Emma from the nightstand. She looks so pretty and innocent. I am flooded with memories of Emma and think of how much I want to solve this case for her. And yes, admittedly I want to beat the sheriff too. Out of nowhere I hear a voice, "Is everything okay Miss Tess?" My heart jumps and in my mind I spring ten feet in the air like a cat that has been frightened, fur puffed out with a big long hiss. Somehow, I manage to keep my feet on the floor and speak calmly, "I love this picture of you and Emma." I act as if I am taking a picture of it so Jack can print one for me to have. I continue stammering out my lie. "I'm sorry, I should have asked first."

Cody seems more sad than angry. "You can just take that one. I'm never going to get her back anyway." We walk toward the door to leave.

"Don't say that. Just keep doing well and give her time." Jack leads the way down the steps from the loft and I know he is thinking we have taken enough chances with this part of the investigation as I pause to give Cody a little more advice.

When I catch back up to Jack, he asks what the last words were with Cody. "I told him that he should call you."

Jack's eyes widen. "Call me?"

I lean onto Jack's shoulder. "I told him that Emma was the catch of a lifetime and he needs to fight for her. That if he wants to know how to make a lady feel more special than anything in the whole world, he should call you for advice."

I feel Jack's sweet lips on my cheek. "I called out the second time."

"I know baby, I was just focused on finding things and I did get a lot of pictures."

Jack gives me a concerned look. "His reaction could have been a lot different when he caught you. I don't like you taking chances like that."

Jack's concern brings a smile to my face. "Don't worry, baby. It's part of being a detective, and you are a good assistant. And after taking that kick-boxing class, I think I can take little Cody if I have to." I flex my arms like a muscle model.

Jack sighs but can't hold back a giggle as he reaches out to take my hand in his.

I add with a little grin, "And you were a killing machine in that game."

"A detective and a comedian. Can we go home now?"

I reassure him, "You get to sit the next one out. Girls only." He looks a little worried as I suggest, "Why don't you go to Rohan and see if you can get an update on Marcus?"

"Gladly, I might get an order of the spicy fish toes." He laughs as he crosses the street. "Try to stay out of trouble. And stay safe, no risks."

I yell back at him, "And don't go to the hat store."

I had texted Victoria for help on the next part of the mission, which was going to take place at The Devotional Grind. She shows up in distressed jeans with small rips in the legs and a long, light blue Kimono. Always classy and stylish. Victoria distracts the rest of the garden club ladies and I easily convince Mrs. Jones to show me how to make her special latte. Mr. Jones is in his office in the back of the café, conducting an interview with a new prospect for a barista position. One of his employees will be leaving for college soon and he needs her replacement. Victoria chats up and charms the ladies who seem happy to have a new person to share in their meeting.

After making drinks, Victoria and I stay with the ladies for about thirty minutes and brag about Mrs. Jones's barista skills. I leave feeling proud of our undercover skills, but Victoria says she is going to kill me because the garden ladies are begging her to join.

Jack and Rohan were just finishing up a plate of spicy fish toes when I enter Sandy Toes. Thinking of their toe shape kind of makes me nauseous as I was already queasy after the dirty laundry incident, but after trying one at the behest of Rohan I agree they taste better than the name implies. Rohan loves his novelty items, especially if they can be named to tie in the restaurant theme. Jack asks if my latest mission was as exciting as our visit with Cody. I announce to him that it went off without a hitch. His eyes tell me that may have hurt his pride a little and he may be concerned that Victoria will replace him as my lead assistant.

I rub Jack's sexy arm as the wind whips through the Impala on the way home and assure him with a wink that I prefer the added benefits of my sexy man as my lead assistant. And my lead assistant did well today. Jack picked up an interesting tidbit from Rohan that at least part of Marcus's jail time was due to drugs, as we had feared.

We take Emma a daily special from Rohan, her favorite. We need to check on her and she could use some nourishment for her and the baby. We had stopped by Ed's beforehand to pick up a few groceries for her, too. We peek through the crack in the blinds to make sure Emma isn't resting before knocking on the door. She is sitting on the couch reading a book about baby names. That melts my heart.

Emma looks stronger, has a little color back to her cheeks, and she is too cute in her little Sandy Toes T-shirt and shorts. We tell her that we visited Cody and ask if he has reached out to her. She holds up her phone, "Several texts."

I ask if she has responded.

Dryly, "I did."

I tilt my head to the side. "He is trying Emma."

Emma replies with a slightly softer tone. "I know. I'm just not sure that I can trust him to stay clean and I'm not having my baby around that."

I softly lay a hand on her shoulder. "I understand and respect you for that, but he has never done anything like that before right?"

Emma is enjoying her Sandy Toes special with a helping of the new fish toes on the side. "Not until that stupid Billy started coming around again."

"Again?"

Emma takes another bite. "Yeah, I had asked Cody to not have him over to the loft."

I look at her curiously. "Why did you do that?"

"I just don't like being around him." Emma keeps her eyes down to her plate.

The familiar food seems to be making Emma more like her old happy self and I don't want to push her too hard, so I drop the subject. "Why was Cody taking all the extra shifts?"

A smile almost creeps across Emma's face. "I just wanted to fix up the loft, but Cody was talking about getting a bigger place."

That raises a concern in me, and I glance toward Jack. "But you never told him that you were pregnant?"

"I wanted to wait a little longer in case something went wrong." Emma holds up a fish toe for inspection. "This is definitely a Rohan idea."

Jack laughs. "Fish toes. Trust me, the taste is much better than the name."

Emma continues, "I was told that my mother lost two babies before she passed during my birth." She pauses. "I just didn't want him to get excited too early."

"I'm so sorry, Emma." Rohan had told us the story, but we had never heard Emma say it out loud.

Thinking I better change the subject again, "How about Marcus? Other than being cranky, why don't you two get along? We have never known you not to get along with anyone."

"He isn't that bad. He just always tries to boss us around."

"Us?"

Emma is making the special disappear and it worries me that she isn't getting enough to eat. "Me and Cody. He is always interrupting our lunch to tell Cody he needs to get a better job, or learn a trade, and that we need to save money. I guess he means well but he is hateful about it." Another bite. "The fish toes are pretty good."

Jack jumps in. "He seems to be doing a good job for Rohan."

"He is a hard worker." Emma pauses. "And a pretty good cook," as she scrapes the bottom of her plate and smiles.

My mind goes to the chef on the boat, then straight to Gabriella.

Emma laughs again thinking about the fish toes. Her joy of life is infectious even in these difficult circumstances. So many people in Sandy Strips talk about how she makes their day better whenever they see her. Victoria always described Emma as having a positive vibe that you could feel when in the room with her.

Jack and I hug Emma, she flinches, though less than before. I glance toward the door letting Jack know that we should go, and out of the corner of my eye I see a face in the window and scream! Jack and Emma both jump. It is gone now, but I know I saw someone looking through the window. Jack runs to the door, yanks it open quickly and runs out to find the mystery person. He and Lucca run smack into each other. They both stumble sideways and catch their balance against the door. "Well, hello Tess, Jack . . . Emma."

I am still trying to figure out what just happened. "What are you doing Lucca?"

Lucca straightens out his shirt and looks toward Jack. "Sorry about that buddy. I was coming to get my jacket that Rob gave me. I think I left it here the other night when I brought some of my special Italian spaghetti for Emma."

Jack looks at him. "You must be in a hurry to get it."

Lucca leans in and whispers, "I peeked in the blinds to make sure not to interrupt your time."

I feel my brow raise. "Is Rob doing your clothes shopping now?"

Lucca slips the jacket on and models it for us. "Got to support the local kid." It is a baseball jacket from Rob's nephew, Robbie.

Jack looks puzzled. "I thought you and Rob had not been seeing each other so Linda wouldn't catch you."

Lucca snickers, "I didn't see him. He must have snuck out and left it on my deck. He knows I love Robbie and would want to support him at the big game."

I fiddle with the clip in my hair. "I thought Rob was out of town for work."

"He is. It was in the yard at the side of the house. He probably left it at the back door before he went out of town and the storm blew it away. I found it the other day when I was picking up debris from the storm."

Lucca glances over to the empty plate. "I've been trying to get her to eat more. Looks like you guys found the right thing with a good ole Sandy Toes special."

I start to slide between Lucca and the door. "Come over later and hang out at the pool if you like." I hadn't planned to ask him, and I am not sure where the words came from.

Lucca grins. "We do need to finish what we started the other night."

"Oh, I thought you did finish." I felt the warmth in my cheeks.

All three of us look at Emma and say in unison, "Massage."

Lucca, never one to let it drop, "I've heard that special lotion I used on you is very good for your skin."

My face is getting hotter, but I don't want to let him win. "If it's that good, then maybe I do need more; that is if you have extra to spare."

"Finding extra for you will be no problem at all." Lucca winks and he is proud of himself for that one.

Thankfully Jack breaks up the banter. But it does feel that we are all in agreement that we need to finish what we started.

39

JACK

I STOOD ON THE DECK looking at the breaking waves and far beyond, thinking. Is all this change worth it? Even to get me better, has it been worth the sacrifice? So much has happened over the last few days. How did we get here so quickly? Is Tess as happy as she seems right now? Is she too happy with all this? Am I really okay with the things that have happened and the things that may still come? Was the doctor right about my insecurities? Are Tess and I both okay? Will I stay "fixed" with or without our extra adventures? Does Tess need the extra now, or is she okay with it being just us?

It has always been us standing together against the world, just me and Tess. I have never wavered in my faithfulness to Tess, and I know with all my heart that she has been every bit as committed. Are we throwing all that away? Have we already? Tess seems so happy and excited right now. I know that is a big part of my recovery, temporary or not, but it is more than that. She has more energy, more vigor, and more passion. She has been doing things that she has wanted to do before but didn't think she could, being more open, taking more risks, even being a private investigator for crying out loud.

Our intimacy has always been such a wonderful part of our life together. We stay respectful and caring of each other's wishes and mix that with fun and surprises. I have never thought of it as routine or dull like Lucca talked about with Martina. Tess has always said that she didn't need to instigate our intimate time because I am constantly "after" her, and that is a good point. But my conservative southern girl has been much more aggressive on this trip, at least since the first visit to Lucca's. But all of this is what we have tried to discuss so many times during the past year. All in the name of helping me get better and to make her happier. All for us and our intimacy. So, it had to be okay, right? And I do have a spark growing inside, anticipating what may be coming next. From what I have seen, Tess is experiencing the same fire and maybe we just need to make the most of this next chapter of our journey . . . together.

Tess's voice startles my thoughts back from the horizon, over the water, across the beach, landing back on the deck to view her beauty. "I thought you may want a sneak preview."

Her silk robe hangs open revealing a peek at the outer edges of the blush circles on her heavy breasts that hang against her pretty ivory skin. Beads of water still float on her skin and my eyes follow the occasional tiny stream that drifts downward across her curves before fading away. "No one in their right mind could pass up an opportunity to enjoy that beauty."

Tess takes a few steps forward and does one of my favorite moves. Raising one knee and pointing her toes to the ground, as an offering for me to love on her. I kneel and let my cheek come to rest on her damp thigh while my hands softly roam her leg from top to bottom. I gently rub over her foot and heel, slowly letting my fingers glide up her leg, feeling every curve and muscle along the way. I love it when she invites me to enjoy her like that.

She then lifts her foot to the chair and flashes those pretty dimples.

I reposition and eagerly accept her offer with pleasure. We make eye contact as I kiss her gently. Her fingers grasp my hair, and she pushes me deeper to her while releasing a small moan from her lips. "Save some for later, baby," as she hesitantly pulls away. She flips up the back of her robe, flashing her gorgeous round butt as she slowly strolls back through the sliding door. I want her so badly.

From the window we can see Lucca approaching the house. This is it, we are going all in with no return to how things were. I am so nervous. Having second thoughts, almost sick to my stomach, but all the discussions and ideas are now exhausted, and it is time. If we are ever going to take this step, now is the time. And we both do have that spark, that fire inside. I take a deep breath and struggle to make my legs take me to the door.

I pull the front door open slowly, as if it weighs a thousand pounds, and Lucca greets me with a smile. Before I can get any words past my lips, Sheriff Fry greets us both from the steps behind Lucca, though not with a smile. Lucca is just as shocked as the rest of us.

"I've been told that I'm like a ninja even though I'm a big strong guy," the sheriff announces with great pride. "Hate to interrupt your little party, but I thought I may find you over here when you weren't home."

Disgustedly Lucca asks, "What is it you want now, Sheriff?"

The sheriff pulls up his belt like he does when he is on the verge of a big announcement. "Your bail has been revoked and you are comin' with me, back to jail where you belong."

We are all shocked, none of us more than Lucca. "Why was my bail revoked?"

"I convinced the judge that you were a flight risk to return to Italy." Sheriff Fry smiles with satisfaction. "Since you don't have a wife or a business to keep you here."

"What a jerk!" The words blast through Tess's unfiltered lips as all heads turn in her direction. "We will get you out, Lucca."

The sheriff puts the cuffs on Lucca once again. "And I have your golf club with Emma's blood. I've got you this time, boy." The sheriff tips his hat. "Ma'am, Jack." Tess and I stand speechless in shock.

As they walk out, I hear the sheriff whisper to Lucca, "I told you when you left, I would bring you back sooner than later."

Tess and I curl up on the lounger under the pool lights and the setting sun to try to come up with a plan. She is angry and upset about the whole mess. I am too but there is a small part of me that wonders if the sheriff could possibly be right. Maybe he saved us from making a big mistake. Though now is not the time to mention that to Tess.

I can see the wheels turning in Tess's head right before she stands. "Let's go see Emma."

I know there is no stopping her, that she needs to feel like she is doing something productive. "Why don't you try to talk to Emma alone again? I can go back through all the notes and see if anything new jumps out."

Tess slips on her cover-up and gives me a kiss. "I won't be long, baby."

I crank up some smooth jazz and begin reviewing our notes. It's so peaceful outside by the pool. I begin working through each step from the moment we were told what happened. Had anyone acted differently than normal? What would be the motive to hurt Emma? Who would have been out in the storm? Who knew where to find her?

A noise from inside the house breaks my concentration. At least I think that I hear something from that direction. I quickly lower the music and sit quietly, still staring at our notes. There it is again. I am sure this time, there was a noise from inside the house. I move quickly to get out of sight from any windows.

I ruffle through Rob's collection of expensive water toys to grab a boat oar from the carport storage and stay close to the wall as I tiptoe quietly up the back steps. I listen closely for more sounds as I get near the top. On the deck I stoop low and lean over to take a quick peek into the window. My heart jumps and I duck quickly back out of sight. There is someone in the house!

I tighten my grip on the oar and crawl low enough under the window to not be seen until I reach the sliding door. I can feel my heart pounding in my chest as my grip tightens on the wooden weapon. I gather my thoughts and my courage. I have to be fast. Mentally, I make a quick plan: rise, fling open the sliding door, and cock the oar back ready to attack, all in one motion. Don't hesitate Jack. You can do it. Ready. Go!

All in one smooth motion, I spring up, fling open the sliding door, pull the oar back like a batter ready to swing at a fastball. Then yell. I'm not even sure what I yell, and it's probably nothing that makes sense, but I am like a crazed maniac as I enter the room. My eyes dart to the left, then to the right. Quickly again, back and forth. Left, then right as I try to move like a ninja through the room. If I watch this in replay like we do footage from our basketball games, I am sure that my movements are far from ninja-like. But right now, I feel stealthy and ready. Trying to be quiet, I move toward the kitchen, hands digging tightly into the wood held above my shoulder.

Another sound and I make a fast spin around the corner of the kitchen wall and pull the oar back more, ready to swing with all my might. The screen door bounces closed, and I see a figure in dark clothes leap down the front steps. I hurriedly follow through the door and yell, but again I have no idea what words come out. The shadowy figure has disappeared, nowhere in sight. I stand tensely and scan all directions, but see and hear nothing. I am trying to decide whether to pursue the intruder when . . .

Words come from behind me and my heart jumps out of my chest as I spin around and start to swing the oar with all my might.

"Jack!!"

All the muscles in my body tense to stop my movement mid-swing. It is Tess and Emma standing in the doorway. I drop the oar to my side and feel a twinge in my back. I strained it with the force of stopping in the middle of the swing. I wince as I let my arms drop. "Hi, baby. What are you guys doing?" I try to sound as calm as possible.

Tess steps forward and puts her arm around me. "What are you doing, Jack?"

I lead Tess inside with one glance back. "Nothing, baby, just thinking we may want to take the canoe out before we leave and you startled me."

I am pretty sure Tess is not buying that story, but she goes with it . . . for now.

Tess looks at me concerned. "Emma came over to hang out with us."

I smile at Emma. "That's great. It will do you good to get out of the apartment for a little while." I prop the oar against the wall and open the fridge. "You guys go out to the pool and I will bring a pitcher of tea and cups."

40

TESS

EMMA SELECTS THE MUSIC WHILE she sips a glass of iced tea. I lie back on the lounger and begin rereading my notes while Jack flips through the pictures on his laptop. Emma occasionally tells us about one of the new artists she is playing and suggests, with a giggle, that we may like their music if we give them a chance instead of just listening to our oldies. I ask Emma a few more questions from my notes to verify information, but mostly try to let her relax.

I have spent my whole adult life taking care of my family. Putting any career dreams on hold. I have no regrets at all as I have loved the chance to do that, but now this is something I want to do. Something I need to do. I am determined to solve my first case and to prove to everyone that I can do it. To prove it to Jack. To help Emma . . . and Lucca. To beat that annoying sheriff. And to prove to myself that I can do something that makes a difference outside of taking care of my family. There are so many unanswered questions, but I must figure this out.

It is nice to hear Emma laugh and it's nice to talk about anything besides the assault. She is so much fun to be around. I notice Jack is looking more at pictures of me than the case, but I know he needs a break to enjoy his time. I can't wait to find out what he was doing on the porch with an oar, but I decide to let him tell me when he is ready. I figure it may be something he doesn't want Emma to know. When he thinks the time is right, he will share it. I lean over to look at one of the pictures and whisper, "Are you wishing you had a skinny girl?"

Jack looks at me so sweetly. "You know perfectly well that I love my little curvy girl more than anything."

I love the way he adores me. The night is so good hanging out with Emma until that shrill, chalkboard scratching voice sounds again. "You gonna give me those pictures now or am I gonna take you to stay with your friend?"

Jack closes the laptop without looking up from his chair. "Do you have that warrant yet?" Jack is such a calm peaceful person but there is a limit to his patience, and I am worried the sheriff is about to see a completely different side of my husband. One that we rarely see, only when he is in protective mode for me or the kids.

"Don't need it to charge you with obstruction." Apparently, he has done his homework since the previous visit.

Jack goads him anyway. "Why did it take you so long to figure it out? Did you go ask your daddy for help?"

"I'm the sheriff now and you better show me proper respect," he says as he wrestles to free the handcuffs from his belt.

I know Jack has reached his limit and I am worried as he pops up from the lounger with anger in his eyes and steps toward the sheriff. Thankfully, he is interrupted by another surprising voice. "If you arrest him, I will sue this town for every penny you have and then some." We all turn to see Devin walking through the gate.

A startled Sheriff Fry struggles to respond. "Excuse me Mr. Blake, I'—I'm just trying to bring justice to poor little Emma."

Devin moves face to face with the sheriff. "You already have the wrong guy. I suggest you don't compound that mistake."

The sheriff fidgets and tries to choose his words carefully. "Respectfully sir, please leave the investigatin' to the qualified professionals."

Devin leans even closer, nose to nose with the sheriff. "That's exactly what I'm doing." He glances at me. "She will get it solved for you soon."

I try to hide the shock from showing on my face as the sheriff searches cautiously for his next words.

Devin doesn't wait. "I'm sure you don't want to interrupt these good people any longer than you already have. You can leave now."

Sheriff Fry looks away from Devin and glares at me, then Jack, then Emma before hanging his head and mumbling, "Yes sir," as he shuffles back through the gate.

Jack asks Devin what just happened, and I have even more questions. Devin explains that he and Gabriella were working out at the gym and Victoria had filled them in on everything that happened to this point. Jack had received help from Devin with the software enhancement, but we didn't want to bother him with all the details of the story.

Devin also noted that when they purchased the home here, they had made a sizable donation to the town and to the sheriff's office, and had been continuing supporters. "Have you seen the new SUV that Fry is so proud to cruise around town in?" Devin tells us that he came over to see how he could help after Lucca used his one phone call from jail to ask Devin for assistance.

I chime in, "So you and Lucca are friends?"

"Oh yeah, we have gotten to know our neighbor well since we moved here."

Puzzled, "How did this never come up when we were all together?"

Devin chuckles. "I don't know honey. I guess we all had other things on our minds."

I am trying to process what everyone knows or may have discussed when Jack jumps in. "I love her, but you do know that Tess is not a real detective?"

"She is more real than that fool." Devin makes a good point.

I force a nervous smile. "Well at least I am trying to find out what really happened."

Devin agrees, "That should keep him off your backs for a while."

Jack shakes hands with Devin. "We owe you one."

Devin glances over to Emma who had sat quietly through the whole conversation. "Hope you are feeling better."

Emma offers one of her wonderful smiles. "How could I not be with so many nice people trying to help me, thank you."

Devin turns back to me. "Solve this and get Lucca out." He lets the gate snap closed behind him before turning down the sandy path toward home. "Then we can all celebrate together."

I feel my cheeks warm. Does he mean that how it sounded? Does he know about the massage? How close of friends are they with Lucca? Did he post Lucca's bail? So many unanswered questions. One thing I know, more than ever, I need to solve this case . . . for so many reasons.

41

JACK

IT IS STILL EARLY, BUT Tess is not in bed when I awake. I feel sluggish, as if I had slept most of the night with one eye open. Probably because I had, and with an oar beside the bed. I knew Tess needed to get some rest so I had put off telling her about the disturbance last night.

I stumble sleepily into the den and my eyes pop wide open at the sight. Apparently, Tess has been up for a while. One wall in the den is covered with two large pieces of poster board with hand-drawn stick men. Each stickman has a large circular face with plenty of notes off to the side . . . kind of like smiley faces but with a little more detail. My wonderful wife has many talents, but drawing is not high on the list, so I am surprised to say the least.

I wipe my eyes as if to make sure what I am seeing is real. "What in the world is that?"

"It's my suspect board," she proudly announces. "Every good detective has one."

I try to hide my confusion. "Where did you get the board and markers?"

Tess keeps staring at the board, writing notes and drawing more lines connecting one person to another. "I did a little snooping through the closets and storage this morning."

I step in for a closer look and as I see the faces up close, I think Tess has done a pretty darn good job. I point to the one at the top right. "So the one with the cowboy hat and ponytail must be Billy."

Tess is proud of her work. "Yes, it is, glad you can identify him. He was jealous of Cody and obviously Emma was uncomfortable around him. Last night when I went to see Emma, she mentioned that Billy had showed up to the loft a few times when he should have known Cody was at work." It was obvious that Tess had her share of caffeine this morning as she kept going without taking a breath. "Speaking of last night, what were you doing with that oar? I forgot to ask with all the other happenings."

I'm not sure why but I lean in as if I need to whisper the answer to Tess. "Someone was in the house last night."

Tess's eyes widen. "What? Who? What were they doing?"

I laugh at her energy. "Maybe you need to ease up on the coffee, baby," I say as I pick up her unfinished mug and take a drink. "I don't know the answers to any of that."

Tess becomes even more excited. "We need to call the police!"

I stare at her board. "Think about what you are saying. Do you really want Sheriff Fry here investigating that?"

Tess quickly agrees that is not going to help. "Should we call Linda?"

I shift the mug away from Tess's reaching hand. "I think you have had enough, baby. What good would it do to call Linda?"

Tess walks through the likely outcome of that, then agrees with me with a shrug of her shoulders. "Well, what do we do then?"

I kiss Tess on the cheek, "Let's solve your case. That may give us the answer to who our intruder was."

Tess gasps, "The photos!"

I make a calming gesture with my hand. "You know I always hide our photos well. They are fine." I want to get Tess back to focus on her board. I point to the next one. "And this one with the ball cap, the small mustache and four little chin hairs is Cody."

"Right again, good job," she says as she studies the board. "He could have been under the influence of drugs or just angry that Emma left him. He may have even found out about the baby and become irrational. Either way, the ex-boyfriend on the list is a must have."

I place my hand on my goatee, contemplating. "The chef hat is Marcus, but are we sure he needs to be on the board?"

She glances at me then back to the board. "His past record for one thing, and the picture of him and Cody. Maybe he had Cody trying to get pills from the clinic. Or possibly Cody owed him money from a drug deal and Emma got caught in the middle. Maybe something more nefarious that we haven't even thought of yet."

"Nefarious, huh?" Tess is using big detective words now, but I nod in agreement at those possibilities. "Is the one in the gardening hat Mateo?"

"Yes, and beside him in the scarf is Celest. I have always liked her scarves." Tess continues, "We don't know why Mateo had the envelope of money with Emma's initials, so he must be considered, and if something was going on with him and Emma and Celest had discovered it . . . well, we all know about her bad temper. And Emma has yet to mention anything about Mateo or the envelope during all our conversations."

I nod again in agreement. "All of that is true."

Tess puts a finger on the drawing with wavy hair and a partial scruffy beard colored in. "This makes me feel guilty because he is our friend, but I had to include Lucca too. Victoria said he hadn't been himself since Martina was diagnosed and he did know where Emma was staying."

I wrap my arms around Tess from behind and her hair tickles my face. "I'm sure he is innocent, and you are only trying to be thorough." Though I am not completely sure I believe my own words. I attempt to break the somber moment. "Is that a fedora with a feather and wrinkles on the face?"

Tess lets out a chuckle. "You always have to include the one who was first on the scene, and technically he was the only one who knew that Emma was expecting."

I shake my head but agree with her logic. "So, what about these two?" I point to one with a fancy necklace and the other with a gold watch and much rounder face.

"You should know those two easily, Rob and Linda with their expensive accessories." We laugh together. "And I found a watch behind the trash can in the bathroom when I went to Emma's last night."

I remind her that neither of them was in town when it happened.

She gives me a true detective answer: "That's what we think but until we know, they go on the board."

One last drawing of a blank face remains. I point and shrug my shoulders.

Tess studies her work. "That represents someone we either haven't thought of or don't know yet. Maybe our intruder."

I told her that person couldn't have done it because they didn't have eyes. She chuckles but doesn't take her eyes from the board. I must admit that I am impressed with her hard work even though the drawings are a little funny. She does have an official suspect board with a timeline. She has included everyone she could think of and their motives. It's hard to think of people that we know being capable of doing such an awful thing, but do we really know people as well as we think?

People have private lives with secrets and challenges we can't imagine, even the closest of friends. No one would have ever thought that Tess and I would be doing some of the stuff we have done . . . and are considering doing. I am so proud of Tess. Maybe she is going to be better at this private eye business than I originally gave her credit for.

She sounds so professional. I look into her baby blues. "I would really like to make love to a middle-aged private investigator."

"Funny, now help me look this over to see what I'm missing. And don't think I missed that middle-aged comment."

"I am being serious. Let's go do a car photo session and then I will jump in and help you. I promise."

Tess looks at me sweetly. "You have a one-track mind, baby."

I smile. "Thank you."

We drive ole red to a deserted road at the very end of the island closest to our house, and since it was determined that the possibility of flooding was too great, there are no houses built in the area. We had walked down to the end of the island and circled back up this road several times over the years and had never seen anyone there. It isn't a particularly pretty spot with the brush and trees growing unattended, but it is very private. A perfect place to take sexy pictures of Tess and old red.

Tess is wearing a classy little black dress that contrasts beautifully with the bright red car and its white interior. I get several great shots from mild to a little more fun. The wind lifts her dress, exposing Tess's sexy legs. She provocatively bends over the hood, and then poses sweetly on the trunk. She is the sexiest woman ever in my eyes.

The second set is in her black bra and panty set that we determine could pass for a swimsuit if we do have unexpected company. Tess helps me with the creativity since I am too excited to think of specific poses. She does some shots with heels and a few shots barefoot, some behind the wheel and still others sitting on the top of the back seat like a pageant winner. Even a few topless, and she says the girls love being free in the breeze. She effortlessly spins her hair up to a knot, making her eyes and cheekbones pop for the pictures. I love the ones that show her muscular back and arms as she holds her hair up and exposes the back of her pretty neck. She looks so classy like that. By the time we wrap up I crave her badly. Just like the night on the beach, I assure her that we are in a private area, so we can get in a quickie at least. Even though that night didn't go as smoothly as I had hoped, what are the odds of getting caught twice, right?

It takes some convincing, but I finally talk her into making love under the blue sky in old red. I tell her that it will be nostalgic in an old classic, like a free love couple back in the sixties, as if it that really matters to her. It doesn't take long to discover that we aren't as young and flexible as in our younger days and we roll, smush, and elbow each other to find a suitable position.

Finally, we stop snickering long enough for Tess to climb onto my lap facing me in the back seat. I tell her how sexy she is sitting on my lap. We kiss passionately. I love hearing her sounds of happiness as I fondle her breasts. The gentle breeze feels wonderful swooping through the car and over our bare skin. Tess reaches up and loosens her hair, letting the cool silver fall across my face. I get so lost during our intimate times and so focused on my wife that I wouldn't notice if sirens were approaching, and Tess becomes lost with me as our bodies move together.

My hands clutch Tess's sexy hips and feel her movements, the muscles in her legs tense against my body, I breathe in the scent of her hair. I feel her nails dig into my chest when she rises up. I move my hands over her muscled arms and watch her fleshy mounds sway with our movements. Our bodies in perfect sync move in the sweet rhythm of familiarity together. Being one with Tess in this moment is indescribable, the happiest place in the world for me. Tess throws her head back and lets the beautiful silver locks fall deep down her back. As our bodies meld with one another, our eyes meet and scream I love you to each other. The sounds of happiness and excitement come from her mouth and bring me joy like listening to a favorite song that brings back wonderful memories.

It is exhilarating, exciting, and sexy. Everything I had dreamed of when I leased the old Impala. Two lovers together in another time with nothing else on their minds. I fill Tess with all my intense joy. Then Tess screams out. Loudly. I love when she calls out during our lovemaking. Her sounds reinforce that she is enjoying herself, and that excites me even more. Another loud scream and I begin to question what I am doing that is so good. I want it so badly to be caused by my sexual prowess, but something tells me that isn't the case as I have stopped all movement. It seems to be more of a distress call than one of ecstasy. Not exactly the feeling I am striving to give her.

Tess leans over to one side and digs her nails into my shoulders as she continues to cry out. I just know someone is coming and she is trying to hide herself, but I can't understand why she is being so loud. I lift my head and my eyes scan all directions to find who is interrupting our special moment. I can't help but think it must be that stupid sheriff. Then finally Tess yells it out, "CRAMP! A cramp in my leg!" Between catching our breaths among the uncontrollable laughter, we manage to roll each other over to our sides and finally stretch out her leg, granting her some relief. I massage the spot trying to ease her pain.

We wipe the happy tears from our eyes, and I work through the laughter to get the words out, "We aren't as young as we used to be."

Tess pulls me on top of her. "But we still got it done. I love you, Jack."

42

TESS

LUSCIOUS LEMON ICE CREAM MELTS in my mouth, my favorite summer flavor. Victoria's black raspberry chocolate is delicious too as we share a taste of each other's cup. Jack and I try to make it to the ice cream shoppe as much as possible when we are in town. I feel guilty indulging without him, but he had been asked by a former player to help write a résumé for his dream job, and I am not good about leaving him alone when he is working. He normally won't allow our time to be interrupted when we are on vacation, but he said it was such a great opportunity for the young man who had turned his life around during his time at college.

I'm so glad Victoria agreed to meet me so I could ask her about Billy, and if I am being honest with myself, so I can talk to her about other things. Victoria kids me that she agreed to our meeting for Jack because he will never meet the deadline with me talking, showing him things on my phone, and putting my feet in his lap for a rub. She knows me too well. I'm so used to always having his attention that I am not very good when he is focused on anything else.

I share my concerns with Victoria of how Emma acted when I asked her about Billy, hoping she can shed light on why. Victoria admittedly doesn't know Billy well but is quick to say that she gets a bad vibe every time she has been around him. I trust her instincts so that is all I need to hear for me to not trust him. She adds that Billy and Cody were always together growing up and they stayed that way until Emma came into the picture. Cody was smitten from the first time he met Emma, and they spent every minute together away from work.

She went on to say that Cody is a much nicer person with Emma than he ever had been when he and Billy were running together. Victoria is surprised at how much Cody changed for the better over the last few years. She says Cody has finally seemed to grow up, but Billy is still stuck in his wild party days.

When we finish our treat I ask Victoria to walk on the beach. Jack needs a little more time, and I am still trying to get my nerve up for a deeper talk with her. We are having such a peaceful walk on a beautiful day until I hear a voice that I recognize too well. "Hey sparkles, I didn't know you were in town."

It was BK, or Big Kahuna as he liked to be called. Owner of the local rental store and self-proclaimed sexiest man on earth. I have managed to avoid him the entire trip, until now.

BK leans against his surfboard and as usual, he admires his own body as if seeing it for the first time while talking to any female, practically begging for a comment on his muscles. "Did you finally get rid of smooth G and you're ready for a younger, more exciting guy?" BK tells me every year that I am too hot to be tied to any one man. Certainly not one that just turned fifty, ancient to BK, and that I need a young guy. That I should be playing the field. He gives me a dirty feeling every time I am near him.

Everyone in Big Kahuna's world has been given a nickname. Jack and I had been assigned ours on our first visit to his store many years ago. Big Kahuna was so impressed with Jack's kindness and good manners that he renamed him smooth gentleman, quickly reduced to smooth G to sound cooler, I assume. My new name earned me much aggravation from Jack because he always tells me my smile sparkles off the walls of the room like diamonds reflecting in light. Jack is so sweet, but can be a little silly when it comes to describing me. I believe Big Kahuna was referring more to my long hair that he seemed to be obsessed with when I first met him. And letting it turn gray has not bothered him at all. He always wants to touch it, which is very annoying. "Jack is here with me." I try to keep the conversation short and not so sweet when dealing with BK to keep him from thinking that I have the least bit of interest in him.

BK rubs his abs. "Ah, that's too bad. You are too hot to be tied down, baby."

His comments are always so difficult to respond to. I never know what to say. "I bet you are busy at work." It's the best I could come up with.

BK flexes his quads and looks to Victoria and me to see if we are going to comment. "Never too busy for you, baby. You should swing by and let me teach you how to paddle board. We would have a great time." Of course he adds a wink.

I try not to gag. "Maybe sometime, Jack and I are pretty busy."

BK smiles. "That's the problem, babe. You need more playtime and less dull time with an old guy."

I want to tell him about our adventures just to shut him up, but decide that is not only a bad idea, but it would probably backfire with BK.

Victoria intervenes, "We are going to let you get to your surfing, Egbert."

BK immediately turns and hurries toward the water.

I am so confused. "What just happened?"

Victoria explains to me that BK annoyed her so badly with his constant studly act that she had a friend do some research into his history. Turns out his real name is Egbert, and both his parents are science teachers with no interest in surfing. Victoria says she has just been waiting for the right time to use that information. She says that she has a picture of him from a middle school science fair. "You should see his big round glasses and nerdy haircut." Victoria and I laugh so hard at how terrified BK, or Egbert, looked when she called him that.

After a few minutes of walking along the edge of the water, Victoria tells me to let it out when I am ready. She does have good instincts. I start stammering and beating around the bush and she interrupts, "After all these years of friendship and what we shared together the other day I can't believe you are struggling to say anything to me. Have you killed someone?"

I laugh. "Like I could do that." I then add, "You look so beautiful in the cover-up and your black suit." Victoria is not going to let her beautiful skin get too much sun.

She gives me a "thank you" smile but is not going to let me dodge the conversation. "Then spit it out. You know that I am not going to judge my dear friend."

I take in a breath and blurt it all out at once. That seems to be the best way for me. I'm afraid if I stop, I won't get started again. I confess it all. I tell her what happened with Lucca and Gabriella without giving too many details so it wouldn't sound like an erotic romance novel.

Victoria is quiet, too quiet. Finally, after what seems like too long of a delay she giggles and places her arm around my shoulder. "I'm so proud of you honey."

"What? Proud? Why?"

The smile remains on her face. "Because you took a risk, let your passion loose and enjoyed yourself."

I stop to look at her. "You did hear that it was with another woman?"

Victoria continues walking with her eyes forward. "I certainly did my dear."

"And you don't think that is awful of me?"

She looks over to me. "Oh honey, I did grow up in a pretty free love time."

"Yes, but this isn't my younger days."

Victoria stops to take a seat in the sand. "Not only in my younger days."

I pause and let her words process in my brain, then my mouth falls open. "You and Martina?"

She smiles. "It's a different kind of wonderful. Not one that I prefer all the time, but I am so thankful I didn't miss out on the experience."

I stammer, "How are you so calm about everything?"

Victoria calmly responds with, "Why are you concerned with what people will say or think? They are going to talk no matter what you do, or don't do."

She keeps going, "Tess, in this big, crazy world we live, this just isn't that big of a deal. I think it's great that you tried something new. Even better that you enjoyed it. And the best is that it was good for you and Jack. So why are you concerned with anything else? The people you are worried about would be the first to NOT want to talk about their own actions."

Again, Victoria has helped me to put things in perspective. It is easy and nice to be able to talk with her knowing that I am not being judged, and having confidence that she will be honest with me instead of just going along with anything I say. In the past she has gracefully pointed out areas in which she thought I was not looking at things the right way.

I ask Victoria if she is up for a little shopping as I decide that Jack and I will need to go undercover for our next mission.

43

JACK

A FLANNEL SHIRT AND COWBOY boots, topped off with a black Stetson hat and a large belt buckle with bull horns hanging across my Levi's is all part of the outfit Tess has chosen for me. She and Victoria had gone on a shopping spree at the thrift stores for our mission tonight. I feel so out of place when we turn off the small two-lane road into the Sand in your Boots honky-tonk bar just across the bridge from the island. I do feel good in the Stetson though, which helps me get into character.

Trying to look the part, I walk slightly bowlegged into the rowdy club that is packed with cowboys and cowgirls from wall to wall. Tess tells me that I may be trying too hard. My outfit, my walk, even sticking my thumbs into my front pockets still does not make me feel like I fit in as Tess and I look for a seat while live country music plays from the big stage at the front. Several people are dancing on the main floor area, so we weave our way around the outer edge until we find a tall table with two stools available along the wall.

Tess, on the other hand, looks so cute in her cowgirl boots, button up plaid western shirt, hat, and tight blue jeans. And her booty looks so good in those jeans. As I look around the room I wish that she had kept the cleavage to a minimum because I can easily envision an all-out brawl with these drinking cowboys if they get too flirty with her and my protective tendencies kick in. Tess waited until we parked to put on the boots and is already saying she is going to need a foot rub when we get home.

Our mission is to gain any intel we can on Billy, who has been working here for several years. Exactly what intel I am not sure, but I am just the assistant following Tess's orders and trying to keep her safe. We have never officially met Billy and are confident that he won't recognize us in these outfits even if he has seen us around town at some point. Tess had clipped her thick silver up and tucked in under her cowgirl hat. She looks so precious. Tess wants to learn more about him since Emma seems uncomfortable when his name comes up, so here we are listening to the latest country hits along with some classic oldies.

No alcohol for me tonight, which is not going to help me fit in with this tough crowd, but I am driving, and I want to stay ready in case things get a little too wild. We enjoy a couple of dances to mingle and watch Billy from a distance before going back to our seats to grab our drinks and a few peanuts that have been delivered to the table. The people-watching is great, and Billy, a large-built guy that fits the description of a bouncer, is enjoying working the ladies in the room. He has long greasy hair tied in a ponytail just like Tess's drawing and seems to be familiar with most of the crowd, especially the women.

Tess and I jump back on the dance floor when one of our favorite oldies plays. It is not looking like we are going to gain much information other than reaffirming that Billy does work here and enjoys partying as much as anybody in the room. But I am having a fun night of dancing with my girl looking great in her tight jeans and flashing sexy cleavage. That is until this group of three older ladies who seem to have already enjoyed several drinks grab me away from Tess on the dance floor, promising I will be returned safely.

They are a friendly bunch, maybe a little too friendly at times. They dance a circle around me with drinks in hand while I try to keep a watchful eye on Tess to keep her from facing the same fate with some rodeo riders. Tess seems to think it is all funny as she mingles in the crowd, talking to anyone who can hear over the music.

As long as I can see Tess, I feel comfortable. I just try to make the best of the situation and add it to our list of crazy adventures on this vacation. I even let out a few "Woo-hoo" yells with the three ladies through the first dance. The hat-wearing fun-loving girls grab the back of my Levi's a couple of times, but I just go with it to try to get what we came for. I hope Tess doesn't see the flirting and become the one to start the brawl that I am trying to avoid tonight.

As the second song ends, I am looking for an escape route from the dance floor when I hear the dreaded announcement over the speakers. It is amateur karaoke time, and my three new friends immediately wrangle me like roping a bull and drag me to the stage. One of the ladies is screaming, "We're first, we're first," as we climb the steps into the spotlights. She seems to be recognized as enough of a regular that she has some influence to get to be first. I am frantically searching for Tess to bail me out. Finally, I find her in the crowd by her nice butt that I would know anywhere, but she is disappearing to the back of the bar. I am thinking she is most likely going to pee, but it could be that she just can't bear to watch the agony of what is about to happen.

I have to be encouraged by the ladies again when we get to the stage, then I see our assigned song and feel my cheeks warming up. Our quartet sings a classic about a woman standing by her man, loud and proud. I figure if I'm going to be up in front of everyone I may as well give my best effort. The ladies pour themselves into the singing as if it is an audition on one of those shows where stars are discovered. I am so relieved that I survived as we close out the song. The rowdy crowd chants for another song since we, well since the ladies, are putting on quite a show.

Thank goodness our next effort is a popular song that entices a lot of singing help from almost everyone in attendance. I am giving it my best country music star rendition. I am also wishing that I had partaken in a cold beer, or several, to give me more confidence. The entire bar becomes involved, and the place is rocking. I notice Tess crossing the back of the room about halfway through the song and I know she is going to have so much fun with this later tonight, and beyond. I love seeing her hair falling from under the brimmed hat. She is just so pretty in every kind of outfit.

Me and my new friends make our way off the stage and to the dance floor. The ladies yell out to Tess to join for the upcoming line dance, and she happily takes her place with us. The entire dance floor immediately gets organized and begins the dance in sync with one another. Tess and I are not too experienced with this type of dancing, but I must admit it is a lot of fun with the energy of the crowd.

Mercifully, my night of stardom does finally end, and the ladies walk us back to the table and tell Tess thanks for letting them steal me. They all three leave a big mark of red lipstick on my cheeks. Tess compliments us on our great singing, and I give her a sarcastic look. Tess kisses me on the lips and moves her thumb up to rub the makeup from my cheeks but pauses and decides she wants a picture first. We squeeze in with our new friends for a fun picture of the memorable night when the lead lady says, "You did much better than your landlord."

The picture captures my stunned bewilderment. "Our landlord?"

"Yeah, aren't you the out-of-towners that rent Rob's place every year?"

So much for our undercover outfits. We admit that we are and wonder how in the world they know that. "How often does Rob come out?"

One of our new friends laughs. "You know Rob, he works a lot, but he usually makes it in every couple of weeks or so."

Tess is in full detective mode now. "So when was the last time he sang with you?"

"Just a few nights ago." She looks over at one of the other girls to ask what night. She seems like a person that doesn't bother herself too much with days of the week unless it's tied to what music is playing.

The other lady thinks for a moment before saying, "Oh, that's easy. It was the night of the big storm, remember? He was staying down the road at the little hotel and really cut loose that night."

The first lady chimes back in. "But not as good as ole Jack did tonight. Next time you're in we've got a date on the dance floor and the stage, honey."

Tess loves it. "Don't worry, Jack won't miss a chance to sing and dance with you fun ladies again."

Tess says she has all the information she needs and is ready to get out of there. I am more than ready. We make our way through the crowd again, waving goodbye to our new friends on the dance floor, when all of a sudden, Billy steps in front of us. He grabs Tess's arm and asks her to tell him the real reason she was messing in the back room. I have no idea what he is talking about, but my defenses are on edge seeing his hand on her arm.

I look him in the eye and calmly but firmly state, "Get your hand off her." I am thinking we have made it this far without incident and we just need to make it the last few steps to the door.

Billy holds tight as Tess tries to pull away. "Not until she tells me why she was in the back room."

Tess blurts out, "I already told you. I was looking for the restroom."

Billy growls, "I don't believe you."

I reach over and place my hand on Billy's arm, still calm, at least on the outside. "I'm not going to ask you again."

Billy's eyes move from Tess to give me the once over. "I'm head of security here."

I quickly respond, "I don't give a damn who you are. Get your hand off my wife!"

A gleam comes to Billy's eyes, and I know this is probably not going to end well. "She isn't going anywhere until I get answers."

I have come too far to turn back now, and I am burning with rage to defend Tess. "Last chance."

Billy chuckles. "You really think you're big enough to take me."

I'm far from being a violent person, just the opposite really, but when it comes to protecting Tess, I am willing to do whatever is necessary. In one quick motion I swing my arm down, snatching his hand from her arm, and forcefully twist his wrist. Billy is quickly folded like a pretzel and the big man drops to the floor in front of us. I apply more pressure to his arm when he attempts to rise. Tess is always signing us up for new things to try, and I am happy that martial arts training has been one of our recent experiences.

I look down at Billy. "We are walking out of here. It can be peaceful or painful. It's up to you."

Our three new friends approach with a group of cowboys. "Let it go, Billy."

Billy ponders his predicament for a moment then reluctantly agrees to let this go . . . for now. I am relieved because I really don't want this to get out of hand more than it has already. I hold him in the grip until Tess passes through the door. I thank my singing friends and their buddies and keep my eye on Billy as I let go and start to follow her.

The ladies yell as I go through the exit, "Don't forget, we have a date when you come back."

"Can't wait." I am thankful that our honky-tonk night has come to an end with everyone in one piece.

As we cross the bridge in old red Tess tells me that she had snuck into the back and found Billy's locker while everyone was caught up in our big moment on stage. She is having too much fun with all of this, but I remind her that I am not happy with the risk she took. She moves right past that comment to tell me what she found.

In Billy's locker Tess discovered several small baggies of pills in his jacket pocket. A dark blue jacket with the bar name and the year it was established. And a photo of Emma hung on the inside of the door of his locker with pictures of several other girls. I tell her she could have easily been caught and I almost run off the road when she tells me she had been. Billy had walked in but thankfully she had closed the locker by that time and was a few steps away. She had told him she was looking for the restroom and he bought it because he was only interested in flirting with her. She says he reached an arm around her waist and said that he would take her to a private bathroom in the back. I find myself wishing that I would have broken his arm.

She said the first thing she could think of as she swatted his hand away and told him she only danced with other women.

Tess looks at me with concern. "Jack, the jacket I saw could be the one in the picture."

"It could, but we don't know that." I try to remain objective after our confrontation with Billy.

Tess points out, "He has a temper and definitely doesn't seem to respect women."

I agree with Tess on that observation.

I lecture her about safety the rest of the way home, but she looks at her makeup and hair blowing in the mirror, not hearing a word I say.

Tess touches my arm and shares the dimples that I love so much. "You look sexy in the boots and hat."

I smile, liking the thought that she is thinking about me in that way, especially during the mission. "Thank you, baby."

Tess gives me one of her mischievous looks. "Maybe I can ride Johnny Bravo when we get home." Color spreads across her cheeks.

I can't hold back my grin or my words. "Oh, Johnny would love to give petunia a ride."

"You naughty cowboy."

I take her hand. "Maybe we should do some pictures of you in the hat and boots." I give a little wink. "And nothing else."

"Relentless," Tess sighs. But I see the dimples appear again as she lays her head back against the seat to enjoy the breeze.

I give her a good long foot massage once we finally get to bed.

44

TESS

IT'S NOT LIGHT YET, BUT I can't sleep thinking of the case and all the craziness that has happened on our trip. Jack always says that he can feel the tension when I am awake, even if I lie perfectly still. I guess he feels it this morning too because he rolls over and asks me what's wrong, even though I have not moved a muscle.

I giggle. "Just a lot on my mind, baby."

Jack is still half asleep as he pats me on the leg. "It's all going to be okay, sweetness."

That is pretty much his theory in life. It will all be okay. I tell him that everything I do is not okay. That I do mess up and and say things I shouldn't, but he always takes my side in anything that happens. Once, I had been fussing with our young son, Sam, and he stormed into the room and asked his dad why mom NEVER gets in trouble. It was so difficult to hold back our laughs. But he did have a point: Jack just supports me no matter what.

I feel guilty about disturbing Jack's rest after having him at the bar late, but I can't help myself. I slide my leg up over him and begin to rub it over his manly area. I know how much he loves this, and I smile at how quickly this affects him. I feel Jack's excitement grow as I flex my calf over him, and his hand begins to rub my leg. I love it when I feel his hips begin to shift.

I reach for the bottle of love voodoo and lean over to let it flow slowly over his core. With my hand now rubbing his chest, I move my toes gently over his hardness. I know Jack cannot resist this loving. My arch glides easily over his oil-covered passion and his hand clutches my calf. He loves to feel the flex of my muscles and I am happy to give that to my sweet husband. I massage and pinch his nipples while my foot moves up and down easily over the oil. I know that he won't last long and I soon feel his warm happiness cover my toes.

I lean over to kiss Jack's cheek and listen to his deep breaths of satisfaction. "Thank you for taking my mind off things, baby."

Even in the dark, I can feel his smile as he pulls me closer. "I am so happy to help you clear your mind."

With a pinch to his side, "That's so sweet that you are willing to make that sacrifice for me."

"I'm always here for you, baby," he says as he covers his sensitive chest when I try to pinch his nipple.

Jack goes out on a morning run with Devin, and I am determined to get Emma moving again to get her out of her depression and speed up her recovery. I peek through the broken blinds of the pool house apartment and can see Emma curled up on the couch with a bowl of cereal. Most likely her favorite, Fruity Pebbles.

Understandably still nervous from the attack, she looks through the peephole before opening the door for me. I am proud of her being cautious, even while I haven't been. Jack had given me another lecture about that before leaving on his run this morning. Emma greets me with that sweet smile. "Hello, Miss Tess."

I give her a hug and tell her that she looks so cute in her pajama shorts. "Get ready, we are going on an adventure."

Emma instinctively ducks back into a shell like a turtle. A shell that had not existed in all the time I had known her. I know it is hard for her to try to move forward but she needs to if she is going to overcome this awful event.

I coax her, "Come on, we will have so much fun."

Emma walks back toward the couch. "I don't really feel like it today, Miss Tess."

"I know, baby, but I haven't gotten to play pickleball in so long and I need you." I cheat a little because I know that she has a hard time not helping someone in need, even if it is as minor as this.

Emma chuckles. "I'm no good at that game."

I take her hand gently and lead her toward the bedroom. "That works because I'm not very good either."

She gives me one last look of protest but knows that I am not going to let her off the hook. Emma digs through a drawer and retrieves a bright blue one-piece suit. "Are we playing on the beach?"

"Yes, that one will be perfect." I pull open my cover, showing her the one-piece skirt suit I am wearing that Jack likes so much.

Always the sweet girl she says, "You look so good, Miss Tess."

I laugh. "Flattery is appreciated but it is not getting you out of this." I start to step out of the room but Emma asks me to stay. Even after several days the bruises to her pretty skin look so painful, mostly still dark blue and purple but lighter than before. They are all around her little pooched tummy and her sides. The thought of this sweet little girl getting beaten breaks my heart.

She stops dressing with her suit just below her swollen tummy and smiles, "Would you like to feel her?"

I move to her quickly with my hand out. "I would absolutely love to." Gently I touch my hand over her bruises and feel a tiny flutter. "She is excited about pickleball."

Emma laughs. "She may be fussy about me moving off that couch."

I look at Emma's sweet brown eyes. "Do you know it's a girl?"

"Not yet, but that's what I think in my heart." Quickly adding, "But I will be happy either way."

I give her a gentle hug. "I know you will. And she will be so lucky to have you as a mommy."

As we make the short walk to the beach, I tell Emma that I have never played beach pickleball and will probably keep letting the ball hit the sand. I mark off the lines of a reduced-sized court with my racket handle and tell her we will go easy since she is still sore. After a few minutes we find our rhythm and can keep our volley going for several shots. Emma seems to be moving well for all she has been through.

I tell her that I am mad at her for being so freaking cute while she is pregnant. I share that I gained so much weight with my last baby that I have been trying for twenty-five years to lose it.

Emma lets out one of her signature laughs. "You have always looked so pretty, Miss Tess."

I love that girl. We shuffle through the sand, hitting the ball for a good thirty minutes laughing over our stumbles and the fact that I won't chase an errant hit more than a couple of steps. That and my slips of the tongue when I miss an easy one. Once we almost collide going after a pop-up that lands between us and both fall trying to avoid each other. It is so good to see Emma having fun.

We take a break after our near collision and sit in the sand with our feet at the edge of the water.

"Thank you for making me get out today," Emma says as she leans her head on my shoulder.

"I've had fun, but I don't want to push you too hard." I wrap my arm around her shoulder.

Emma squeezes my hand. "I feel good, and it has been so fun to run and laugh again."

I laugh. "Well, I'm always up for pickleball so you just let me know anytime you want to play."

We sit quietly leaning against one another for several minutes as we feel the gentle waves roll over our feet. I fight back tears thinking of all this sweet little girl has been through in her life and then being left lying in that storm beaten so badly. My sadness mixes with anger. I want to bring whoever did this to justice.

Emma lifts her head and looks into my eyes. "I know that you are a great mom, Miss Tess, because you are such a good person."

My tears break through and roll down my cheeks. "Thank you, baby, and you will be a great mom too for the very same reason."

She places both her hands around mine. "I wish you could stay here with me and teach me how to be a good mom."

My tears flow freely now. I sniffle. "Me too, honey, but you are a natural caretaker with so much love in your heart. You will be a great mother." I pause and add, "And a great wife."

"I sure hope so, Miss Tess. I'm going to try my best and I hope I can be fun like you too."

That makes me laugh and breaks up the tears. "You mean crazy like me."

Emma snickers. "Maybe a little of that too."

We giggle as we hold each other close and watch the water run higher up our feet.

45

JACK

I PAUSE TO LOOK AT Tess and Emma sitting arm in arm on the beach before going up to stretch and shower after my run with Devin. I can see Emma improving each day, and Tess's love is no small part of that. Tess is such a sweet and caring person. They both are, and it touches my heart seeing their friendship with one another.

Tess surprises me by slipping into the shower with me. We take turns rubbing the suds over each other and share a wet kiss while the water rushes over our heads. Tess massages my core aggressively with both hands and it's tearing me all to pieces. I love touching and kissing Tess's wet skin as much as I love the feel of her hands on me. I am getting worked up from all the fondling and I think maybe Tess is heating up from hearing about my conversation with Devin.

Devin was very forthcoming about his and Gabriella's open marriage and about how beautiful and fun he thought Tess was. He talked of how sexy it was to watch Gabriella and Tess through the window the other night and how much he loved the pictures on the boat. Though I still feel a little guilty about watching Tess and Gabriella. Devin said even before he had proposed to Gabriella that she was open with him about her enjoyment of playing with others. Devin loved her so much that he didn't let that stop him for asking for her hand in marriage and he emphasized that their intimacy had been very exciting from the first day.

He was very comfortable with having the conversation about Tess and me and said that he hoped we could all get together soon. It was difficult for me to be as open or relaxed about the topic, even with the experiences of the past few days. I did confess that watching Gabriella and Tess was exciting, but I didn't really respond to the four of us getting together. Though, I know that is a very real possibility, especially the way Tess and Gabriella are getting along.

I can see Tess's interest pique as I share the conversation. After I dry off she stays in the bathroom drying and trying different styles with her hair. I maneuver around on the bed trying to find the perfect magazine model pose. I laugh at myself as I spin all around trying different positions before settling on my side with the sheets tucked between my legs, barely covering my privates. I prop up on my elbow and wait in anticipation for Tess to come into the room with as sexy of a look on my face as I can conjure, again laughing at myself. Tess is right that posing is not easy work, and I feel a little foolish.

Tess strolls in staring at her phone with her robe untied, looking so beautiful. She stops cold in her tracks when she glances up to see the pose that I have worked so hard to perfect. The dimples I love so much appear. I am pleased that my effort doesn't cause her break into laughter, it certainly could have happened. A couple of quick pokes to her phone and we have some sexy music followed by a beautiful tempting strip tease from Tess. I love when she plays with me like this. She lets me see a few peeks of bare shoulder before easing the robe down near that sexy bubble butt with a sultry over-the-shoulder smile. Finally, Tess lets the robe drop to her feet and twists her wonderful booty. She spins around and teasingly covers her breast with one arm while placing the other hand over her intimates.

She sensually sways her hips slowly to the sound of the sax, offering another sweet smile. With a slow-motion walk Tess makes her way over right next to the bed. She reaches for the bottle of oil on the nightstand and pours it slowly across her chest. Tess runs her hands all over her sexy body, eventually coming to rest, cupping her heavy breasts. She massages, squeezes, and pinches her nipples while continuing to move with the sound of the horn. She even pushes one breast upward and paints circles around the areola with her tongue. Gazing at me while clamping her mouth around the flesh and ever so slowly stretching her nipple between her plump lips before releasing. She knows exactly how to drive me crazy. She has reversed my plan of tearing her up and I am now ready to jump from the bed to grab her, but Tess raises an index finger telling me to stay put.

Tess slowly moves over and places her soft lips to my neck. Chills immediately overtake my body. Her kisses trail down my chest, sides, and stomach with the cool touch of her silky hair gently brushing over my skin. More chills. Mercy! I am all to hell. She lets her heavy silver strands flow across my pulsing excitement as her lips attack my inner thighs. I begin to think she is going to make my love flow without ever touching me there.

Tess repositions between my legs, now marked with love bites, and looks up through her messy hair to meet my eyes. Her eyes hold onto mine as her tongue slowly, incredibly slowly, draws a circle around the tip of my desire for her. As if watching her frame by frame on my camera, she traces around, downward, and leisurely back up again. Tess's eyes do not let go of mine, and her silk strands brush softly over my skin. My innermost wish is granted when I feel the warmth of her mouth take my ambition. The movements of her cheeks with me inside is so beautiful. Glorious. Amazing. Wonderful. I cannot take my eyes from Tess.

She easily moves her kisses further downward to take my orbs into the heat, awaiting past her lips. An oily hand wraps around my intense arousal. Her eyes stay locked onto mine as her grip squeezes, but stills flow easily with the oils mixed with the remainder of her kisses. I love watching the flex of her arm as she strokes me. My hips follow the flow of her hand. I am mesmerized by my wife. The details of her beauty come into focus even more. Her plush lips wrapped around me, her painted fingers moving over me, the silver locks spread over my skin, her eyes staring into mine. Those beautiful blue eyes whispering I love you.

I am overwhelmed with yearning, passion, and love for her. She too easily brings me right to the edge of ecstasy before easing away. Dimples appear on her flushed cheeks, and I want to scream, please don't stop!

Tess spins her body gracefully to lay on the bed beside me facing my direction. She lifts her feet, rubbing them up my chest and softly landing on my cheeks. No words are necessary, I know what my baby wants.

Who is this girl? Tess is always fun, I love the way she plays with me, but this take-charge aggression and teasing is new. It is so different from her normal submissiveness in our intimate time. I eagerly accept the request and begin placing kisses all over her feet and ankles, thinking of how wonderful she made me feel earlier this morning. Rubbing my lips through her sexy arches and around her heels then grabbing kisses from the soft skin of her heel behind each foot. I take each of her toes deep into my mouth one at a time while rubbing her calves and shins ever so slightly with my fingertips. Chills emerge on her legs as I suckle from her big toe to her little toe and back slowly. Looking at her with grateful love through the whole wonderful journey.

My lips enclose several of her sexy little toes inside at once for kisses and suckles as her hand slides between her legs. That fuels my excitement even more. Tess gently spreads her moisture across the tenderness of her velvety skin and her painted fingers disappear inside the warmth. I continue to explore her feet more intently as my gaze stays locked onto her every movement.

I feel her calves flexing as the intensity of her self-massage increases. The scent of her skin, the intimacy of loving on her feet, and the view of her hand on herself is so erotic. I want her so badly right now. Tess opens her legs wide, granting me the most wonderful view of her painted nails disappearing into her beautiful flower. I am dying! She offers a gravelly whisper, "Show me how bad you want me, baby."

I start to move toward her, but she holds up her hand as a stop sign. Another gravelly whisper, "Like I'm showing you."

Oh my gosh, I'm not good at being watched. I am the one behind the camera, but how can I even think about resisting her request. I can't. Tess slides her fingers from the heat below and moves them up to slowly rub across her lips. My hand grips myself and glides over the oily shaft as I watch her every move intently. Her hand moves back between her legs and resumes with great earnest.

Her baby blues lock onto me, her legs spread wide, her pretty hand massaging herself, and the beautiful feet that I just made love to are all making my hand move faster. Her dimples are the last straw, and the excitement pours over my hand just as I see her leg muscles tense and her hips rise. I see the shudder travel through her body, and I know that she has joined me in happiness.

Tess moves to me, gently lifts my hand and takes my fingers between her lips. I feel her tongue circle them as he gives me the sweetest of smiles. She then offers hers to me which I eagerly accept.

What an amazing woman.

46

TESS

EVEN THOUGH I HAVE SEEN him twice I have forgotten to include one suspect on our list, probably because I am more concerned with avoiding him. Before we leave the house, I add BK's drawing with long flowing blond hair to the board. Jack and I wear our swimsuits to help sell this undercover mission As Jack pulls old red into the parking lot of Try Me Rental Shop, I reach for my clip but drop it back into the console, thinking I will have a better chance of gaining information from BK by leaving my wind-blown hair loose. I feel a little more confident questioning Big Kahuna now that I have a little embarrassing history on him if I need to use it.

We walk under the sign, which is a giant surfboard with a surfer riding a large wave. Below the wave is the store slogan, "You Will Like Me." Once you meet the owner you understand the real meaning of the sign. Big Kahuna greets us as he swoops his long blond locks from his face and begins to speak with his laid-back voice, "Sparkles and Smooth G, cool to see you."

I wasn't even sure if anyone on the island knew his real name or the story of how a surfer in his twenties moved from the opposite coast to this tiny strip island to open his business. That is until Victoria let me in on some of the secret earlier. The mystery has certainly raised a lot of eyebrows and I am sure that Mrs. Jones and her club have been working diligently for the information. But as the friendly folks of Sandy Strips are inclined to do, they welcomed Big Kahuna with open arms, especially Rohan, who benefits greatly from the extra tourists coming to rent equipment and be trained by the Big Kahuna himself.

It is difficult for me to use the name he went by without getting tickled, so I try to avoid it and I call him BK mostly. He always seems to make a good first impression on strangers because he is so approachable. But it doesn't take long for people to see that he is certainly on the cocky side, typically strutting around with no shirt to show off his tan six-pack abs and muscled chest. That's just one more trait of his that gets on my nerves. I can't imagine that he ever works out between running his business and playing in the surf the rest of the time, but he still looks like that. It just isn't fair.

I shrink back as he approaches to give Jack a greeting with a fist pump and then annoyingly wraps both arms around me in a bear hug. I can't stand it, but I know it's coming. I am not special, he just fancies himself the desire of all women so he thinks any lady will feel privileged to receive that greeting. I am not sure if it is because Jack is with me, or because of what Victoria had said earlier but BK doesn't even mention our earlier meeting.

Our plan is to pretend to be interested in a rental of some kind to see how Big Kahuna reacts when I bring up Emma's name. Pictures of rental items are lined along the wall with signs that say whether they are available or not since many of them are too big to fit into the shop with the clothes and gifts. The shop stays so busy that it will be easy for us to find an item listed as unavailable so Jack and I can get our investigating completed and get out quickly. BK tries to talk us into the jet skis he has available, but we tell him that Rob has some at the house. I notice the "unavailable" sign on the paddleboard picture so I ask about those. From previous conversations BK knows that I am genuinely interested in paddleboarding, so it is a believable request.

You can see the disappointment on Big Kahuna's face as he glances at the empty wall while I am asking him how well he knows Emma. He casually responds. "She is a hot girl, Sparkles."

It is so difficult to keep him focused. "Do you hang out with her often?"

BK smiles. "Ooh, I would like to. Can you hook me up?" He stops to admire his own body in the mirror. He is so frustrating. "Have you guys surfed or anything together?"

"I see Bella Treasure on the beach sometimes." Bella means beautiful, so beautiful treasure. That is an appropriate nickname for sweet Emma.

I am working on my next question when Big Kahuna lets out an unusually energetic, "Rad! Let's go, Sparkles."

Confused, I look the direction that BK starts walking and see one of his employees coming through the door . . . with a paddleboard of all things.

"I'm going to teach you how to ride today, Sparkles."

My panicked eyes shift to Jack. Before either of us can think of anything, much less get a word out, Big Kahuna grabs my hand and leads me out the door with the board under his arm.

BK looks back at Jack. "You can hang out here, Smooth G."

I know that Jack is not staying behind and I keep glancing back at him, hoping he will think of something to get me out of this predicament, but BK is excited to get started. We step into the inlet with our board and I see Jack snickering as he watches from the edge of the water. My surfer teacher is a little too handsy for my liking as he helps me up onto the board. I am even more uncomfortable as he places his hands on my hips as I paddle us out.

I love paddleboarding as much as I thought I would, and I am surprised by how well I am balancing, at least early on. Big Kahuna eases back slightly, but his hands remain uncomfortably on my hips, and I wish Jack was sharing this experience with me instead of the self-proclaimed God's gift to women. I am still asking BK about Emma, and I am surprised that he is talkative about her as we paddle north. Jack follows along the shore.

Out of the blue, BK squeezes me a little tighter and whispers, "I bet you were still sexy when you were pregnant like Emma is now."

I snap my head around to look at him and that causes me to become unsteady on the board.

He quickly responds by tightening his arms around me and leaning against my backside. I temporarily regain control. That is until I feel the throb of Big Kahuna's . . . well, his big kahuna against my butt. I am shocked and somewhat rattled as he rubs up against me.

Then, for some reason, I guess because of the craziness of the situation, I become tickled, and there is no turning back. When I get started laughing nothing can stop me. The laughter is rolling up from within and I start to wobble. Uncontrollably. We hit the water with BK still trying to hold onto me, but the scramble to the surface separates us.

BK grabs the board as I make my way to shore. Jack meets me at the edge of the water and looks at me with concern, maybe even panic as I walk toward him with tears in my eyes and unable to speak. I'm sure he thinks I am hurt as he rushes to me, and I try to keep the laughter from getting completely out of control. Big Kahuna remains in the water and knowing why is not helping my attempt to hold back the laughter.

Jack nervously looks me over. "Are you okay?"

Still struggling to get the words out and doubling over, I say, "Yes, baby . . . I'm good."

Jack looks confused as he holds me but then finally realizes that I am laughing and not crying, which gets him started too, even though he doesn't know why.

Big Kahuna finally eases from the water. "Whoa, that was quite the wipeout, Sparkles." His bulge says that maybe he should have waited a few more minutes in the water but Jack doesn't notice. BK says he needs to get back to the shop and I whisper the secret of my laughter to Jack as BK jogs away.

Jack laughs even harder. "Watch him run with his stiff board."

I double over again unable to stop giggling. "You are going to make me pee."

Jack keeps piling on. "Hope you didn't enjoy paddleboarding as much as his Big Kahuna."

"I loved paddleboarding, but no, not near as much as he did." As I try to gather myself again, I look back at Jack. "Can you believe that craziness?"

Jack raises his eyebrows. "Of course I can believe it. I tell you all the time how sexy you are."

We start walking back to the car. "He is just a young guy with lots of hormones."

Jack squeezes my hand. "And you are a beautiful lady."

Ole corny just won't let it go as we approach old red. "It's hard for a guy to be that close to a sexy woman like you."

"Stop it." I scowl at him trying to keep from smiling.

"Stop what? I wasn't the one doing anything."

As we climb in the convertible, I reach over and grab Jack tightly between the legs. "Does watching me paddleboard have the same impact on you?"

Jack smiles. "All day, every day."

My sweet hubby isn't lying about that, and I am thankful that I make him feel that way. As the wind blows my hair dry going down the road, I can't help but think I am surprised that I affected a young guy like that. I never think of myself as being sexy, no matter how many times Jack tells me. In fact, my response when Jack tells me is that it is him that makes me sexy. He tells me that is a silly thing to say. But I AM seeing myself in many new ways on this trip.

47

JACK

WE BOTH HAVE OUR SECOND shower of the day, me because I sweated while watching the paddleboard show and Tess because of her spill into the water with Big Kahuna. We decide to share this round of cleaning in the name of conserving water and saving time. Tess's skin feels so slick and soft with the suds washing over her curves. Once again, my hands roam over every inch of her body and enjoy the loving caresses in return.

Tess is playful again with our touching in the shower, something that is becoming normal on this trip. I wonder if it is just because of our bodies sliding against one another in the shower or if some of it is coming from a younger guy being so excited about her. Whatever it is, I am enjoying the increased aggression and passion from her.

Watching her get ready has always stirred me up, and the short black silk robe against her pale skin is just too much as she sits at the dressing table brushing her hair. The contrast of the black gown on her ivory skin ignites a fire inside me as I approach her from behind. I kiss her sweet little ears and let my warm breaths linger before giving passionate kisses to her neck. She is so sensitive there. I feel the chills arise on her skin. My hands move across her soft shoulders sliding the silk away and reach around to brush over her hard nipples and massage her breasts.

The flash drive of photos plays in my mind. Tess in the burgundy dress on our first night, all prettied up and posing just because she loves me. The mini massage at Lucca's, and how she seemed to enjoy it, going wild when we got back home. Strutting around Rohan's looking gorgeous in the white dress. Every step she took was a show of her glorious body in slow motion. Her beautiful smile. The swimsuits, the photos on the boat and in the car. The incredible massage at Lucca's and the joy spread across her chest. Watching her first experience with Gabriella. She could not hide her happiness during that special time. Tess's touches, smiles, dimples, laughs, her eyes, her love for me, her sacrifice for me. Her determination to solve the case. I love this lady. And I want her to know how much. I crave her with all my heart and soul, and I must show her. I want her right now, out of necessity. Not just because I love her and think she is beautiful, but because I need her to survive.

Tess's body trembles as I reach back around to pull on her hard nipples, and my kisses became more forceful on her neck. She slides one hand back to feel my urge for her. I want her. Right now. I need my wife. I'm taking her. My hands slide down over her body, my fingers find the moistness between her legs, and I know that she wants me too. I smooth the wetness all over her soft intimate skin and feel her knees tremble as she rises from the chair. My lips trace the diagonal line of freckles across her back before guiding her to bend over the dressing table. I am going to show Tess my uncontrollable desire for her!

Then she surprises me with a whisper, "Give it to me Jack." We talk and sometimes laugh during our special time. Especially the one time our old bed fell apart in the middle of lovemaking and we finished at a forty-five-degree angle after finally catching our breath from laughter. But Tess is more likely to say something naughty and funny instead of blunt sexual talk.

I lift the black silk over her beautiful round bottom, letting the cool material lay across the deep curve of her lower back. I fill my hands from the bottle of Tess's love oil. I massage the scented slickness abundantly into her voluptuous backside, sliding all around her before guiding her hips back to touch mine. My hands glide across her shoulders, flow down the inward curve of her waist, and I clutch her hips forcefully. I easily but eagerly enter her with my desire. Not Tess's favorite style of intimacy, but it's what I want so badly right now. There has been so much buildup to this moment, this will not be our normal sensual romantic lovemaking. This is an uncontrollable lust for my wife.

Our bodies collide together urgently. Her silver hair moves across her back, bouncing from the jerking of her body. The view in the mirror of her breasts swaying vigorously with our intense love is beautiful. I reach both arms around to grab them tightly as my fervor grows with each clashing of our skin together. I aggressively tug on her firm nipples causing her to wince, but I can't stop myself. My need is too great. Her backside jiggles as I frantically try to convince her of my hunger. My hand moves down to feel her muscled thigh tense. I love seeing her triceps flex as she steadies herself on the table while my fervor grows. A bottle falls and rolls from the dressing table. I begin to rub oils into the heat of her core.

Tess is filled, my fingers from the front and my throbbing hunger from behind. Her sounds grow louder. And she surprises me once again, "Harder, baby." I love hearing those words and my thrusting intensifies. My hand pushes into the fire between her legs while I fill her beautiful backside with my love. I love Tess so much!

One last long, full scream of satisfaction from Tess magnifies my insatiable desire for her. Tess's joy is my greatest thrill. She continues to brace herself for several minutes, allowing me to enjoy her. Finally, I ease myself from all her insides, leaving one last splash of joy across the flesh of her gorgeous bottom, which is marked with my fingerprints. I love watching the proof of my satisfaction slowly ease down the back of her leg. I hold onto her as if she is about to fall from a mountaintop so I can capture this moment of her image in the mirror. And to steady Tess from her shaky legs. I take in all of Tess's wonderful details as she leans over in front of the mirror and lifts her eyes to meet mine in the reflection. Dimples. Messy beautiful silver hair. Flushed and beautiful cheek bones. Love marks on her tender neck. I am so happy just staring at her.

A few moments pass then Tess calls out, "The pool guy!"

I am shocked and a little disappointed, maybe even slightly jealous. "That's who you were thinking of just then?"

"No!" Tess turns to face me. "I love you. I loved that. But you said there were no signs of forced entry into the house, and we would have seen anyone getting into the back of the house from where we were sitting at the pool."

I listen intently, but tiredly. "Yeah."

Tess continues, "We thought it could have been someone with a key, right? I suggested Linda's maintenance guy, but you said the intruder moved like a younger person."

I nod in agreement. "Like one of my basketball players."

Tess is right. We had only seen the pool guy a couple of times, but he is young, and his size is about right for the person I saw in the house last night. I suggest we do a little recon on our pool boy after taking another look around the house to see if we can determine what was taken.

We scour the house—all levels since we don't know how long whoever it was had been in there. We are convinced that it has something to do with the investigation since some of Linda's valuables that were out in the open seem to be undisturbed. But it is difficult to determine since we don't know if the intruder found what he was looking for.

As Tess goes into the laundry room to get her cover-up that is hanging to dry, she reminds me that we have agreed to meet Victoria at the beach this evening.

I think it will be a great break from the investigation and the intruder and will give me time to help think of a plan for us to find out more about the pool guy. Tess looks so good walking toward me in her see-through cover as she pauses with her hand on the light switch.

I watch her curiously for a moment as her eyes scan the room. "Is everything okay, baby?"

She nods her head and flips the light off. I am hoping that Tess is thinking something fabulous about our intense intimacy, but something tells me that there are more serious thoughts bouncing around her mind as she gives me a hug before we leave the house.

48

TESS

WE ROLL OUT OUR MATS on the flatter and harder surface of the sand, close to the water. Sunset yoga on the beach with Victoria always relaxes me and is helpful to clear my mind from the onslaught of thoughts during our trip, and the uneasy feeling I just had in the laundry room. A smile creeps over my face as I watch Jack stretching in his tight shorts in preparation for Victoria's class.

After a brief warmup, Victoria leads us in our first vinyasa. This is one of the easier classes she will teach, meant for a time of calming the body and mind amid the gentle breaking waves. Jack enjoys this with me every time we take this class. He needs to relax too, but I can feel his stares as I move into the first downward dog in my swimsuit. Jack may be missing out on the "free your mind" part of this. But I am too, thinking of his strong hands clinging to my hips and our eyes meeting in the mirror just moments earlier. He needed my love so badly right at that moment. I love to have that impact on him, but I push myself to concentrate on the moves we are working on and the sound of the ocean.

Victoria's body flows effortlessly through the movements, and she is like a statue with her balance poses. Jack and I have some wobbles, but we hang in there with her. I see Victoria smile a few times and look over to see Jack working harder to stare at me than the poses we are in. I decide I am the only one that is even trying to calm my mind. I try to keep my focus, but my eyes keep wandering to Jack and his muscles flexing, so I guess I am just as guilty as he is.

We are holding steady in our warrior three pose when the peace and tranquility are interrupted. "Count me in." Big Kahuna strolls up beside me and goes right into the pose too close to my space. He smiles. "Do you need help balancing, Sparkles?"

"No thank you." I try to sound as polite as I can, but the sarcasm is there.

BK looks at Victoria. "You don't mind if I join do you, Graceful?"

There is another nickname he has spot on, so maybe I am not giving him enough credit for that talent.

Victoria smiles. "Be our guest, California."

I am surprised that Victoria is joining in on the nickname game as well as the fact that BK is facing Victoria after she used his real name earlier. I can't help but wonder why he is choosing to be in Victoria's presence after running away so fast earlier. I want to figure out why it is so important for him to be here. Surely it isn't anything to do with our paddleboarding incident earlier.

BK removes his shirt, taking a moment for himself and anyone else who may be interested to admire his body before joining. I must admit though, he looks almost as graceful as Victoria as we continue through the class. I guess the calm focus and balance is what helps make him such a skilled surfer.

As we come to the close of our session and rest in corpse pose while listening to the peaceful sounds of the water BK taps my hand and whispers, "Let's finish our board session, Sparkles."

So much for peace and relaxation. My insides wince and I am determined that I will not do that again no matter what it takes. I am also thinking that BK better be quiet because Victoria does not like her classes interrupted, even informal beach classes, and she has let him slide once already. We all lay still and breathe deeply, me thinking of a way out of another paddleboarding adventure with Big Kahuna.

As we close and shake the sand from our mats before rolling them up, I try my best to tell Jack that I need saving from BK without using words. I raise my eyebrow and look over my shoulder while trying to mouth, "Get me out of here." Not knowing that BK brought up the paddleboarding, Jack just looks at me, confused. I continue my efforts by shifting my eyes dramatically, looking toward the house, even moving my hips slightly in attempt to mimic the balancing on a paddleboard.

Jack's eyes finally light up as if he understands. BK asks if I am ready to hit the water and immediately Victoria responds with, "Sorry California, they are going on a walk with me."

BK won't challenge Victoria and he is not one to join what would be to him "a boring walk on the beach." BK turns toward me before leaving. "Why did you ask all those questions about Bella Treasure today?"

I am surprised that he was paying enough attention to even notice that all my questions were about Emma. "I was just wondering if you know her well."

BK gives a glance to his biceps. "Yeah, she just wanted you to see if she has a chance with me. Tell her to come see me if she wants some adventure." BK glances past me to Jack. He whispers, "And you too, if you ever want younger and more exciting."

I should have known. He braved seeing Victoria and me again just because he thought Emma may have interest in him because of my questions earlier. "I will let her know, BK."

Once BK hits the water, I thank Victoria for the save, and we store our mats at the end of the path going back to the house before heading out on our walk. The sun is close to disappearing as we begin, and I ask Jack why he looks disappointed. He confesses that he thought I was trying to hurry back to the room for some playtime, and I can't help but let a little laugh slip out. "How did you get that from my very specific directions on needing help with BK?"

"Specific, huh? I specifically heard that you wanted to hurry to the house."

Jack chuckles and adds, "You moved your hips in the 'I want you' motion."

"Because that's what you wanted to hear," Victoria laughs with me this time.

Victoria steps between Jack and I. "You guys are so precious together."

We each put an arm around her as we stroll down the beach, sensing she is missing Steven a little more tonight. Victoria talks openly with us about the moments of sadness that overcome her at the oddest times. She speaks about many of their fondest memories and catches me off guard when she includes the exploits over their last couple of years his life. I think Jack is even more surprised than I am.

I had heard most of the story before and shared it with Jack, but Victoria shared more of the details. How Steven felt that he had exposed her to something she would have never done on her own, but seemed happy to have experienced. Victoria confirms that Steven was right in all those assumptions. Victoria has such a way of making conversations about sensitive topics so comfortable and Jack seems relieved, maybe even happy, to have someone to speak to about all of this.

The sun disappears leaving us with a moonlit beach walk that somehow is helping all three of us with our next steps in life.

49

JACK

WE HAD TO BE THE cleanest people in Sandy Strips after our third shower of the day. Tess flat out tells me that there is to be no hanky-panky this time, because she is starving and wants to get to Sandy Toes for more of the baked salmon. I reluctantly obey her wishes, but it is extremely difficult when she chooses the little black dress with a low scoop top. The silver 'T' is nestled right next to my favorite little freckle in her cleavage. I love it when she wears all the extra bling. Her thick silver mane is pinned back over the ear on one side with a turquoise clip, and left down on the other. Probably my favorite style. My heart is not the only thing to flutter when she turns and flashes her little dimples.

Tess's puffy, moist lips gently kiss my cheek. "Don't even think about it. I'm so hungry."

I smile and feel the slickness of my cheek with a finger. She adds, "I see it in your eyes, baby."

She is not wrong. I want to make love to her again right now. "Is it in my eyes that you see it or the same place you saw it with the Big Kahuna?"

Tess tilts her head. “Not funny, let’s go.”

I watch her round bottom twist through the door and down the hall. “How do you think surfer boy knew Emma was pregnant?”

My sexy investigator turns. “He has probably been getting information while chasing the garden club ladies.”

I chuckle. “He does seem to have an affinity for the mature ladies.”

Tess’s eyes pierce me as I try to snuff my laugh. I remind her that Victoria says frowns cause wrinkles but that does nothing to change her expression.

She moves quickly down the steps. “You better get old red started before you get in trouble.”

At the risk of facing my southern girl’s wrath, I snap a couple of photos of her legs crossed in the front seat as her look tells me I better get ole red moving, and quickly.

As usual, Rohan’s place is hopping and we enjoy the music while eating our delicious meal. Hattie comes over to visit while Tess and I split a slice of cheesecake with fresh strawberries and a drizzle of chocolate. Hattie and Tess are cut from the same cloth, as the saying goes, when it comes to speaking their mind, or speaking truth as they describe it. The personality match has helped them build a good friendship and strong bond over the years. Plus, Tess loves Hattie’s long flowery outfits that she wears with such grace while keeping her fiery personality. Many people have underestimated Hattie’s intensity due to her fancy dress and small build. She is a sweet lady, but you don’t want to cross her as she will quickly put you in your place.

Hattie excuses herself to find Rohan, probably to take him to the dance floor, which Tess and I think he likes much more than he will admit. Tess and I enjoy the people-watching and the music before deciding to hit the dance floor ourselves. Tess is so beautiful with her silver hair flowing over the black dress and sharing her sweet smile. Her laugh almost always buries my worries, and it makes me so happy to see her having fun. My hand rests against the soft skin of her bare back and it warms my insides as we slow dance. I breathe in the wonderful scent of my wife. There are so many changes and challenges right now but my love for her continues to grow stronger each day.

As the song ends, I feel a tap on my shoulder and turn to see my old nemesis, Sheriff Fry. Devin's scolding and threats had given us a nice reprieve from his annoyances recently, but he is back with a big grudge this evening. He begins speaking loudly over the next song, telling us that he is going to contact the state authorities if we don't hand over the evidence: the pictures of Tess. The sheriff says he has friends in high places and that our buddy, Devin, will not be able to protect us for forever. I wonder if the break-in has something to do with him looking for the pictures since we haven't found anything missing.

I look into the sheriff's eyes and try to pull out my best old western cowboy accent before using another of my favorite movie lines, "You're a daisy if you do." Again, I'm not sure what makes me say the things I do sometimes. Maybe it's living with Tess and her unfiltered thoughts all these years.

I shake my head, clutch Tess's hand, and we jump into our dance moves to a song from one of our favorite seventies bands. The sheriff's face twists into a scowl and turns bright red while he waddles around in a circle trying to step between Tess and me. His hands are fighting to keep his revolver and cuffs in place as he is now hopping in circles. He screams for us to stop at the top of his lungs. We continue to dance. His determination to get face to face with me while I dance with Tess has led him to unintentionally boogying with everyone else around us.

Several cell phones point in the sheriff's direction, capturing his hand-waving and hopping in circles as the music blares through the crowd. To make it even funnier, the lyrics are about dancing and sex. It is quite amusing as Sheriff Fry looks for an opening to get between me and Tess while quick stepping, as he holds his cap with one hand and pulls his belt up with the other. The crowd loves it and soon forms a circle around the three of us, clapping their hands to the beat as I lift Tess's hand for a spin. The chants begin, "Go sheriff, go."

Finally the sheriff, who has been busy screaming at me, realizes that he is at the center of attention along with our dance. His face glows even brighter with a mixture of anger and embarrassment. His hat is crooked and his shirt untucked. Furiously, the sheriff reaches for my arm only to have Hattie's hand intercept him.

The stone-cold stare of this little feisty lady meets the sheriff's eyes with determination. "Time for you to go, Sheriff."

The sweating, red-faced sheriff puffs his chest toward her. "You can't make an officer of the law leave, Miss Hattie."

Hattie motions her arm toward the exit. "Goodbye, Fry."

The crowd responds wildly in support of Hattie. The chants begin at once, "Goodbye Fry. Goodbye Fry!"

I can see the sheriff's mouth moving as he waves his arms furiously, but the chants drown out any chance of him being heard. The crowd is so deafening that Marcus even comes from the kitchen to see what the ruckus is all about. Marcus pushes his way through the crowd and speaks directly into the sheriff's ear. The sheriff looks around at the onlookers and quickly rushes toward the exit, followed by the crowd roaring in unison, "Goodbye Fry."

One more loud cheer from the group as Rohan and Hattie join Tess and I on the dance floor. We switch partners for the last part of the song and the chants of "Hurricane Hattie" drown out the music. Finally, we make our way from the raucous party to the kitchen to thank Marcus and Hattie who had followed behind.

Curious, I ask Marcus what he said to the sheriff. Marcus says he simply shared that he had seen prison riots start over circumstances less serious than this and reminded the sheriff that this crowd loves Hattie. Marcus lets out a rare laugh and the rest of us join him as we talk of how fast the sheriff waddled toward the exit.

Marcus winks at Hattie. "We won't let anyone mess with Miss Hattie."

Hattie thanks Marcus, apologizes to us about the interruption and adds, "That sheriff doesn't have the sense of a chicken."

I kiss Tess as I rev up the engine on old red. "You look so sexy tonight."

Tess gives me her usual reply when I can't shut up about her beauty. "You make me sexy."

"That is crazy! I don't make you sexy, you just are sexy." A smile creeps across my face. "Seeing you across a room like that tears me up."

"Really?" Her sarcasm is apparent; I have only told her that about a million times over the years.

Her hair blows in all directions as I pick up speed. The black dress rises up her thighs and her pretty arms flex as she fights the hair from her face and her beautiful cleavage calls my name. "You aren't hungry now, right?"

Tess's baby blues look at my hand on the steering wheel and her dimples appear, "Oh, I'm hungry all right."

I drive a little faster, hoping that the sheriff isn't waiting for us on the road home.

50

TESS

I SET UP MY MAT next to the pool for some morning yoga. Jack is usually happy to join in, but this morning he said he needed a run since we have been eating more than normal while on vacation. It's such a peaceful day, and the stretching feels great on my muscles. I am relaxed in corpse pose at the end of my session when I hear a catcall whistle. My eyes squint open against the blue sky and I don't even want to look to see who is disturbing my tranquility.

A shadow blocks the sunlight, and it takes a second for my eyes to adjust. The first thing I notice are long, beautiful brown legs leading up to a short skirt, which I am positioned to see right up. I let out a happy scream, "Hi, Gabriella!"

"Hello, sexy lady." Gabriella offers a hand to help me up.

I can't hold back a smile. "I thought I had fallen asleep during my corpse pose and was dreaming of your sexy legs."

Gabriella laughs. "You are so sweet . . . but a little crazy."

"Just a little? Want something to drink?"

"No thank you, baby. I went for a short walk and was thinking how much I missed you so I thought I would pop over for a sec."

"I'm so glad you did. I wish you could stay for a while."

Gabriella shares a sad face. "I wish I could, but I just have a few minutes. Devin wants to drive inland to shop. You know we can't turn men loose with shopping on their own."

I laugh. "That's for sure. I'm so glad you came over. I miss you too."

"Let's have another fun night soon."

I feel my cheeks flush. "I would love to." I still can't believe I did that, and I still have trouble talking about it.

We chat for a few more minutes before Gabriella rises from her chair. "I will call you soon." Then Gabriella surprises me again as she leans in and gives me a long sexy kiss with her hand nestled into the back of my hair. Followed by a love tap on my butt. Then another deep kiss with her hands clutching my hips.

I am so flustered that I can barely get out a goodbye. But I liked it.

I am rolling up my mat when I hear the gate open. My sweet hubby is back from his run and I thank him again for being my protector last night on the dance floor. Jack says he ran into Emma on the beach and asked her to join us at the baseball game tomorrow. He thinks it may be easier for her to make her first public appearance after the attack with everybody in one setting instead of having to face one person at a time and be forced to answer the same questions repeatedly. Jack adds that it would be good for us to be there to support her. Emma said yes, so she must have agreed that it was a good idea, or she was just trying to appease us. Either way we are glad she is getting out of the house and it will hopefully help her get back to normal in some way.

I feel apprehensive about going to a game when an innocent person is locked up and I need to break the news to Jack that I have another detective mission for us this afternoon. Jack really wants to relax alone with each other, so I am going to need to find some good motivation to sell him on my idea.

We go back to the house to clean up and have a snack. Jack is gathering up our stuff to relax at the pool the rest of the afternoon, so when I return from my shower wearing a short leopard dress and heels, he almost drops the plate of finger sandwiches he had just sweetly made.

"Why are you dressed up, baby?"

I spin around to model the dress. "Do you like it?"

"Oh, my goodness, you look amazing! But what is going on that I don't know about?"

I plant a sweet kiss on his cheek and rub my leg up the front of his body. The plate of sandwiches begins to slip from his hand and I barely save it from crashing to the floor. "I have something I want to do with the case."

"Oh baby, I thought we were going to relax at home today."

I smile. "I will make it worth your while with a special treat." I follow with a little wink.

"That's not fair. You know that I can't tell you no, treat or no treat." He quickly adds with a smile, "But I will take the treat option."

I tell Jack to drive ole red to the dead end before going into town. On the way, I place my high heel on the dash, making my dress ride high up my thighs and slowly rub lotion onto each leg. I gently remind him to please not wreck the rental. As we near the end of the island, I lean over and squeeze the front of his shorts firmly, whisper into his ear how sexy I think he is, and that I want to show him how badly I want him. I feel the bumps of the tires go off the road momentarily.

By the time Jack parks at the private dead end I have his shorts unfastened and all his yearning in my hand. I lean across the seat and lay my head in his lap, looking up into his anxious eyes. He is pulsating against my cheek. Jack slides the seat back, and my tongue tastes his desire, already wet from anticipation.

I brush the thick hair back behind my ear as I enthusiastically move my lips to engulf my man. I know that he loves to see my cheeks and lips when I am sharing the deepest of intimate moments with him. My short dress has slipped upward, and I feel Jack rest his hand on my exposed backside. My lady region is warming as I vigorously share my passion and desire for my husband.

I can feel the muscles in his legs tense as I quicken the pace. I tighten my lips around his smooth, hard shaft and enjoy the sensation of his pulsing excitement. His length presses against the inside of my cheek then glides deeper into my throat. I am so aroused by his obvious joy, and I move my body to have easier access to swallow as much of him as I can. My knees are bent in the passenger seat. I can feel the breeze flow across my exposed butt stuck straight up in the air.

My head bobs at a more feverish pace. I barely notice Jack's hand gently pulling my hair back from my face as the wet messiness of our passion oozes from my mouth and runs down my chin. Slurping sounds fill the air. I don't care. I am lost in the moment of joy. Nothing matters but pleasing Jack. I love the way he fills me. I want my man and all his lust for me. He eagerly obliges my wish, and I take all his salty love I can.

The remainder drizzles down his beautiful penis and over my hand resting on his smoothly shaved skin. I slide my tongue over the full length of him again. I savor his taste and the closeness we have with this special lovemaking . . . and I can't let any get on his shorts and deter our upcoming mission. I was not thinking of that until afterwards. I raise to meet his eyes and wipe the remainder of his sticky happiness from my chin. Jack sweetly cleans more from my cheek as I press my lips tightly against his.

"Would you want that again, baby?" I smile at my handsome husband. His flushed cheeks are so darn cute.

Jack's sweet, loving smile tells me that he loved his special treat, and that he loves me. I kiss him deeply again before sitting back in my seat and wrangling my dress back down. His eyes tell me of his appreciation for me.

Jack reaches over and wipes my cheek again. "You are the most amazing woman in the whole world. I will take you wherever you want to go."

We drive into town and park several parking spots from Sandy Toes and put the top up to be less visible as we sit and wait. I feel Jack's eyes on me and remind him that we are now working. He can't help himself though. Marcus exits the restaurant and walks in our direction. We expect him to stop at Food for Thought to buy groceries to deliver to his mother but instead he turns to enter the bookstore. Shortly after, he reappears and surprises us by walking directly toward where we are parked.

Marcus is moving right at us with a tote in hand. Jack and I are getting nervous that he has spotted us or somehow knows that we are watching him. Closer and closer, looking in our direction. I panic and yell, "Duck!" without thinking that there is only so much room for a person to get down inside the front seat of a vehicle. Both my and Jack's heads go down quickly toward the middle of the seat. *Thud!* Our foreheads collide and I temporarily see stars. Instant headache.

To make things worse, as we lie side by side with our throbbing heads, we both get tickled about the plight we find ourselves in. We can't stop the laughter from coming. It is like when you are in school and know that you should be quiet while the teacher is talking, but you just can't. And once you start laughing, you just can't stop. Our first official stakeout has been reduced to our heads laying together on the front seat, laughing like little kids. Then comes the wrap of knuckles on the passenger window.

At least the uncontrollable laughter stops as I rise with dread from the seat to face an angry Marcus. For the first time ever, I am thankful to see Sheriff Fry. Well, sort of. I roll down the window and try to smile away the throbbing in my head as he leans down to look inside the car. "Everything okay here?"

"Yes, yes, we are all good here," I say as I try to maneuver my hair to cover what surely must be a knot on my head.

He grunts. "You guys are acting a little strange."

I assure him that everything is good. "We were trying to find my hair clip that fell on the floorboard."

The sheriff's eyes study me intently, which is not unusual for him. "Isn't that your hair clip on the back of your head?"

Well crap. "Uh, yes, yes, it is but that isn't the one I dropped. A girl needs a backup clip, sheriff. Just like you need backup tools on your belt." Which is uncomfortably right in my sight line now as the sheriff raises up to stretch his back.

He stretches his back further as he lets out a thinking hum, leaving his belly among other things filling my window view. I struggle to fight back another laughing spell when Jack gives me big eyes. Finally, the sheriff leans his head back down to the window. "People in this town can't protect you two forever. I am going to keep a watch on you." He points two fingers toward his eyes and then back toward Jack and me. "And I am gonna get those pictures soon."

I don't doubt that he will be watching me as he has since that first time he peeked through the planks of the outdoor shower when he was a teenager. He walks away, giving us the "I'm watching you" sign one more time.

We look around just in time to see Marcus exit Cody's loft with empty hands and we wonder why he would be visiting him. Then we see Billy coming down the sidewalk and the two men stop face to face. There is what seems to be a heated exchange before Billy turns to head back from the direction he had come. Jack and I share a puzzled look.

Marcus enters his car and begins to drive. We keep plenty of distance behind Marcus's, car not sure if he had spotted us downtown and we are aware of the fact that this car is easily identifiable. We know that Marcus will be going to his mother's house so there is no need to take a chance of being spotted. By the time we arrive at Marcus's mothers house, he is putting her trash into the back of his car. As we drive past her house and turn at the next road, I see Marcus's mother give him a big hug that she is still holding on to as we drive out of sight.

Victoria had texted us a small bit of information on Linda's pool guy Javier, and I talk Jack into driving by his house just a little further down on this end of the island before going back home. This part of the island is not as nice as the fancy rentals on the other side of town. This area has more affordable and smaller houses where many of the workers live, but still beachfront.

Many of the homes do not have house numbers, causing us to miss Javier's place on the first drive-by. As we circle back to find the right house, Jack and I are surprised to see Billy parking in Javier's driveway. I state the obvious, "This isn't good."

Jack concurs, "Definitely not."

I know Jack doesn't want to hear the next part. "We have to get a closer look to see what's going on in there."

"I don't know, baby. That could be dangerous. We know Billy is bad and we don't have much information on Javier." Jack looks worried as he turns at the end of the road to make another pass.

"Please baby, we have to find out who did this to Emma." I reach for Jack's arm. "And what if it was Javier who broke into the house?"

I see that Jack is still contemplating, so I shamelessly go with what I know will work. "There may be more surprise treats for you."

Jack pulls into a public beach parking lot a couple of blocks away and hesitantly puts the car in park. "Only if you agree to call this off immediately whenever I feel it has become too dangerous. I want to protect you."

A big smile crosses my face. "Agreed. Thank you, baby. Let's go investigate!" I giggle under my breath knowing that the treat would work.

51

JACK

TESS AND I TALK THROUGH our plan, deciding to approach the back of the house from the beach. There is enough natural landscape growth to give us some privacy at the back of the house. The next problem is that we are not dressed appropriately to blend in with others at the beach on this hot day, so I take off my shirt and decide that my casual shorts will work good enough as a swimsuit to not draw any unwanted attention from this busier section of the beach. I double-check for any remaining signs from our earlier dalliance in the car. All clear. Even in the heat of the day, I get chills from the thought of how amazing Tess was earlier. Focus, Jack.

Tess's outfit is a different challenge. That sexy leopard dress is much too fancy to be on the beach, especially in this area. Tess is known to have just about anything that you could need in her car back home, but we don't have many extra items in the rental car.

Tess screams out, "Oh, wait!" She leans over the back seat, and I can't help but touch her sexy butt that is stuck straight up in the air while she reaches further into the back floor. She flinches as my hand runs up between her legs. "Yes!"

I continue to rub her. “Glad you like it.”

She pops back down to her seat and proudly holds up one of her cover-ups. “I thought I left this in the car when we took photos the other day. And yes, I did like that.”

I look at her quizzically. “You are going to wear that over your dress?”

“Of course not! Instead of my dress. Over my bra and panties. They look enough like a swimsuit.” Tess pulls up the bottom of her dress to expose her black panties. “See.”

I enjoy the view and remind her that we are in a busy public place. “Hmm, I am not sure that will pass for a bathing suit. Looks like sexy panties to me.”

She pulls the dress back down. “I will have the cover-up on.” Tess holds it up again.

I smile. “Uh, it is partially see-through.”

Tess pulls the dress over her head. “It will be fine.”

Damn, she looks so sexy sitting in the front seat of the car in only her underwear that I can’t get my eyes off her long enough to make sure that no one is approaching in the parking lot. Her changing right there in a busy area makes me nervous, though I should be used to it as she has lifted her shirt more than once to remove her bra during our travels, even a few times while waiting in a drive-through. Tess always says boobs are nothing but globs of fat and no big deal, but she is much shyer than she acts. At least most of the time. But then again, there have been a lot of changes in her actions this trip.

We walk the couple of blocks on the crowded beach before reaching the back of Javier’s house. I am not sure what our plan is and the only things I brought with me are my phone and the car keys. I can’t stop checking Tess out knowing that it is her panties and bra I am seeing through the cover-up. Once we identify the correct house we step through the overgrown brush between the house and the beach. The path has obviously not been used very often which is unusual for the houses in the area, and we have to stoop under the overhanging brush and slide through a small opening to enter the backyard.

It’s not a large area and we are close enough to the house to hear voices but not make out what they are saying. We walk casually and close to the shrubs at the side of the house and decide if we are seen, our excuse will be taking a shortcut to the road to find our car. I am more nervous with each step, knowing that Billy and I are not exactly best buds, and we have some unfinished business from the bar.

The voices seem to be coming from a room at the back of the house. The blinds are closed but the window is open, so we duck down and quickly make our way up against the house and settle directly under the window. We hear who we think is Javier say, "I'm not going back."

Tess and I mouth silently in agreement that it is Billy, who responds, "You didn't get what we needed, so you have to go back man!"

The two continue to argue for a few more minutes, and I motion to Tess that we need to leave. Tess raises a finger, asking for just a little more time. She tries to shift her weight to her other leg, but her foot gets caught on the bottom of her cover-up and she loses her balance. She falls back slightly and bumps into an old foldout chair leaning against the house. The chair scrapes its way down the vinyl siding, landing on the sandy grass. Tess and I flatten ourselves as much as possible as we hear the rattling of the blinds just above our heads. We hold our breath and try to remain perfectly still.

Billy yells angrily, "Is anyone else here?"

Javier replies, "Nobody is here man, probably a dog."

Billy responds with the words we didn't want to hear, "I'm going to check around the house. You need to learn that you can't be too careful in this business."

My heart is thumping. I must keep Tess safe. I whisper to her, "Let's make a run for it." She reminds me both that Billy and Javier know what we look like and will easily identify us even if we are running away. My mind is racing. I can't think of anything reasonable, and we are quickly running out of time, so I speak with urgency while still trying to keep my voice as low as possible. "Let's cover our heads and run!" We can only hope that they don't see our face or Tess's silver hair, and that we are far enough away from them that they may not recognize us.

Tess looks at me confused. "Cover our heads with what?"

I survey Tess with only the cover-up and her panties and bra, then myself with just shorts and underwear. I can't think of anything else. I hear the screen door slam at the front of the house. We are out of time. I slide my shorts off and wrap them around my head and uncomfortably shove my phone and the car keys in the top of my underwear. I notice that I do have remnants from the special treat that Tess gave me in the car earlier. Happiness. Tess follows by quickly tightening the knot in her hair, removing her cover, and wrapping it all around her head and part of her face.

We hear Billy's footsteps as he approaches from the side of the house. He is getting close. Too close! Tess and I take off running. Fast as we can. Well, as fast as she can. I stay behind her just in case Billy catches up to us. We swerve to the left to stay out of Billy's sight line as long as possible and it takes him a couple of seconds to yell, "Hey! Get back here!"

Tess and I continue running, and I can hear by the heavy breaths of Billy's next words that he is now in pursuit. I am happy that Billy is more into his partying than exercising. We have a decent head start and try to keep our pace while squeezing through the hole and under the overhanging brush leading out of the yard. Tess and I both take a bump to the head as we go through the tight opening and make our way toward the crowd. Unfortunately my shorts, or my head cover, stick to the hanging limbs and I am now running down the beach in just my underwear. Tess's cover-up must have been loosened by the same bump to the head and flies off her head in a gust of wind. Now we are both inappropriate in a large group of people just trying to enjoy their day at the beach.

By the time Billy gets to the opening in the landscape, Tess and I have made it to the edge of the water and mingle in with hundreds of others. We slow to a walk to keep from standing out and with a quick glance back, I can see Billy standing at the edge of the shrubs. His head is feverishly scanning left and right as he holds one hand to shade his eyes while the other holds my shorts. The shorts that I was wearing while having such a wonderful time not too long ago.

Then I notice the reason for such a big group of people. Big Kahuna is doing tricks on his surfboard and the islanders turn out to watch when he brings his talents to this area of the beach. Tess and I are out of breath, partly from the running but mostly from the adrenaline of almost being caught, and we are not safe yet. We stop in the middle of the crowd to act like we are watching the show, and hopefully stay hidden from Billy. It seems the safer bet right now because if we break out from the crowd, Billy, with Javier now beside him, will definitely spot us.

There we stand amongst hundreds of beach-goers in our underwear. All ages of people are there to watch Big Kahuna. Since the only clothes Tess has left on are so skimpy, I hold her close as we start to weave our way through the crowd, trying to get back to the car. Then I hear Billy arguing with someone not far behind us. I tackle Tess in the edge of the water and begin making out with her, hoping that Billy will only be looking for someone running away.

Thankfully it works. Billy jogs right past us, irritating everyone he runs into along the way. I hold Tess close and we laugh at our skills at dodging the big oaf of a security manager. I kiss Tess again, and we lay still in our embrace while trying to determine when Billy is far enough away to resume our trek to the car. We are just about ready to get up and make our final getaway when the unthinkable occurs.

I guess it was bound to happen; someone had been offended by two older people making out in a lack of swimwear, or lack of clothes in general, and called the police.

We hear him before we see him. "Step aside, step aside. I have this under control." Sheriff Fry appears before us once again.

52

TESS

HANDCUFFED IN THE BACK OF Sheriff Fry's official police SUV . . . in our underwear. Jack and I managed to avoid another confrontation with Billy, but not with the sheriff. The last several minutes have been a blur, but I do vividly recall the sheriff putting his hands on my hips to spin me around to apply the cuffs. The next thing I knew, Sheriff Fry was rolling in the edge of the ocean like a beached whale, fighting desperately to get to his feet.

I had just barely managed to grab Jack before he pounced on top of the sheriff. I was able to calm Jack enough to not go full crazy on the guy who has irritated him for years. But the damage was done, and assaulting an officer will be added to the indecent exposure charges. The sheriff's fear seemed to show by the extra wetness on the front of his pants.

Jack had finally allowed the sheriff to cuff him, but only after the sheriff agreed to let Jack place the cuffs on me. And only after assuring the sheriff that he would finish what he started if the sheriff laid a finger on me again, even with his hands cuffed. I don't think the sheriff had any doubts about the validity of Jack's statement. Jack finally placed the cuffs on me, though not with the same gleam in his eye as when he places the restraints on me during our play time.

My zeal to be a detective is what landed us in this mess. In the back of Fry's SUV in our underwear. I have caused Jack to almost get in a bar fight and now to have an assault charge. He has never been in any kind of trouble his entire life. I have failed Emma by not getting her justice. Failed Lucca by leaving an innocent man in jail. At least I am almost positive that he is innocent. And Devin, he went to bat for me to solve the case. And Jack, most of all Jack. He went along with everything just to support me. All these thoughts race through my mind at a furious pace.

And I had gotten sidetracked from the real reason that we came on vacation to begin with: to help Jack get better. He is better, but at what cost? Did it make him happy, or did I do most of this out of selfishness? Have I damaged our relationship permanently? I should have stood on my initial feelings to NOT do anything the doctor advised. To not chase fantasies. To not change anything. To not take any chances. I have never liked taking risks. What would it be like when we got back home? If we ever get out of jail.

And I let the irritating sheriff win! What was I thinking. I am not a detective. I should have just focused on Jack and helping him get better all by myself. Tears begin to fight their way out. Tears will hurt Jack even more. It destroys him when I am sad or upset. He tells me that he would rather I get angry and exercise or punch something to get my feelings out. That's why he hung a punching bag in our gym years ago. My hands are cuffed, and we don't need another assault charge, or I would gladly punch the sheriff right now.

I begin to sniffle to try and pull the tears back in, but I am losing that battle too. The tears start to flow until it's a full-on cry, which is very unusual for me. Jack looks at me with a stoic face, I know that he must be silently agreeing with my thoughts that I haven't even turned into words yet.

He leans over to me as much as possible while strapped into the seat. "Look on the bright side baby, at least the sheriff is not in his underwear." Jack makes a face as if he had just eaten something terribly sour. "I mean, can you just imagine him rolling around the sand in his whitey tighties."

Jack busts out laughing . . . and I do too, even though it's through tears. His ability to make me laugh is one of the first reasons that I fell in love with Jack. Sheriff Fry looks in the rearview mirror. "Shut up back there!" His eyes remain on my breasts long enough that I am sure we are going to wreck.

Surprisingly, we make it safely to the police station, and even though his uniform is wet, the sheriff is beaming with pride as he opens the back door of the SUV to show us off like his prized catch at the annual fishing tournament. I am afraid that the sheriff may say or do or touch something that will still cause Jack to go after him. I know that the earlier joking was for my sake, and that Jack is still seething inside.

The sheriff unbuckles me after lingering too long, acting as if he couldn't get the seatbelt unclipped until Jack leaned over within inches from his face. The sheriff tells me to stand at the end of the car while he lets Jack out. He is enjoying taking his time to cause as much embarrassment as possible, leaving us standing outside, almost nude. He even pauses to wave at a passerby. Finally, the sheriff leads us into the small jailhouse to process the paperwork. The air conditioner is running full blast in the sheriff's office, and we can hear prisoners talking beyond the door of the room we are in. Jack asks the sheriff to give me a cover-up, which Sheriff Fry quickly declines.

Jack stands, and I urge him to please not do anything, that I will be fine. The sheriff places his hand on the club strapped to his side. Jack tells him if he pulls it out that he will always be known as the man beaten with his own stick by a prisoner in cuffs. The sheriff ponders that for a brief moment before his hand shakingly lets go of the club. I see it as more of my own failure. Jack never acts like this; he is always calm and reasonable, a peacekeeper.

The sheriff finishes his paperwork and leads us through the door, down the short hallway to the last of four cells. The other three are occupied, including one with Lucca. The cell beside me and Jack is occupied by a young person who, by the sound of his rambling, is only recently admitted for intoxication. The other cell across the hall from us is an older man who is sitting quietly. He just keeps staring into our cell after the sheriff removes our cuffs, locks the door, and exits. Jack places me behind him to block the strange man's view which causes him to mumble something I am thankful I can't make out.

Lucca calls out, "What in the world are you guys in for?"

Jack answers curtly. "Trying to get you out."

I can hear the distress in Lucca's voice. "I'm so sorry to both of you. Did the sheriff take your clothes?"

Jack is in no mood to talk. "Don't want to talk about it Lucca."

Lucca pauses, then calls out one more time. "Here, take this." He carefully aims and flips his shirt to the front of our cell.

The weird guy mumbles something else and Lucca yells for him to shut up. Jack reaches through the bars, retrieves the shirt, and hands it to me. I call out a thank you to Lucca.

Jack and I cuddle together on the bench, him still blocking the man's view. I start the whole process over again in my mind of how I have messed everything up. I just want to get out of here, go back home, back to our ordinary days. I don't care about being a detective and I don't want anyone but Jack. The tears come again.

53

JACK

I AM SO UPSET WITH myself for letting us get into this situation. I did not protect Tess in her detective endeavor or in our marriage. I am a failure.

An argument interrupts my pity party. We hear loud voices coming from the office on the other side of the door. One is Sheriff Fry, but I am not sure who he is arguing with. The young sheriff, who suddenly appears more like little Freddie from the Peeping Tom incident years ago, nervously follows behind the older balding gentleman, leading the way through the door. "They are prisoners, indecent exposure and he," pointing to me, "assaulted me."

Retired Sheriff Fry, or Frank, or Freddie's dad, grabs the keys from Freddie and opens the door. "Good grief, boy! Go get two blankets right now." Young Sheriff Fry drops his head and slowly walks back down the hall.

I didn't know old Frank well, but I remember helping him board up windows before the bad storm years ago. Frank opens the door. "I have been trying to let that boy figure things out on his own, but I swear I am not sure if he is ever going to grow up. I am sorry to you good folks. Freddie will be dismissing all charges."

Young Sheriff Fry returns with the blankets and starts to respond but Frank cuts him off with a wave of his hand. "You need to learn who is really trying to help you and who is using you for their own benefit."

As we walk down the hall Tess stops to hand Lucca his shirt back with a sweet smile and thanks him again. Tess and I glance at one another quizzically about that comment, but right now we are just appreciative to have been saved by Frank. He offers to drive us by our house to get some clothes then back to our car. Again, we express our gratitude.

On the way to the house Frank explains that Freddie is a good boy, but he is struggling to follow in the footsteps of Frank and his grandfather, who was also the town sheriff. He says that Freddie thinks he needs to solve a big case to earn the town's respect even though he has been told that it is the small things that earn trust and respect. And that he has told Freddie that he must make his own path, and not worry about what everyone thinks of every little thing he does.

It seems that advice keeps being repeated on this trip . . . and it is most definitely a good rule to live by.

Frank drops us back at old red and I have one last question for him. "How did you know that we were arrested?"

Frank smiles. "I was sheriff in this town for a long time, fortunate enough to help a lot of people and build many special friendships. I still have many people that let me know anything that is happening in town, especially with Freddie." Frank taps his fingers on the steering wheel. "And honestly, you guys have made a lot of good friendships here, too. The people of this town have always seemed to watch out for one another."

We thank Frank again for all he did for us and start to exit his car when he says, "One more thing. Don't give up on searching for the real attacker. But be careful, that is a known drug house that you were sneaking around. Bunch of bad guys in there."

I am too surprised by the comment to get any words out, so I just nod and thank him again. I was still thinking that Tess's short-lived detective career needed to end.

Frank follows with, "It's never wrong to try to help an innocent person, especially a good friend."

I know he is right about that, but how can I let Tess continue with all the danger I have let her be in already?

I agree and close the door with another thank you. Frank rolls the window down. "And if you can find it in your heart, try to give Freddie another chance. He really isn't a bad guy; he's just trying to find his way in this world. He lost his mom when he was a teenager, and has struggled to find his way ever since. I am trying to teach him that it isn't only about rules, and that sometimes people are not who they seem to be, so investigate everything diligently. And most of all, don't make decisions on what you think people will think."

More familiar advice from a wise, experienced person.

Tess and I talk about how you never know what kind of challenges people are facing that may affect the way they act as we lower the top on ole red and let the wind blow in our faces on the way home.

Neither of us feel like a big dinner, so we make popcorn with plenty of butter and pour in peanut M&M's, and cuddle up on the couch for a movie. We watch silently through the first portion, both of our heads filled with thoughts of what we had been through and where we should go from here.

Finally, I interrupt the quiet. "Are you wanting to try new experiences without me?"

"What are you talking about?"

"I saw you and Gabriella at the pool today." The same image that was so thrilling to me nights before . . . at least after I recovered from the initial shock, had ripped my heart out this morning, thinking that Tess would rather pursue these new adventures without me.

"No way. Not at all. She just stopped by for a second, and you know how she is with rash surprise moves."

"It looked like you were enjoying it . . . and her."

"Oh, Jack, no. I mean yes, I do like her, and my time with her, but no, I do not want to have adventures without you . . . ever! You are and always will be the most important person in my life."

"I don't want to hold you back from your happiness Tess. I may have done that for too long. But I don't want to lose you either."

Jack, if they lined up all the forty-five-year-old men in the whole world, I would pick you every time."

"Baby, you do know that I am fifty years old, right?" Tess always uses a random number for that saying of hers. So much in fact that I wonder if she really has lost track of our true ages.

Tess laughs. "Whatever age they line up, I will choose you . . . again and again."

"Not a twenty-seven-year-old muscled surfer, that obviously likes curvy mature ladies?"

Tess squints her eyes. "You are about to get in trouble Mr. Walker."

"I love you, Tess. I just want you to be able to do and try new things you like and not hold you back. But not lose you either."

"Everything I try is going to be with you. And you are not getting rid of me. You are my heart walking around outside of my body. We are meant to be together forever."

I smile and thank my sweet wife. "Baby, I'm so sorry I didn't keep you safe."

Tess sits up from her relaxed position. "Are you serious? I am sorry for dragging you into all this nonsense."

I take Tess in my arms. "I am not sorry at all. You have done a great job trying to help people while trying to figure this out."

A tear forms in Tess's eye. "I haven't solved anything. I have just wasted a lot of our vacation and stole time away from me and you."

I gently wipe the tear from her cheek. "Oh baby, that's not true at all. Emma and Lucca don't have anyone else trying to find the truth and help them." I let a small laugh bubble out. "And I have had a great time with you in all our adventures. I mean, how else would I have seen you in a cowgirl outfit, or moving around the room in that sexy dress at Rohan's?"

Tess's lips part slightly to let a small smile peek out. "I love you, but you are just trying to make me feel better for getting us arrested."

I kiss her on the cheek. "Riding in the back of a police car almost naked was pretty darn sexy too. And handcuffed at that."

She lightly punches me on the shoulder. "You are a crazy man. Really, I am sorry for spending so much of our time on this when you needed me."

"Baby, I have not only had a blast doing all this with you, but I am so proud of you for taking this on. For chasing something that you want to do. Don't you dare be sorry for that."

Tess leans in for a long, loving hug. "I love you, Jack." While still holding me she says, "But all this other stuff we have done. Is it okay? Are you happy? Are we going to be okay?"

"My sweet Tess, I love you with all my heart. Of course, we are good and will continue to be good. I have loved everything, especially seeing your happiness and passion. That's all I have ever wanted for you."

Tess wipes her eyes again. "But we have always been so traditional with everything in our lives. Just me and you together."

I agree, "Yes, we have, and I have enjoyed every single second of it with you. I wouldn't change a thing, but if the next part of our journey breaks from 'normal,' that is just fine with me, as long as you are happy, and we are together."

Tess squeezes me tighter. "But I don't know if it's right or if it will mess up what we have had all these years."

I tell Tess that I can't breathe from the death grip of our hug, and she laughs but doesn't let go. I assure her that we will do everything possible to not let anything divide us. And that our love will remain strong, and nothing can ever separate us, that we need to pursue things that make us happy. And that we have not only made it through so much, but thrived when so many said that we wouldn't. I don't want to admit to her that I am still struggling a little with my own insecurities with our new adventures. I feel that I need to continue to work through this on my own while supporting Tess, so I don't hold her back from her happiness.

Tess lays on my shoulder as we finish our movie and popcorn. I listen to her breathe and I inhale the familiar and beautiful scent of my wonderful wife. I know that she will fall asleep if I let her sit still for too long, so I invite her to go lay under the stars.

54

JACK TESS

WE LAY ON THE DOUBLE lounger under the stars of the upper deck situated on the roof of the house. It is a beautiful cloudless evening, an almost-full moon, not too humid. The waves roll gently in before drifting back out. A sound that Tess and I have always enjoyed together. Our minds drift into the night sky above, away from any stress or worries. Holding one another tightly.

Jack and I have discarded our clothes in the privacy of the upper deck. Outside, being naked feels so freeing and intimate with my husband. My mind is empty of everything except Jack. No thoughts of health scares, of emotions from the past year; not even thoughts of the adventures of this vacation. Just alone with my hubby under the stars.

My hand softly follows the beautiful curves of Tess's body. I treasure the feel of her velvety soft skin. Her hand caresses my chest lovingly, knowingly. I love her touch. I cherish her plush lips melting into mine. Her familiar scent. The subtle curve of her lower back under my hand.

Jack's fingers glide smoothly through the strands of my silver hair, then downward. The touch of his beautiful hand caressing my skin causes my heart to flutter. Our bodies press together, my leg automatically wrapping over his hip, pulling him tighter. I can't get close enough. I feel his want for me. I ache for his love, his sensuality. His hand slides to the flesh of my backside and I push my hips tighter into his.

Side by side, holding onto the wonderful taste of her kiss. Tess's leg squeezes me closer, wrapping us together. Her sensuous love travels through my veins. My lips pass over her ear, pausing to whisper my undying love for her. My desire. My need.

Jack's warm breath sends chills across my body. My hand brushes over his shoulder and holds the tensing muscles of his arm. I lean my head slightly, offering more of the nape of my neck to his kisses. I need him. My husband, my lover, my best friend, my safety. My whole world.

Her wonderful and familiar scent envelopes me. It's the oxygen that gives me life. My lips glide across her ivory shoulder as my hand presses against the sexy muscles of her upper back, leaving no space between our bodies. Bound in devotion to my wonderful wife.

I must have my husband. I am going to have him because I know he wants to please me. He always wants to please me. My hand descends to his tight little butt, gripping and guiding him on top of me. The muscles in his shoulders and arms glisten under the light of the moon. He hovers over me. Handsome, strong, sexy. His smile, his happiness is all I want in life. The security of always having his love.

I'm lost in her blue eyes that sparkle like the stars. Her thick silver mane spreads beautifully across her perfect ivory skin. Our eyes meet in a loving embrace and hold. Plush lips part slightly as we become one together. Connected intimately.

I am filled with my husband's love and eagerness for me. His blue eyes screaming that I am all he wants, the only thing he needs. That he cannot live without me. Without my love. My legs raise, asking, no begging, for more of him. His soft lips attend to my lower calf. A slight smile crosses my face, knowing that he will think of this very moment when he sees my legs in the days ahead.

Our bodies move as one, knowingly, familiar. Tess's eyes look deeply into my soul, sharing her devotion for me. The intimacy intensifies, our fury increases; there is a rush of emotion. Warmth, a flame, a fire. Tess raises her beautiful strong legs, inviting me to continue kissing her calves. My lips move across the arch of her foot and across the bracelet on her ankle, finally clamping my lips to her lower leg. The taste of her skin is so wonderful.

I feel the increased rise and fall of my chest. Jack's hand grips my ankle. The other firmly at the back of my opposite knee. Holding me open for his pleasure. I feel Jack deeper and deeper inside. I love us being one together. I need all of him. My body rocks. Furious suction to my calf.

Breasts swaying fiercely, flowing to the movements of her body. Beads of sweat beginning to glisten across her heaving chest. Tess's legs lower and wrap tightly around my body, the force pulling me closer to her. Silver flows back as her head lifts to my chest, lips circle my nipples. Nibbles, then bites. Colored fingernails dig sharply into the flesh of my back.

I am so close. I know every detail of my husband. All his sensitive spots. I know how to tease him, every move of his body, every flex of his muscles tells me a story. I know just how to touch his body and where to kiss to give him the ultimate pleasure and happiness. Not just his sexy body, but his heart, his fears, his dreams. And he knows me the same way. We are made for each other.

Tess's intimate sounds whisper to me. Her every need, desire, and pleasure. I feel the slightest change in her movements, the tension of her muscles. She is beautiful, starlight twinkling across her sweaty body. Her kisses on my chest have taken away any control I thought I may have had. All that I am is hers. All hers.

Our bodies speak to one another in the most intimate of ways. Our hearts connected. Our thoughts. Every part of us. We come together as one. One body. One life. One soul. One happiness. One love. The breaking of the waves is louder, roaring through my insides. I give all my love and passion to my husband. It's all his.

We hold tightly to one another. As if the next breath of life depends upon it. The inner waves calm. The stars and the moon dim slightly. Bodies, hearts, souls pressed together. Breaths slow, eyes gently relax and close.

Our bodies entangled, we sleep naked under the stars all night.

55

JACK

THE EVENT IS AS BIG as advertised. The earlier postponement due to the storm on our first night here has not dampened the spirits or the enthusiasm of the sell-out crowd that has arrived. And the clouds have cleared for tonight's game.

The stands are full and the crowd is raucous as the Disco Duckbill mascot dances on the field in the team's bright yellow colors with black trim. Everyone in the home stands and many of the opposing fans are doing their best disco dances.

Tess and Emma look precious in their baseball caps, Tess with a ponytail poking out the back. Everyone is so happy to see Emma and her smile. She has received so many hugs, I lost count. There is a vintage car show out front, but Tess had discouraged me from entering ole red. Balloon-making clowns roam through the stands, and there are plenty of games for the kids and the adults. About any kind of food that you can think of is offered for sale. It is a circus atmosphere.

As the team expected to win, the Manatees clad in dark blue and silver are more serious as they take the field. They know there is more riding on tonight than just putting on a good show for the fans as baseball scouts are in attendance to see if any Manatee players are ready to move up to the big leagues. A great night for some of their players can mean the chance of a lifetime, including the local hero Robbie, Rob's nephew.

The game is competitive and Robbie, an outfielder wearing number thirty-three, already has two hits at the halfway point including a three-run homer. Tess and I scan the crowd between innings—well Tess scans the crowd during the entire game. This is a people-watching extravaganza for her. We are able to find almost everyone we know from town. Mr. and Mrs. Jones are sharing cotton candy which Tess thinks is too cute. It seems Tess has forgiven the preacher's wife for stealing her panties.

Mateo, who is a former minor league player and a huge baseball fan, is standing at the fence down the first base line. It takes us a few minutes to find Celest, head wrapped in a bright yellow scarf about ten rows up behind him and sitting with her mother. She is looking at a magazine and apparently does not share Mateo's love of baseball.

The fans that won a chance to participate as cheerleaders bring one of the biggest applauses of the night when they take the field to dance during the seventh inning break. We even see Cody laughing along during the exhibition. Victoria is her usual elegant self, dressed classy as always and sitting with a young lady that she is mentoring to be an instructor at the gym. Probably to take her place soon. Tess and I are saddened to think of Victoria finally considering retirement.

We even spot Frances from the bookstore and What's the Scoop has a mobile truck set up with people lined up for ice cream almost the entire game. We never see Ed, and I assume he let some of his young staff come to the game while he stayed back at the store. Devin is back from a short business trip and he and Gabriella are in the press box that has his company name, DEVGAB Tech, in bold letters across the top. His software is great for keeping stats for sports games.

Other than poor Lucca, Rohan and his crew are some of the few we know that are not present as they prepare for the large post-game party. Rohan never misses an opportunity to capitalize on events such as these. His advertisements are posted all over the stadium. Some with "Try our new spicy fish toes" written boldly across them. Sandy Toes will be packed after the game.

We find Billy pacing the edge of the outfield fence in his security manager jacket. We doubt that he is really working and guess that he instead is trying to show off for any girls that will look his way. Speaking of getting girls to look, Big Kahuna is strutting back and forth in front of the main bleachers . . . shirtless, of course.

The Ducks have a one-run lead with only two innings left. I am sitting on the edge of my seat, tense from the exciting game and Tess pokes me, saying she and Emma would like some nachos. Robbie hits his second home run, and the crowd is going wild as I pass the vendor stand. I get caught up in the excitement, and seeing Robbie's name and number on jerseys, hats, and jackets for sale makes purchasing a souvenir seem like a good idea at the time. We know Rob and Linda so well that if his nephew makes it to the big leauges, I would like to have something with Robbie's name on it to show that I was at the big game. The last hat sells to the guy in front of me and the only jersey left is an extra-large, so I am stuck with purchasing the most expensive souvenir. Tess looks at me curiously and shakes her head when I return in my Manatees jacket with the nachos, and is not impressed when I share that the salesman told me it was the first time they had sold merchandise with a player's name instead of just the team's name. I share that all this merchandise has just arrived in the last few weeks. Tess remains unimpressed. I assume it is partly because we have so much of our college clothing around the house as it is. I remind her that we use ours for recruiting players.

Robbie goes on to make the game-winning hit in the last inning, and even the Disco Duckbill fans cheer for the local kid. Young Robbie has made quite an impression on the scouts and media in attendance.

Uncle Rob meets him on the field to celebrate.

56

TESS

I UNTIE MY PONYTAIL AND let my hair down for Jack to enjoy on our drive back into town. I know Rohan must be pleased as we search several blocks to find a parking space around the restaurant. Emma laughs when I make Jack take that silly jacket off that doesn't match the rest of the nice outfit I assembled for him to change into after the game. We had only made it one block walking toward the restaurant when I realize I have forgotten my hair clip. I tell Jack and Emma there is no way I am walking into that crowd with my hair having been under a hat for several hours, then blowing in the car. I scurry back to the car and move everything around the seat to find my clip. I am fast-walking to catch up to Jack and Emma—and it hits me. "I've got it . . . I'VE GOT IT!" I begin to run.

I slow to a walk when I catch up with Jack and Emma. I picture my suspect board and think that I have discovered who the attacker is. However, there is enough doubt that I would rather wait to talk it through with Jack one more time first. But I don't have the luxury of time. Our vacation is ending soon, and this is my best chance to have everyone together at one place. I will be taking a huge chance if I go through with the plan that is coming together in my head, and we just got out of one big mess with my risk-taking. But Jack said that he was proud of me for trying to help Emma and Lucca. He encouraged me to keep going. Jack and I have tried many new things on this trip, many of which have worked out quite well. Taking risks is what this trip is about. Risks and not worrying about what everyone else thinks. I'm ready to go for it.

We find Rohan and congratulate him on the great turnout. He is so excited that he hugs us both instead of just Jack. If I didn't have another agenda, I would tease Rohan about my first ever hug from him. I hold Rohan a moment longer and whisper into his ear. He meets me in the kitchen five minutes later for further instructions.

You can always count on Rohan. Another thirty minutes later and he has rounded up everyone I asked for and leads them to the "Hurricane Hattie" party room. I am fairly sure that he may have tricked them by saying a prize is involved based on the pieces of paper with a number in everyone's hands. But I don't care how he got them there. An elderly gentleman—a familiar friend—slips into the back of the room late and unnoticed by most everyone else. I try to prepare myself and gather my courage. A courage that I would never have had if I had not stepped out of my comfort zone in so many areas these past two weeks.

Jack and Rohan take their place in front of the two doors on opposite ends of the room, putting on their best security faces. Jack has been a nervous wreck since I gave him a brief summary of my plan. I can see the concern on his face. I thank everyone for coming and boldly tell them we will be identifying Emma's attacker tonight. Something the old "take no chances" Tess would never have done. The smiles fade from the crowd and murmurs fill the room. Victoria stands by my side and requests that everyone have a seat. I believe the only reason no one leaves is less because of the security at the door and more because they are afraid of looking guilty. Billy defiantly refuses to sit but stops short of trying to leave.

I begin by pointing out that Preacher Jones is the only one who officially knew that Emma was expecting at the time of the assault. I add that her injuries follow a pattern of someone trying to hurt the baby. I continue to describe the beating in more detail. She had two hits to the head, causing a concussion, and several bruises to her arms and back trying to defend against the blows. And because of my hugs and from playing pickleball, I had discovered on my own that much of the damage was to her stomach and sides. The room falls silent as they hear the brutality of the attack. I remind everyone that Mr. Jones is the one that found her in the brush.

Mouths are open in disbelief as I continue, "But Preacher, we all know that you have spent most of your life helping others in need, and that you are a kind person incapable of an awful attack. I believe that you kept your word to Emma by not sharing her secret with anyone . . . not intentionally at least."

My attention turns to Mrs. Jones. I admit that she and I share a weakness of being a little nosey. I offer a smile to ease the insult I just hurled at such a nice lady, even though she did steal my panties. "I know that you didn't mean any harm, but you overheard some of the conversation between your husband and Emma while making your special latte. You shared what you heard with your garden club friends." I pause. "Isn't that correct, Mrs. Jones?" I hold firm in the uncomfortable silence that follows, an effective trait that Jack has taught me many times over the years.

Just when I think I might lose this silent standoff, Mrs. Jones breaks. The preacher's sweet wife admits that she had overheard pieces of the conversation, including Emma's condition and where she was staying. Another moment of silence followed by, "And yes, I did tell some of my closest friends but only so we could be ready to help when needed." I attempt to hide my relief. If I had gotten this part wrong, I wasn't sure the rest of the story would come together. I am shooting from the hip through much of this. Now it's safe to assume that word had gotten out to several others around town, which opened the suspect list.

Without looking toward anyone, I share that we know someone was giving money to Emma. Another gamble as I have not figured out what the story of the envelope from Mateo's box is and Emma has not mentioned it during any of our conversations. I tell the audience that mystery money could suggest there is a secret that could have spurred an attack on Emma. I let the room sit quietly again while everyone tries to sneak glances at each other to figure out who I am talking about.

Another long uncomfortable silence before Mateo finally blurts out, "I was only trying to help her. I know the difficulty of growing up poor and Emma is a good girl and a hard worker." He smacks his hand on the table as he continues, "I know the value of someone believing in you and everyone needs a little help." Mateo turns to Celest to apologize.

Celest stares back at him intently and we all hold our breath, waiting for that infamous temper to show itself. "Did you really believe that I didn't know about the money? I keep up with everything in our business Mateo."

Mateo looks shocked, scared, and relieved all in a matter of seconds.

Celest straightens her scarf and adds, "Emma IS a good girl, and I am proud of you for helping her. I made her stop working for us because I had heard that she was expecting." She glances toward Mrs. Jones. "I didn't want her loading those heavy boxes." Then with an intimidating scowl toward Mateo, "Don't you ever try to hide anything from me again."

Mateo hugs Celest tightly, undoubtedly happy that he survived his secret.

Now I turn my focus to Cody. I tell him I was so upset at him when I heard that he hurt Emma with his poor decisions. I share that when we came to visit and I saw the condition of the loft, I was ready to beat him myself.

I continue that my first thought when I saw his meeting with Marcus behind the restaurant was that it had to be a drug deal. I apologize to both for jumping to that conclusion. "Jack and I have family members that have struggled with addiction and sadly too often everyone's first thought is to assume that a recovering addict has fallen back into their old ways. Then I thought you had become aware of Emma's pregnancy when I saw the clinic papers. But I did not think they would share that information with you, and it didn't make sense that you would share that with Marcus.

So Jack and I followed Marcus." I look apologetically to Marcus. "I'm sorry for that, too." I explained how I saw how he blocked Billy from coming in the loft and how sweet he was to his mother, how he protected Hattie, and I am convinced that he has a good heart under the rough exterior. "Plus, Rohan would notice if anything was amiss with your job performance, and we all know how good the food is here, even the fish toes." That brings at least a little chuckle to the crowd.

"I thought about how Emma told us how bossy Marcus was with her and Cody, and how he talked to Cody about getting a better job to take care of Emma." I look back over to Cody. "So I believe that Cody was showing Marcus proof that he was staying clean, which made sense due to Marcus's past battle with those demons." Zooming in on the enhanced photo helped me see that the paper looked like a drug test. I let them know that, at first, I could not figure out the reason for the book delivery, but then it came to me when we were in the restaurant kitchen. With the business at Sandy Toes continuing to grow and Rohan wanting to cut back on work so he can spend more time with Hattie, Marcus is looking for an assistant. Cody needs a career change, so it is a perfect match.

Marcus and Cody look shocked, and Marcus claps. "You DO make a good detective, Mrs. Walker."

I smile at Jack and thank Marcus, thinking that is not too bad for an amateur, but there is still a long way to go. It appears from Emma's glance toward Cody that her heart softens a little as she hears that he had stayed clean and was looking for a new career.

I take a deep breath. "I know that you are thinking that all I have done is to confirm who didn't do it. But eliminating suspects is an important aspect of the investigative business."

Sheriff Fry clears his throat loudly and mumbles that he already has the attacker locked up. I ignore him and continue, "And this shows that none of these people had a reason to hurt Emma, much less her unborn child."

I look to the back of the room and lock my eyes on Billy. I am surprised that he has stayed in the room this long. "But you, Billy. You did have a reason to be angry with Emma." First, I speak of how Billy's jacket matches the one we saw in the picture as I flash a quick smile toward the sheriff. This causes a slight stir as not many people know about the photo shoot from that night. And I feel a little flushed as the words travel across my lips. But I continue and speak of how Billy needs help with his drug use. I say that I am convinced that he has a crush on Emma, that he has acted inappropriately to her, and that he is a bad influence on Cody. Billy's scowl grows, and he takes a couple of steps forward. Hattie tells him to take a seat, but he ignores her and starts toward the front of the room. Marcus steps in his path and without saying a word dares him to try and pass.

I nervously persist. "Billy is capable of anything with his drug use and bad temper. And I believe he is jealous of Cody, but I don't think he is capable of planning an attack like that. I believe he would just roar in and fight without any thought of the consequences." I pause for a brief moment as there are some snickers in the room. Several people seem to agree with that assessment of Billy and find the description humorous. I add. "I also can't believe that even Billy would set out to hurt an unborn child."

The information we learned about the drug house on the night of our arrest helped me to conclude that the conversation we heard between Billy and Javier was about a drug deal and nothing to do with the house break-in. I tell Cody that he can try to get Billy professional help but that he should cut ties with him if he continues the drug use and keeps making Emma uncomfortable. Marcus agrees emphatically.

Billy growls at Cody as he points toward Emma, "You let little miss goody tell you everything. You need to get tough and put her in her place."

Gasps fill the room. Cody stands and looks up at his much bigger cousin. "I love Emma!"

Billy laughs. "That little tease has made you a wimp."

Then the unexpected happens: little Cody rises from his chair, crosses the room quickly, draws his right arm back and swings with all his might, connecting squarely on the side of Billy's jaw knocking him backwards a few steps. A chorus of "oohs" lifts from the attendees and then a stunned silence.

I can see the steam coming from Billy's face once he gathers himself. He takes two large steps forward and towers over Cody while rubbing his cheek.

"You asked for it, now you're going to get it, little fool." Billy draws back and forcefully starts his big arm forward. Marcus's hand catches Billy's fist just short of Cody's chin. And for the second time I see the big brawny security guard taken to his knees. The sheriff cuffs Billy and makes him stand next to him at the door.

57

JACK

MY HEART IS THUMPING AS Tess works through her theories. I want to help her, protect her. I am confident that she can do this without me, but it is difficult for me not to intervene. I know she wants to do this herself. She needs to do it herself. But if she gets stuck or off track, I will be there for her in a heartbeat. I will happily take all the anger from the crowd. I will do anything for Tess.

But this trip has been all about Tess facing her fears, chasing her dreams, and embracing her desires. I must let her do this alone . . . unless she gives me the look.

It is killing me that I don't know for sure if she has the correct person identified as the attacker, but I trust her. If by chance she is wrong, then that will be okay too. We all get things wrong, do things wrong, say things wrong. It's okay. Life goes on.

Just like our other decisions of letting Lucca and Gabriella into our intimate lives these past two weeks. Tess making the right choice of who committed the assault is not the most important part, because everyone gets things wrong at times. What is important is that we make our choices together and with good intentions. And trust and support each other whatever those decisions are. That we remain committed to one another, no matter what happens. And we will change course together as one if necessary. Sticking together in Tess's reveal of the assailant, in our intimacy, and in our lives, whether our decisions prove to be right or wrong.

I am ready to go after Billy again, but I chuckle inwardly that I am getting dangerously close to getting a reputation for being a troublemaker after the incidents at the bar and with the sheriff on the beach. So, I hold myself back and let Marcus and Cody take care of that big oaf.

I know Tess will get through this and whether she gets the right person or not, I am so proud of her working so hard to solve the case and help Emma and Lucca. She did not let fear stop her from seeing this through and she has always had good instincts when it comes to identifying people's character. I am so proud of Tess's beautiful and kind heart. Her intelligence. Her care for me, our family, and other people. I am the luckiest man in the world.

I stand back and let my wonderful wife continue without getting in her way. I love her so much.

58

TESS

I LET THINGS SETTLE A moment, then make eye contact with Big Kahuna, but decide to not even address him. I am sure that he is not guilty, and I don't want to stir him into speaking. Big Kahuna is too interested in having fun to get involved in something violent. Letting him talk would most definitely get me sidetracked on the mission of revealing the attacker.

My eyes turn to Rob. "Rob, I hope you will accept my apologies in advance for some of the things I will be sharing in front of your friends and neighbors."

I take in another deep breath and begin to speak. "You and Linda have been trying to generate more income. Typically, your house would be booked every week of the peak season, but your business, like many others, has slowed, and Lucca mentioned that you have been laying off employees recently. And I think you may have priced yourself out of the market with the latest rent increase. That is why you practically begged us to stay two weeks this trip. Let's face it, your house is beautiful and offers so many extra benefits because Linda not only has great taste, but a desire for nice amenities, which makes your home such a nice rental. And Rob, you have a desire for those same nice things. Rolex watches, boats, fancy cars, and so on. I also think that trying to keep up with the new neighbors has been another financial burden for you. There is nothing wrong with any of that but with the instability of the economy your sales commission and rental income must have taken a dip also. Add in the survey mishap that lowered the value of your property and the delays with the remodel of the pool house and I believe finances have become tight. Then you and Linda decided not to rent out the pool house after investing that money and I'm sure that added even more stress."

The tension is palpable as I continue, "Lucca mentioned that he helped you get back home several times after a night of too much drinking."

Linda clears her throat as she glares toward Rob. "I told you not to talk to Lucca."

Rob's head remains down as I keep going. "Lucca would find you on the beach or on his deck and would try to keep you quiet to not wake Linda as he got you home."

An embarrassed Linda speaks again, "I don't know if you are trying to blame Rob, but he wasn't even in town the night Emma was beaten."

I feel bad for Linda and her comment causes me to take a deep breath before taking my next big swing. "Actually, Rob was in town that night. Robbie's big game was originally scheduled for the first night Jack and I came to town, but the storm caused it to be postponed until tonight. There was no way Rob was going to miss his nephew's big game and the prediction of the path of the storm was too uncertain for him to take a chance on not being in town."

A slightly more defiant Linda interrupts again, "You have no idea what you are talking about."

I continue, "We have witnesses that place Rob here the night of the attack." A slight smile pushes across my lips as I think of Jack's singing friends.

The rest of the room stays quiet as I continue, "Rob was indeed in town, staying at the It'll Do Motel just a little down the road from the bar."

Rob's worried look confirms that our information is correct. I let out a deep breath because if I missed that, the rest of my theory may not come together. Before this trip, before trying my hand at being a private investigator like I have always wanted to do, and before I learned to try new things, I would not have considered taking that chance. I am surprised that I enjoy the adrenaline rush of all this.

Linda huffs, "Congratulations, you know Rob has been running around like he always has, but that doesn't mean he hurt anyone."

More mumbling drifts throughout the room.

I flip my attention back to Rob. "Rob, you posted bail for Lucca, didn't you? Because you knew that he didn't do this to Emma."

Rob's eyes remain staring at the floor. "Yeah, I knew he didn't hurt Emma."

I hold up my phone to Rob, showing the picture I had taken at the pool house. "And this is your watch on the floor of the pool house bathroom, right?"

Rob nods his head in agreement.

Linda seethes as she shifts in her chair.

Emma's sweet voice speaks for the first time. "Nothing happened."

My stomach leaps. I think I may become sick right here in front of this room full of people I had assured we would be revealing the attacker tonight. She said nothing happened. Emma would not lie, would she?

How could I have gotten this wrong? Sweat forms on my forehead. My confidence fades to doubt. I know Rob was in town and I know that was his watch in the pool house. He had been drinking a lot and roaming around the grounds at night. Emma alone. He had to be the attacker. But why would Emma lie about that?

Figure it out, Tess. I feel everyone's eyes lock onto me. It feels as if the silence lasts forever, but the thoughts are rolling through my head so fast it has only been a moment. Come on, Tess, you can do this. You have put yourself out there . . . in so many ways. You have faced your deepest fears. You have leapt out of your comfort zone with no net to catch you. Don't fail now.

Jack's sweet baby blues meet my eyes and I can feel his encouragement, telling me I can do anything I put my mind to. That he is with me no matter what. My eyes leave the safety of my husband to dart desperately around the room and for some reason they stop at the familiar face in the back. He shares the slightest smile and puts his hand to his heart before glancing toward Jack.

Breathe Tess. Think. Slow down your thoughts. Deep breaths. What matters most, more than anything else in the entire world? Even if I don't get this right, Jack will still love me. Look at all we have been through together in our lives. All sorts of trials, family addiction, health issues, death. Look at the things we have tried that we never would have dreamed of during this trip. So far out of our comfort zone. Things I feared my whole adult life. Things that I never thought I wanted to happen. Things that could have destroyed us. But they didn't. And they won't.

But I knew the whole time deep within my heart that none of it would destroy us, whether it cured Jack or not. I knew that he would love me forever no matter what we did or did not try. I am so thankful for the kind of love and bond that we have together.

THAT'S IT! Love! Love and passion make you do crazy things. The breath I have been searching for finally returns. My eyes shift to Linda.

I stare confidently at Linda. "But you were in town too, Linda."

Linda becomes even more defiant. "That is ridiculous. I was staying with my sister-in-law."

"Were you? Because someone with a key entered the house the night of the storm. You left a little mud next to the washing machine and dropped a towel in the brush between the house and the pool apartment. Jack found a key under the washer. I found the towel . . ." My mind goes back to twigs sticking me in the butt. "Well, it doesn't matter how I found it. The towel hadn't been there too long because it wasn't faded. You took it the night of the attack with the intention of returning it to the house later and panicked when you lost it in the brush. So, you came back into the house to take out the rest of the set so it couldn't be matched if found later. Then a vision of Emma twirling her pool house key while watching the game tonight came to me and I gain even more confidence in this new theory. You didn't put the key back then because you thought you needed to put the golf club you used to attack Emma back into the storage room. At some point while waiting to return the key, you decided that you could pin this on Lucca."

My thoughts go back to when I grabbed my cover-up from the laundry room. That's why something seemed off to me as I was walking out of the laundry room. I have just now thought of what the intruder was doing in the house. I couldn't pinpoint the reason I had paused when grabbing the cover-up at the time, but I now realize it was because there was another key on the hook by the washer. I explain that Linda sent Javier into the house to put the key back in the laundry room when she became afraid that I was getting too close to solving the case. That's why Jack and I couldn't find anything missing. Javier didn't take anything, he just returned the key and almost got caught.

My eyes remain intently on Linda. "And you wore the Manatees jacket on the night of the beating before putting it on Lucca's deck. That and using his old golf club to hurt Emma helped you kill two birds with one stone. Beating Emma and having Lucca take the blame was too perfect. Isn't that right, Linda? And your cousin, Sheriff Fry, was all too happy to listen to whatever ideas you threw his way." I believe that is what Frank Fry meant when he said the sheriff was listening to the wrong people. Linda was manipulating the young sheriff into thinking that it had to be Lucca, and he fell for it.

An angry Linda replies, "I hope you and Jack enjoyed your last stay at our house."

"Oh, we certainly have, thank you." I smile at Jack. Then I look at the sheriff. "Where did you find the weapon, and in what interrogation did you discover the tip?"

The sheriff stalls to gather his thoughts. "An anonymous note was left on my car."

"And the weapon?"

He hangs his head. "I received an anonymous text telling me where to look behind Lucca's house." The sheriff paused. "Linda confirmed that it was Lucca's club." The sheriff hung his head, I assume from embarrassment that he had actually not done any work to solve the case.

I continue. "If we go to the pool house storage room I believe we will find the rest of the set of golf clubs that match the assault weapon and the rest of the towels that match the set Linda probably used to wipe her fingerprints from the club."

I look at Jack and smile. "That key is now hanging in the laundry room. My sweet husband worried so much about the leak and the key."

Linda screams out, "This is absurd, and no one is going in my house or the pool house!"

I politely remind her that the pool house belongs to Lucca, and I'm sure he will be happy to let us cut the lock off if needed. Uncomfortable silence. Linda holds strong as I push a little more. "The only thing I don't understand is why. I know that you have misplaced anger toward Lucca because of the survey but why Emma? Why would you hurt her or her baby?" As I wait patiently for Linda to reply the final piece of the story becomes clear to me, and I share the thought, "Because you aren't secure enough in your marriage." I think of how confident I am in my own marriage. "You thought that something was going on between Emma and Rob and you weren't sure that Rob wouldn't leave you."

Linda stares at Rob, then looks at me with her face turning red. "I wasn't going to let Rob have a baby with that slut and waste our money, or even worse—leave me alone after all these years."

Gasps fill the room. Rob tries to gather himself. "What are you talking about?"

Linda becomes slightly less defiant, maybe even a little sad looking. "Several nights I would come looking for you when you were out drinking. One night I saw you in the pool house with Emma through the window with the broken blinds. You didn't come home until the next morning. I knew her and Cody had broken up and we hadn't exactly been getting along lately. And you were drinking a lot."

Emma repeats, "Nothing happened Linda."

Linda glares at her. "I saw you two all over each other on the couch, you little tramp. Then I found out you were pregnant. The time frame matched you two being together in the pool house. Why does everyone think you are so sweet?"

Rob jumps back in. "I passed out on the couch and Emma stayed in the bedroom. I remember falling into her several times on the couch while telling her about my problems. She could have kicked me out but was kind enough to listen to my drunken complaining, and promised to never mention it to anyone."

That promise and Mateo's envelope were both promises Emma kept.

Rob adds, "I had no idea she was staying there until that night."

Cody crosses the room, sits by Emma, and takes her hand in his.

Linda is deflated as she looks around the room, then at Rob, then finally to Emma. "But I thought . . . I was sure." Her hands cover her face as she seems to finally understand that she had everything wrong about Emma and Rob. She had been angry for no reason, worried about what everyone else would think, and let her thoughts run away with her instead of talking about it with Rob. I have a moment of sympathy for her as I understand how easy it is to avoid talking about difficult things. Linda wipes tears from her cheeks as she looks at Rob, "I'm so sorry." A long silent pause before she looks to Emma. "I am truly sorry. What have I done?"

Murmurs fill the room.

Jack leans over to the sheriff. "And that's how a real detective does it."

As the sheriff leads Linda and Billy from the room and the air fills with whispers and mumbles, Sheriff Fry's father approaches me and extends a hand. "Great detective work, Mrs. Walker."

With all sincerity I respond, "Thank you so much . . . for everything. Especially the hand to the heart hint."

His hand still gripping mine, he says, "Maybe you can teach my boy a few things. He sure could use your help." A kind chuckle follows.

"Jack and I are going to follow your advice on giving extra understanding to all that Freddie is facing." We know as well as most that you never know what personal challenges people are fighting.

It was Frank's point to the heart followed by a glance toward Jack that had not only calmed my nerves but pointed me to a crime of passion. Only desperation could make someone hurt Emma or a baby. Without the same assurance that Jack and I share, Linda had snapped.

I am so thankful for Jack, for our marriage, for us.

59

JACK

TIRED FROM ALL THE EXCITEMENT the night before, Tess and I sleep late. Well, we are awake, but stay in bed for some affection and pillow talk. Sweet conversation of our lives together, the tears of challenges and the celebrations of joy. Exciting trips and ordinary days. The journey over the last year. The surprises of the last two weeks. I love the closeness of our talks, memories, and sharing of dreams. Tess's messy hair, her sleepy natural beauty when just waking, and her warm familiar scent. I hold her and caress her through every word. Her voice gravelly from just waking and all the talking from last night's reveal of the crime. She rubs her soft foot all over my legs. One of my favorite things. Finally, we decide to rise and face the world together, as we always do.

We agree to spend our last full day of vacation on the beach. Aside from a few small interruptions, we have our little corner of beach all to ourselves for most of the day. Tess looks so sexy in her skimpy leopard print bikini. Such a wonderful treat for our last day.

I keep making her repeat the story of how she figured it all out and exactly when. The Manatees jacket and the details the salesperson had told me when I bought it had clicked with Tess when she went back to the car to get her hair clip. She had seen the number thirty-three on the sleeve and the Manatee's logo which gave her more confidence that she was right. She thought Rob was guilty until she was in the middle of talking in the Hurricane Hattie room and the jealous woman theory had kicked in with a little help from Frank, and his gestures. I am so proud of her. Tess finally tells me to stop asking her to repeat the story and to quit bragging about her investigative skills and to stop telling her how awesome she is in the leopard print. But I can't.

Cody and Emma are the first to stop by to thank Tess for her help and kindness. Cody has come to help her load up her things to move back to the loft. They look very happy together, Emma's great smile is back in full force, and we are glad to hear that Cody has accepted an offer to be Marcus's assistant and apprentice at Sandy Toes. Many thanks, hugs, and a few happy tears are shared. Emma's short wavy hair ruffles in the ocean breeze as she and Cody bounce joyously hand in hand toward the pool house.

Lucca was released earlier this morning after the judge processed his paperwork. He sits with us for a while profusely thanking us for saving him not only from jail but from the depression he had been fighting. He knows it will be a continuing battle, but he is taking steps in the right direction by reopening his massage business in Victoria's gym. He pleads for us to let him know anything at all that we want or need so he can repay us. And of course, he banters a little with Tess about wild leopard print clothing and lotion for her skin.

Our third visitor is a bit of a surprise. Sheriff Fry shuffles through the sand to apologize for not listening to us earlier, among other things. Tess and I are convinced that Frank or Devin or both have forced him to do it. He tells us that all charges have been erased from Lucca's record and that Linda stayed in jail last night. Emma had come by early in the morning to drop the charges against her, so she has now been released, but the judge is going to make her do three-hundred hours of community service for other charges. He admits that Emma is a better person than most to be able to forgive Linda for what she has done. It is certainly a humbler version of the sheriff, but he still can't control his gawking. I find it difficult to hold that against him because I haven't been able to take my eyes off Tess all day. Tess and I have an empathy for him that surprises us. We laugh after he leaves that it is only a slight empathy, but we will work on being better about that.

After some cooling off in the water we receive our final visit of the day: Devin and Gabriella. I must admit that Gabriella is striking in her white string bikini and dark skin, and Devin looks even more fit and muscular without his shirt than I had noticed before.

As usual, we have a great time hanging out with them even if it is limited today. Gabriella and Tess are as mischievous as ever as they sit together, whispering and giggling. I wonder if they are going to invite us to a celebration for Tess solving the case. I am also curious as to what Tess will want to do. About an hour later, everyone hugs goodbye after they insist on letting Tess and I enjoy some private time.

I mention to Tess that I am surprised there had not been an invite to celebrate the success of her first—and hopefully last—detective case. Tess gives me one of her little smiles that means she has something to share. It makes sense that she and Gabriella would have set something up without needing to include me or Devin in the conversation.

I smile. "So what time are we going?"

Tess says innocently, "Going where?"

"Funny. To Devin and Gabriella's."

"Oh, we aren't invited to anything with them tonight."

I look at her curiously. "Why the smile then?"

"Gabriella told me the night that we were, um, together that I needed to experience the feeling of another woman. And she was so right." Tess's cheeks begin to color.

"Okay. And the smile?"

Her face glows a little brighter. "Today Gabriella said there were other experiences that I need to have just as much."

I look at Tess, confused.

Her cheeks now a bright red. "What would you think about inviting Lucca over tonight?"

I kiss her warm cheek. "I'm in if that makes you happy."

60

JACK TESS

LUCCA HAS BEEN AT THE house about an hour, and we have enjoyed our time together talking and laughing like we had so many times in the past with him and Martina. I am nervous and still questioning if I can go through with this. Obviously, Tess wants to try this new experience, but I don't even know how to transition if we are going to do it. Before, we had the massage that started like any other massage would . . . even though it ended quite differently. This is completely different, and we don't know what we are doing. But Lucca does.

Lucca looks at Tess. "Do you remember three, maybe four years ago when you and Martina were playing darts against me and Jack?"

Tess quickly replies, "We beat you with a bullseye on the last throw and you and Jack had to jump into the pool naked while Martina and I sat on the deck and enjoyed our margaritas."

"Yeah, that purely lucky bullseye you hit."

"Lucky? Whatever makes you feel better."

Lucca sits up in his chair. "I want a rematch. All three of us, on our own this time." He pauses with a mischievous smile. "With different stakes."

Tess giggles nervously. "I'll be happy to beat you guys again."

After some fun trash talk, a couple of drinks, and a few rounds of strip darts, Tess is still in a tank top and her panties while Lucca and I are left only in our briefs. My last dart lands just outside the bullseye to give me the win and cause Lucca and Tess to lose another article of clothing.

Tess smiles sheepishly and steps toward me. "Would you like the pleasure?"

We share a long kiss as my hands slowly lift her top past her stomach, across her breasts, and finally over her head. My hands automatically move to massage her chest as I taste her puffy lips again.

I feel Lucca's chest press against my back and his hands squeeze my backside as Jack kneels before me, softly drawing circles around my areolas with his tongue. I am glad for the gentle touch as I recall the soreness from our last dalliance. Jack then slides my panties down my waist, and I feel the silk material brush down my legs to my feet. I place a hand on his shoulder as he helps me step out of them. Lucca's warm breath flows across the back of my neck and drifts across my entire body like a settling fog. Have I always had this fantasy buried deep within me?

I rise to kiss the front of Tess's neck and my hands feel the chilled skin as they roam the curves of her hips and waist. Her chin lifts, inviting my kisses to the front of her neck. I see Lucca's kisses glide to her shoulders and his hands to her arms. Tess is tightly sandwiched between us. Her hand wanders across my body to below my waist and she grasps me through the only piece of clothing remaining on any of us. Tess's knees begin to bend, and she slides downward. I feel the increasing beat of my heart. She looks so beautiful and yet so vulnerable kneeling below us.

I lower to my knees and with one smooth motion discard the last of the material keeping me from Jack. I am so happy to see and to feel his excitement, and it is obvious that he is enjoying the extra firmness and aggression of my touch as I massage his desire with both hands. After a few moments, Lucca steps to my side, silently requesting the same attention. It jolts me as I realize this is the first time in over twenty-eight years that I have even seen, much less touched another man. I take a deep breath and slowly reach a hand for Lucca. I am a bit apprehensive as I feel his firmness for the first time, while my tongue traces the familiarity of my husband. Slowly up and down, then gently around the tip while gazing up into his eyes. I feel shivers traveling through his body.

Tess's bracelets jingle as the hand NOT touching me moves. My eyes deflect from her beautiful lips encircling me to the rings on her fingers that are gripping Lucca. I am about to lose my nerve. I wonder if I can continue, or if I am going to punch him. I can see that Tess is lost in the moment, and I try to save this image of her passion in my mind. She takes me deeper into her warm mouth, her lips pressed around me, bringing me so close, but knowing just when to ease up. Tess knows every detail of me intimately. She turns her attention to Lucca. With uncertainty I watch the traces of her tongue again, only this time it is not with me. Tess must sense that I need the affirmation of her devotion to me, and silently sends that message through a loving squeeze to my hand.

I take a deep breath to gain confidence as I am still a little bewildered to be this intimately close to another man. My breath escapes and my lips part as I lean in to take Lucca. I close my eyes, somehow thinking that will help me continue. The unfamiliar scent and texture of his skin is peculiar to me. My hand feels the muscles in his backside tighten as he slides between my lips. I am trembling with nervousness. He feels different inside, not bad not good, just different. I am not sure what I am thinking or if I should be thinking at all. I persist. I feel Lucca's knees begin to tremble as my motion becomes faster with the increasing movement of his hips. I can hear his moans and I feel my cheeks flush when occasional slurping noises escape. I know he doesn't want me to stop but I pull back and let him slide from my lips before standing to lead them both to the adjoining bedroom. They follow obediently.

Tess looks amazing lying on the bed presenting herself to us. I flash back to the massage table, almost wishing that is where we were now. Lucca clearly wants more of her special kisses as he quickly moves to his knees beside her shoulder. I understand why as Tess is so skilled and tantalizing with that part of her love. She obliges once again, taking him into the warmness past her glistening lips. I trace the curves of her legs with kisses as my eyes are held spellbound by the movement of her cheek as Lucca disappears into her. Tess begins to struggle for breath with her lips wrapped tightly around his fullness. Her eyes move to meet mine, and I am unsure if she is confirming her pleasure or trying to ensure that I am okay to keep going. Even with my excitement, I am not sure that I am, but it feels as if I would be trying to stop a runaway train at this point.

My body shudders for an instant when I first feel Jack's lips between my legs. Warm and gratifying. He always makes me feel so good with his special kisses. My thoughts bound back and forth between Lucca pushing through my lips and the tender pleasure below. I wish that I could see my husband pleasuring me, but I am pressed too tightly against Lucca. The extra stubble feels strange against my lips instead of Jack's smoothness, and his scent is unfamiliar. I pause, wondering what I am doing and because my jaws are tiring as Lucca's pace and force quickens. Suddenly, I can breathe again as Lucca withdraws allowing me a reprieve. His warm spray splatters across my cheeks and nose with some landing in my hair. I indulge his offer of the remainder to my lips.

I ease myself through the slick cream that remains on Tess's billowy lips as Lucca follows my earlier path over her shapely legs to the heaven between her thighs. I watch her take me enthusiastically and I wonder if she is just trying to make things even, giving me what she just gave Lucca. Tess's legs rise into the air and there is no doubting her pleasure at this point. Tess lets her feet land on Lucca's muscular back. Her calves flex as she presses her toes hard into him causing her hips to rise and fall. Moans rumble from deep inside Tess and slip through her filled lips. The warmth engulfing me, the sight of the movements of her hips, and the flexing of muscles in her legs prove to be too much, and soon Tess is swallowing my passion. Tess makes most of my happiness disappear, and what remains drizzles a trail connecting her slippery lips back to me. A small amount runs down to puddle against her neck and settles into her silky silver strands.

I love receiving the gift of the warm taste of Jack's love. I want to tell him how sexy and handsome he is, but I can't get the words out. I feel him, partially hardened, brush against my already messy cheek. Lucca's intensity is rising, and my muscles tense. I am at the edge when I feel Jack's mouth encircle my swollen nipple. It is the final nerve and I return the favor of my love flow to Lucca's lips. My chest rises and falls.

Again, Tess is a picture of beauty lying before us, but Lucca is quickly ready for more and opens Tess's legs wide. He desperately presses himself inside her and the intoxication overtakes him. His thrusts are powerful, and Tess's breasts rock back and forth. She squeezes my hand and grunts with pleasure at each clash of their bodies together.

Lucca furiously pounds between my legs as my arms spread wide, one hand squeezing Jack's and the other grasping the sheets, bracing myself. My tender boobs bounce frantically until a panting Lucca pulls from me. I am mistaken in thinking he needs a break. He places his hands on my hips and guides me to roll to my hands and knees. Lucca anxiously takes his place behind me, and I smile as I look into Jack's eyes, thinking of how much he loves it when I do this pose for him during our photo sessions. Lucca thrusts himself inside once again.

Lucca's hands grasp Tess's hips tightly and yank her toward him as he drives into her furiously. The white sticky residue reflects from Tess's lips and cheeks with a small trail down her chin. Her smile asks me to join so I move to my knees before her, and she takes me between her lips once again. I love it when she lets my excitement grow inside her warm mouth. I have gone from not being able to be excited at all to being ready again in just a few moments on this trip. It's the why that worries me. Tess's hanging breasts sway beautifully but more violently as Lucca groans with every clash of his hips against her backside. The softness of Tess's lips feels so good as they tighten around me. I brush sticky strands of silver away from the shiny streams on her cheeks.

The force of Lucca lowers me to my elbows and Jack slides his body down with me. My lips press tightly against my husband's smooth skin. Breathing becomes difficult with the fullness of my husband and the fury behind, so I release Jack and lay my cheek against him. I love the closeness this makes me feel with Jack. My bottom is still up in the air and Lucca's intensity stays vigorous. I think of how uncomfortable I feel when Jack takes photos with my big butt in the air, but here I am offering it to another man. It's been so long since Lucca has had the chance to be with a woman and it shows. His force finally crashes my body to the sheets, but Lucca doesn't slow. He parts my legs wider with his knees and remains inside my soaked lips. I can feel the jiggle of my bottom with each crash of our bodies together. I lift my hips as much as I can for him. I am biting Jack's thigh now and inhaling the familiar scents of his body. Finally with a loud moan Lucca pulls out and I feel hot streams landing over my backside. I lay on my stomach with my legs spread wide and Jack stroking my hair.

It is impossible for me to not indulge with Tess lying on her stomach, legs spread wide. I grasp her hips and pull her back up to her knees and elbows and continue where Lucca stopped. I love seeing her in this position. Calves tensed, beautiful butt jiggling, and the white cream sprayed across her backside reaching up to her mid-back near the diagonal line of freckles is fueling my fire. Soon Tess's tired body collapses again and I fall against her back. Her moans are louder and match the pace of our bodies clashing together. I want so badly to continue but I feel that Tess needs a break, so I make myself ease from her and roll to her side.

I lay still to catch my breath as four hands run across the backside of my sweaty body, making me remember the massage a few nights earlier. The soft touch of their fingers feels so good on my skin, but I can feel their tension. They won't wait, they can't wait much longer. And if I am honest with myself, I don't want to wait either. Hands roll me to my side where Lucca lays facing me. Lucca pushes my hand back toward the sheets, but I surprise myself and I push Lucca to his back instead. Who is this aggressive girl inside of me? I eagerly lift a leg, swing it over Lucca's muscled stomach and came to rest straddling him. My hand moves to guide Lucca where I need him, and where I know he wants so desperately to be. Lucca's eagerness glides inside my wet skin easily. His hands grasp my sides and pull me forward, causing my hands to land on the front of his shoulders, swaying the heavy flesh of my chest over his face. He offers relief from the weight by cupping each in his hands.

I push Tess's hair back from her face again as she rides Lucca wildly. Tess raises, stiffening her back and letting her heavy breasts rest against her body. They have such a gorgeous full shape and her areolas have widened and taken a deeper color with her excitement. She lets out a full-blown scream. I know that she loves the feeling when she is on top. Lucca raises his head to smother himself between her irresistible breasts, squeezing them around his cheeks. Tess's body bounces fiercely, and her long moans tell me of her undeniable happiness as I hear the wet sounds of joy between their bodies. Tess's back arches and she throws her head back, letting the sticky silver strands fall deep behind her. Her hands reach back and grip Lucca's thighs as she rides to his rhythm. Her full suction-marked hangers fall against her skin as they bounce to her movement. I lean in to kiss her forehead.

I pull Jack closer to me, turning my upper body slightly to rest my hands on his hips. I guide his hard love against my cheek and press to him. I need to feel my husband. I kiss Jack's stomach and hips relentlessly. I want him to know how badly I want HIM. The depth and the angle of the penetration on top makes me succumb rather quickly, but I allow Lucca time to for his own pleasure. Finally, I lift my leg and roll off Lucca, my body limp as I fall to my back. The teasing and the restrictions from the massage night along with no sex for a while have made the wolves desperate for more. Jack slides between my open thighs and becomes one with me again. He is most definitely cured. I lift my legs into the air and spread wider giving all of myself to him. Jack goes deeper and harder while kissing the calf of my raised leg. I smile knowing that he loves seeing my calves when we are out somewhere and thinking of this very moment. I fight through his bites of passion. The pain, the pleasure, and the emotions flow out of me once again. I have lost count of how many times. Jack eases my legs back to the bed before moving up to straddle my stomach. He slides himself between my breasts and I push them tight against his beautiful penis. We won't need the oils since I am slick from the two men's passion and sweat. I love the feel of him gliding between my flesh. He finishes quickly and covers my chest even more with his love and happiness.

Tess's chest heaves while she lies on her back with arms and legs spread wide, beautiful silver matted with stickiness, and her chest shining from the covering of sweat and love. I love her beautiful flower open from the passion we have shared. I know that Tess is tired, but her dimples tell me that she isn't ready to stop yet. I step quickly into the next room to get bottles of water for everyone. It doesn't feel right to leave her alone for more than a moment. I return to find Lucca straddling her head with his legs. He buries his face deep between her thighs and consumes her like he is an animal thirsting to death in the desert that just found an oasis. Tess takes him deep into her throat and he presses his body tighter to her. Her moans match the movement of his hips as they become faster and harder. Tess grunts and gags but continues to pleasure Lucca as her hands hold onto his backside. He plunges his face deeper between her intimate lips and drinks her bliss wildly. Tess's hands finally must push Lucca off to catch her breath. She strokes him just above her face, taking his dangling pendants in her mouth, as he raises his wet cheeks and begins sucking her inner thigh. Three fingers push inside her soaked lips, her feet dig into the bed, muscles flexing, hips raising, and I can see her happiness come again through the shutter of her body. Lucca swings a leg from around her head landing at her side. He takes her painted fingers and wraps them around himself, then places his hand over hers. Soon his head falls back, and her breasts and her fingers become painted with more of his love cream.

I am beyond exhausted yet determined to give myself to my husband last on this night. I rub their love lotion into my breast as my eyes request my husband to come to me. I glance downward, guiding him with my eyes as I open my legs for him once again. He ever so sweetly and gently moves to unite with me. To bind us together. Our lips come together and our tongues slow dance while he is inside making sweet, wonderful love to me. Our eyes meet and I whisper that I love him. I know when my husband is ready. My hands grasp his nice little ass and pull him tightly to me, feeling the fullness of his desire. I eagerly accept his love. His passion fills me. I feel the overflow of his love run down my skin and puddle at my butt. I wipe sweat and cream from my hot cheeks as I smile at my husband. "I love you, Jack." Wow, this night is truly amazing. I am surprised at how exciting this was to me. As I let my exhausted body rest, I almost chuckle as I look at the guys covered with my scratches on their backs, chest, and arms. The wolves look like the prey may have gotten the best of them on this night.

Lucca thanks us with such sincerity, and is considerate to leave Jack and I alone to hold one another, to think, to talk. To just be together. And to drink water. I need water.

61

JACK

WE ARE ENJOYING OUR PLATES of pancakes and fresh fruit with many of our home away from home friends in the Hurricane Hattie room during a bustling late breakfast hour at Sandy Toes. Victoria is still fussing at Tess that the ladies of the garden club are driving her crazy to join. I can't hold back a laugh thinking of her mixing with that group. It is Cody's first order as a chef's assistant, and we all agree that he has a bright future. As I pick up a strawberry, I ponder aloud if we have bought enough fresh fruit from Mateo to take home.

Victoria smiles. "You can always come back sooner, Jack."

I return the smile as Victoria looks over to me and continues, "You guys had quite the adventure on this trip."

I agree and contemplate if she already knows about last night. The thought of her knowing surprisingly doesn't bother me. I am not sure I understand who this new person inside of me is, but I am happy and feel free instead of concerned about what everyone else is thinking. I like this feeling. This morning was another time of sweet intimacy for Tess and me, convincing us both that we are indeed enjoying this new journey. It did make us have a later start but our enchantment on the upper deck during the sunrise was well worth it.

Rohan had asked to get a picture of everyone together before we left to commemorate the special happenings on this trip. I set up the tripod in the front of the room and smile as I think of the things that happened that Rohan does not know about. We all huddle around the table together: me, Tess, Victoria, Devin and Gabriella, Rohan and Hattie, Emma and Cody, Lucca, Mr. and Mrs. Jones, and even Marcus and Big Kahuna who was picking up an order and just dropped in to join the photo. Mario and Celest are normally too busy at the market, but Rohan had lined up Sara to help just long enough for them to make it for the photo. I have a moment of sadness thinking that we have lost our friendship with Rob and Linda, not to mention our standing rental. But then I smile as I think of this photo possibly going onto the wall in the Hurricane Hattie room, adding to the story. And what stories there are in this mix of people.

Tess and I glance at one another during the timer countdown and just before the shutter clicks, we ask each other THE question. About last night, about this whole trip. After the series of automatic photos have taken, we answer each other with a smile and a kiss.

As the group walks us out, we see flowers laying across our convertible. The accompanying note reads: "Thank you for restoring my passion for life. Martina would be so happy for all of us. Until next time."

Victoria is as soothing as ever as her and Tess share a long hug. Rohan sniffles and wipes his eyes as he hugs me goodbye. Emma doesn't hold her tears back as we squish her between me and Tess for a final hug. We remind her that we want to see the very first baby pictures. Cody yells at me to practice my gaming before coming back.

We drive slowly down main street. We see the preacher hustle over to the café and standing at the front door tipping his hat with Mrs. Jones waving as we drive by. As we look down both sides of the street we see many of the shop owners temporarily stop their busy work to bid us farewell. There are so many wonderful people in this town. Tess and I are now the ones fighting back the tears. We even receive a quick siren and flash of lights from the sheriff's SUV as we pass. Ed is in his green apron and stops sweeping long enough to give us a salute. Mateo sits another bag of peaches in the back seat as we slowly move past the market. We even got a smile and a wave from Celest in her bright orange scarf. The kids having an early ice cream on the sidewalk wave their sticky little hands, and Frances the book lady steps to the door to share a smile.

I choke back tears, and with a gravelly voice whisper, "This really is our home away from home." Tess wipes my cheek with her thumb and giggles. "You are so sentimental."

We clear the downtown area, and the wind picks up as we cross the bridge leaving the island. Tess wraps her hands around my arm. "Oh yeah, Gabriella and Devin did have an invitation for us."

I glance over to Tess and lower my sunglasses slightly. "Well, I guess we missed it."

Tess laughs. "Oh no, we haven't. They have invited us to spend the week with them in their New England cabin, to enjoy the fall foliage."

"I knew you and Gabriella had to be conjuring something up."

She kisses me on the cheek. "I can't wait."

Tess pulls the clip from hair, props her painted toes on the dash, and flashes those wonderful dimples at me. "I love you so much, Jack."

Every day with Tess is the best.

ACKNOWLEDGMENTS

I MUST BEGIN BY THANKING my wonderful and amazing wife, Tammi. She has been my inspiration, my love, and my soulmate for almost four decades. I would never have been able to complete this book without her unwavering encouragement and support. Every click of the keyboard took place with Tammi and our sweet bluetick coonhound at my side.

I would like to thank Myles Schrag, my fantastic production editor from Mascot Books, who quickly became a friend as much as a manager. A special shout out to Caitlin Smith, my cover designer who not only provided beautiful ideas that complemented the story, but exhibited incredible patience with my multiple changes to the photos. Thanks to the entire Mascot team for their professionalism and guidance throughout the process of editing, proofreading, and bringing this book to market.

A special thanks to Savannah Gilbo, book coach and developmental editor. Listening to Savannah's podcast and subsequently taking her writing course gave me confidence and direction on how to get the story from my thoughts to paper. She has a wonderful teaching style that emphasizes detailed organization, while still allowing authors freedom of creativity.

Last, but certainly not least, a sincere thank you to Elissa Wood. Elissa is a wonderful photographer whom Tammi and I had our first boudoir session with. She made us feel so comfortable from the first time we met her, and we have scheduled other sessions since. Elissa's work has given me many great ideas for my amateur photography hobby, and some of her work is featured on the cover of this book.

And finally, thanks to so many more people who have impacted my journey that led to this joyful moment of having my first novel published.

ABOUT THE AUTHOR

JOHN (J.W.) WOODWARD HAS LIVED in several areas in the eastern United States, but the place he calls home has always been in the beautiful mountains of southwest Virginia. He enjoys writing alongside Tammi, his wife of almost four decades, nestled in a cozy cottage.

John loves his family of three grown children and several grandchildren, and is always advising them to enjoy the journey of their lives and treasure the small moments together. He is an avid reader and enjoys amateur photography, with his wife being his favorite subject to capture in the lens.

John has always had a passion to write, and is excited to debut his first novel, *Every Picture Has a Story to Tell,* after a small detour of forty years in the business and finance industries. He is living his mantra to never give up on your dreams!